Praise for S. L. Viehl and the *StarDoc* series

"I don't read much science fiction, but I got ahold of a manuscript copy of *StarDoc* and just loved it. Don't miss this one." —Catherine Coulter

"Space opera somewhat reminiscent of C. J. Cherryh's early work." —*Chronicle*

"An entertaining, almost old-fashioned adventure. . . . The adventure and quirky mix of aliens and cultures make a fun combination." —*Locus*

"Viehl has created an excellent protagonist . . . and she's set the stage for an interesting series of interspecies medical adventures." —Space.com

"Space opera and medical melodrama mix with a dash of romance in this engaging novel . . . a rousing good yarn, with plenty of plot twists, inventive scene-setting, and quirky characters to keep readers thoroughly entertained. . . . *StarDoc* is a fun adventure story with an appealing heroine, a lot of action, a sly sense of humor, and wonders aplenty." —SF Site

"A fascinating reading experience that will provide much pleasure to science fiction fans. The lead character is a wonderful heroine." —*Midwest Book Review*

"Viehl's characters are the strength of her novel, showing depth, history, and identity." —*Talebones*

continued...

Beyond Varallan

"[Cherijo is] an engaging lead character. . . . Viehl skillfully weaves in the clues to build a murder mystery with several surprising ramifications." —Space.com

"A riveting tale no connoisseur of excellence can put down without finishing. With more than a few surprises up her sleeve, this rising star proves herself a master storyteller who can win and hold a bestselling audience." —*Romantic Times*

Endurance

"An exciting science fiction tale . . . fast-paced and exciting. . . . SF fans will fully enjoy S. L. Viehl's entertaining entry in one of the better ongoing series today." —*Midwest Book Review*

"[*Endurance*] gets into more eclectic and darker territory than most space opera, but it's a pretty engrossing trip. Recommended." —*Hypatia's Hoard*

"A rousing medical space opera. . . . Viehl employs misdirection and humor, while not defusing the intense plot development that builds toward an explosive conclusion." —*Romantic Times*

Shockball

"Genetically enhanced fun. . . . Cherijo herself has been justly praised as a breath of fresh air—smart [and] saucy. . . . The reader seems to be invited along as an amicable companion, and such is the force of Cherijo's personality that it sounds like fun."—Science Fiction Weekly

"Fast-paced . . . an entertaining installment in the continuing adventures of the 'StarDoc.'" —*Locus*

"An exhilarating science fiction space adventure. The zestful story line stays at warp speed.... Cherijo is as fresh as ever.... Fans of futuristic outer space novels will want to take off with this tale and the three previous *Star-Doc* books, as all four stories take the audience where they rarely have been before." —*Midwest Book Review*

Eternity Row

"Space opera at its very best.... Viehl has created a character and a futuristic setting that is second to none in its readability, quality, and social mores."

—*Midwest Book Review*

"S. L. Viehl serves readers her usual highly entertaining mix of humor and space opera. This episode is enlivened by the antics of [Cherijo's] daughter, Marel, and by an exploration of aging and immortality. As usual, I look forward to the next in an exciting series." —BookLoons

Blade Dancer

"Fast-moving, thought-provoking, and just plain damn fun. S. L. Viehl has once again nailed it."

—Linda Howard

"A heartrending, passionate, breathtaking adventure of a novel that rips your feet out from under you on page one and never lets you regain them until the amazing finale. Stunning." —Holly Lisle

Bio Rescue

"Like Anne McCaffrey, only with more aliens . . . entertaining." —SF Crowsnest

"Viehl does a good job of telling the story, with believable alien as well as human characters and with more romantic emphasis then you usually see in SF." —SFRevu

ALSO BY S. L. VIEHL

StarDoc

Beyond Varallan

Endurance

Shockball

Eternity Row

Blade Dancer

Bio Rescue

Afterburn

REBEL ICE

A StarDoc Novel

S. L. Viehl

A ROC BOOK

ROC
Published by New American Library, a division of
Penguin Group (USA) Inc., 375 Hudson Street,
New York, New York 10014, USA
Penguin Group (Canada), 90 Eglinton Avenue East, Suite 700, Toronto,
Ontario M4P 2Y3, Canada (a division of Pearson Penguin Canada Inc.)
Penguin Books Ltd., 80 Strand, London WC2R 0RL, England
Penguin Ireland, 25 St. Stephen's Green, Dublin 2,
Ireland (a division of Penguin Books Ltd.)
Penguin Group (Australia), 250 Camberwell Road, Camberwell, Victoria 3124,
Australia (a division of Pearson Australia Group Pty. Ltd.)
Penguin Books India Pvt. Ltd., 11 Community Centre, Panchsheel Park,
New Delhi - 110 017, India
Penguin Group (NZ), cnr Airborne and Rosedale Roads, Albany,
Auckland 1310, New Zealand (a division of Pearson New Zealand Ltd.)
Penguin Books (South Africa) (Pty.) Ltd., 24 Sturdee Avenue,
Rosebank, Johannesburg 2196, South Africa

Penguin Books Ltd., Registered Offices:
80 Strand, London WC2R 0RL, England

First published by Roc, an imprint of New American Library,
a division of Penguin Group (USA) Inc.

First Printing, January 2006
10 9 8 7 6 5 4 3 2 1

Printed in the United States of America

This book is for
my friends in New Zealand,
Teulon and Teresa,
who graciously allowed me
to borrow their names
for this story.

Before

When the healer came to my world, I felt pity for her. I wept for her.

Then I took justice for what had been done.

She arrived on the vessel that appeared just before dawn. I saw it at once as it came hurtling out of control, a thin white streak against the fading purple of the sky. Like too many others, it had been wrenched from its flight path by the kvinka, the fierce wind streams of the upper atmosphere, which shield the surface of Akkabarr, my homeworld.

"So cold." My apprentice, Enafa, joined me at the window I had chopped in the thick blue ice. As she shivered, she also peered, trying to see what had caught my attention. "Is that a ship, Skjæra?"

"Quiet." I measured the plume, silently calculating the rate of descent as I watched it elongate.

She hopped from one foot to the other, slapping her arms with her mitts. "Should we alert the crawls?"

"Wait." I watched it fall until it bloomed with a flash just over the north fields. That decided the matter. "Bank the heatarc and put on your outfurs."

As Enafa obeyed, I heard her murmur "Die quickly," one of the more traditional Iisleg prayers.

"They will." All the newly outcast pray, but I did

not ridicule her as one of our skela sisters might. Truth be plain, I envied her that faith. It would probably not last through another season on the ice. "Finish your tasks."

"Perhaps I will be singled out this time." She sounded excited rather than frightened at the prospect. "My mother often chose me over my sisters, you know. When I lived in our iiskar. She favored me."

I pulled on the thick pile of outfur I'd made for myself during my first season on the ice. "Yes, as you have told me." *Too many times.*

Her vain wish would not come true, of course. Enafa had been among the skela for a mere three suns. Our headwoman preferred seasoned handlers on the ice. My apprentice's fears and hopes, like her memories, reminded me of how different we were. She still clung to that once-life as if it were yet hers.

I had been dead for a long, long time.

At times I wondered if my own five seasons of exile had numbed the life out of me. I no longer felt sorrow for what I had been, or disgust for what I had become. It would not matter if I had. As long as I worked, none of the skela cared what I felt. Enafa had yet to learn that, but I had no desire to be her teacher in those matters.

Watching over the child and keeping her from killing herself through stupidity was work enough.

Together we trudged from the watch place back through the bitter cold to the crawls. Skrie Daneeb, our headwoman, had not yet risen from her crawl, where I glimpsed her wedged between two old ones. Likely sharing her prodigious heat with them, I thought, and sent my young apprentice to warm herself at the great heatarc in the central cavern. Daneeb never openly showed sympathy for the young or the ancient among us, and I knew she would not appreciate being discovered off guard by a newling.

"We show no mercy," she told every outcast when they came to the skela. "No one shows it to us."

I walked a few yards beyond Daneeb's space and pretended to have an irritated throat. She appeared a moment later, balancing by resting one hand against a thermal pad on the stone wall while she pulled her trousers over her leggings. "What is it, Skjæra?"

"A crash, Skrie. Four kilometers past Golihn Ridge." I hesitated as I recalled the plume, and the flash. If I was in error, handlers might be wasted, or needed. Also, there was much I could not say within the hearing of others, particularly Enafa. "The ship flashed just above the surface."

Daneeb grunted, then shrugged into her outfurs and strode out to the central cavern. A moment later, I heard her bellow, "Crawls five, seven, nine, rouse yourselves! Work awaits!"

Forty-three of us occupied the caves since the latest outcasts had arrived two suns before. I determined our numbers the same way everyone did: not by counting faces, which would have been rude, but by the division of food. Our headwoman's predecessor once secretly doled out extra rations to whoever brought in the most bodies, and hoped to recruit those she indulged as her personal protectors. Daneeb herself discovered the crime, dragged the headwoman from the cave to dark ice, and staked her out there.

I knew because hers was the first body I ever saw

claimed by the jlorra, the enormous felines with which we shared our world.

"Forget life," Daneeb often told me. "You are skela now."

Abandoning hope and one's memories was the price of becoming a dead handler. What had any of us left to dream over or remember fondly? My once-life had been taken from me, as well as my second chance among the Iisleg. Skela could never return to their iiskar, or see their families, or touch another living Iisleg for as long as they breathed. Even after our deaths, only another dead handler could touch us. To be cast into the skela meant enduring an unclean existence, one that rendered us forever despised and exiled.

In most ways, that was worse than dead.

I knelt beside Enafa before the great heatarc to warm my limbs. No longer pinched by cold, her young face glowed smooth and plump, but drowsiness made her eyes heavy. "You should sleep while we are gone. You will have watch again with me this night."

This made her pout, and resentment filled her eyes as she watched Daneeb leave the crawls. "Skjæra, can you not ask the skrie to take me with you this time? I want to go."

Barely beyond her first bleeding year, cast out from her iiskar for stealing food, and now making demands like a spoiled child. Enafa needed more curbing than I had afforded her as yet. "No."

Her mouth drooped. "You do not care for me."

"No," I lied. "I do not."

It did not pain me to watch her scurry away, cringing, rejected. She did not know that I had done her a favor.

One of our sisters emerged from crawl nine, groaning as she dragged the thermal wrap from her head. "Why do they never come down *after* the first meal?"

On top of my dealing with my apprentice, the mild complaint irritated me. The ferocious winds forced down any offworlder vessel that attempted to land on our world, and perhaps the *ensleg* deserved it for trying something so idiotic, but to care more about food seemed atrocious. "The kvinka has no regard for your empty belly."

A big shadow fell over me, cast by Galla, the beast driver. Light from the heatarc made her shaggy, heavy outfurs glow red. "Malmi, get up or starve a day." She moved her gaze to my face, and her silver eyes narrowed. "You, outside."

I followed the beast driver at a cautious distance. Once our boots touched ice, Galla made an impatient gesture toward Daneeb, who was already out by the sleds, balancing skids. "She waits for you."

Galla did not like our headwoman or me, but like most beast drivers, she disdained anything that stood on two legs or threatened her position. Someone had once made light of her devotion for the jlorra, who still preferred me over Galla. The beast driver's response had left deep scars. I made a brief, courteous nod to her before I strode to the sled.

Daneeb looked up from the wide alloy blade that would keep us from falling through the sheet crust. "Tell me the rest."

Very reluctantly, I did. "The stardrive may have imploded in the upper atmosphere, but if it did, they must have ejected it. The explosion was too small to be from anything but changes in the interior atmosphere. The vessel itself appeared to be League, military, not very large, possibly a leader's transport."

Daneeb knew my discomfort had nothing to do with reporting these facts to her. My unease came from the same source as my familiarity with offworlder ships: the time when I had lived and worked as a physician in the windlord cities.

My once-life, when I had believed myself to be Toskald.

I would still be among the windlords, living as one of them, had the records of my birth been destroyed. I would never know why my parents kept the data, which showed that I had been born Iisleg. Perhaps they never thought anyone would find out that they had secretly purchased me as an infant from a slaver. Had I been aware of my origin, I would never have allowed it to be discovered after their deaths in a lift accident. But I had not known, and so the magistrate presiding over my parents' estate used the information to seize possession of my inheritance. It had further amused him to send me to live on the surface with my mother's tribe. My attempt to treat the wounds of an Iisleg female beaten badly by her husband resulted in my being cast out of the iiskar.

Iisleg women never went to the skim cities, unless they were sent as tribute to the Kangal. They could not be healers, nor were they permitted any form of proper education. It was blasphemy for a woman to even think of such things; thus I was walking blasphemy. The headwoman had discovered my abilities quickly enough, and occasionally made use of them, but extended more of the mercy she claimed not to have by helping me to conceal my forbidden upbringing and knowledge from the others.

Even the godless skela would stake out a heretic like me.

"A League leader. Daévena." The headwoman's spit froze before it struck the ice. "The gjenvin must be on their wind skimmers by now. Go, help Galla harness the beasts."

The ice caves of the jlorra squatted beside the skela crawls, and were guarded only by the enclosures necessary to discourage the beasts' nomadic nature. I carefully latched the entry gate behind me before picking my way through the skeleton yard and entering the largest of the passages the jlorra had licked out of the ice.

I called out my presence. "Galla, I am sent to help."

"Bring more retainers," was her breathless reply.

I took down the head straps and leads from the hooks Galla had driven into the ice wall, and carried them farther into the darkness. My eyes adjusted rapidly, but the weight of the retainers nearly made me stagger. Something growled to my right, but I kept going. I had nothing here to fear but Galla. The jlorra had been my friends since I had come to this place.

Offworlders called our pack beasts snow tigers, and admired their appearance and strength. The jlorra were immense, long-bodied creatures with six agile appendages and splayed paws edged with sharp digging claws. I suppose to ensleg eyes they appeared quite attractive. Their sleek pelts changed with the color of the snow crust, at times dark blue like the endless night of sunless seasons, only to grow as pale as drift crystal during the long rising.

A number of traders once attempted to export them for labor to other ice worlds. The Iisleg were quite willing to sell their beasts, and then send the gjenvin later to recover the crashed skimmers and round up the outraged jlorra, who slaughtered their buyers.

From this sort of foolishness came the Iisleg saying "Death cannot be made a servant."

I came upon Galla attempting to wrestle a retainer over the massive head of the pack leader, who was resisting her touch. Seeing the other beasts becoming restless, I carefully placed the harnesses I carried on the floor.

"Allow me to serve," I said, and held out my hands.

Galla flung the retainer at me. "They should be beaten and starved."

"I would not recommend you try." The jlorra padded over and rubbed the top of its heavy skull against my side in a gesture of affection.

I looked into the beast's large, silver eyes, and saw again what Galla could not. The jlorra would never go hungry. If the skela did not provide adequate food for them, the big cats would simply break through the ice separating our caves and dine on us. It was their nature, and had spawned another, more menacing proverb among the Iisleg: "Death never worries about its next meal."

We reached the crash site after the gjenvin from the nearest iiskar had arrived. As skela were not permitted to approach the living, we waited a short distance beyond the ring of debris. The ship was almost as I had predicted: of League military design, but not a leader's vessel. It was of similar size but, from the lack of bodies and the large amount of visible salvage waiting to be recovered, more in the way of a freight transport.

But why would the League use such a small ship to transport their weapons? It seemed inefficient, almost ridiculous.

I murmured an apology to Daneeb, who only shook her head. "I have never seen or heard the like, either, Skjæra. It was not for you to know." She pointed to one of the others on the skimmer. "Look after her."

I climbed down, and saw Enafa waving a mitt at me. Despite my harsh words, somehow the girl must have persuaded Daneeb to permit her to come with us. My numbness intensified. "I will, Skrie."

Once we came into view, the chief gjenvin recalled his team to their wind skimmers. According to our laws, the wreck could not be salvaged until the dead were removed, and for that, he had to yield the site to the skela.

"Why do they not stay?" Enafa asked as I took her arm and led her toward the debris field.

Had this fond mother of hers never instructed her on anything? "They cannot work if we are near."

She made a haughty sound. "Daévena, so they fear us."

"No." I turned her to me, my hands tight on her arms. "They do not wish to be contaminated by us. We are unclean. They are not. If you stray too close, they will kill you. Do you hear me?" Enafa's eyes went large as she nodded, and I let her go. "Stay by my side, watch, and learn."

My apprentice held her tongue, and kept her eyes on the ice. When the last of the salvagers had retreated,

Daneeb turned to face the gjenvin skimmers and sank down on the ice—an expected obeisance as well as a warning that our work was to begin—then rose and snapped out orders. The rest of us moved in to begin our search through the twisted wreckage for bodies, and I showed Enafa how to rummage through alloy and snow.

"Their blood freezes instantly, so always look for color on the ice." I told her. "Remember, they are mostly offworlders, so it may not be red, like ours. Harnesses or retainers are usually torn, but may lead to where they were flung on impact."

"How many have you claimed?" she asked as she pawed through the debris.

"I do not count." Yes, I did, but I had no intention of telling her I had recovered and skinned 1,040 bodies of worgald.

Some of the younger gjenvin watched us. Enafa stiffened when the wind carried their whispers and sniggers to our ears.

Look at them.

The soiled ones.

Perhaps they are hungry.

"They speak as if we were jlorra," she said, glaring at the skimmers. "They know we do not eat the dead ensleg."

"We amuse them." Had she not reacted, I doubt if their contempt would have registered with me, so accustomed to it was I.

"The beast driver does not like it." Enafa nodded toward the big woman approaching us.

Galla shuffled past, scowling. "Should stake them down and let loose the beasts."

I shoved a twisted panel aside. "That would be useless."

"Like this teat sucker Daneeb latched on you?" The beast driver grunted a laugh. "I thought you done with nursing the weak, Skjæra."

Enafa's cheeks darkened. "I am not a baby! And Skjæra is a healer!"

"She is nothing but shit, like the rest of us. You, newling, are less than shit." Galla pulled the body I had uncovered from the snow, and used her dagger to strip it of its worgald. I tried to urge Enafa past, but the beast driver glanced up at me. "She will watch." She began to work on the head.

As Galla slid the flat blade beneath the ensleg's skin and began removing his face, Enafa made a choking sound. "What are you doing?"

"The work, useless." She flipped her knife to clean it, hard enough to splatter both of us with blood crystals and bits of frozen flesh. "You must take it whole."

My apprentice stumbled a few steps away, then vomited. I supported her as she heaved, until her belly calmed and she could stand alone. Rather than thank me, she clutched at my arm with fierce fingers. "Why do you not stop her? She desecrates him!"

"Galla does our work. The windlords require the intact facial skins of ensleg dead be sent to the skim cities," I told her. "Offworlders will pay handsomely to identify their dead."

"They sell ensleg scum to the ensleg scum," Galla corrected as she rose to turn the male over. "At least the jlorra and the rothawks dine well on what is left. Look at this poor bastard, Skjæra. He's mostly intact.

You might have saved him with your witchery, were you not shit now."

Referring to my ability to heal often amused the bitterest among the skela, who had honed mordacity to an art form. That I should end a handler of death was perhaps the ultimate irony. Over time I had grown accustomed to it.

Galla's sneer had a far different effect on my apprentice, however. "As well you might have been grinding beneath him tonight!" she snapped.

It was well-known that Galla had been an ahayag who repeatedly serviced every male in her iiskar. Being a harlot was accepted, if not particularly admired, but dallying with ensleg traders was not permitted. Galla had been caught with the wrong color male in her furs. Since becoming beast driver, she liked to pretend she had never been a prostitute. She made sure everyone else kept up the pretense, as well.

I stepped in front of Enafa to take the blow meant for her, and managed to stay on my feet. I clutched my aching belly as I gasped out, "She does not think . . . before she speaks. . . . Forgive her . . . beast driver."

The knuckles in Galla's bloodied mitt bruised my breast as she shoved me back against a portion of the ripped hull. "Get out of my way."

"Do not hurt her!" Enafa snatched at Galla's arm. "Let her go!"

"Galla." Daneeb appeared out of nowhere. "Release your sister and return to your labor."

The beast driver took her hand from me and pointed to my apprentice. "She called me a whore."

"The child is mistaken. You *were* a whore." The

headwoman folded her arms. "Take the body and pile it with the others."

Galla slung the dead ensleg over her shoulder and, after a final snarl in my direction, strode off.

"Enafa, go and work with Lati." Daneeb waited until my apprentice moved away. "I vow, Skjæra, that woman would have you staked before the season is out." A large hand helped me to my feet. "Do not give me reason to permit it."

"It will be as you say, Skrie." I breathed in deeply, willing the cold to ease the pain.

"Over there seems a likely spot. Go and search it." Daneeb nodded toward a chunk of the fuselage far from Galla. "Work quickly. The salvagers become impatient."

I waded through piles of useless components and grid housings before I reached the fuselage, and put my lever bars to work on an intact compartment.

You might have saved him.

The remarkably undamaged alloy refused to give, apparently once a door panel that had been secured.

Staked before the season is out.

I wedged the tip of one bar into a seam and pulled back with all my weight. The physical work was difficult for me most of the time, perhaps because my hands had been trained to repair, not to destroy.

Do not give me reason to permit it.

The panel slid open, and something fell out. An arm, glistening wet and red, horribly broken and yet still attached to a body. I stepped back, astonished not by the limb, but by the fact it was *still moving.*

I moved in to have a closer look. "Mag Dǽvena."

The ensleg was small, slight, and apparently Iisleg. It wore offworlder garments, so I assumed it to be human, like the ancestors of the Iisleg, whom the Toskald had abducted and brought here to Akkabarr centuries ago. Impact had mangled its puny body, judging by the broken bones and torn flesh showing through jagged rents in its garment. Blood masked its face, and for a moment, I thought someone had already claimed worgald from this one. But no, more red blood still pumped from the wounds, and gushed from a deep crater in its skull. I drew in my breath when I saw the gray-and-pink brain showing plainly through silver-sheened dark hair. Odd, broken lengths of chain encircled its wrists and lower limbs. They did not rattle, as the blood on the alloy links had frozen them together.

And despite all of this, the shattered arm still moved, the broken hand still reached. *A miracle.* I found myself unconsciously reaching down to cover the hand with my mitt.

Enafa appeared at my side. "Skjæra, it lives!"

Her voice jerked me back to reality, and I snatched my hand away in revulsion. What was I thinking, trying to touch it? "Not for long."

We would have to wait for it to die.

But my young apprentice was already kneeling beside the ensleg, shouting, "Skrie! Here! Over here!" She looked up at me. "Skjæra, can you heal it?"

I hesitated, eyeing the terrible head wound, knowing what I might have done for it had I my instruments and medications. "I could try, but . . ."

Daneeb hurried over. "What now?" She halted, and stared. "Daévena yepa, it cannot be."

I turned to Enafa, who was touching the ensleg, and took in a swift breath. "Skrie, no one has yet seen this."

"I will tell them!" My apprentice jumped to her feet and ran for the wind skimmers, leaping over debris.

Daneeb and I immediately took off after her, trying to stop her. But Enafa was young, and swifter than both of us, and threw herself down before the chief gjenvin's hovering skimmer.

I was terrified—Enafa had not listened to me when I had told her that skela are forbidden to speak to the gjenvin unless spoken to—and ran faster.

She was already pleading with the chief when I sank to my knees in the snow beside her.

"You see?" She held out her bare hands for the chief to see the frozen crystals of ensleg blood glittering on them. "It lives."

"You put hands on it?"

She nodded eagerly, and I closed my eyes briefly.

The chief turned to Daneeb. "You are headwoman?"

"Yes, Kheder." She knelt beside me. "Forgive this transgression. The fault is mine."

The chief, an older male with much experience on the ice, nodded. "I trust you to see God's work is done." He tossed a pistol to her, which she caught neatly. "Now take your filth out of my eyes."

Enafa opened her mouth, foolishly trying to protest, but Daneeb jerked her to her feet and hauled her away from the skimmers.

I kept pace with them, desperately trying to think of how to stop this. "She did not know, or think, Skrie. Her first time in the fields—I did not anticipate that she would—I am the one to be punished, not—"

"No more words, Skjæra." She gave me a furious look. "He had just cause to put us all to the ice."

Daneeb ordered the others to gather at a clear spot beside the fuselage. Someone gave her two of the jagged stakes we used to fix things in place, and then the headwoman threw Enafa down on the ice and drove the stakes through the palms of her mitts.

My apprentice screamed with pain as her blood spilled on the ice. "No! What did I do? Why do you do this?"

Galla came to watch. "You have offended the God of the living, and contaminated the ears of the faithful, newling." She smiled. "For that, you die."

"Skjæra!" Enafa turned her face toward me. "Please! Stop them! I don't want to die!"

Daneeb came to me. "Your blade, Skjæra."

I removed it from my hip and stared at it. The blade had been given to me for one reason. One for which I had not yet been made to use it. "I cannot."

"Do this, or we all join her."

I looked over my shoulder. The gjenvin had their crossbows loaded and pointed at us. If the chief gave the order to fire, every skela on the ice would be shot and killed. Which he would, if the transgressor was not punished.

I did not have to rudely count faces to know it was one life or twenty-six.

The chief gjenvin shouted something, and a crossbow twanged. Galla shrieked, clutching the bolt in her chest, and then fell over into the snow.

I could not walk to her under my own power. Tears froze on my cheeks as Daneeb guided me over to Enafa and made me straddle her body. The child stopped screaming and her eyes went wide as Daneeb seized my wrist and hoisted the blade over her chest.

"Jarn," Daneeb said against my ear, her voice low and urgent as she used the name I had not been called since my once-life. "You cannot save her, but you can save her suffering. Guide my hand."

It was not Daneeb's duty to do this. It was mine. Unlike the other skela, I was meant to do more than drag the dead from the wrecks of their ships and strip the faces from their skulls. I was special among the skela, for my knowledge of the living body, and for knowing precisely how to remove life from it as quickly and efficiently as possible.

I was Skjæra, the Death Bringer.

Enafa did not scream when the blade came down, thrust through her heart, and pinned her body to the ice. She gurgled my name, and then went limp.

In the distance, the gjenvin lowered their bows.

Daneeb jerked the blade free, and made me rise with her. No one looked at us. Since Enafa was skela, no one came to take her face. As Galla was dead, one of the sisters released two of the jlorra, who rose and lazily padded over to us.

Daneeb used her body then to block the sight of the snow tigers. Her gaze was hard on my face. "God's work must be done. Take the ensleg." She slapped the gjenvin's weapon in my left hand. When I did not move, she added, "You are no longer a body healer, Skjæra. You are a dead handler. Take payment for Enafa's life."

Slowly I walked back to where the ensleg lay, still groping the air with its ruined fingers. It could not survive such injuries, I knew that. Enafa's terrible mistake was not in thinking I could save it, or trying to plead for its life.

She had touched it with her hands. Touched the living.

I tucked the weapon under my arm and shook the mitt from my left hand, which I wrapped around one of the ensleg's. I no longer cared if any of the skela or gjenvin saw me. *If this be offensive to God or Daévena, let them stake me out beside her.*

The ensleg's eyes were open in the frozen red mask of its face. Blood rimmed those dark eyes, and suffering filled them. Then it gently curled its battered fingers around mine. Tears, not blood, inched down the frozen gore over its cheeks. They did not freeze.

Knowledge came to me in that moment. Knowledge that the ensleg was a female, like me, and that she had seen everything.

"Her name was Enafa. She was born twelve seasons past, and her mother often favored her above her sisters." Gently I placed her hand over her heart. "I could not favor her above mine."

It was then that I saw the mark on her garment: the coil and staff symbol of an off-world healer.

I should have felt anger. If this ensleg healer had not survived the crash, Enafa would still be alive. The chains on her body meant she had been imprisoned on this vessel, so she was doubtless a criminal. But despite all of this, I could not hate her. Enafa had died trying to save her. That meant something, surely.

The fact that she was a healer had to mean something.

I touched one tear on the ensleg's cheek before I rose to my feet. I felt pity for her. I wept for her.

Then I lifted the chief gjenvin's pistol and took justice for what had been done.

Now

ONE

Two forms drifted. Had frost taken shape and life to cross the windward ridge, it would look much like this pair. They were not ghosts, but moved as spirits might, their pace fluid and indifferent. The two made for the best vantage point above the vacant plain, but they also stopped every ten paces. The man turned his head from side to side. The feline watched the man. When they moved again, scythelike claws and spiked serrats pierced the brittle crust of solidified snow, but neither made a sound.

Death, the Iisleg said, no longer walked alone.

Raktar Teulon stopped at the peak of the ridge and performed a complete thermal scan of the surrounding area before removing his face shield. He squinted, making his ghostly eyes shrink to pale slivers between dark lids, and took in the view from north to south. At minus thirty degrees centigrade, the surface air attacked his white and blue outfurs, eager to freeze the body beneath and render it into a statue to tower over the tallest of Iisleg men. It had to be satisfied with leaving scrolls of frost on his weapons, an Iisleg dagger fastened to his right forearm and an offworlder sword with seven curved, congruent blades strapped to the back of his left shoulder.

Do not go, my heart, a memory whispered. *I fear for you.*

Another answered for him. *You no longer have the privilege of choice, slave.*

Once Teulon saw the outlying fields were empty and no ships edged beneath the kvinka overhead, his vision shifted within himself. Like the whispers, he always carried the images inside him. They had come with him to this world, as silent and disconnected as he. Frozen in time they were, and would have made little sense to anyone but him. The soft, pallid hand of a Terran. Green blood on that same hand, tightened to a knotted fist. The noiseless flare of pulse fire. Glittering blades. Darkness. A whip in midarc. Another hand, harder, insistent.

Red blood on blue claws.

Do not go. Her voice, as sweet as summer rain, always faded away before Teulon heard the obscenity of his. *You no longer have the privilege of choice.*

My heart. Slave. My heart. Slave. The whispers rode his breath now. Swelling in. Rushing out. Never ceasing. *Heart-slave-heart-slave-heart-slave-heart—*

And beyond them, there were others. Others he could not hear. Voices that would never speak again. Voices from the void that was as dark as this place was white. Voices forever trapped there, between path and embrace, the voices of the blood, his blood, not of this world but his own, their own, all of them gone now, obliterated, beyond bodies, beyond dust, as if they had never been, and those lost voices shrieked at him, demanding their blood debt be satisfied, their honor known, their path returned to them—

I fear for you.

Teulon glanced down at the big cat, which stood motionless and alert. A familiar yearning glittered in those remote, silvery eyes. "Soon, my friend."

The jlorra bore a thin, diagonal slash of scar tissue that neatly divided the dark fur of his face and wound around to disappear in the full ruff beneath his mouth. The white streak became jagged whenever the cat bared double rows of dagger-shaped blue teeth in a silent snarl. Long ago this particular jlorra had proved too feral to serve the Iisleg who had snared him and then tried to kill him for his furs. The attempt had scarred the cat and stolen his voice, but it had cost the Iisleg two beast masters and five warriors.

The wounded cat had escaped. Roaming the ice fields alone, the jlorra healed, becoming even more dangerous, killing so efficiently and indiscriminately that the Iisleg named him Bsak, after the insatiable, soul-eating god from their oldest legends.

So it was until the day Bsak returned to the Iisleg, walking like a pampered pet at the side of their Raktar, from whom he had not been parted since.

After performing a second scan, Teulon covered his face with the triangular insulated shield plate that protected his skin from the cold and masked any shine from his eyes and teeth. The jlorra paced him as they left the ridge and slowly descended to the snow plain. There waited five figures: Hasal, his second-in-command, and four Iisleg hunters from the Iiskar Elsil, the first of the surface-dwelling tribes to join the rebellion.

Only Hasal dared look directly at him.

Teulon touched his glove to the top of Bsak's head, and the cat sat down on his haunches. "Send them."

Hasal raised one arm and brought it down with a

slashing motion. Snow erupted in countless geysers as one hundred surface skimmers discarded their frost sheets and shot up into the sky. The skimmers' engine-heated shrouds shed meltwater, which fell in a frozen rain and made tiny pits in the ground crust.

In the wake of the launch of the scouts, ground troops in rebel-bleached outfurs swarmed over the plateau to begin setting up camp. Only four figures cast color on the snow, and did not join in the work, but instead came to stand a short distance from Teulon and his lieutenants.

Teulon watched the cluster of skimmers separate and form a reconnaissance line before sweeping up and over the ridge. All the pilots carried beacon finders that had been adapted to locate and mark the position of subsurface bunkers. They would perform a single pass of the designated area before returning. Because the skimmers were of Iisleg design, their presence would not trigger the drone monitors guarding the bunkers.

Teulon knew that the fully automated storage units contained enormous stores of ordnance: surplus and emergency weapons caches from thousands of different worlds, closely guarded, held in reserve until needed.

"No patrol ships," one of the Elsil muttered, scanning the empty horizon.

"The Tos' don't patrol the trenches," Hasal told him.

The Toskald had always had good reason to feel confident about their surface armory. Drone monitors, programmed to fire on anything that attempted to access the trenches without a code, guarded each cache. Codes were changed at random intervals by means unknown to the Iisleg. Even if the monitors could be disabled, there were the internal sensors and inventory scans. If one cache was discovered disturbed, the provisions of food and medicine sent down from the skim cities would stop for a month. If two were disturbed, nothing was sent for a season.

Teulon knew no tribe had ever tried to access more than two caches. Imagining what would happen if they dared had kept the Iisleg obedient for more than five centuries.

One of the first things Teulon had shown the Iisleg had been how to build food synthesizers that rendered most organic materials into edible nourishment. That ended the tribes' dependence on their Toskald masters' supplies. Eradicating the threat of starvation had been the first stage of the rebellion, after the Iisleg had elevated Teulon to Raktar over the rebel forces.

This was the last of the northern territory to be inspected and mapped. When the skimmers returned, they would add their data to that which Teulon's cartographers had already gathered. This would result in a complete, highly detailed map of every armory trench in use on the planet.

Teulon intended to take them all.

A soldier approached and made a polite sound, drawing Bsak's attention. He eyed the big cat with the wariness of one who had seen what a jlorra could do to a strong, armed man.

"What is it?" Hasal demanded.

The soldier nodded toward the waiting hunters. "The emissaries from the eastern iiskars wish to bid the Raktar permit them join us."

Teulon studied the four unfamiliar, waiting men.

Theirs was not an unexpected request. The eastern tribes were considered outlanders, small fringe clans too poor to buy a place for themselves in the crude coalition that had constituted the Iisleg's only form of government. Before Teulon became Raktar, the only security they could afford was through obtaining the uncertain favors of the Toskald princes. Now that the flow of tithes to the skim cities had been disrupted, the outlanders needed to court his protection.

They did not yet understand that Raktar Teulon could never be placated or appeased.

"Bring them," Teulon told the soldier. The easterners would have to be evaluated, trained, and watched, but the Iisleg learned quickly. He could use the additional men to fill in for those who would soon leave to join the others waiting in the northern territory.

The soldier made a quick gesture and the four approached them. One inhalation told Teulon that they had not yet been through any sort of useful field training; they hadn't even bothered to mask their bodies' odors with smoke. Two wore shabby outfurs that sported innumerable mended patches, the mark of low rank. One wore the thermal garments and footgear of an offworlder—likely salvaged from a wreck. The fourth had pristine furs and turned-skin boots unscarred by the ice.

Bsak shifted, and Teulon touched a gloved hand to the back of the cat's neck. The jlorra padded over to the emissary with the offworlder garb and sniffed before doing the same to the one sporting the newer garments. Both men were wise enough to remain still and silent. The big cat moved on to inspect the two shabbier figures before returning to Teulon's side.

Teulon rested his hand on the jlorra's head as he watched all four faces, noting the tiny changes in skin color, sweat odor, and eye lines.

Feeling safer now, New Furs took a bold step forward and bobbed his head. "From Iiskar Bjola I am sent. Many more victories in your name, Raktar."

The other three glanced at each other, as if trying to decide who should go next, and how to at least match the Bjola's honorific perfection. Addressing the Raktar was already a delicate business; this made it only more complicated.

"All have seen the blood of the Tos' on the ice, marking your new kingdom," the Bjola said, his words not as rushed now. He appeared confident, as well, a man who had enjoyed a fortuitous beginning. "Our tribe eagerly welcomes the coming freedom."

Hasal made an indistinct sound. Some heard it as a hiss of impatience, others as the whistle of Iisleg contempt.

Teulon waited. The scent of body odor thickened and changed. Bsak stirred.

None of the outlanders could interpret the Raktar's silence. The Bjola decided to seize the awkward moment as a new opportunity and turned to Hasal. "We would not hide like fearful women in our shelters, of course. Our rasakt would know—would beg know—how many of our men may be sent to serve the Raktar?"

Hasal answered the question with, "All who can carry a bow."

The only Iisleg males who did not carry bows were the rasakt of each iiskar, boys who could not count fifteen seasons, and the dead. The rasakt would have to send every man they had.

The requirement stole what was left of the color in the Bjola emissary's face, but he recovered and made his obeisance by moving a hand diagonally over his chest. The step back he took did not appear as confident as the one he had taken forward, but the outlanders had known nothing of the rebel forces or how to serve them.

Now that they did, the worst part seemed over. The other emissaries relaxed. One attempted to smile.

Teulon lifted his hand. Bsak dropped his head low and fixed his silvery eyes on the four men. His paws flexed, digging retractable claws into the ice, while his body flowed into the posture of an animal ready to spring.

"It would appear," Hasal said in a flat, bored tone, "that one here does not seek to serve."

The four men displayed the stunned expression of innocents. Their stammered-out protests of loyalty died as the jlorra's angular jaw dropped into a silent snarl, displaying blue fangs as long as battle daggers.

Teulon waited.

It was then that one of the pair in the shabby furs decided to act. A pulse pistol appeared in his hand, and he leveled it at Teulon's head.

"Die, offworlder demon of—" The rest became a choked, liquid gasp as Teulon's dagger sank into his neck.

Startled eyes moved from the hilt of the dagger to Teulon's face. No one had seen the Raktar move.

A moment later the pistol hanging limp in the hand of the assassin went flying as Bsak landed on the traitorous emissary and dragged him down into the snow. Jlorra did not waste time toying with their food, and as Bsak fed, the remaining three outlanders looked away.

The snow around their feet turned to pink, then red slush.

Teulon walked past them and nudged the cat aside long enough to retrieve his dagger. He flipped the blood from the blade before it could freeze on the alloy, wiped it clean on the dead man's outfurs, and slid it back into his forearm sheath.

"Hasal." Teulon walked toward the temporary shelter that had been erected for his use.

Inside the Iisleg hunting tent, the heatarc's coils glowed amber through their distribution mesh. Hasal removed his gloves to warm his thin hands. "Ice eaters. They become bolder by the day."

Teulon used a piece of cloth to clean the faint traces of blood still clinging to his blade. Iisleg blood was very thick and tenacious. "Desperation."

"The most dangerous of men are. And these easterners—I know their kind." Hasal crouched to scoop clean ice into a melt pot and placed it on the cookmesh. "Even the ones who believe in the rebellion would rather kiss Kangal ass than fight. The Tos' bounty on your head has gone from extravagant to extreme."

Teulon watched his second prepare a strong, dark infusion of tea plant and idleberry grown in skim-city greenhouses. The Iisleg were addicted to the drink, which was also their only source of certain vitamins, without which they suffered a form of scurvy. The ingredients were among the many foodstuffs he had taught them to grow over the last year in the abandoned amory trenches, now transformed into hydroponics labs, to supplement what could be produced from the synthesizers. "Deprivation consumes honor."

"As you say, Raktar." Hasal filled a transparent server carved from clear airstone so as to resemble a chunk of ice, and took a sip to check for poison before bringing it to him.

"Are they ready?"

Hasal nodded. "You have but to give the word." He tugged back his hood and fingered a tuft of pale hair over his right ear. There was a tiny, brittle snap, and he plucked a crushed insect from one strand and showed it to Teulon. "This is the soul of an eastern tribe, Raktar." He flicked the dead insect into the heatarc, where it was instantly vaporized. "Lice, all of them."

Teulon drank some of the tea. Idleberry gave the infusion a fruit scent and a faint sweet taste, but not enough had been added to mask the intense bitterness of the tea plant. The Iisleg deliberately brewed it that way, Hasal had told him once, not to save the idleberry, but to remind themselves of the nature of life.

The tea, like the outlander tribes, was an unpleasant necessity. He watched the light from the heatarc refract through the convoluted airstone, where it created the distorted image of a face trapped in glass. The mouth of the face yawned as if trying to gulp down the dark steaming liquid of the tea. "We need them."

"We shall be blessed if they do not first barter us off to the Kangal." Hasal started to say something else before he dragged in more air and thought about it. "It is said that they make half their women skela in order to collect more worgald."

Teulon had heard little but bad jokes and expressions of disgust toward the dead handlers. Iisleg collectively regarded them as little more than excrement with limbs. He personally had no use for them. "I do not want their women."

"What if these men betray us?" Hasal asked.

Teulon's fist contracted, and the airstone server shattered.

One hundred miles to the east, Rasakt Deves Navn, headman of Iiskar Navn, listened as his most experienced tracker relayed the details of his latest excursion.

"I saw no caravans for ten kim," the scout said. He had shed his outfurs, and was still using thermopacks to warm his red, snowbitten hands. "No sled trails in the air. We know Skjonn has not descended for weeks."

The two men were the only occupants of the rasakt's shelter. Amber light from the heatarc made their faces ruddy and kept the cold pinned to the layers of stretched skins and salvaged alloy panels that formed the thick, flexible walls. Above their heads, trickles of icy air that had slipped in through tiny cracks in the wall seams and around the top of the rolled hide of the smoke flue danced with the rising heat.

"What of his forces?" Like other Iisleg, Navn did not speak the name of the Raktar out loud. To do so was considered equal to shouting for the gods to visit death upon the camp.

"The army is but four suns' journey from us, moving east," the scout said. He was a man of middle years, a veteran of crossing the ice, and bore the scars of countless skirmishes with man and beast on his skin. No emotion showed in his flat eyes. "Perhaps as many as ten thousand men surround him. Reserve battalions flanking them on all sides, ready to supply replacements."

"Twenty thousand he has, then." Sizable, but not enough to challenge the Toskald forces. Cold made Navn's own fingers ache, but to warm them over the heatarc in front of a subordinate was a show of weakness, something he especially guarded against. Instead he tucked his hands into the ends of his sleeves, assuming a pose of wisdom and patience. He long suspected the pose had been invented by one of his own ancestors, perhaps another rasakt with appendages equally vulnerable to chill.

"More than twenty, Rasakt," the scout cautioned. "I counted the reserves at four to one, and more arrive with each passing sun."

Fifty thousand men. Rasakt Navn forgot about his personal discomfort and regarded the map of the eastern territories. On it were red marks indicating the reported sightings of the central rebel army, but there were so many now, the map skin appeared riddled by pox. "Where do they go?"

"I cannot tell you." The scout's eyes changed, and his voice went low with shame. "They vanish from their camps before dawn, and they leave no track. It is as if they conjure a path from one place to the next." He made a protective sign over himself.

Navn restrained a sigh. The rebels were obviously using some manner of surface transport vessels, which were regarded as magical creatures by the outland tribes. Only a few headmen like Navn were educated enough to know that the flying ships did not actually devour men and belch flame.

This is not for them to know, Navn's father, the former headman of the iiskar, had instructed him. *Most ignorance is unnecessary, but some serves as a means of control and rule.*

Using surface-to-space transport on Akkabarr had never been possible. The only ships that came to the surface were flown by the Toskald pilots, the only ones who knew the secret to successfully navigating through the mile-wide, vicious kvinka currents of the upper atmosphere. Once, a tribe had captured a ship, intending to force the pilot to take them to the skim city, but the ship had mysteriously exploded before it ever left the ice, killing everyone on board. The remainder of the tribe was denied supplies and slowly starved to death.

Navn did not know how the Toskald had convinced so many worlds within the Tryg Quadrant to use Akkabarr as a storage depot and central armory, but that trust had never been betrayed. Shipwrecks of those who tried to raid the planet provided the Iisleg with the bulk of their tithe wealth. Since offworlders constantly tried to get at the billions of weapons stored in subsurface armory trenches, crashes were frequent.

Not that the crashes would do them any good now with this rebellion brewing.

Among the eastern tribes, Iiskar Navn held a superior position. It was the largest and oldest of the tribes. Some thought that Deves would imitate his father's warlike ways, but the younger Navn learned that no one could eliminate every enemy, and to die covered in glory still meant one was dead.

When Navn had taken over as headman, he had demanded moderation and reason instead of battles and glory. His warriors became competent hunters, and his salvagers kept the tribe's tithes modest but regular. Some of the older Iisleg had been scathing and even whispered Navn the Younger was a coward, but time was on Deves's side. His tribe grew, as did his stores. In time Kangal Orjakis had selected his men to serve as caravanners to transport and present the worgald and tribute from this region to Skjonn.

Navn did not want rebellion, not after all those years of careful work. Yet unless he chose sides, he and his tribe would end as victims of both.

Shouts surrounded the headman's tent, and the scout automatically drew his bow and went to the flap. "An intruder, come into camp," he said, but he lowered his bow. "A woman."

Navn had no time for females, visiting or his own. It was the odd look on his scout's face that drew him to the flap to glance outside.

His men had formed a protective barrier before his tent, but beyond their shoulders he saw a small, sticklike figure with tattered, rotting furs hanging from her body.

The female appeared as human as the Iisleg, but she was not a native. Her hair had been grown as long as a man's. He had never seen a woman so thin, either, not even during the Famine of Disobedience. She did not speak, but tottered about, reaching skeletal hands toward his men, who moved out of reach.

If she had been a man, they would have helped her, but women held little value for the Iisleg. They earned a small bride-price for their fathers when they were of age to be purchased for marriage, but that was their only real worth. The gods had created women without souls so that they would be content to provide care and warmth for men. Wives could be trusted with simple, menial tasks, like cooking, weaving, and purifying water. Until she married, a female shared her mother's work, or sorted in the gjenvin tents. A few who were unsuitable for marriage for various reasons were permitted to serve as ahayag and provide physical relief to the unmarried men of the tribe.

Navn did not care about the woman, or her pitiful state. It was the twisted symbol, still visible on the breast of her ragged undergarment, that struck him to the core.

That, he had seen before. It was the same as the mark on the garment of an ensleg female the gjenvin had brought back from a crash site. A woman with a terrible head wound, who had been covered in blood and dying.

But it could not be her. That female was dead. Had been dead for two years now.

"It is a walking shade," his scout whispered, raising his bow to dispatch it.

"No." Navn covered the bow sight with his hand and stared hard at the manacle around one of the female's bony wrists. That, too, was familiar to his eyes. "I will see her."

The scout appeared astounded by this, but moved to one side. Navn secured his skull wrap before stepping out. As he moved through his men, they parted as new snow before the storm.

"How does she live?" one of Navn's hunters asked

no one in particular. "She carries no furs, no food, no weapons."

"The demons protect her." Another raised his bow.

Navn stepped between the bow and the woman. "No."

The female, evidently exhausted, stopped and sank to her knees in the snow. Her fingers were ghostly sticks, colored and stiffened to gray claws by snowbite. Navn reached and caught her by a length of her snarled dark hair before she toppled. Her eyes rolled up into her head for a moment before she focused on his face. Her lips moved to shape something, but it was not a word he understood.

Navn thought of the ensleg female who had come two years ago. Who had worn the same symbol. Who had been dragged into his tent by the chief gjenvin, who had claimed the skela could not kill her. Unlike this one, her face had been caked in frozen blood and gore. He could not tell from the features if this woman was the same one.

No, that one who came before is dead. Navn, who had lost his faith when he had become headman, made a sign of protection over himself. *I myself watched the jlorra drag her out of camp. They must have devoured her. They would not permit a dying thing to live. She was nothing but food to them.*

He seized her arm and brought it up to examine the manacle around her wrist. The alloy cuff was of off-world making and had slots where chains could be attached. The other ensleg female had been wearing two manacles identical to this one, with broken lengths of chain hanging from them.

This is not the same one. It cannot be. "Who are you?"

She did not answer him, or rouse at the shake he gave her.

There were legends about the vral, faceless spirit beings made flesh that could not be killed. The gods sent such things to prove a man worthy. Navn had never believed in such tales. Everything died.

He stared down at the unconscious female. She was flesh. She possessed a face. But if he tried to kill her now, and she would not die . . .

Navn released her and gestured for two of the women hovering at the edge of the group of hunters to come forward. "Carry her to the visitors' tent," he told them. "Have Hurgot examine her." After a momentary hesitation he added, "If she can be saved, she may live."

No one looked directly at him—one did not make eye contact with the rasakt—but his instructions sent a wave of shock through those present. An ensleg could come to Akkabarr only from a crashed ship. The subzero conditions on the planet usually killed any survivors. The Iisleg did not rescue ensleg; alive they had no value to the tribe.

Navn was never happier in his rank. As rasakt, he was not required to explain himself. He did not have to inform his tribe that the woman wore the mark of an ensleg healer. Nor did he have to share the decision as to whether to send tithe to Skjonn, the skim city of Kangal Orjakis, whose taste for ensleg females was notorious.

"Rasakt, shall we send the gjenvin to look for her . . . for a ship?" one of the hunters was brave enough to ask.

"No." Things would only grow worse when they did not find one. The rasakt turned his back on the unconscious female. "Take her."

Two

Encrypted File
092002573

She sleeps as I write this.

Her quarters are far from my own, but I have not planted any recording drones to watch her. Close proximity and remote surveillance have never been necessary—I have been aware of her from the first, and the connection between us grows stronger each day. She is unaware of it, or deliberately ignores it.

I cannot. She is always with me now.

Duncan Reever stared at the words he had recorded during his last year serving as linguist for the multi-species colony on Kevarzangia Two. The year he had met a Terran surgeon, Cherijo Gray Veil, who had saved his life, and had given him many reasons to live again.

But she was no longer with him. Cherijo was gone, taken from him two years ago—

Go.

Find her.

Hurry.

Those four words had sustained him through the long, frantic months of searching for his missing wife.

They had begun as a silent prayer and grown into a merciless directive. Presently they formed the taut, four-ply thread of will that enabled control in a situation where he had very little left.

Go. Find her. Hurry.

These days, those four words were all that kept Reever from going mad.

Logic provided the only structure and reason that he would accept in his current state. He had to go. If Cherijo had been capable of returning to him, she would have done so by now. He had to find her. Something had prevented her escape, something she could not overcome on her own. When he found her, he would free her. He had to do so quickly. He could not stop, could not rest, not for a moment. Thanks to his wife's unique genetic qualities, she was the most hunted, coveted fugitive in the galaxy. If Reever did not find her, someone else would.

Logic provided direction on the path, according to the Jorenians, but no comfort. They referred to it as "the indifferent whip across the soul's shoulders."

The whip made no difference. Reever had made a vow all those years ago, a promise to protect Cherijo and watch over her. To stay with her for as long as he lived. As long as there was even a remote chance that she was alive, he would not stop searching for her.

To stop would be the same as walking through an open air lock into space.

That Cherijo was more than a wife to Reever was something no one understood. He had never attempted to express what he felt for her to anyone but her. Even with her, words failed him.

Why do you love me, Duncan?

He felt the only adequate answer he had given her had been after another of her endless double shifts in surgery, when she had been too tired to strip out of her bloodstained scrubs. He had been obliged to undress her and help her into the cleansing unit.

He pulled the bloodstained tunic over her head. *You are what I have always wanted.*

I'm an arrogant, bad-tempered—she brushed back some hair from her eyes to look at him—*inconsiderate shrew, and that's on my good days.* She placed one slim hand on his shoulder to steady herself as she stepped out of her trousers. *You should work on your wish list. You know, just in case something happens to me.*

Aware that the intensity of their connection and his own feelings often frightened her, he hadn't told her that there would never be anyone else. She had frightened him, too. It was all there in his old journal files.

> The detail is astonishing; when I concentrate, I can feel the adrenaline pumping in her veins and the precise focus of her thoughts as she works. My limbs ache with the ghost weight of her exhaustion after she finishes a double shift in Medical. I can count her breaths, smell her scent, and occasionally—to my dismay—even taste what she eats.
>
> Through her, I have discovered needs that I never knew existed. They twist inside me, these peculiar, foreign demands—and I am almost certain they are not coming from her. The old priest Arembel, who cared for the injured after bouts in the arena, once told me how it could be, but I did not expect this.
>
> I did not expect her.

His gaze drifted toward the end of the entry, where he had written, *The good doctor dreams of me.* To his knowledge, no one had ever done that—dreamed of him—and at first it had puzzled him.

Does she still dream of me? Does she miss me? Does she wonder, every waking moment, if I am well? Is she frightened? Have they hurt her?

If nothing else, Reever at last understood the killing rage the Jorenians felt whenever their kin were threatened or harmed.

He shut down the console and went to finish his last task. Halfway through his packing, the door chime rang. "Come in."

Xonea Torin, a seven-and-a-half-foot-tall Jorenian and captain of the Torin HouseClan's ship the *Sunlace*, entered Reever's quarters and closed the door panel behind him. "Linguist."

He had been expecting this visit. "Captain."

"You will not find her."

"I already have." Reever stowed another weapon in his gear pack and glanced through the viewport. Below the ship's orbit, the white-and-blue sphere that was the planet Akkabarr swelled like a bubble of ice. "She is down there."

"You cannot know this. There has been no word of her on this world, or any other." Xonea, who was also Cherijo's adopted brother, came to stand beside him. "No one from the League will confirm that the slaver transport crashed here."

The League had never confirmed anything since the Jado Massacre, which had occurred just after Cherijo had saved two worlds and had subsequently been sold to a pair of Rilken slavers. She had overpowered her diminutive abductors, had taken control of their ship, and had been flying to rejoin Duncan and Marel on the *CloudWalk*, HouseClan Jado's ship. While she was en route, the Jado ClanLeader had left to meet with the League, and then had transmitted emergency orders for the *CloudWalk* to open fire on the League ships.

That signal was the last thing Reever clearly remembered before waking up in medical bay on the *Sunlace* and being told that Cherijo's ship had vanished during the battle. The League placed Cherijo's name on the official list of those who had gone missing and were presumed killed during the Jado Massacre.

"The computers salvaged from the transport were sold by the Toskald." Reever had personally hunted down and interrogated the Bartermen involved in the transaction. "I ran the logs myself."

"The logs simply showed that the ship was one of many in the vicinity of Oenrall at the time of the massacre," Xonea reminded him.

"That transport received orders to depart Oenrall for Akkabarr on the same day Cherijo was abducted. It arrived. It never departed. She was on it." And she was down there, waiting for him. It was all very logical.

"The Mother of All Houses prove you right." The big Jorenian rubbed a dark blue, six-fingered hand over his brow. "You cannot land on the surface. It is too dangerous. Every pilot who has attempted it is dead."

Reever glanced briefly at him before he selected a dagger from his weapons storage unit and tucked it into his sleeve sheath.

"Very well, what say you somehow succeed where so many have not, and make a successful landing."

Xonea stepped between Reever and the storage unit before he could take out another blade. "The surface dwellers are in revolt against the Toskald. If they find you, they will kill you."

"They can try." Reever knew precisely how dangerous the natives were; he had been studying all known aspects of Iisleg culture, along with their origins, for weeks. They might try to kill him, but many had tried, and all had failed. Besides, he had other plans for the rebels.

There is only one thing better than defeating an enemy, the old priest Arembel, another Hsktskt captive who like Reever had been forced to fight in the slaver arena, had told him. *Make the enemy work for you.*

"You may go to your death for nothing. We have not seen her for—"

"Two years, forty-six days, nine hours, and eighteen minutes." Reever reached around him and took out two more knives. These were Omorr-made, and slid into the sheaths strapped to the outsides of his thighs. He preferred fighting with Omorr weapons in subzero conditions; extreme cold did not affect their brilliantly forged steel.

"Duncan." Although the Jorenian people were accustomed to making frequent physical gestures of affection, Xonea did not make the mistake of touching him. "You must be prepared for the worst."

"That is why I am packing." On impulse, Reever picked up a handheld voice recorder and tucked it into a pocket.

Frustrated, the larger man made a careless gesture toward the viewer. "So you survive it all, to do what?

Find what is left of her? You would scan every pile of bones down on that ice ball for her DNA?"

The ghost of Cherijo's first love, Kao Torin, looked out at Reever from Xonea's solid white eyes. Before becoming Reever's wife, Cherijo had bonded herself briefly to Xonea, as well, a time when Reever had thought her lost to him forever. He would not revisit that private torture chamber again. He already existed in a far worse place. "She is not dead."

The captain of the *Sunlace* wasn't finished. "What say you if she is? What do you then, Duncan? Will you lie down with her remains? Will you embrace the stars while you hold a corpse in a bed of snow?"

"She is not dead." He couldn't explain why he was convinced of it. He knew only that if she had died, he would have felt her go. He was sure of that.

As sure as he knew that he would do exactly as Xonea predicted if he discovered he was wrong.

"There is nothing I may say that will persuade you to abandon this quest, is there?" Xonea, not expecting an answer, turned to leave, and then hesitated. Without looking at Reever, he said, "I say these things not to wish her gone, Duncan. I honored her. We all of us honored her."

There was no Jorenian word for *love*. The closest to it was *honor*, which still did not equate the same word in every other language Reever knew. Jorenian honor meant far more than mere admiration or respect. It encompassed a degree of personal devotion greater than most humanoids were capable of feeling.

Reever's wife had lived with that sort of honor. He had lived for her, and now he lived for those four words.

Go. Find her. Hurry.

The door panel opened before Xonea reached it and a petite Terran child with bubbly blond hair darted into the room and dodged around Xonea to fling herself at Reever's legs. Her small arms formed a tight cinch around his knees. "Daddy, don't go."

"Marel." Reever gently loosened his daughter's grip and lifted her up, holding her carefully as her small arms encircled his neck. The child buried her face against his chest. She smelled of the Jorenian herbal cleanser that bore close resemblance to Terran vanilla.

Xonea gave him one final, wordless look before he left them alone.

"Please, Daddy." Marel's voice trembled even more than her diminutive form. "Please don't go away. Please."

Some Terrans still believed in hell. Reever could see why.

"I am not going away." He carried his daughter to the chair where once he told her bedtime stories, and sat down with her. How long had it been since he had held her like this? He could not remember. He had been so busy looking for Cherijo. "I am going to get your mother."

"I don't want you to." Marel lifted her small face and stared at him with eyes that changed color from blue to silvery gray, just as his own did. The shape of her eyes, however, was identical to her mother's.

"I am the only one who can find her, Marel." Reever had to make her understand. He was the only one who could go. The only one who could move fast enough. Who could safeguard her. Who would kill for her.

His daughter's brow furrowed. "Daddy, everyone says Mama is gone to the stars."

He had heard the same, many times. He had simply not realized the Torin were saying it when his child could overhear them. Or perhaps he had not reinforced his own, contrasting view. Truthfully, he could not recall the last time he had held Marel like this, or had spoken to her about her mother. "No, she has not. She lives."

"If she's not with the stars, then why did she leave us alone for so long?" The child's hands became small, hard fists. "You said Mama loved us."

"She does." Cherijo had been gone too long for Marel to retain any substantial memories of her. To his four-year-old daughter, "Mama" had become the face smiling out of a two-dimensional photoscan, the central character in one of many tales, lovingly told.

Marel was not aware of what her mother had done to save and protect her. Cherijo had been utterly ruthless about concealing their daughter, pretending to lose her during a miscarriage, while in reality having Marel successfully transferred to an embryonic chamber. She had even kept that from Reever for more than a year. Cherijo had since erased all of Marel's medical records and had enlisted the Jorenians in concealing Marel's existence. He knew that his wife would go to her death rather than let anyone harm their daughter.

Reever had not told Marel any of this because he had always felt that it was not his story to tell. That may have been an error on his part. "Your mother loves us very much, my delight."

"Then why doesn't she come back?" Marel demanded.

For his daughter's sake, he wished again he could be anyone other than who he was. Not a battle-hardened warrior and telepathic linguist. Not someone who could kill with his bare hands, fly combat missions, and translate words and concepts into several hundred thousand languages. The man he was could not give his child the reassurance she needed.

You could start, Duncan, Cherijo would say, *by telling her the truth.*

"Marel." He waited until she met his gaze. "If you were lost, and could not find your way back to me and the HouseClan, would you wish me to come and find you?" She gave a reluctant nod. "That is what I believe has happened to your mother. She is down there, on that planet. Her ship crashed there, and the winds above the surface are so strong that she cannot leave. That is why I must go and find her, and bring her back to us."

The child thought this over. "What if *your* ship crashes?"

He had refused to think about what his death would do to his daughter. As much as he loved her, even the prospect of making her an orphan could not stop him from going to Akkabarr to find his wife. Nothing could.

Go. Find her. Hurry.

It was for the best. Soon there would not be enough left of him to make even an adequate pretense of being a father to Marel.

The Torin will protect her and care for her. "I am a better pilot than your mother," he said, quite truthfully. "Mine will not crash."

Marel pressed her cheek against his chest and

closed her eyes. "Take me with you. I'll help you look for Mama. I'm good at helping."

"You are." Reever stroked a hand over her soft curls. "But someone must stay here and look after Jenner."

As if hearing his name as a summons, a large, silver gray cat with blue eyes walked into the room. He was followed by his mate, Juliet, a completely black female with large golden green eyes. The two felines looked at Reever, then at Marel, and came over to sit at Reever's feet.

Marel sat up and gazed down at them, her bottom lip pushed out and trembling. "Jen has Jules to love him. If you don't come back, I won't have anyone." Before Reever could respond to that, she flung herself against him once more. "I love you, Daddy. Please find her this time."

Reever, who had never learned how to weep, felt his eyes burn and saw his visual field blur. "I will, Marel. I will."

Two decks below Reever's quarters on the *Sunlace*, Senior Healer Squilyp stared at the patient charts waiting for his review. The modest stack contained routine cases being supervised by the Omorr's medical and surgical residents, all of whom were extremely capable and hardly in need of his direct supervision. He always reviewed the charts anyway; being the primary physician and chief surgeon on board the *Sunlace* was a responsibility he took very seriously.

Cherijo Gray Veil had been the Senior Healer before him. One did not follow in the footsteps of the best cardiothoracic surgeon in the galaxy without feeling a certain sense of inadequacy.

What had he said to her when she had selected him to succeed her? *I will get even with you for this.*

Dark blue, slanted eyes had rolled in an insolent fashion. *Dream on, Squid Lips.*

Beyond the stack of charts, the upper hemisphere of Akkabarr filled the bottom half of the exterior viewer panel. Many who knew nothing about Akkabarran slavers considered the remote ice world intriguing and beautiful. To Squilyp's eyes, the planet was as attractive as a pus-filled boil.

You care deeply for her, do you not? Duncan Reever had once asked him, seemingly on impulse. There was something in his eyes, however, that told the Omorr that Reever had given much thought to the question.

Squilyp had tried to answer honestly. *She is my best friend. Of course I do.*

He had not been entirely truthful. He had cared for Cherijo, looked after her, and respected her. He had even grown strangely fond of her temper, annoying as it was. Yet he had also envied her, and had been regularly exasperated by her. No person he had ever known had possessed her talents, or had cared so little for them. Her capacity for compassion routinely shamed him, and then she would do something so blindingly stupid he would be propelled into shock.

Squilyp had acknowledged long ago that Cherijo had been one of the most important and influential people in his life. He counted himself fortunate for that.

He also wished that he had never met her.

She is down there. She had to be; all the evidence

Reever had uncovered indicated that she was. If she was still alive, Reever would find her.

If she is . . .

Squilyp reached with one of his three arms to take the first chart from the top of the stack, and watched with mild surprise as the entire stack instead went flying off his desk and landed with a noisy clatter on the deck. At nearly the exact same moment, his door panel opened, and a tall female Omorr hopped in.

Garphawayn, the Lady Maftuda, stopped a few feet from his desk and surveyed the clutter of charts. The meter-long, prehensile gildrells that covered her mouth flared like a nest of agitated white snakes. She was tall and elegant, a female Omorr in her prime, with healthy pink hide and strong, shapely limbs. A slight bulge beneath her sternum bones disrupted the elegant line of her torso, but the evidence of her unborn child's growth made her seem only lovelier to Squilyp.

He stared at her, the woman he loved. Garphawayn and their child were the main reason that he prayed Cherijo was dead. He loved them more than his life; surely he could be pardoned for wishing to keep them alive.

Cherijo, who had tried to kill herself more than once to save Reever and Marel, would forgive him.

Her dark, round eyes shifted to study his face. "Perhaps this is not the ideal time for us to discuss why you are still working, or the desiccated condition of the evening meal that I prepared for you several hours ago."

"Close the panel," Squilyp told his mate.

Garphawayn closed and secured the door. "Is this

show of temper and reluctance to complete your shift a response to some offense I have unknowingly committed?"

Squilyp used the membranes on the end of one arm to rub his tired eyes. "Reever leaves within the hour for the surface."

"I see." His mate glanced at the viewer panel. "You are not accompanying him." That part was delivered as both a statement and a warning; Garphawayn had no qualms with asserting her rights as his mate and debating his decisions.

Squilyp could not go with Reever. He was the Senior Healer; he could not be spared to risk his life on a foolhardy quest that would likely end in disaster before it began.

That was the official reason, anyway. "I am not."

Garphawayn's expression softened. "I am glad to know it. You are needed here, husband." She turned her back on the viewer. "Do not misinterpret that remark as a show of indifference to the feelings of others."

"Your sentiments are known to me." A year of marriage had enabled Squilyp to learn precisely what lay beneath her proud, remote manner. Her capacity for understanding and affection often staggered him.

Just as Cherijo's had.

"I feel much sympathy for Reever, and indeed for Cherijo, too, if she still lives," his wife said carefully, as if she knew she was treading on sacred ground. "Yet someone must think of the child. Of both children."

Squilyp rose and hopped around the desk. "The children are always my concern. Marel is like my own daughter. As is Xan . . ." He couldn't think of the boy or look at the planet anymore. "It does not matter now. I do apologize for being inconsiderate and ruining dinner."

"It is only food. One can always prepare more." Garphawayn touched him in the way of Omorr mates: a light and discreet brush of two of her gildrells against his. "You must stop blaming yourself for what happened. You did everything you could when she disappeared. We all did."

"It is not that." Squilyp *had* blamed himself for months after the Jado Massacre, but when Cherijo did not reemerge and the standoff between Joren and the League stabilized, those feelings had grown into a shameful relief. "I pray that Reever is correct, and that she is down there on that planet. She was—is—my best friend." He would keep reminding himself of that.

"That is very kind, but that is not all you feel."

Guilt made his voice grow tight. "I cannot deny that it would be better for Marel—for everyone—if Reever fails."

"Squilyp." Garphawayn took a step back. "You cannot mean that. Reever would never recover from the loss, and neither would the child. As for Cherijo, what has she done to deserve such a fate?"

He shook his head. "You do not understand what it will mean if she is found."

"Of course I do," his mate snapped. "What her parent made her to be is not her doing. Cherijo deserves to live freely. Reever needs his mate; Marel, her mother."

"This is not about what Cherijo is, or what she means to those who love her," Squilyp said. "The Jado were slaughtered. The League has unequivocally stated that the *CloudWalk* attacked their ships and they were only defending themselves when they destroyed it. They provided a recording of the Jado ClanLeader giving his ship orders to fire on them."

Her gildrells became stiff spokes of outrage. "The League commander is a liar, and that recording was falsified."

"We cannot prove it. There has never been any proof that the League ships did anything but defend themselves, and every League officer has provided sworn testimony of the same. The recording has been examined by both sides and declared to be authentic. Reever and the children never saw or heard what happened." His shoulders slumped. "Cherijo is the only witness left who may confirm or deny the official version of the events."

Garphawayn made a disgusted sound. "You know as well as I that the League fired first."

"I know that the Jado had no reason to attack. They were there to negotiate peace." Squilyp remembered the strong, stoic expression of the Jado negotiator. "Unless they knew that the League had captured Cherijo before the firing began. She was—is—a member of the Jorenian planetary Ruling Council. If the Jado knew she was in danger, they would have immediately abandoned the negotiations in order to get her back."

"To get her back by attacking the ship on which she was held?" His mate sounded incredulous. "By destroying it? I think not."

"An enraged Jorenian does not often think clearly," he assured her.

"That may be so, but I still do not understand how it can be better that she is never found," Garphawayn said, her tone flat now. "She was there; she knows the truth. That truth must be told."

This was what everyone thought, what everyone felt. Cherijo, the ultimate truth seeker, had become a symbol of it. Everyone admired her and loved her; few thought of the practical matters, like the actual consequences of such a revelation.

"Until her body is discovered, Cherijo remains a member of the Ruling Council. If she is found, she will confirm whether or not the League fired first. If they did, they massacred an entire HouseClan." Squilyp swallowed a surge of bile. "You do not want to know what the Jorenian response to that will be."

"If the League fired first, they deserve whatever the Jorenians do to them," his mate stated flatly.

"It is not only the Jorenians." Squilyp touched the wall panel and switched the viewer panel from clear to opaque. "There are worlds outside the League and the Faction who want this war to end. They view the Jorenians as admirable for remaining neutral through it. If it is known that the League massacred the Jado, that will be the final outrage. Those worlds technologically advanced enough will use it as impetus to take up Joren's cause as their own."

His mate's eyes flared wide. "How many worlds would do so?"

Squilyp enabled the viewer panel, changing the magnification to show the dark, glittering expanse of the surrounding quadrant.

He left his mate staring out at ten thousand stars.

THREE

Hurgot did his best to hide his anger as he stripped the rotted rags from the body of the unconscious ensleg female. It was a waste of his time, this examination, but the rasakt had ordered it done. There was no question of refusal.

Still, what was Navn thinking, showing such attention to a half-dead ensleg, and a female one at that?

He felt no pity as he studied her pathetic condition. Malnourishment or starvation had feasted on her flesh, leaving her with limbs like well-worried bones and a slightly swollen belly. She had not the intelligence or sense to cover properly before venturing out on the ice. Offworlders seldom did, which was why so many ended as stiff white blobs covered in snow. In the old days that stupidity alone would have earned her a slit throat, had she been Iisleg, to eliminate all possibility of her reproducing equally brainless offspring.

Before Hurgot touched her, he covered his hands with thin hide mitts. *Navn be sliced,* he thought. *I will not contaminate myself with whatever offworlder vermin she carries.*

Her skin responded to his prodding with more resilience than he expected. That she had suffered from waterlack rather than coldsleep was evident. Her lips and eyelids were swollen and chapped, but her belly felt warm. She had probably tried to eat snow for water, unaware that she could not afford to lose the body heat required to melt ice crystals in her mouth. Yet from wherever she had come, she had not traveled far; the snowbite on her fingers and toes showed a sickly gray that would heal, not the black that promised flesh rot.

"The gods smile upon you, ensleg." It was only another reason to resent her. She had shaleev, that rare and blind luck the deities for their own amusement sometimes afforded fools and incompetents. But divine intervention was scarce enough, and desperately needed by all men; to waste such on a woman was akin to the gods showing affection for a pack beast.

As Navn had. Did the headman not remember that a healer's talent was supposed to be devoted exclusively to caring for the men of the tribe?

Hurgot parted the ensleg's long dark hair to check for parasitic infestation—if she was permitted to stay, one of the tribe's women would have to shear her properly—and frowned at a mass of scar tissue beneath a swath of shorter, silvery white hair that measured as long and wide as his hand. *Such a wound should have killed her.*

A soft groan emerged from the ensleg's mouth, and her eyelids fluttered open. Her eyes were tilted like an Iisleg's, and she was obviously human, but that only made her seem all the more unnatural. It was appalling to think that his people shared a common ancestry with such an ensleg being.

He waited for her to focus on his features before he

gave her some water from a skin to moisten her mouth. "Tell me your name."

A line formed between her dark brows, and her lips pressed together, opened, and then closed again. The way she regarded him seemed to indicate that she did not understand his speech.

"Do you not speak Iisleg?" What a foolish question. She was an offworlder; of course she did not. It only made the situation that much more frustrating. The only manner in which he might communicate with her would be through a language translation device, such as those the windlords used, but the Iisleg were not permitted such things.

He tapped his shoulder. "Hurgot." He repeated the gesture and his name several times, and then nudged her shoulder and gave her an expectant look.

The ensleg appeared more confused and now perhaps a little afraid.

"Do you not remember?" The head wound she had suffered in the past had been grievous; he had known men with such wounds to lose all knowledge of themselves, their tribe, and the world. Some had been reduced to a perpetual state of infancy, unable to control their limbs or bowels. Those who were unable to care for themselves were removed from camp during the night and taken to the nearest jlorra cavern.

"Dahktar." The female struggled to sit up. "Dahktar."

The word held no meaning for him, but was uncomfortably close to *Raktar*. "Be still. You will only lose your wits again if you try to stand." He pushed at her scrawny shoulders with his hands to emphasize the words.

The ensleg peered up at him and pointed at his shoulder. "Hurgot."

"Yes."

She pointed at her shoulder and looked expectantly at him. It was a perfect mimicry of what he had done, but she wasn't mocking him. She was making the same request of him.

"I don't know who you are." He saw a flicker of disappointment cross her features, but that was the sole reaction she showed. The few ensleg he had encountered during his lifetime had been male slavers, but like other windlords they were as children and flaunted their emotions. It was one reason the Iisleg regarded their former masters with complete contempt.

"Hurgot?"

He turned to see another woman standing inside the flap of the tent. Would the camp's females begin pestering him for a look at the oddity? "I am occupied."

"Even for word from our rasakt?" The female dropped her face wrap, revealing the vivid, sensual features that had once enchanted every male permitted to see them. Over time lines of petulance and malice had scored the beauty, but Sogayi was still considered the loveliest of women. Of course being taken by Navn as kedera had only made her seem more desirable; the headman had his pick of women for first wife, and had paid Sogayi the ultimate compliment of never taking a second.

Hurgot was more interested in being politic than being pulled under the spell of a female, particularly one with as much influence over Navn as Sogayi possessed. "Never, Kedera. How may I serve?"

Sogayi stayed where she was and let her gaze drift over him, lingering on his white hair, wrinkled face, and gnarled hands before she made a rude gesture toward the ensleg. "The rasakt would know the state of this thing."

An answer to be carefully considered. If the headman wanted her to die, Hurgot could arrange such, but Navn would not have sent his woman to make such a request. Also, Sogayi showed little affection toward members of her own gender. The phrasing she used might have come from her own distaste and not Navn's.

He decided to be cautiously honest. "The female is malnourished and dehydrated, and suffers from moderate snowbite and exhaustion. If it pleases the rasakt to provide for her needs, she will live."

This did not please Sogayi, whose eyes measured the length of the ensleg's hair. "We do not need women who ape men in this camp."

"No," Hurgot said. To point out that Sogayi herself wore her hair to her shoulders, and in other ways often stepped beyond the bounds of suitable female behavior, would have been uncivil, and possibly dangerous. Hurgot could prove nothing, but he suspected Sogayi had sent many women and more than one man to the ice by pouring her sweet poison into Navn's ear.

"I will send women to care for her," Sogayi said, as if it were her decision. "Tonight you may present her to the rasakt."

Hurgot forgot discretion and raised his eyebrows. "It is likely that she will not be well enough to walk such a distance for several suns."

Sogayi wrapped her face, but not in time to hide her

smile. "Then you may carry her." She slipped out through the flap and left it open and fluttering.

Had any other woman in camp spoken to him in such a fashion, Hurgot would have been within his rights to immediately order her to be beaten. As Navn's kedera, Sogayi was not exempt from proper behavior—on the contrary, she was expected to set an example for the other females—but making any issue of her disrespect was the same as telling Navn that he had made a poor choice in wives.

Given the rasakt's blind affection for his wife, Hurgot was not inclined to be so reckless.

"Well, ensleg," he said to the woman, who was watching his face, "at least you do not weigh very much."

The events of the day had left Navn with a sour belly and an aching head. Neither was improved by the last two duties to be performed before he could retire for the night.

"Our hunters brought down seven ptar," Skuyl, Navn's storekeeper, said as he made his report on the day's hunt. "No cave marms were taken, so Yakop has set new trench traps. Wem reports the jlorra are kept well fed but seem restless."

The pack animals had not been out on the ice for weeks, thanks to the rebel blockades. "Have the beast master release unmated pairs so that they may hunt." Navn felt impatient. The rebellion had everyone so preoccupied that they were forgetting to use common sense. "Wem loses one day's rations, so that he might contemplate his work and not his fears."

Skuyl nodded and made two notations on the

scraped-clean portion of the plas panel that he used for writing before he continued. "The renser have filled the quota tank and Umot has made repairs to the cleaners. The gjenvin master has uncovered an old wreck site and requests additional females for the sorting sheds. One of the ahayag has delivered a male child; Gonnur claims knowledge of her and has no sons of his two wives."

Traditionally, married men were not supposed to use the camp's ahayag, but if both wives proved barren, it was considered an acceptable alternative to getting children. Gonnur would not have put this before Navn if he doubted the boy's paternity. "He may take the child weaned. I want that tank kept filled. Anything else?"

The storekeeper hesitated and looked over Navn's left shoulder. "I have all but your orders as to the disposition of the ensleg female."

"There is nothing to be done presently. She is under my consideration." Navn's head was throbbing miserably. "That is all I wish to hear now. See to the needs of the tribe."

Skuyl bowed and left the shelter. Always attuned to his moods, his wife slipped into the main room and attended him with silent and gratifying care. Sogayi had a soothing broth prepared and personally served it to him, humming a wordless, pleasing tune as she made the graceful presentation. As was proper, she refused to take sustenance herself until he had finished his meal, and then drank only a few dainty sips from the dregs in his bowl.

"You are a good woman," Navn said when she

knelt to remove his boots and massage his feet with a piece of warming cloth.

"I belong to a great man," Sogayi said, giving him the shy smile that pleased him most. "Your wisdom and kindness have shaped me."

Navn suspected the misfortunes of her youth had been rather more influential, but allowed the flattery to remain unchallenged. Sogayi need not be reminded of how much her beauty and talent had caused her to suffer. "You should retire now, wife. I will join you after I have dealt with this ensleg."

"May I not stay?" Sogayi pressed her forehead to the top of his feet. "I have so little time with you as it is, and I may perhaps be of assistance with the ensleg female."

Navn didn't wish to face the ensleg alone. It was a weakness to admit that, but so it was. He needed a shield, and permitting his wife to be present could be the next best thing. She would remind him of his position, and would help him maintain his dignity. She would also not broadcast his weakness to the rest of the camp.

He waited a respectable interval before saying, "I will allow it."

"You are all that is good and generous." Sogayi kissed his feet before replacing his boots and fetching his kederash from the wall niche where his more formal garments were kept. "Should I summon hunters to stand guard?"

Navn shook his head. "She is no threat to me," he lied. The tent flap moved, making the attached bells chime, and he raised his voice. "Enter."

Hurgot stepped into the shelter. At his side was the

ensleg, now properly garbed, and the healer removed her face wrap to show her features. Hurgot supported her with one of his arms, Navn saw, but quickly released her and pointed to a spot on the floor. The ensleg dropped down onto her haunches and pressed her forehead to her knees. She was so thin that the day robe she wore billowed out around her.

Navn could not look directly at her. To do so would be to give her attention she did not deserve. Because she was Terran, she was shaped and smelled like other Iisleg females. The only true oddities about her were the garments she had worn, now gone, and the long hair, which could be cut off. Yet even as he ignored her, Navn felt the strangeness of her presence stretching and growing, until it seemed she might fill all the space in the shelter.

She is nothing, he reminded himself. *A weak, sickly female with no one to feed or care for her.* He owed her nothing, either. Allowing Hurgot to tend to her had been entirely magnanimous of him. If anything, his choosing to be merciful might damage him more than her presence.

Navn could feel the weight of her glances. The ensleg was studying him, but making an effort to conceal it. Such a show of manners from an offworlder was unexpected, and somewhat heartening. *Perhaps you will survive this night.*

As was tradition, Sogayi came forward with a steaming cup of tea for Hurgot. Her movements were unhurried and fluid and turned the ritual greeting into a small dance as she presented the drink. After a respectful glance back at Navn, who gave her a nod to allow her to speak, she added a smiling, "The rasakt will hear you."

The healer followed custom and refused the tea before addressing Navn. "Rasakt, I present to you the ensleg female." Hurgot bobbed his head. "If it pleases you to know, I may tell what I have learned of her in this short time."

Navn accepted a cup of tea from his wife. "Tell me."

"The ensleg is a young adult female in her parts and, like us, from human stock." The healer grimaced, as if this was undesirable but could not be helped. "This one does not comprehend our language, so it was not possible for me to interrogate her, but I have had limited success with using drawings and gestures."

"Indeed." Navn felt new tension cording his muscles. "What have you learned of her?"

"Very little. This one has suffered a serious head wound, along with others, within the recent past. All have healed, but the one to the head may be the reason why she cannot say who she is or how she came to be here. Such wounds sometimes cause the mind to be scoured clean." Hurgot's gaze shifted briefly to the ensleg. "Despite this, she is obedient and quick to learn. It took me but five minutes to teach her the proper posture for her presentation, all done without words. If this one is permitted to learn our language and serve the tribe, she may be of some limited use to you."

Sogayi smothered a sound.

Annoyed by the distraction, Navn turned to his wife. "What is it?"

"Pardon my startled reaction, husband, but this thing is ensleg. Worth only as much as can be had for its worgald." Sogayi regarded the other female briefly before shuddering and turning her head. "To allow it to live and work among your women . . . such a practice would be unsafe, would it not?" She gave him an anxious look—a female in need of direction.

Navn saw that his clever Sogayi was also giving him an easy solution to his problem. He could have the ensleg killed for the worgald, and all that might be said was that he did so to soothe the fears of an overly nervous wife. Truly he was blessed in his choice of women.

But what if she cannot be killed? What if her face is taken and she still walks and talks, as before? The image of recreating such a horror made the rasakt want to puke up his broth. *This is not the same female. She cannot be.*

Hurgot shuffled his feet and cleared his throat. When Navn gave him his attention, he said, "Ensleg females are known to have special value to the Skjonn Kangal. It is said that he will pay double for one such as this."

"The rebels will not permit anyone to send the usual tithe offerings." It was something that had needled Navn to no end.

"Now they will not." The healer made a rocking motion with his head. "Should the windlords prevail . . ."

Navn did not need Hurgot to finish the thought. If the rebels lost the coming war, the Iisleg would have to work hard to regain the favor of the windlords. Tithes might have to be tripled—and Navn's men would be the ones to face the Kangal's ire directly as they delivered them.

He faced the ensleg. "You, woman. Rise and let me look upon you."

Hurgot tapped the ensleg's shoulder, and she rose awkwardly to her full height. Without hesitation the healer released the shoulder folds that kept her day robe in place, and allowed the garment to fall to the floor. Beneath it she was naked.

Navn studied her form. She had two breasts in the usual position, although they were not very large, and a triangle of dark hair over her woman's cleft. There were no marks of childbirth or abuse on her, and the unblemished condition of her pale skin was equal to that of a child.

"She is scrawny." Navn knew the Kangal liked his women with some meat on them. Yet after so many voluptuous beauties, perhaps this ensleg would prove something of a novelty, or serve those of the Kangal's court who preferred young boys, given that she had the same basic shape. "Is she open?"

"Yes, Rasakt," Hurgot said.

So she had known at least one man. Navn saw little beauty in her, but knew offworlders had tastes even more perverted than the windlords. "Did you find any signs of disease or pregnancy?"

The healer hesitated for a moment. "None, Rasakt."

"But?"

"There is white in her hair, so she may not be as young as she appears." Hurgot tapped the ensleg's wrists, and she held out her palms. "The wrist of her eating hand is slightly swollen, and she cannot use it as well as the other. Her fingers are callused. These indicate she was once . . ." He trailed off, searching for words. "Skilled with her hands."

"She may have used ensleg weapons," Sogayi murmured, her eyes wide.

"She may have used ensleg cook pots," the healer replied as he pulled the day robe back onto the ensleg's shivering body and dressed her like a child. "With her mind so damaged, we will likely never know."

Navn's wife stiffened. "I am sure it is as you say, Healer. Yet I have heard whispered tales of such ensleg women. They are permitted to act as their men, even join their armies and fight in their wars—"

"Enough," Navn said. He would not tolerate such obscene talk, and to allow any further speculation about the ensleg's origins was wholly unacceptable, as well. "This is my decision: I permit this ensleg to live and to serve the iiskar. When she learns our language and proper behavior, her status will be that of marked tribute for the Kangal."

Hurgot bobbed his head. "Where shall I put her to work, Rasakt?"

"She may go to the gjenvin." Among the salvagers, she would have the least amount of contact with the camp women, and working salvage, she could not sicken anyone, as she might with ill-prepared food or contaminated water. Navn saw Sogayi's expression and knew his wife thought he was being too generous. In a harsher tone he added, "If she does not speak adequate Iisleg within the moon, she is to be given to the ice."

Hurgot bowed and backed away, tapping the ensleg and gesturing for her to accompany him. The ensleg female gave Navn and Sogayi a highly discourteous, piercing look before she followed the healer out of the shelter.

"I regret my insolence in speaking during your

business." Sogayi's tone was only slightly apologetic. "You are wiser than I and must see much in this ensleg that I cannot."

"Were we not on the brink of war, I would play the skela and skin her myself," Navn said. Sometimes, like now, his wife needed to be reminded of the absolute power he wielded over her and every soul within the iiskar. "Her life remains mine."

"As does my own." Sogayi crouched at his feet, completely subdued now. "Forgive my foolishness. I know it will be as you say."

Navn felt his ire soften. Sogayi's devotion was one of the few things in this life he could depend on, and he would not shrivel her feelings with too much harshness. "I cannot discount any advantage now," he told her. "These are dangerous times, and it is prudent to plan with great care." He rested a fond hand on her head. "Do not be afraid of this female. She is nothing to us."

"As you say," his wife repeated as she pressed her cool cheek against his knee.

Four

Duncan Reever had not told Xonea Torin or anyone on the *Sunlace* that ten years past he had successfully piloted a weapons transport more than once through the brutal winds of both the upper and lower atmospheres of Akkabarr. To admit that he had once flown to the skim cities as well as landed on the armory planet would mean relating details of his life still unknown to anyone but himself and TssVar, his former friend and the Hsktskt lord who was now commanding the Faction's central armies.

If he failed, on the other hand, someone should know.

He took out the handheld recorder and switched it on. "It was TssVar who sent me to Akkabarr to spy for him, just as he had sent me to Kevarzangia Two. The Faction had never been able to determine how the Toskald had turned their world into an armory for hundreds of other species. There were concerns about the League using Akkabarr as a front for their own move against the Faction. I was sent to infiltrate the Toskald and scout the planet for its potential to be taken."

He paused the recorder. Coming to Akkabarr all those years ago had been Reever's first contact with free humanoids since being enslaved by the Faction himself. Yet while the Toskald were warm-blooded humanoids, their emotions seemed limited to self-absorption, ranging in intensity from greed to paranoia. Among the Toskald, appearances were everything, and Reever had no difficulty blending in. They had prejudiced him, though, and for years afterward he thought all humanoids were equally as trite and shallow.

Until he had met Cherijo.

Reever switched on the recorder. "I gathered evidence that showed Akkabarr's violent atmospheric conditions rendered it impervious to scanning and impregnable to any attack force. Then I learned the secret of the shifting dead-air zones, and how the Toskald pilots located and used them to get from space to their floating cities, and from the air cities to the surface of the planet and back again. Those facts I did not relate to the Faction, as part of the balance for what had been done to me."

As a spy, Reever had betrayed the Hsktskt countless times. It was payment for the three revolutions they had forced him to fight in slaver arenas. Saving lives seemed the most adequate expiation for the many he had taken.

Hala!

Reever thought of his former owner, a centuron with a heavy fist who liked to beat her slaves as much as she enjoyed starving them. She had been the one to give him that name after he began killing on the sands. Her cronies had taken to chanting it every time he had entered the arena, when his reputation for efficiency had begun drawing larger crowds.

Hala in Hsktskt meant "death," and death was what he had given them, until the day he had saved TssVar from an assassination attempt, and had been elevated from slave to the Hsktskt OverLord's equal.

"Being made TssVar's blood brother took me into the ranks of the most powerful raider division within the Faction," he told the recorder. "His protection and trust gave me the opportunity to sabotage the Faction from within, which I continued to do until he sent me to evaluate Kevarzangia Two. That was when I met you, *Waenara*. When you saved me."

He was talking to her, not the recorder now.

Reever shut off the unit. He knew he now had to erase the voice file; he couldn't risk the Toskald's confiscating the unit and learning when and how he had spied on them. He couldn't find Cherijo if he was imprisoned or dead.

I should have told her.

There was much about his past that Reever had concealed from his wife. In the beginning, it had been caution that kept him from confiding in her—he felt vulnerable enough, forming such a rapid and intimate connection with a female who was a total stranger to him—and then a curious dragging, weighty sensation that his psychological database indicated could be guilt or shame. Because Reever's childhood had been spent on a succession of alien worlds, and his Terran xenobiologist parents had left him entirely in the care of drones or the nearest sentient species, he had never learned how to feel human emotions. Meeting Cherijo had changed that, but Reever was still something of a novice at recognizing them.

Akkabarr's white and blue colors filled the launch's

viewer panel. Reever's hand clenched, and then he pressed the key that erased the voice recorder's storage chips.

When I find her, I can tell her everything.

"Disengage autoflight stabilizers," he told the helm computer as he left orbit at a near-parallel course with the surface of the ice world. Once the launch was under his manual control, he bypassed the safeties and angled the nose down four degrees.

The launch shuddered as it began the long slide into the lethal upper atmosphere.

The ride was still as much of a bastard as it had been ten years ago; Reever had to fight to keep the launch from rolling as he located, and then maneuvered the ship in the exact center of, a narrow conduit of dead air between two of the widest, most powerful upper wind currents. The secret of penetrating Akkabarr's atmosphere was not to enter the kim-wide wind streams, but to slide along their periphery through the dead-air zones and use their enormous energy at precisely the right place and moment to jump through an interior vortex to another, lower pocket of calm.

Starry darkness blackening the port and starboard viewports lightened to deepest violet, streaked with white and silver striae: streams of icy dust that had been trapped forever between the endless winds.

"Recommend reverse course," the helm computer advised him. "Increase engine output to achieve escape velocity."

Gradually Reever made his descent, the launch bouncing and rocking as he used the Toskald technique of sliding from one elongated dead-air pocket to the next. *The same manner in which throwing flat rocks permits them to skim the surface of a body of water,* he thought as he skirted a current strong enough to disintegrate the launch around him. Another solitary practice he had taken up as a youth during the four years his parents had forced him to spend on Terra in an educational facility.

Something tightened inside him. "I never told you that I know how to skip stones, either, did I?"

"Unable to process," the helm panel replied. "Please restate request."

Give me back my wife. "Cancel request."

The launch lurched wildly as Reever forced it through a vortex almost too small to be useful. At the other end lay a fury of blasting hail that buffeted the hull with the force of pulse fire. Although this airspace was as dangerous as those above it, Reever relaxed. Reaching the hail stream meant he had descended through the last of the upper atmospheric currents. Beneath the hail lay the region that the Toskald occupied with their habitat vessels, and from there it was only a short and violent flight through the far more dangerous lower atmospheric currents to reach the surface.

He had yet to transmit his final relay to the *Sunlace.*

"Queue encrypted file ADR-14 on preset channel. Prefix file ADR-14 with following message: Xonea, this is Reever. I am not landing on the surface immediately. The data which follows explains why." Something else he had not told the captain of the *Sunlace.* "I will contact you when possible. End prefix. Transmit file ADR-14."

"File transmitted."

Hail dust occluded the view panel for a few more minutes before the launch leveled out in the clear, temperate zone. Beneath the calm air, the lower winds permitted only the briefest glimpses of planet Akkabarr's glacial features.

Reever could not feel her from this distance, and still he reached out with his mind to her. *Beloved, I am here.*

There was no answer. There never was.

After a long moment of staring at the vacant ice fields, Reever engaged the sensors and scanned until he obtained the position of Skjonn and altered his course to intercept.

The immense suborbital cluster of vessels, satellites, and artificial domed biospheres, commonly known as a skim city, ballooned on the horizon. Reever knew that the Toskald were no more indigenous to Akkabarr than the Iisleg's ancestors were, but they had evidently come here far better equipped.

He knew from the cultural database that five thousand years ago, the swelling of the Toskald homeworld's sun into a red giant had forced their exodus. They had selected Akkabarr for its isolation, unique atmospheric conditions, and biospheric compatibility with their species. On this new world, they knew they would have no neighboring inhabited worlds to trouble them, their cities would be guarded by planetwide walls of winds, and they faced no risk being eradicated by some exotic alien microorganism hostile to their physiology. They had brought with them the technology that had allowed them to survive on their homeworld for centuries after that planet's surface had become too seismically unstable to support life. In the process of adapting their city-sized vessels to better match the challenges of Akkabarr's frozen climate and vicious atmosphere, the Toskald had evolved into one of the most advanced species in the quadrant.

Reever admired the instinct for survival in any species, but successful adaptation and technological development were simply not enough to satisfy the Toskald. Once they had restabilized their civilization, they turned their efforts to eliminating any possibility of a second exodus. This resulted in Akkabarran slavery and arms dealing.

Such paranoia could be dangerous. Yet as Reever had discovered, with a little preparation, it could also be readily manipulated.

Reever opened his relay channels and transmitted a stanTerran approach signal, requesting permission to dock. He cycled the relay to repeat in Toskald and several other quadrant languages, the same way a diplomat would. He watched his panel as his sensors tracked a highly focused scan beam passing over the launch. The Toskald would read the standard array of defensive weaponry along with Reever's vessel identification.

The dock supervisor still transmitted a terse inquiry. "What business have you in Skjonn, Terran?"

"Official business," he replied. "The matter is confidential."

"That should cost you," the supervisor informed him. "Standard visitor regulations are being transmitted to your database. You are not permitted to carry weapons, enslaved beings, biologics, or materials classified as hazardous under InterPlan Schedule one through two thousand four hundred sixty-eight. You will not be permitted to leave your ship until you have acknowledged understanding and voluntary adherence to these regulations, violation of which will result in your immediate detainment, prosecution, and punishment under Toskald law. Confirm or deny."

"Confirmed." Reever noted that the turret cannon mounted above and below the docks tracked his approach, and the focused scan remained continuous until he disengaged the launch's engines. He unfastened and removed his flight suit, straightening the uniform it had concealed, before sending the required agreement to the visitor regulations. Only after two biodecon sweeps was he given permission to disembark.

Two heavily armed security drones were waiting at the bottom of the ramp for him. "Identify," one of them said.

Reever held out his identification. The drone took the chip and inserted it into its memory panel to read it. It seemed a long time before it said, "Confirmed." It removed and returned the chip to Reever. "Destination?"

He produced a second, encrypted chip. "I seek an audience with the Kangal Orjakis on a matter of interplanetary security."

This time the drone took only three seconds to verify the data from the chip before its programmed demeanor switched from interrogative to deferential. "This way, sir."

"I see Janzil Ches Orjakis, Kangal of Skjonn. Presentation of prospect seven-nine-seven."

Janzil Ches Orjakis, Kangal of Skjonn, reclined as

the newest candidate for his personal use and amusement walked to the oval of polished stone before his chaise and halted there.

Above his head, a panel reflected the image that pleased him most: his own. Many long hours had he devoted to achieving his physical excellence; maintaining it required continual vigilance. His father, Orjak Ches Stagon, the Kangal Before, had impressed this on him as nothing else.

You are to be the Next, Stagon had told him when he had taken Orjakis for his first treatment. *You must show care in this, for the people have expectations to be met.*

Having his young bones stretched and his small muscles stimulated by the offworlder machines had been painful, something Orjakis had never known, but he did not weep. Not in front of his father, who endured ten times as much treatment without a murmur. Orjakis's caregivers had made him understand the dangers of his position, too. There were others his father had sired who could easily be named Next, others who would not whine or complain about the rigors of physical duty.

Now he was Kangal, and a man grown, he felt he had surpassed even Stagon as the embodiment of the ruler perfect.

Orjakis turned his head to admire how golden threads of light chased each other through his dark hair. The angular countenance of boyhood had vanished, replaced by features that were a harmony of all things sensual and commanding. Countless Toskald had fallen in love with their Kangal merely after one glimpse of his face.

His face could not compare with his body, naturally.

His body had driven a number of his lovers, both men and women, to commit suicide after they had been discarded. At times he found this to be convenient—not to mention a suitable homage to his prowess—but was still careful to make his addresses at the commons from behind a screen that showed nothing from his neck down. To be adored was his due, but to protect the masses was his duty.

Envy and desire should never be fatal.

Orjakis lifted a hand mirror and through it regarded the slave. She was watching him, of course, and had remained silent. Someone in Acquisitions was putting more effort into pretraining these prospects. The slave slowly raised four graceful arms while she undulated beneath the sultry column of air streaming down from one of the ceiling portals. Her rather sedate garment actually consisted of long strands of sparkling tube gems, the flared joints of which caught the heated stream and caused the strands to fan out in pleasing patterns. As the strands moved, oiled brown-and-purple-striped flesh appeared.

"What is she?" Orjakis asked his chamber drone, which had announced the prospect.

The drone consulted its database. "Hybrid of as yet undetermined species, slave-born Garnotan, Kangal. Purchased from the Common Trade Platform by Acquisitions."

Orjakis tilted the mirror. She had no hair or nose, and her double-lidded eyes had a black reptilian gleam to them that he found mildly repulsive. No breast mounds or nipples, either, unless they were on the back of her, but her ample hips were supple enough. *She can keep her eyes shut*. Orjakis found the extra limbs rather novel, and wondered if she sported any additional orifices. "Screen and clean her."

Unfortunately, the female chose to drop into a complicated crouch that involved balancing on one palm while continuing the elegant movements of two arms. The fourth arm snaked down and worked her remaining hand in and out of her body.

Although it was evidently meant to entice, the show of manual dexterity immediately killed Orjakis's interest. "Wait." Professionals always left him cold; he preferred to do his own training. "Cancel the prep work and send her to the garrison. Send in our notch."

The slave made no sound, but her black eyes shimmered with realistic tears as the drone hauled her out of the chamber.

Orjakis's notch, a retired trader who had sold himself to the Kangal to satisfy the last of an inherited debt, entered with recorder in hand. He had been so adept at his work that no one could remember his name anymore; he was simply the notch. "I see Janzil Ches Orjakis, Kangal of Skjonn. Your desire, Kangal?"

What he desired was an end to the monotony. "We would see the tithe that has arrived from the surface. Arrange it."

The notch's face became more wrinkled. "I cannot, Kangal."

Orjakis sat up and put aside his hand mirror to grace the notch with a direct look. "*What* did you say to us?"

"I cannot arrange a viewing, Kangal, as there is no tithe." The notch nodded toward the edge of the city. "Acquisitions reports that those which Kangal does not wish to hear mention of ever again during the

Kangal's lifetime have prevented all of the tithe-bearing caravans from reaching the transport lifts."

"Impossible."

The notch said nothing. A slave did not argue with the prince of the city.

"No tithe." Orjakis rose and held out both arms while his wardrobe drone draped him in a robe. "We gave the order to withhold all supplies to the surface, did we not?" "The surface" was as close as he would come to referencing those Iisleg animals.

The notch consulted his recorder. "The Kangal issued such an order." He read out the date and time Orjakis had done so, and added, "Nothing has been sent to the surface since the Kangal's order took effect."

"Then *where* is the *tithe?*" Orjakis shouted.

The notch cringed. "I would theorize that it is still on the surface, Kangal."

Orjakis strode past his slave and out of his chamber. A short corridor led to his private reception room, where more drones and several slaves waited at their posts. A chamber drone darted around him to release an orange-red-tinted spray.

"Janzil Ches Orjakis," the chamber drone announced. "Kangal of Skjonn."

The presentation scent, blended exclusively for each Kangal, eradicated the smell of anyone and anything else in the room. The color of the spray was supposed to be a gracious signal of the Kangal's present mood, but the drone had made the erroneous choice of vigor-orange.

Offended as Orjakis was, it should have been tinted an ombré of purple-dignity and yellow-ire.

"We want all of our advisers in here. Now." He

dropped down on the only chair in the room, a throne made of offworlder materials and gemstones. The cushions automatically adjusted themselves to his body, providing the perfect support and comfort.

It took Orjakis's advisers three minutes to report en masse to the reception room. They took their places according to rank and importance and knelt on the floor, heads held in a position roughly equal to the height of Orjakis's knees. Those who had a clear view of his face fixed their gaze there. Those who did not stared into the room's reflecting walls, all of which had been installed at angles to show Orjakis's throne, and were programmed to turn and track his movements if he rose and moved about the room.

When the Kangal was present, no one looked at anyone or anything but the Kangal, or the image of the Kangal. That was law.

Yet even the Kangal had to adhere to certain requirements. "We will hear the daily report from Development."

Development was the only drone adviser within the court, as its work was too important to be trusted to a mere courtier. It rolled forward and halted at the correct, respectful distance from the throne.

"I see Janzil Ches Orjakis, Kangal of Skjonn," the drone said, imitating its living counterparts. "Development reports that all is well within the city, Kangal. Fifteen new works depicting the Kangal's image have been installed in bereft areas. Seven male children born in the last day were given names paying homage to the Kangal's reign. The exterior renderings of the Kangal's wisdom which were wind-damaged have been repaired. All will be well within the city, Kangal."

Seven males born—a good omen, Stagon would have said—and all named to honor Orjakis, even better. He permitted such homage children to possess a second, personal name by which they were to be addressed; otherwise the city would be overrun by hundreds of "Kangal's Tributes" and "Glories to Orjakis."

"Acquisitions," Orjakis said, and Tamor stood. The tall male hunched over slightly but kept his eyes on the Kangal. "The notch tells us that no tithe has arrived from the surface. You may inform us as to the present location of our tithe."

"I see Janzil Ches Orjakis, Kangal of Skjonn, but I regret that I do not have an answer for the Kangal." Tamor, who had a high, rather feminine voice, swallowed before he stumbled on with, "The rebel blockade—"

"Close your mouth. Return to your place." He turned his head to regard the next ranking adviser. It was unlikely that the man had gone insane, but one never knew for certain with those outside the species. "Provisions, have you disobeyed our orders?"

"I see Janzil Ches Orjakis, Kangal of Skjonn. I have followed the Kangal's orders and stopped all transfer of supplies to the surface, Kangal. As have all the Kangal of all the other skim cities." Magnu, a dwarfish ex-slaver, moved his shoulders back. His habit of squinting as he talked annoyed Orjakis to no end, but it seemed to be a nervous habit that the man could not shake. "Not a crumb has been dispatched, on this I swear."

"That is all that preserves your hide at the moment." Orjakis tapped a fingernail against his teeth as he thought. "Defense, what has been done to eliminate the interference with our tithe?"

Gohliya, the general in charge of Orjakis's army, did not move from his position on the floor. "I see Janzil Ches Orjakis, Kangal of Skjonn. I would ask if I have the Kangal's expressed permission to rise and to continue to speak?"

"Of course you do," Orjakis snapped. "We asked you a question. Answer it."

"Nothing has been done about the interference, Kangal." The old man said it with a queer sort of relish. "The Kangal's last orders regarding the matter were to starve those who have created it into submission."

The general had been an adviser since Orjakis's father had ruled as Kangal of Skjonn. "You knew what was ordered had not restored delivery of the tithe?" Gohliya nodded. "Yet you said nothing to us."

"I was ordered by the Kangal not to speak or rise until the Kangal's displeasure with me had abated." Gohliya removed the long blade at his side and placed it on the inlaid stone floor. The gesture had some sort of ceremonial meaning, one Orjakis could not recall. "I am shown unworthy, and beg the Kangal release me."

The old man wanted to step down; that was why he had laid his blade at his feet. Only Orjakis could grant his request; he could use the sword to dispatch the general, or bestow it on his replacement.

He might indulge the old warmonger, but not until the matter of the tithe was resolved. "You are not released. Pick up your weapon." He waited until Gohliya had obeyed him. "Defense has displeased us.

You will do whatever is necessary to restore delivery of our tithe."

Gohliya had the effrontery to break eye contact with him. "That would require we go to war with those who once offered tithe to the Kangal."

The insult was deliberate. Had Gohliya ever once looked away from Orjakis's father, Stagon would have snatched his blade and beheaded the old man on the spot. Orjakis could easily imagine doing the same, this very moment. Then again, a headless man could not lead the army.

It was quite the dilemma.

"I see Janzil Ches Orjakis, Kangal of Skjonn." A drone cleared to bring important business to Orjakis entered the reception room, ablaze with high-alert indicators. "Official inquiry has been made."

There were only a handful of dignitaries with enough rank to activate the drone's urgency protocol, so Orjakis rose from the throne. As was proper, shoulders hunched and heads bent to insure that the Kangal stood tallest in the room. It also enabled him to see the drone at the entryway.

To the drone, Orjakis said, "Elaborate."

"Allied League of Worlds Colonel Stuart, Andrew Robert, has arrived and requests a private audience with the Kangal," the drone stated. "Encrypted access to further details has been provided."

An offworlder? No appointments had been made; no ships were in orbit. "Who brought him in?"

"He flew in alone, Kangal."

The few offworlders who knew how to traverse the upper atmosphere piloted slaver ships, yet this male claimed to be a League officer. The League publicly condemned slavery, but select members of its militaries often came to Akkabarr, seeking discreet solutions to personal difficulties.

It could be that this Stuart person worked for one of them.

"Drone, notch, you will stand by and remain. The rest of you, get out." Orjakis sent for proper garments and his headdress before accessing the remaining data the drone carried. "Good. Very good. We will see this man now."

The drone departed and returned with a Terran dressed in the drab brown garments of League military design. The Terran dropped into the formal presentation position without being instructed to do so.

"Rise." Orjakis was pleased to see his new allies had at last briefed their officers on how to show some proper Toskald protocol. He took a moment to admire the Terran, who was tall and fair-haired. Although he was perhaps a little old for Orjakis's personal taste, he possessed the physique of an experienced warrior.

The eyes, too, were incredible.

Such men were as delicious to seduce as they were to bring to heel. *A pity we cannot collar him.* "We are the Kangal of Skjonn. You are the Colonel Andrew Robert Stuart of League Intelligence. Your data and credentials are in order."

Colonel Stuart did not make the common offworlder error of responding to Orjakis's remarks, but waited in silence, his gaze steady.

"You show startling and intimate knowledge of how to behave in the presence of Toskald royalty. We are enchanted." Orjakis gestured to the notch to enable his recorder and returned to the throne. "You may now make your request of us, Colonel Stuart."

The League colonel angled his head up, but not enough to disturb the eye contact between him and Orjakis. "I see Janzil Ches Orjakis, Kangal of Skjonn. I thank the Kangal for providing me with this opportunity to speak in the Kangal's presence," he said in fluent Toskald. "The Allied League of Worlds Intelligence Division has sent me to request permission of the Kangal to search the surface of Akkabarr to locate one of our vessels."

The man could have been a native, lifelong courtier, such was his command of Toskald and proper address. Disconcerted by this, Orjakis frowned. "You know our language."

"Before I joined the League, I piloted a Garnotan vessel."

So he had worked for slavers. An interesting switch of careers. "You said the League sent one of your ships to our planet?"

"The missing vessel was scheduled to dock at Bharova," the colonel said, referring to a nearby skim city that belonged to one of Orjakis's cousins. "It never arrived."

"Why not make your appeal to the Kangal of Bharova?" Orjakis asked.

"The last registered coordinates show the vessel within Skjonn airspace when it vanished." Stuart produced a datapad. "Simulations indicate it would have crashed in territory belonging to the Kangal of Skjonn."

At last, a show of some ignorance. "Nothing that crashes on the surface survives, Colonel. What is left is immediately scavenged by the things that dwell there. Your efforts are in vain; you will find nothing."

The colonel's eyes seemed to change color from green to a light gray. "My superiors believe that a slave being transported may have survived the crash. It is for this slave that I wish to search."

The absurdity of the request pulled a laugh from Orjakis. "You search for a single slave? What is it? Hsktskt?"

"It is a Terran female. A physician."

"A human woman physician? There are such things?" At this rate, his mirth would never end. "This becomes more intriguing by the moment. Colonel, tell us, what female—physician or otherwise—could possibly merit such an effort?"

"This slave female has knowledge of certain events which, if manipulated by our enemies, could prove damaging to League treaties," the colonel said. "I have been ordered to find her and bring her to Intelligence Headquarters for interrogation and detainment."

"Certain events?"

"The Jado Massacre."

"Ah." Orjakis vaguely remembered the debacle, which had nearly drawn Joren into the League-Faction war. He would not have paid any interest to it if not for the Jorenian involvement. He had only ever owned one himself, a prime male that he had been forced to have put down.

That particular execution had broken Orjakis's heart; none of his other slaves had the physical beauty that one had possessed. Acquisitions should have warned him that, like the Hsktskt, the species was unsuitable for life in bondage. Yet such were the difficulties and deprivations that he endured as Kangal. "We are sympathetic toward our allies, as always, but your slave has doubtless gone the way of your missing vessel."

"My superiors understand that I may not find this slave alive." As he produced a small sack, the colonel's tone remained even and as colorless as his eyes now were. "If I may, the League offers a small return for the Kangal's generous gift of time and patience."

"You offworlders have such bizarre priorities." Orjakis made a languid gesture, and the notch took the sack from the League colonel. "We find we are in a mood to indulge you, Colonel, as long as your compensation proves adequate."

The notch emptied the contents of the sack—a dozen large, flawless black diamonds—onto his recorder, and scanned them. He nodded toward Orjakis, silently verifying they were genuine.

Such gems were rare and coveted by many for their beauty and technological value; a single black diamond could purchase one hundred choice slaves. Orjakis found the size of the bribe even more intriguing than the colonel. *Who is this female, and what does she know that compels the League to offer so much simply to look for her?*

Colonel Stuart was not telling him all. He would have to be watched.

"We grant you permission to search on the surface for your missing vessel and slave," he told Stuart, "but you are to go with one of our pilots. A weapons trader who is familiar with conditions in the lower atmosphere and on the surface." He smiled, knowing precisely whom he would send. "To insure your personal safety, of course."

"I would be glad of the escort," the colonel said. "The Kangal's generosity is greatly appreciated."

He watched the Terran's mouth as he spoke, and thought of how it would look above the silver alloy of a slave collar, or filled with something more interesting than diplomatic lies. *What color will his eyes be when I take him?* "We will remind you of this when you return, Colonel. You may take your leave of us now." He extended his hand, palm up.

Stuart hesitated, and then bowed over the Kangal's hand.

Orjakis knew then he would have to die.

FIVE

On the day after she found the people, the one called Hurgot gave her a name.

"Resa." He touched her shoulder. "Resa."

At first she thought he would make the gestures and facial expressions to help her understand the meaning of what he said, as he had before. He only prodded her again and repeated, "Resa."

She understood name words, although her name remained, like almost everything, lost to her. "Hurgot." She pointed to his sagging shoulder, and then her own. "Resa?"

He nodded and said more words. She didn't understand their meaning, but eventually she would. The language he and the people spoke sounded like something she had perhaps known once, in the time before she woke up on the ice.

Resa did not remember anything of that before-time. A black shroud enveloped all that had been before the ice and the cats. When she tried to see into that suffocating darkness, her head hurt, her wrist throbbed, and her stomach wanted to empty itself. The pain and nausea convinced her that whatever had happened in the past was best forgotten.

The only word she remembered—dahktar—seemed

to be one that Hurgot did not know, or that frightened him. He gave her the strangest looks when she said it, so she kept that word to herself.

Resa did not think much of what had been, anyway. Everything was new to her. Hurgot, the shelter, the robe she wore, the food she ate. Even the water tasted strange. And there were so many things in this place of people, things to eat and drink and wear and hold and look at and listen to and smell.

Not all were pleasant, but even those things unpleasant were better endured than being alone out on the empty ice.

The people's shelters did not seem much like the caves of the cats. Many things had been fastened together to make them, from hard flat things the color of dirty snow to dried animal skins. They also contained so much heat that Resa felt stifled at times, but that, too, was more tolerable than the cold.

Resa did miss the cats, but she did not want to go back to live in their cave. She had felt small and helpless there, and while she did not know who she was or from where she had come, she knew that she did not belong with them. Her body told her that she was the same as the people. Surely she was meant to be here, with her own kind.

She only wished the people were not so strange to her.

Listening to Hurgot speak to her and mutter to himself taught Resa many more words. She learned the way his face looked when he was asking something of her. Very quickly she learned the meaning of "yes" and "no" as well as what Hurgot and the people called water, food, and leader. The leader word—*rasakt*—was the one she noticed that Hurgot spoke without his face changing.

The rasakt dwelled in the largest shelter. Hurgot had taken her there and made her disrobe and crouch down before him. She did not understand why, but it seemed to be important to Hurgot.

While Resa was there, the rasakt and his beautiful woman said words that sounded familiar, too. Yet Resa did not feel comfortable near them, especially the woman. That one's mouth had stretched and curved while her eyes burned, and she had not made her mouth so when she had come alone to speak to Hurgot.

Resa also did not wish to be left with the strange women in the shelter where Hurgot took her the third day after she found the people. When she tried to follow him out, he pushed her inside the shelter and said words that sounded angry. Hurgot had given her water and food, and she did not wish to make him angry, so she stayed.

The women within the shelter stared at her for a long time. Some of the older ones gestured toward her and said things that sounded strange. Others only made the *huh-huh-huh* sound. When Resa wondered if she would be made to stand there all day, one of the youngest ones came up and touched her hand.

"Resa, come." She tugged on her hand and gestured toward the glowing thing in the center of the shelter that made warmth.

Resa went with her, and sat as she did, close to the warmth. She waited until the younger woman was looking at her face, and then touched her own shoulder. "Resa." She pointed to the other woman's shoulder.

"Ygrelda. That is my name." She looked into Resa's eyes as if to see understanding. "Ygrelda."

"Ygrelda-that-is-my-name." Resa ignored the low *huh-huh-huh* sounds made by the other women. "Ygrelda."

"Ygrelda is *my* name. Resa is *your* name," the younger woman explained, making more gestures and speaking in a slower fashion.

Resa mimicked her again but understood that she had to reverse and separate the words. "Resa is *my* name, Ygrelda is *your* name."

Ygrelda's mouth stretched and curved. "Yes, very good."

That day Resa learned that "yes" and "very good" indicated that she had done something to please one of the people. "No" and "you must not" meant she had made a mistake. There were many mistake words at first, but never for the same thing.

The women of the shelter did not sit and talk and make the *huh-huh-huh* sound for long. After sharing food from a pot, of which Resa was given a bowl, they rose from their places and went to the snarled things piled between flat, raised platforms.

"Salvage," Ygrelda called the snarled things. "We sort them."

That which Ygrelda wished Resa to do was not difficult. *Salvage-we-sort-them* meant work. The work was untangling one thing from the pile, examining it, wiping it dry and clean, and placing it in another, new pile with other things like it. Before Resa was permitted to do the work, Ygrelda showed her things she was not to do, like pressing buttons or removing pieces of the things. Those not-to-do things were "dangerous" and "forbidden to us," whatever those words meant.

Resa stood at Ygrelda's side and did the work while she listened to the women talk. She could remember and repeat everything said to her since she had come to the people, even if she didn't understand the meaning of the words, but she did not speak. Absorbing the talk seemed more important now than attempting to make it herself.

"Resa, come," Ygrelda said after a time, and led her by the hand to the source of warmth again. The women did not sit around it, but they stood as close as they could while they ate different kinds of food.

"You must eat now." Ygrelda accepted a bowl of steaming liquid from an older woman and placed it in Resa's hands.

The smell made Resa's mouth water, and the warmth soothed her chilled fingers, but she waited until Ygrelda had her own bowl and drank from it before she did the same. The liquid contained flesh and plant matter that had been rendered soft. Resa would consume anything edible, but thought the contents of the bowl tasted much better than the raw, bloody food that the cats had brought to her.

She looked at Ygrelda and raised the bowl a little. "Very good." She made Hurgot's asking face.

The younger woman nodded. "Very good soup."

"Yes, very good soup." She recalled the words one woman had said to another after receiving assistance with two badly snarled things, and wondered if they would be appropriate now. "I thank you."

Ygrelda turned to the large woman who had laughed at Resa. "You see, Mlap? She learns."

"Like a beast does." A peak formed in Mlap's top lip. "Better you hitch her to the jlorra master's pack sled, or you may find yourself carrying her about like an unweaned babe."

Resa thought of what Hurgot had said to her after the burning-eyed woman had made her lip do the same thing and used the *carry* word. Perhaps what Hurgot had said to her then would also please this woman who had shown her kindness.

"At least you do not weigh very much," Resa told Ygrelda, using the same vocal intonations that Hurgot had.

Every woman in the shelter stopped talking and stared at her. Mlap's chin sagged and her face grew red, but the other women made the *huh-huh-huh* sound, quite loudly, as did Ygrelda until her eyes became wet.

Feeling yes, very good, Resa drank from her bowl.

Teulon's dream always began with the League general's words.

There will be never be peace, and it is time that your people learned that.

The guards had come out of nowhere. Later, Teulon would kill them and many of the others who came to take their place. But hearing the general's first words had left him too stunned to react. He had been invited to the League ship as a neutral moderator, to bring peace between two old enemies.

Teulon had tried to warn them of the consequences.

If you kill me, my HouseClan will not rest until you are dead.

The mouth of the League general stretched out. *That is easily remedied.*

Darkness swallowed him, and then the world filled with voices blending anger and terror with words that still made no sense. *It will make it appear as if the stardrive malfunctioned. . . . Fire on all League vessels within the vicinity of the ship and destroy them. . . . I have given the order to defend the fleet. . . .*

Even then, Teulon had not fought. He had fallen to his knees. He had begged for them. *Be merciful. Spare them.*

Hold him up. I want him to watch. I want him to remember—

White light filled white eyes.

Teulon woke to the taste of blood and the sound of Hasal's voice. He sat up and removed the leather strap he had tied over his mouth while his eyes adjusted to the darkness. "What is it?"

"Recon sighted by our sky monitors." The silhouette of his second appeared near the shelter flap.

Although the heatarc had been banked for the night, sweat soaked Teulon's hair and slicked his skin. The center piece of the leather strap bore many indentations from other nights; this time his teeth had bitten through it and torn at his lower lip.

He closed his hand over the strap. "How many?"

Hasal stood with his back toward Teulon. "Ten Tos' scouts and thirty tankers."

For a moment Teulon contemplated summoning his forces and taking down the skim-city invaders. Forty vessels meant nothing; Skjonn's skyforce consisted of thousands of ships. He knew why Gohliya had sent them. A skirmish now would serve to pinpoint the location of the central encampment, which Teulon had been careful to change every twelve hours. Once the Kangal's general knew where they were, he would immediately send more, better-equipped troops down to attack.

Attack us. Teulon's fingers became claws.

As tempting as the prospect of battle was, the coordinated assault on the occupied trenches had been planned, and had to be executed before the next phase of the rebellion. Confronting the Kangal's army—and beginning the war—would have to wait.

"Maintain cover," he told his second. "Track them until they have returned to Skjonn."

"There is also report of an offworlder vessel that came unescorted from orbit and docked at Skjonn earlier today," Hasal said.

Had the Kangal sent for support troops? "Vessel type?"

"A small passenger transport launch. The pilot used an open-channel, multilingual relay to request permission to dock."

The League would not send a diplomat experienced enough to traverse the kvinka merely to pay a courtesy call on the Kangal. "Track the League transport, as well. If it attempts to leave the planet, shoot it down." Hasal took a step but hesitated at the flap. "What more?"

"It is cold." Hasal inhaled slow and deep. "Men do not sleep alone in the cold. In all things Iisleg are as one. We would see to our Raktar's comfort."

Comfort on Akkabarr was a synonym for *women*.

Many of the Iisleg had brought their women with them, but their rigid, misogynistic customs prohibited the females from fighting or participating in any manner of aggression. Indeed, the tribes had more rules about what women could not do than what was permitted them. Teulon had tolerated the presence of the Iisleg females because they stayed out of the way and kept to the shelters, where they prepared meals and provided sexual relief for the men.

From the beginning, the troops had believed that Teulon would take two women from those who were still unclaimed and keep them in his shelter. That he had not yet done this had generated a great deal of talk and growing concern.

More warriors were sending for their women, and the ratio of females to males was close to doubling. Another annoying aspect of Iisleg culture was that every man was entitled to two women.

"I have no need," Teulon told Hasal.

His second gave him a curious look. "It is the way."

Like most customs of the Iisleg, polygamy dated back to when their ancestors had been brought as slaves to Akkabarr. Evidently there had been an imbalance among the captured humans, with twice as many women as men. The Toskald also learned that the female slaves were less able to withstand the rigors of working on the ice. Better shelters were provided, and the women assigned to domestic duties, while each male slave was ordered to take two mates.

Teulon imagined that enlarging the slave population more rapidly had also appealed to the Toskald. With two mates, a normal male could expect to sire at least one child per year. There was no question of noncompliance from the slaves; the Toskald believed in swift, harsh punishment. Any order that was protested or disobeyed resulted in immediate execution.

Teulon could have ordered Hasal from the shelter, but he needed to put an end to this. "It is not my way."

Hasal gestured to the flap. "The men do not understand this. Neither do I. They are only women."

Teulon's second was not unique in his attitude. Iisleg indifference to females had been growing for centuries, ever since the Iisleg's ancestors forgot their former monogamous existence on Terra and began to evolve a new society. Over the centuries what had been a rapid breeding strategy became a foundation for preferential treatment that evolved into a brutal gender bias. Males not only considered themselves more valuable than females; they utterly subjugated their women. Eventually the Iisleg were permitted more freedom, but the females never enjoyed it. By that time their social status had been completely eradicated, and it never improved. Even now, the females were as much slaves to their men as the Iisleg's ancient ancestors had been to the Toskald.

"I am not Iisleg," Teulon said. "The women would be frightened by my differences."

Hasal made an impatient sound. "Their fear means nothing. If they do not please you, they will be punished."

Any woman who disobeyed a man was immediately and permanently outcast from the tribe. Most were beaten to death or driven out to die on the ice.

I have killed enough women.

"Do none of the women here please the Raktar?"

Hasal asked, misinterpreting Teulon's lengthy silence. "Should we send for other females?"

"No." Explaining his true reasons for preserving his solitude would be worthless; the Iisleg were not capable of understanding it. His claws distended, straining against his flesh, and then he thought of something. "You have no women in your shelter."

"I desire men, not women," Hasal said, very matter-of-fact.

Same-gender sex, too, was an accepted practice among the Iisleg. Teulon could not lie and claim to have the same preference; his second would simply bring him males from which to choose. He had to find words to explain that there was no viable alternative to his solitary state.

"It is that you desire no one, woman or man," Hasal said, as if the thought had been spoken aloud.

"Desire." On Teulon's homeworld, it was not used in such references. "My people Choose a single woman. That Choice is for life." He made the hand gesture of bonding, to emphasize this. "Two become one. One that never becomes two again."

It was, perhaps, the longest speech Teulon had ever made in front of his second, who was now gaping at him. Hasal could not understand what Choice meant to the Jorenians, or that it was a privilege.

You no longer have the privilege of choice, slave.

Teulon's second stared at him as if seeing him clearly for the first time. "I think I understand." He made a protective sign, directed at Teulon rather than over himself. "What is done can never be undone."

No, it cannot. "Go now."

"As you command, Raktar." Hasal slipped out of the shelter and secured the flap from outside.

Not yet.

Teulon's claws became fingers once more, and he replaced the blades he had taken from his forearm and chest sheaths. The strap was bitten through; he would have to make a new one.

This made the seventh strap he had gnawed through in his sleep.

Hasal had been the one to introduce Teulon to the strap one morning some months past, when he had seen his general washing blood from his mouth. "This you may find useful, Raktar."

He had examined it and saw how it was made of a single long piece of leather wrapped around a small cylinder of salvaged plas. "How so?"

"We give it to those who are wounded." His second had sounded a little too casual. "It helps them when they cannot . . . be silent."

Since that time Teulon had rarely slept for more than an hour at a time, but when he did, he tied the strap over his mouth and set the center piece between his teeth. Crude as it was, it worked as well as the restraints and silencers that had been used on him on the journey to this world, where he had been brought to be sold as a slave.

You no longer have the privilege of choice.

Teulon rose and went to sluice the sweat from his skin. He had modified one leg of the heatarc to accommodate a shallow basin, in which he melted snow for cleansing. When he had first come to the Iisleg, they had thought his hygiene practices strange. That changed after he and Bsak demonstrated how much easier it was to track a man who did not bathe than one who did. Now all the heatarcs in the camp were modified with meltwater basins, and every man bathed before leaving camp.

Hygiene had not been a priority during his brief time as a Toskald slave. *Do not clean him,* was the first thing Teulon's owner had said. *We like how the blood and the sweat make his skin gleam.*

Teulon thought it a pity he could not peel back his skull and cleanse that single voice from his mind. There had been a time when he might have tried, but for the other voices. The ones that repeated what had been said in the past, and the ones that drowned in silence, unable to speak again. Both reinforced the necessity of carrying on and continuing along the path that had brought him here.

He could not deny them. He could not fail them.

He used his damp shirt to remove the excess moisture from his body before he put on dry, clean garments and his outfurs. The outside temperature had dropped, he saw when he extracted the weather stick Hasal had inserted into one of the shelter's seams. The Iisleg coveted the fossilized twigs, which contained ancient resins that expanded with heat and contracted with cold. Learning to read the tiny beads enabled one to measure the climate with incredible accuracy. At this hour, no resin bubbled through the stony grain of the stick that had been exposed on the other side of the seam. That meant that the outside air temperature had dropped enough to damage unprotected derma and lung tissue, a night when no sane man would venture far from warmth and shelter.

It is good that I am no longer sane.

From his weapons cache Teulon took a long slender spear and his seven-bladed sword. He was not sure why he kept crossing the ice to visit a small, abandoned ice cave. He had found it, and the thing that haunted it, purely by accident. He could not say if the spirit of the cave was real or something his mind had invented. It never spoke. He had never brought anyone to the cave to learn if others could see the ghost.

Instead, Teulon went there regularly. Illusion or ghost, whatever inhabited the cave comforted him simply by being something that defied explanation.

Outside the shelter, the sky was a remote, dark hand holding back the vicious kvinka. Across it lay faint, many-colored light streams, made of starlight refracted and distorted by the upper atmosphere. Bsak lay waiting—like Teulon, the cat needed little sleep—and rose on all six feet when he saw the Raktar.

"Patrol."

The jlorra released air in a short, compressed exhalation—the only sound it was capable of making—and came to Teulon's side. He had tried leaving the cat behind in camp when he went on his solitary treks, but the animal always caught up with him before he traveled half a kim.

Teulon moved through the shelters, automatically inspecting rigging and cover as he went. The men had become adept at securing and concealing their bivouac, but he never took that for granted. Low grunting, the sound of Iisleg intimacy, made him pause by a skim pilot's shelter.

Men do not sleep alone in the cold.

Teulon used the end of his spear to make a slash mark on the outside flap of the shelter. In the hour before dawn, when the rebels collapsed the shelters and moved the camp, the pilot would see the mark and know that he had been heard. He would reinforce the walls of the shelter until they were soundproofed, or abandon it and share another's. Teulon's men had responded instantly to the silent discipline; he never had to make a second slash mark. He turned away, but not before he heard a softer sigh from within the shelter.

I fear for you.

Teulon and the cat walked out of the camp and into the cold night, where the winds scoured away all sound and blended together to become the birth wail of a new world.

Six

"You make my ears ache with your ceaseless chatter, Terran."

Reever glanced at Aledver, the weapons trader Orjakis had sent to accompany him on his search. He had not, in fact, said a word to the young Toskald since boarding, despite the fact that Aledver had made several humorous remarks to illustrate his affability.

A recording drone would have been slightly less obvious, Reever thought. "You wish to converse?"

"I wish not to die of boredom," Aledver said as he powered up the launch's engines. "Forgive me, but I usually deal with species who are nonverbal or interested only in obtaining the best of a deal." His expression changed to one of amused tolerance. "You might have made a better bargain with the Kangal, you know. Perhaps in the future, I might advise you on how to achieve such."

There was another provocative remark, the logical response to which would be to ask Aledver's advice or confide in him.

"Thank you for the offer." Persuasive charisma seemed to be requisite among the Kangal's lackeys, Reever thought. Aledver, however, had the eyes of a man who would use other, less palatable means when his charm failed. *Not a courtier, but adept at playing one.* "How long have you served the Kangal?"

"Of which do you speak? I have served the Kangal Present, the Kangal Before, and the Kangal Once Before." The trader disengaged the docking mechanisms and slowly guided the ship out into the calm corridor of air immediately surrounding Skjonn. "I know what you are thinking."

Reever observed the maneuver, silently completing his calculations for the flight trajectory and how he would deal with the weapons trader once they reached the surface. "I doubt it."

Aledver laughed. "Come now, Colonel. You see before you a young man, but I am at least twice your age. We Toskald treasure perfection in all things, and thus we do not permit our bodies to show the ravages of age."

Toskald body worship was no different from the cultural quirks of a thousand other species, Reever thought. It had roots in the ancient Toskald's reproductive habits, in which males used crude body paint and botanical extracts to make themselves appear more attractive to their females, and thus secure a mate. That it had evolved into extreme vanity and obsession with maintaining an illusion of youth was predictable, if somewhat annoying and often more than a little silly.

"You have achieved a high level of perfection in your own appearance," Reever assured the trader, knowing it was the compliment he was waiting to hear.

"Yes, I know." Aledver released one hand grip and touched the groomed, gilded waves of his hair as his gaze shifted from the pilot's console to Reever's face. "The great mystery is why our Kangal found you so intriguing. Do signal for permission to depart."

Reever engaged the navcomm. "Transport, this is League colonel Stuart. Request permission to depart for the surface."

"Acknowledged, Colonel," a drone voice replied. "You are cleared for city-to-surface jaunt."

"I haven't been on a surface jaunt in months." Aledver moved away from the docking area. "While we're down there, I'll show you around one of the native camps. Iiskars, they call them. You can buy outfurs like mine from them, blend in a bit better. It's incredible to view firsthand the conditions in which they live."

The trader used positioning jets to set the launch at the precise angle needed for the planned descent. The lower winds were more dangerous than those above the skim city, and could easily tear a ship apart before it had the opportunity to crash-land. "It was my understanding that the surface dwellers are preparing to stage a rebellion."

Aledver made a languid gesture. "Oh, that. A trivial squabble over tribute, nothing more."

"The rumors we have heard indicate it is more serious than a 'squabble.'" Reever glanced at him. "It is said that the Iisleg intend to go to war with the Toskald."

The trader produced a world-weary sound. "Colonel, these people are primitives, tribal savages who are entirely dependent upon the Toskald for their keep. Without us, they would have no food, medicines, or comforts. They have no technology, no weapons, and no means of transport off the planet.

They can't even enter one of our cities unless we first descend to the surface to transport them. Do you know what they call us? Windlords. We are deities to them."

Reever listened to the sound of the engines engaging. "You have weapons caches from a thousand different worlds stored on the surface. What if they raid those?"

"They can't access any of our armory trenches. Even if they had the intelligence to try, which they don't, the trenches are constructed deep beneath the surface. They're also fully automated and heavily guarded, and we always monitor them." Aledver leaned forward to look through the front viewer panel. "You're not in any danger, if that is your concern. Orjakis's tribes remain loyal to the Kangal. A few more weeks of starvation and the others will submit, as always."

The launch rocked and shuddered as it left the placid airspace surrounding Skjonn.

"The Iisleg were your slaves once," Reever said while Aledver adjusted the hull's temperature to prevent ice formation and the accompanying drag it caused. "Why did you free them?"

"We haven't." Aledver frowned as the launch lurched, and made another adjustment. "We've allowed them to believe that they are free."

Reever shifted, using his body to block the sight of what his hand was doing under the console. "Shouldn't you level out a few more degrees?"

"I know what I'm doing," the trader snapped.

"Very well." Reever tightened his seat harness. "Why do you permit the Iisleg the illusion of freedom?"

"Convenience, I suppose. They were brought here to dig out the armories, which we thought would kill them. Instead, they adapted in unexpected ways, and proceeded to breed like unchecked parasites." The trader's unlined brow wrinkled slightly as he studied his console readings.

"Many worlds use Akkabarr as their personal armory," Reever said. "Why do so many trust the Toskald not to seize control of their weapons stores and use them for your own purposes?"

"If I told you that, I would have to kill you." Aledver grinned at him. "Let us call it a matter of mutual trust. We Toskald are very adept at turning enemies into allies. Rather like what we did with the Iisleg once the trenches were completed. Our ancestors used the slaves' natural attitudes about female subjugation to work out an arrangement of mutual benefit."

Reever thought briefly of the breeding pens he had seen on different slaver worlds. The most successful were those that catered to the occupants' most intimate desires. "A clever use of existing resources."

"You do not know the half of it. Part of the tithe the tribes are required to bring to the Kangal are women, all of whom they were trained to treat quite shabbily. Over time, you see, the males have grown to regard their females as nothing more than nuisance property, and are quite happy to send their most attractive, competent females as tribute." Aledver snorted. "They believe it to be some sort of honor, as if the Kangal would actually contaminate his flawless body by touching one of their women."

Another revealing comment. "Instead, you sell them to slavers."

"It's all they're fit for, you know. After being raised on the surface, the poor things are completely docile and work hard without complaint. We've become rather renowned for the high quality of female slaves we produce." Aledver stroked the soft fur of his jacket sleeve. "The tribes may not be aware that they breed and train them for us, but they do a magnificent job of it, just as they do with their furs."

Reever imagined Cherijo in such a society, and increased the power to the engines. "None of the Iisleg have ever become suspicious?"

"Why should they? I told you, they're savages. To them, a warm fur is more valuable than a female. If only they knew how much their women earn at auction." A sudden jolt made Aledver scowl and turn his attention back to the helm.

"You do know how to fly through this atmosphere?" Reever asked. "I would like to arrive with all my extremities intact."

"You will." They had reached the midpoint between Skjonn and the surface, and as the position readings registered, a warning claxon sounded.

Reever reached under the copilot's console. "Perhaps I spoke too soon." He switched off the helm power to the pilot's console.

"What is it?" Aledver began punching controls. "None of these panels are responding."

"It may be a systems error. Allow me to investigate."

While he pretended to scan the helm controls, Reever initiated an emergency vent of the shuttle's fuel supply, and launched a small probe to penetrate the stream and ignite it. The result, he knew, would create a long, fiery plume that would be visible from several miles away.

"Stop, there. I see what you are doing." Aledver produced a handheld device Reever hadn't seen since his last sojourn to Akkabarr. The device, commonly known as a tamer, was one slavers used to render the uncooperative unconscious. "You will transfer control of the launch back to me now."

Reever inputted a preset flight code, and his screens went dark while Aledver's lit up again. "The helm is yours."

The trader kept the tamer trained on him as he turned his attention to the now-illuminated screens in front of him. "You idiot, you've brought us in at a ninety-degree angle. And why are you venting fuel?" He began encoding a correction to their course and heading. "You lied to the Kangal. Why are you here? What do you want?"

"Precisely what I told him," Reever said.

The moment Aledver inputted the new codes—none of which were prefixed with the proper enabling encryption that Reever had programmed the computer to respond only to—the guidance system deactivated and locked down. With the helm now inoperative, the launch instantly rolled into a spin and tumbled out of control.

"What have you done?" The weapons trader dropped the tamer and gaped at the viewer. "We're going to crash."

Reever regarded the whirl of sky and land with little interest. "Yes, I know."

Aledver lost his polished facade as he tried to reinitialize the helm. When it became apparent that the controls would not respond, he covered his face with his hands and wailed.

Reever reached under his console and pressed his palm to the scanner he had installed there. His print activated the emergency-landing protocol, which brought the launch out of its spin.

The cloud whips of the kvinka exploded into clear airspace. The surface of Akkabarr then seemed to rush up to meet the launch and swallow it whole in its blue-white gullet. Impact caused the port-side hull to buckle inward and wrenched at the interior seats and harness straps. The force tore Aledver out of his harness and flung him against the flight control panel. Reever, who had reinforced the copilot's seat as well as its harness before leaving the *Sunlace,* remained safely strapped in.

The launch skidded along the surface, sending a giant plume of ice spray into the air. As the skid slowed, the cabin rocked from side to side, and shuddered as the launch came to a full stop.

Toskald blood, red as a Terran's, spattered the interior of the viewer panel as Aledver produced a liquid cough. The pistol he removed from his jacket shook a little as he pointed it at Reever.

"Signal for a recovery vessel," the trader gasped, blood streaming from his nose and mouth as he stumbled out of the pilot's seat, "and if it gets here before the wreck rats do, I will let you live."

"As you had planned to execute me as soon as we reached the surface," Reever said, "I find that unlikely. Put down the weapon or I will kill you."

"With what?" Broken teeth, painted scarlet with blood, appeared as Aledver coughed up a laugh. "You were a dead man the moment you bowed over the Kangal's hand instead of placing your crystal in it."

"Crystal?"

"The keys to Akkabarr, Terran. Had you truly worked for Garnotan slavers, you would possess one. You would have never come near a Kangal without it." He tugged out a chain that encircled his neck, which sported an etched crystal pendant. "They are etched with command override codes for your vessel. Such is the cost of doing any business with the Toskald." He braced his wrist with his free hand and targeted Reever's heart.

The timing and force of the movement Reever used to kick the weapon out of Aledver's hand had taken him a year to perfect while fighting nonhumanoids on the sands of the Hsktskt slaver arenas. It was not a move any humanoid before Reever had ever attempted, and he had paid the Tingalean slave who had taught him with small rations of his own blood. He also managed the reverse of the movement, although it proved a challenge in the restricted space. That lethal blow drove one of the trader's broken ribs through both chambers of his heart.

Aledver was dead before he slumped over onto the copilot's seat.

Searching the trader's body produced four more weapons, two recording devices, and a transponder. Reever kept the weapons and destroyed the tech, and then exchanged garments with Aledver. Removing the blood from the outfurs would take too much time, so Reever transferred a small quantity to his neck and face, to make it appear as if it were his own. He then positioned the trader's corpse in the pilot's seat, to make his injury appear as a natural result of the crash impact.

Reever contemplated the blood staining his hands for a long moment. He had not come here to kill, but the change of situation indicated he might have to do so again. He considered what little he had learned from the trader. *There is more going on here than a native rebellion,* he thought as he took the chain with the etched crystal from Aledver's neck and hung it around his own, concealing it under his tunic. *If the price of a single pilot's doing business with the Toskald is the control of his ship, what is used to pay for weapons storage here?*

Crumpled hull panels had rendered the exterior door panel inoperable, so Reever blew the emergency hatch and crawled through it. The cold outside clawed at his eyes and skin. He dropped three feet down into a bank of snow, ice that had been pulverized by the crash. The hard powder scoured some of the blood from his face as he wiped it away and found his footing.

Silent, motionless white surrounded the launch on three sides. Black-and-gray smoke etched a thick trail across the sky from the vented fuel Reever had ignited. To the north he saw a small blur of movement, figures in heavy furs flying fuel-powered skimmers low over a glistening glacial field.

They were flying directly for him.

"Hunters." Daneeb lowered the magnifiers. "Small band, perhaps fifteen, flying in from the north. What does the box tell you?"

Malmi studied the instrument, which showed the warmth of the living, even while at great distances from them. "Two lights in the wreckage. One red, one purple." She hesitated before adding, "The red moves."

"That explains the hunters." Daneeb nodded toward the devices. "They use the boxes to locate game."

Malmi looked over at the other skela. They stood in a protective circle around Skjæra, keeping the wind from her while she prepared for her trek out to the crash site. "She should wait until we know how it will be."

"That she will not do." Daneeb handed Malmi her pack before she reversed her outfurs and covered them with strange, flowing ensleg garments identical to those Skjæra wore. The ensleg material seemed to crawl against Daneeb's skin, but it had fooled every rebel they had encountered. Since Skjæra had become spirit made flesh, the dead who walked—the vral—such deceptions had become accepted among the skela.

At least, among those who blindly worshipped Skjæra. Daneeb would never feel at ease with this perversion of their work. Yet she knew she alone had been responsible for what had happened to Skjæra, that day on the ice.

The day they had killed Enafa.

The terrible guilt Daneeb felt over what she had done to the child and Jarn trampled down her objections. Two years and better she had lived with the consequences of her actions. She could no more stop Skjæra from her task than she could resist aiding her in it.

When will she go too far? When will I?

Malmi reached to adjust a fold of Deneeb's head

wrap. "You should permit one of us to take your place at her side now and again, Skrie. There are some of us who are not so frightened of her."

A generous lie, for the headwoman had observed that while Skjæra's silent strangeness instilled awe and admiration in her sisters, it also terrified them. It was not natural for someone never to speak a word.

I cannot stop trembling when she is near me, one skela had told Daneeb shortly after Skjæra's transformation. *She never makes a sound. Not so much as a cough or a whisper. And she has eyes like the jlorra's are, just before they spring.*

"It is best I go." Daneeb herself was not very afraid of Skjæra, who might stop death with her bare hands, but who also regularly behaved as if old or simple-minded. Indeed, if she were not constantly reminded and attended, the healer would forget the simplest requirements of life, like feeding herself. One could not entirely fear the helpless.

Malmi looked over at the huddle of skela again. "Can you not persuade her to remain?"

"No." Nothing prevented the Skjæra from making her treks, of course. Not ice storms or predators, not the threat of discovery or blades jabbed at her face by terrified hands. Certainly not Daneeb's threats. The healer went wherever she wished, whenever she pleased, and carried out her masquerade as the vral in order to do her strange work healing the sick and injured instead of being skela and killing and skinning them. One of the older skela had told Daneeb that the reason the vral was beheld as a sacred being was because she would never know fear, deprivation, or death.

Those were also the reasons, Daneeb suspected, that Skjæra was crazy.

No, she blames herself for Enafa and what happened after I killed her. Skjæra probably thought she had been the cause of it, just as Daneeb did. They both had lived with it for a long time.

"There." Malmi tucked in the ends of her head wrap. "One would never know what you are."

Daneeb had never felt shame over being made a skela, either, not for a moment since hearing the words that had ended her once-life.

You are cast out.

The rasakt of Daneeb's natal iiskar had formed an inexplicable grudge against Daneeb's father long before her birth. Her mother had been sent to the Kangal as tribute as soon as Daneeb was weaned. Daneeb's father had been killed on the ice, during an act of cowardice, or so the headman claimed. As a female child with no male to provide for her, Daneeb was made to suffer years of hunger, overwork, and harsh punishment for even the slightest infraction.

Sometimes punishment came even when she did nothing wrong. "Beat her," was the rasakt's favorite order whenever he noticed the thin, silent child she had been.

No one had to ask why. Daneeb was the image of her father.

Daneeb's final, greatest crime had been to refuse to become the rasakt's fifth woman. She had done so deliberately, knowing it would result in her death or exile. At the time she had been quite ready to die rather than warm the bedskins and bear the children of a liar and murderer. Being made skela instead hardly seemed punishment at all.

At least, it had not until Daneeb had been forced to murder a weak and helpless child. A child whose unwarranted death had changed everything, despair into hope, death into life, the familiar into the faceless.

Skjæra into vral.

"Skrie." Malmi touched her arm to tug her from her thoughts. "Stay this time. This is her work. Let her go alone."

"I should," Daneeb agreed as she stepped back and wrapped her hands. "Do you know what I prayed for when I was a little one? A peaceful existence. I wanted it so much that I even gave up my once-life for it. She takes that from me almost every day now."

Malmi's brow furrowed. "I do not understand."

Nor would she, for the younger woman's once-life had been rich with privilege. Daneeb did not begrudge her that.

"Consider what we are," she told Malmi. "There are no men among us, and we cannot have children, but we suffer no true misery. You and I and our sisters are reviled, but we care for each other. We do our work, unpleasant as it is, cleanly and fairly. So tell me, why do I risk losing all this to honor Skjæra's charade as vral, when I might save us all by killing her and truly returning her flesh to spirit?"

The blasphemy brought a soft sound of distress from the younger woman.

"I cannot, and I will tell you why," Daneeb said. Someone should know. "Tarina, the skrie before me."

"I did not know her." Malmi cleared her throat. "It is said that you staked her to the ice."

Daneeb nodded as she strapped serrats to her boots. "For those she had killed. Before I was made skela, she would starve those who were too young, weak, or old to work the ice." She paused, remembering how she had discovered the former skrie's crimes against the skela. It had been too much, and something had snapped inside Daneeb. She had not come to her senses until she had stood over the skrie's dead body and watched her blood freeze on her blade. "Had the sisters not made me skrie, I might be now Skjæra." *And Enafa would yet live, for Jarn would have never ordered her out on the ice, and none of this would ever have happened.*

"I cannot imagine anyone but you as our headwoman," Malmi admitted.

"Truly, I could be as Tarina was. I could give Skjæra what Daévena denies her." She had given enough thought to it. Killing her would definitely end her silent pain. If that was what the silence meant.

"No, Skrie." The younger woman sounded horrified. "You cannot. You must not."

"I am not Tarina." Daneeb now met Malmi's confused gaze. "I have to go with her." She took her pack and shouldered it. "If we do not return within the shadow shift, take the others back to the crawls. We will make camp with the hunters."

"The Skjæra knows them, Skrie, but if the light that moves is ensleg . . ." Malmi could not bring herself to complete the thought.

"I should not have spoken so." Daneeb had not gone a day without feeling her own fear swelling beneath her breast, but she was frightening the girl, and forced her voice to soothe. "No one will harm our vral. Daévena would not permit it."

Such lies, to come from a mouth once so honest.

The prospect of crossing the open ice suddenly seemed much more dangerous to the headwoman. Now she could see how this place resembled the other, where the innocent blood had been spilled and two lives had been lost. Malmi was right to fear the presence of an ensleg, still alive, here and now. Such a cruel reminder might steal what little remained of Skjæra's mind.

Yet the rebellion was all around them. Daneeb did not care about the rebels—if they were foolish enough to make war on the windlords, then they deserved whatever punishment was sent down on them—but the skela might become caught between them. It was not selfish to wish to keep Skjæra safe, and mostly sane, and with them. Not when it meant their very survival.

"Skrie." Malmi nodded toward the Skjæra, who was flanked by two jlorra and now walking toward the ice field.

"You see? She never waits." Daneeb hurried after their healer.

They reached the middle of the ice field before Skjæra glanced at her.

"I know what you are thinking. I need not accompany you. So Malmi said." Daneeb stopped to knock the ice packed between the teeth of her serrats. "I am feeling most unloved this day." As always, there was no reply. "And you, Skjæra? How are you feeling?"

Despite the cold wind blowing in their faces, Skjæra

kept walking, unaffected, uncaring. Like the big cats who walked freely at her side.

Sometimes Daneeb wondered if despite her flesh, Skjæra remained partly spirit. She had almost died, that day on the ice. Since then she never took notice of such things, or complained about need, comfort, or desire. She never showed the slightest emotion.

One of the jlorra, a female, looked up at the headwoman. In her calm, clear eyes was an uncomfortable amount of interest in Daneeb.

Intrigue death, the Iisleg said. *But only once.*

"We saw on the box a red moving light," Daneeb called after her. "An ensleg survivor from the wreckage, it would seem." Skjæra would not wait, and she had to move quickly to catch up. "The ensleg will not know what we are. We could return, wait until it shows its intentions."

Skjæra's pace never faltered.

"I know you think it will not attack, or that the hunters will stop it if it tries to." Always such confidence in their guise. What would happen when the hunters discovered their holy vral was a skela who had refused to carry out her work? "I suppose we do not need them. If it attacks, I will stop it."

Skjæra halted and turned. So did the big cats. What covered the healer's face appeared so like an expanse of smooth, uninterrupted flesh that it was easy to imagine her features gone forever. It was a mask, formed by some sort of living mold that behaved as a cowl. Malmi had found two lumps of the mold in the wreckage, the same day Enafa had been killed.

Skjæra did not have to remove the thing masking

her face or say a single word. Everything about her shouted her thoughts. *You made a vow to me, Daneeb.*

So Daneeb had, many weeks after that day on the ice, when Skjæra had walked into the crawls and proved to all the skela that she no longer belonged to this world or the next by saving the life of the one none of them could bring themselves to kill.

That day, Daneeb had been the first to crouch at the healer's feet and swear to serve her. *I promise you that I will never kill again, Skjæra.*

She had never let her forget that promise, either.

"I will keep my word, but let me go before you." She caught the Skjæra's pack strap to stop her from moving on. "If there is harm to be done, let it be done to me."

The healer regarded her silently.

She wanted to know why, of course. There were one hundred lies Daneeb might have uttered. Skjæra would not have known them as such. Yet it was guilt made the truth tumble, thoughtless and reckless, from Daneeb's lips. "It was I who made you vral, Skjæra. I gave the order to kill the child, to save us all."

Skjæra studied her for a moment before she spoke in a low, clear voice. "Her name was Enafa. She was born twelve seasons past, and her mother often favored her above her sisters."

The ice beneath Daneeb's feet might have split apart to suck her into a crevasse and she would not have felt so horrified. She had to try three times before she could reply. "You remember."

Skjæra glanced toward the crash site.

Daneeb swallowed bile. "What will you do?"

The living cowl Skjæra used to cover her face

seemed to melt away, receding from her piercing eyes and pale skin.

How can she bear to look at me? Why does she not use her blade to slit my throat?

The cowl crept up again, erasing Skjæra's features with the smooth mask of blank flesh.

Daneeb nodded. "You are right—we should hurry. Let us go now, before they cut this ensleg to pieces and feed him to the rothawks."

Seven

Iisleg, Duncan Reever discovered as he crouched behind the cover of the wrecked launch, was a terse amalgam of several Terran Scandinavian languages. The Toskald had never permitted it to be recorded for analysis and addition to any language database, so no offworlder could speak it.

Reever's linguistic abilities allowed him to identify root words easily, but the grammatical structure of Iisleg was complex, and based partially on another, non-Terran language, probably one used by the slavers who had brought the Iisleg's ancestors to Akkabarr. Without the physical contact he needed to establish a telepathic link to absorb their language, he could understand only a limited portion of what the natives who had flown to the crash site were shouting at him.

"Windlord . . . man . . . fight."

". . . liver . . . cook pot."

"Give . . . women . . . sniveler."

As bolts from Iisleg crossbows hammered the hull panel protecting Reever, he made a judicious adjustment on his wristcom that would allow him to communicate. He then amplified the translation device's volume, so his words might be heard over the Iisleg's angry voices.

"I am not a windlord," he told them, speaking slowly and clearly. "I do not serve the windlords. I am a visitor from another world. I search for a crash survivor."

"He searches," one scout said, indicating that much was understood, and laughed.

". . . show him," another promised in a furious tone. "His insides . . . my hands."

The glimpses Reever caught of the natives showed an unimpressive-looking group. Dressed in a ragtag assortment of native furs and offworlder wear, they were all armed with primitive crossbows that dispensed an inefficient amount of alloy-tipped bolts. The blades they carried remained in their handmade sheaths, and Reever guessed they reserved them for use in close-proximity, hand-to-hand fighting. They had arrived on skimmers, but had nothing with them to indicate they had come to salvage the wreck. The skimmers were piled with several bulging sacks stained with dark fluids at the bottom.

Hunters, not salvagers. He had hoped the ignited fuel trail would attract the latter.

"I am searching for a female Terran," he told them. "The vessel in which she was transported crashed somewhere in this area some time ago. She may now be living among your people. She is a doctor, a healer."

An angry voice yelled something mostly indecipherable, about ensleg women being or becoming dead. The man extended what sounded like an invitation for Reever to do the same.

Movement to the south caught Reever's eye, and he turned his attention toward the pair of figures approaching the crash site on foot. Both seemed to shimmer, twin mirages conjured up by the reflection of sunlight on the snow. As they drew closer, their forms seemed to compress and solidify, while the outlines of those forms remained inconstant, vacillating with the rising wavelike patterns of true mirages.

"Ensleg . . . drag you . . . hole?"

A well-tipped bolt penetrated the alloy next to Reever's head, its barbed shaft scoring across his left cheek. He barely felt the burn as he stared at the two figures, who evidently intended to walk directly into the fray.

The natives who were present also took immediate notice of this, for they called to each other to look at the newly arrived pair. There were suggestions made in troubled voices. In the still unfamiliar language, they talked about stopping, cutting, and what Reever thought might be praying.

"No," one said, sounding sick. "Vral . . . vral."

The bolts stopped hitting the launch, and Reever lost sight of the two figures as they passed him and went to intercept the scouting party. Now the Iisleg were whispering instead of shouting, and the one word Reever kept hearing repeated was the one his wristcom could not translate.

Vral.

"Spirit . . . flesh," the male who had earlier been so angry said, his words unsteady. "Man. . . no dying . . . judge."

". . . blood," a harsh voice said.

Reever went still and listened, trying to make out more of what they said and interpret it.

". . . ensleg, holy one," another Iisleg said. His tone

was that of a shamed child, admitting wrong to a parent. "He . . . soul."

"Holy one . . . judge," the harsh voice said.

Snow crunched under heavy steps, and before Reever could move, three native males walked around the launch and confronted him. None of them held weapons, and each of their faces was pale and tight with strain, as if Reever had them pinned down.

"Come," one of them muttered, and made a gesture for Reever to accompany them. "You . . . vral . . . come."

Reever adjusted the volume on his wristcom as he slowly rose to his feet. "Vral?"

"Vral . . . holy one . . . come." The male swung a hand toward where the other Iisleg and the two strangers were waiting. "Blood . . . measure . . . soul." Contempt curled his lip. "You . . . no soul . . .gift . . . head."

Reever understood that *vral* meant the two strangers, evidently revered. He also gathered that they had come to pass some sort of judgment on him, the natives who had attacked him, or perhaps all of them. He considered using the weapons he carried on this trio and making his escape, as he did not have time to indulge in whatever primitive ritual they sought to carry out. At the same time, he wanted a better look at the pair who had caused the others to break off their assault. If these vral were powerful enough to stop a group of furious men intent on killing, they might also persuade them to help Reever.

"Yes." Reever nodded to emphasize this, and the three men turned away. He followed them out onto the open ice and kept alert for any signs of treachery.

The two vral were wearing offworlder robes made of a material Reever guessed to be a bleached form of dimsilk. Spun of light-bending fibers, the fabric cloaked the body while disguising its exact dimensions, which accounted for the mirage effect Reever had noticed earlier.

The other Iisleg stood apart, in a tight group very near to their skimmers, talking quietly and directing furtive, almost shameful glances at the pair.

Reever pointed at the two. "Vral?"

One of the men gaped at him, while a second struck the hand Reever was using to point. From what they both babbled, apparently pointing at the vral violated a taboo.

"Vral," the third said, gesturing for Reever to approach the pair.

The three Iisleg stopped in their tracks as if afraid to go any closer to the mysterious pair. As for the vral, they displayed no interest in Reever until he came to stand before them. He inspected their robes, but the dimsilk concealed everything it covered. Then he looked up into their faces, which were draped with normal cloth that completely concealed their features.

"Ensleg," the larger of the two murmured.

"I am not a windlord, and I do not serve the windlords," he said, giving them a condensed version of what he had told the Iisleg. "I am a visitor searching for a crash survivor. She is a female Terran healer."

The shorter of the two vral lifted one cloaked, gloved hand. For a moment Reever expected a blow to his face, and instead felt a light touch above the bleeding gash on his cheek. The dimsilk separating their skins effectively barred his attempt at a link.

"He . . . not dying," the larger vral said.

The one who had touched him turned and produced a pack from its robes, which it opened. The pack, made of animal skins, contained plas packets, vials, and small cases. The assortment didn't make sense, nor did the small scanner that the gloved hand removed and activated. The supplies appeared completely modern, so much so that they might have come from one of the storage units on board the *Sunlace*. The scanner was even more confusing, for Reever recognized the diagnostic device with one glance.

It was a medical scanner.

"Are you healers?" If they were, they might have heard of Cherijo. They might know where she was at that moment. Reever tensed, resisting the urge to grab and shake and demand.

The vral did not answer, but turned the scanner toward Reever and began passing it in front of his body to take readings.

Being unable to see their faces or touch their skin to establish a telepathic link made communication impossible. He hadn't absorbed enough of the Iisleg language to make himself understood, and the garments the vral wore completely covered their skin. On impulse, he reached out to pull down the material covering the vral's head. The vral stepped away from Reever's hand, but not in time to prevent the wrap from falling back.

Behind Reever, several of the natives made frightened, babbling sounds. He did not try to translate them. He was transfixed by the vision of a being without eyes, nose, mouth, or any other orifice in its head. He would never be able to tell what it was thinking, because the vral did not have an expression. The vral did not have a face.

As the vral turned away, a fold revealed a vertical seam, running around the edge of that blank face. Whatever this being was, it wore a very convincing mask, Reever realized, of material that made it appear as if it did not have a face. *But why? And how can it see or breathe through it? Is it some form of Lok-teel?* Reever had used the sentient, color/shape/texture-changing telepathic mold to disguise his own features, but the Lok-teel were unknown in this part of the galaxy.

Or were they? Cherijo had always carried one with her.

Reever reached out again, but just before his fingers touched the vral's disguise, the larger vral snapped something furious and indistinct and pushed his hand away. It turned its wrapped face toward the Iisleg for an instant as it covered its companion's head.

Reever understood. It was important that the natives believe the vral's ruse. "I won't tell them about your masks."

Some of what he said was understood, for the larger vral went still. The other acted as if it had not heard him speak.

"I will not tell them, but I must learn your language," Reever said to the smaller vral, and held out his hand. Although it wouldn't understand his words, he kept talking. "To do that, I must touch you. I am a telepath, and physical contact will permit me to absorb your language faster. Please."

The vral ignored him and finished taking the diagnostic readings. It studied the scanner's display before going into the pack to retrieve a sterilization kit and a small suture laser. When Reever moved closer, it took corresponding steps to remain out of reach.

"Daévena yepa." The larger vral stripped off a glove, revealing a very human-looking hand, and grabbed Reever's. "Learn it from me."

Reever was accustomed to establishing crude telepathic links with other species in order to tap into the language centers and absorb their lexica. This individual's mind was not as alien as those others, however. It was as close to a Terran's mind as he had ever encountered away from his native planet.

—Daneeb headwoman Skjæra vral skela Enafa ensleg rebels outcast love shame anger guilt fear—

He tried to strengthen the link, but failed. The vral's mind was regimented in odd ways, and it had developed some rather menacing thought disciplines to prevent any access to any but her most recent memories. Daneeb, as she thought of herself, lived only for the day.

There was also an extreme amount of strong emotion Daneeb was presently experiencing, which jumbled language with images and sensations. That, in turn, tugged at the mental connections Reever had established between them. It was all he could do to wade through the turmoil and tap into her language centers. Once he had enough for his uses, he drew back, removing the memory of his intrusion as he left.

He released Daneeb's hand and used what he had absorbed. "I am a Terran, as your people once were. My name is Reever."

Daneeb staggered back a step. The smaller showed no reaction.

"I mean neither of you harm," Reever said. "I need your help."

"You will harm; you won't harm. Which is it?" Daneeb rubbed her hand. "Why did you not speak like this before now?"

"I will not harm you." He realized that explaining his talent might frighten them. "I am out of practice speaking your language. It took a moment for me to remember." He nodded toward the smaller vral, who had removed its heavier mitts and had donned medical gloves. "Who is this?"

"She is vral." Daneeb jerked on her glove. "That is all you need know."

The smaller vral brought a soft piece of warm, damp gauze to Reever's face and carefully wiped the blood from it. The gloves she wore were thin enough to allow him to feel the heat of her skin.

She was approximately the same height as Cherijo. She had a Lok-teel. But if she was his wife, why did she not acknowledge him? Would they be in some danger if she did?

Daneeb became agitated. "Hurry." To Reever, she said, "When she has fixed you, can you fly your vessel and return to the place you belong?"

No such place existed. "If I have time to make repairs, I can," Reever said. "But I will not leave until I find the woman for whom I search."

"You came here for a *woman?*" Daneeb sputtered in disbelief. "Are you such a nothing that you could not find one among your own kind?"

"This woman is special." He only wished he could tell her how, but that, too, might create a hazardous situation. He looked at the smaller vral. "She belongs to me."

Despite the mask over her face, Skjæra seemed to stare at him for a moment, and then dropped the bloody gauze into a small bag, which she tucked into her pack.

"So?" Daneeb made a scathing sound. "You are a man. You can always find another one."

"Have you seen a Terran woman anywhere during your travels?" he asked.

"No," Daneeb snapped. "Our kind are not permitted near the living, only the wounded or dead."

Skjæra applied a topical anesthetic, and then used the suture laser to close the bolt wound.

"You must keep your face dry and clean if it is to heal," Daneeb told him.

"I will. Thank you." Reever saw the Iisleg were growing restless again. He wanted to stay with Daneeb and Skjæra, but the restrictions under which they lived would make his search impossible. "What happens now?"

Daneeb eyed the Iisleg. "We tell the hunters that you have a soul, and are honorable, so they will not kill you here. You will keep your word and do no harm, so they do not kill all of us."

The smaller vral replaced the supplies in her pack.

"They will take you with them to their camp, or perhaps to the nearest iiskar," Daneeb continued. "If you make no trouble, they may let you live. I will talk to them now." She left them and went to the hunters, who watched her approach with visible terror.

Skjæra moved the pack under her robe and hung it from her shoulder. She seemed to notice him at last, and lifted one hand, perhaps in a gesture of farewell. She had not said a single word the entire time she was treating him.

"Cherijo."

The smaller vral didn't respond. Reever wasn't willing to leave it at that, not without being sure, so he reached out and grasped her wrist. "Cherijo, is it you?"

She said nothing.

"I'm going to remove your glove." He exposed her hand and pressed his palm to hers. "No one can hear our thoughts." He reached into her mind.

One thing became immediately evident: Skjæra was not Cherijo.

The woman's thoughts were as blank and smooth as the mask covering her face. If Daneeb lived in the day, her companion seemed to live in the moment. She thought only of walking back across the ice field. There was nothing before that, and nothing after. Reever had left no impression on her mind whatsoever.

Despite his disappointment, Reever realized that the vral was in some manner gravely mentally ill, and immediately broke the link.

"Forgive me," he asked, although he didn't know why. She had been completely unaware of his mental intrusion. As, on most levels, she was indifferent to him.

What happened to her, to destroy her mind so thoroughly? If she had known anything about Reever's wife, whatever had been done to her had destroyed those memories.

That was what disturbed him most. She had no

memory center. Whatever happened to her in the present was all she carried in her mind.

Daneeb rejoined them. "They have agreed to take you back to their iiskar, which is not far from here. Stay with Hathor, the hunter in the gray outfurs. He will see that you are not harmed. We must go. Farewell."

Skjæra said nothing, but simply walked away with her companion.

As the hunters surrounded him, Reever stood watching the vral crossing the empty ice, walking into nothingness. The nothingness disturbed him almost as much as the smaller vral. A woman as small as Cherijo, with a mask possibly made of Lok-teel. Cherijo had carried a Lok-teel. But that blankness—that terrible emptiness in her mind—to have no memories . . .

No memories.

He looked at the hunter wearing predominantly gray furs and pointed to the vral. "I must follow them."

Hathor shook his head.

Reever took Aledver's chain and crystal from around his neck and offered them to the hunter. "Take this as payment."

The hunter hesitated, then took the crystal and tossed it to another man. "You follow them, ensleg—you go alone."

Reever nodded and set out to track the vral.

A week after Resa came to work in the salvage sheds, she had learned enough of the people's words to communicate. Ygrelda, who had been kind to her from the first day, helped by correcting her words and explaining many things. Like the name Hurgot had given her.

"What do Resa mean?"

Ygrelda looked up from the pile of small salvaged parts she was sorting. "What *does* Resa mean?"

Resa nodded.

"It is from the Time Before stories, when we lived on another world. Our people would beseech their gods when a person died, and sometimes that person's spirit was returned to their flesh. When that happened, the person could live again. Spirit made flesh. The word for such a person brought back from death was *resa*."

Resa frowned. "I was not death."

"You were not *dead*, but . . ." Ygrelda sighed and went back to sorting. "It is not good luck to speak of such things. You are here, and you have a name."

Not good luck prevented the people from doing many things. It was not good luck to eat with the hand on the left, or to spill soup, or to touch a sleeping person. It was not good luck to say why. Some of it made a little sense, such as the spilling of soup, for the people never had much food. Not spilling it prevented waste.

Mlap stopped by their table and eyed Resa's pile of sorted salvage. It was twice the size of the other women's. "You make us look lazy, ensleg. Slow down or the gjenvin master will expect us all to do the same."

"Leave her alone," Ygrelda said. "She can work as she likes."

"Not for long." The heavy-bodied woman gave

Resa an unpleasant smile. "The winds whisper that someone wishes a particular thorn removed."

"Someone?" Ygrelda stopped working to turn and glare. "Who?"

Mlap snorted. "Who cannot bear it if she is not the barb embedded in everyone's ass?"

"I know that," Resa said, happy that she had the answer from hearing two women discussing the same thing. "Sogayi."

"Resa." Ygrelda made a silencing gesture. To Mlap she said, "She has done nothing wrong. She has been obedient. She has worked hard. She keeps clean and modest. Why should she be punished?"

Resa had the feeling that her friend was no longer speaking of the headman's woman.

"Why?" Mlap gave the younger woman an incredulous look, and then lowered her voice to demand, "Why do you care? You know what will happen if you cross her. Do you wish to strip dead bodies for the remainder of your miserable life?"

Resa looked from one woman to the other. The woman called Sogayi was the one who belonged to the rasakt. Ygrelda had made her understand a little of how important the headman was, and that to be his woman was a great honor. The puzzling thing about it was that Sogayi's name was never mentioned except in whispers colored by fear or anger. That, too, was how Hurgot had responded to her presence—Resa had never forgotten that. She had felt pity for Sogayi, for despite her privileged position among the people, it seemed she had few friends.

Resa had to be more worried about her own position now, for as Ygrelda and Mlap continued to speak, it became apparent that they were talking about Resa being taken from the salvage sheds and driven from the camp.

It was not fair. She had tried very hard to learn the people's ways, because she did not want them to make her leave the iiskar. She did not think she could return to the ice now, not after living here with Ygrelda and the other women. Even Mlap, who never showed kindness to her, was better than facing that emptiness again.

"I am sorry," Resa interrupted the conversation between the two women, and put a hand on Mlap's arm. "I do better, work harder, Sogayi not be angry, yes?"

"Idiot ensleg." For once Mlap didn't look upon her through angry eyes. "You have no choice in the matter." She glared at Ygrelda. "Neither do you, so you had better prepare her."

"Where?" Ygrelda asked.

"Where do you think? Only watch or Sogayi might flick fresh blood on her first." Mlap trudged back over to her own table and went back to work.

Ygrelda gave Resa a sober look. "Resa, this is trouble."

"I make bad luck?" Maybe by being with the people she had violated one of their customs.

"I don't know." The younger woman frowned at her salvage pile. "Let me think."

Resa worked in silence, excusing herself only to void her bladder once. Had she been with the cats, she would have done so outside the cave, in a hole she would dig in the ice, as the cats did. The people had a special shelter for their needs, which stood over two deep pits, one for urine, the other for feces. Plank benches were propped over each pit and, like the shelter, could be moved to a new spot when the pits were full. Fresh hides and skins were kept for a time in the urine pit, where they soaked for many suns in the collected fluids. Resa had thought this practice odd until Ygrelda explained it was part of the process of making them ready for use.

As Resa left the privy, she walked slowly back toward the salvage sheds. Ygrelda had told her never to look directly at any of the people, especially the males, as it was discourteous. But her trips to the privy were the only chance she had to see anything but the women who sorted salvage, so she could not resist looking around.

There was always much activity within the iiskar. Men moved freely among the rows of shelters, usually in pairs. Those who were hunters often brought heavy sacks of meat into camp, and were greeted with admiration by the other men. Others carried tools and building materials as they went to repair or build onto the shelters. Every man carried a crossbow and a blade. Several carried other, strange devices that resembled some of the salvage Resa sorted.

Although she wasn't supposed to watch the men, Resa enjoyed doing so. Most seemed to like their work and talked openly as they went about it, which allowed her to pick up more words.

The women of the camp always kept their heads wrapped outside the shelters, and did not speak to anyone unless first addressed by a man. They carried water, food, or clothing. None of them possessed any sort of weapon, and Resa had already figured out that women were not permitted to do so. They did not show happiness or any other emotion, but rather behaved in a furtive manner, as if not wishing to attract attention.

Resa paused when she saw a woman chasing after a little boy who had run out of one of the shelters. A big man intercepted and scooped up the child, tossed him into the air a few times, and then set him into the waiting woman's arms. The man then did something Resa had never seen done before among the people: He tugged away a fold of the woman's head wrap, and caressed her cheek with the back of his hand. The two said nothing, but their affection for each other needed no words. After rubbing her cheek against the man's hand, the woman wrapped her face and took the squirming boy back into the shelter.

It happened so quickly that Resa doubted anyone but her had noticed it.

Resa's scalp prickled and felt cold. Ygrelda had cut off most of her hair during the first night she had spent among the women. Resa hadn't liked that, because her hair kept her head and neck warm, but she knew it was to make her look like all the other women.

A passing hunter scowled at her. "Get back to work, ensleg."

Resa hurried back to the salvage sheds. Only when she had stepped through the flap did she release her breath.

Ygrelda came over to her. "What is the matter?" She looked all over her. "Resa, you are shaking."

"Cold outside." Resa made a show of rubbing her hands together. Her wrist was throbbing again, as it had done when she had first come to the people.

"Come and warm yourself." Ygrelda led her over to

the heatarc. She took something from her sleeve and pressed it into Resa's hand. "Here. The chief gjenvin said I might have this." She made a face. "It is pretty, but it serves no purpose. I want it to be yours."

Resa examined the object Ygrelda had given her. It was a small circle of flat, square metal links. The metal was scratched, and exposure to the elements had taken away most of the shine the object must have once had, but it was pretty. "What this?"

"A necklace of some kind. Let me." Ygrelda did something to separate two of the links, and then placed the chain around Resa's throat before joining them again. "There. It looks right on you. It is an ensleg bauble; I thought it would."

Resa tucked her chin in, but the chain of the necklace was so short she couldn't see it. "I thank you."

The midday meal was prepared and served, and Resa left the sorting tables and stood waiting for her portion. She was always last to be given food, but Ygrelda waited with her. Resa noticed how her friend checked her bowl each time, as if to assure it was filled properly. Today the old woman, whom Ygrelda called a renser, handed Resa a brimming portion, as well as two slices of dark, heavy bread. Renser prepared all the food in the iiskar. Since no one else was given the bread, Resa felt confused, and tried to give it back.

"No," the renser said. She gave Ygrelda an odd look. "It is the last, and cannot be divided evenly. Besides, you will need it."

Resa thanked her, which only made the renser look away. Ygrelda's mouth became a hard line when she saw the other women staring at them, but she said nothing.

Certain foods like bread had become scarce since Resa had come to the people, and she felt uncomfortable with being so favored. She liked bread very much, but it was not appropriate for her to have the last of it, not when she was still treated as an outsider by so many. Ygrelda had already given her the gift of the necklace. Her stomach, too, was still clenched after the brief encounter with the scowling hunter. Once Resa and Ygrelda had found a place to sit near the heatarc, she offered the bread to her friend. "I not very hungry," she said truthfully. "You take."

The other women around them looked at the bread, and then at Ygrelda. Some seemed unhappy. Others looked strangely distressed.

Ygrelda's mouth relaxed. "No, Resa. None of us wish to have it. It is all right for you to eat it."

Another kindness. It confused Resa, but she lowered her hand and smiled. "I thank you. Again."

Ygrelda looked away, as the renser had.

Resa wanted to ask so many questions, but she did not have enough words for them. She wanted to tell Ygrelda about the cats, and the ice caves, and how grateful she was to be accepted by the people. How much the kindness Ygrelda and the other woman had shown her meant to her. How hard she would work, if given the chance to stay and earn her place with the people.

She wanted to ask about the big man who had caressed the cheek of the woman chasing the boy. She understood the attraction between males and females—even the cats displayed such—but surely desire among the people was not usually shown so openly. She had never seen such a thing before now, and it confused her.

"Resa," Ygrelda said, her voice low. "We have work to do. Eat."

Resa ate. The bread was a little dry and hard, but she broke it into pieces and dipped it in her broth to soften it. She ate both slices, and drank every drop in her bowl. The other women sitting around them ate slowly, and no one spoke. The silence seemed to press on Resa's ears, so accustomed was she to the women's daily chatter.

She wanted to cry out, *What have I done?* but that was not the way of the people. She was afraid to know, as well.

One of the women nearest the flap suddenly darted away from it to crouch nearer to the heatarc. "Kheder."

Without warning, all of the women stopped eating. Those who were standing dropped down quickly to crouch on the floor. Those who were already sitting tucked their hands into the ends of their sleeves, hunched over, and stared at the floor. Resa looked around until she saw a tall male wearing heavy furs and standing just inside the flap.

"Down," Ygrelda whispered, tugging at her arm until Resa assumed the same position as she. When Resa opened her mouth, Ygrelda quickly pressed her finger against her lips.

"Bring the ensleg to me," the man said.

Eight

The frost-covered body of the dead pilot was hauled out of the wreck by two skela, who brought it before Teulon.

"He was still sitting at the helm," Hasal said as he came to stand over the corpse. "The ship's engines are functional, and there are no signs of failure, although most of the reserve fuel was vented." His eyes shifted to the dead man's whitened face. "He was either a terrible pilot, or a very good one."

"Toskald pilots do not crash." Teulon crouched by the body to examine the dead man's face. He looked over the ensleg garments it wore, pried up the frozen material, and inspected the torso beneath. "What killed him?"

"One must assume the impact, Raktar." Hasal handed him the scanner, which he used to take readings of the dead man's internal organs. "He did not suffer. Death was instantaneous."

The injuries from the crash were evident on the exterior of the cadaver's torso, but none of them were severe enough to cause a broken rib to pierce his heart.

Teulon skimmed the readings on the scanner before he stood and handed it back to his second. He made a brief trip inside the launch to inspect the helm, where he saw blood in two places, and spaces within the storage units to indicate a significant amount of gear had been removed from them. There had also been some tampering with the helm console.

He departed the launch to walk around the site. There had been little fresh snowfall, so the marks left by those who had paid a visit to the wreck were still evident. It had been a small group, perhaps hunters searching for game and picking up the launch's thermal signature. They would have come here on skimmers, and yet there were faint markings indicating at least three had walked out on the ice.

"Track the ones on foot," he told his hunters, who had also noticed the trail.

Hasal joined him. "What do you look for, Raktar?"

Teulon picked up a crossbow bolt near the launch and examined it. "The pilot."

Hasal looked back at the body. "He *is* the pilot."

"He is Toskald, not Terran. His hair has been gilded and there are still traces of cosmetics on his skin. He wears no crystal." Teulon saw faint traces of a dark substance on the alloy-tipped bolt and handed it to his second. "The pilot was shot with this."

"I do not understand," Hasal said, turning the bolt over to inspect it. "How do you know this?"

"The dead man shows care to his body but wears clothing that does not fit his body? See how the sleeves are too short here, and the trousers too tight at the waist. Also, his pants are not fastened properly; they were pulled on in haste. The blood pattern inside the launch tells me that he was killed while near the copilot's chair, and then moved into the pilot's seat. The helm has been vandalized and there is survival gear missing from the storage compartments. The hunters who came here fired their weapons and wounded something that walks on two feet and bleeds red. As a Terran who had emerged from the wreck might." Then they had let him walk away—but why?

"Hunters do not wound," Hasal said, looking utterly mystified now. "They only kill, and they would never allow an ensleg to live." His expression changed. "That is why the Terran switched clothes? To appear to the hunters as a Tos'?"

"Perhaps." Despite the facts he had uncovered, there was still something very wrong with this scene, Teulon thought. "Who hunts this territory?"

"Five, perhaps six different iiskars," Hasal said. "I can send men to check each of them."

It was another hour before Teulon's hunters returned with a Terran male dressed in Toskald garments. The wound on his face corresponded with the bolt Teulon had found. As he was marched over to Teulon, the Raktar recognized him immediately.

"The Terran linguist." It took him a moment to recall the man's name. "Duncan Reever."

Hasal frowned. "You know this man?"

It could not be Reever, of course. The Terran had been on board the *CloudWalk* when it had been destroyed. Teulon had watched him die. Whoever this man was, he was not Reever. Teulon covered his face before facing the Terran prisoner.

"He fights well," one of the hunters told Teulon. "Broke Lapar's arm."

Hasal stepped up to the Terran and gestured to the wreckage. "Were you the pilot of this ship?"

"No. The pilot was killed on impact."

Teulon frowned. The man's voice sounded flat and devoid of emotion—exactly as he had remembered Reever's. "But you took his crystal."

"I gave it to one of the hunters who came to salvage the wreck."

That, Teulon thought unlikely, given that the crystal was his only passage off the planet's surface. The Toskald would never take him back to the skim city without it. "Why have you come to Akkabarr?"

"One of our ships crashed here two years ago. I am here to search for a survivor." He ignored the chuffing sound Hasal made and addressed Teulon. "I was following someone who might have helped me find her when your men captured me."

"Searching for a woman. A crash survivor. On Akkabarr." Hasal spit on the ice. "He is insane, Raktar."

Teulon studied the sky. A storm was brewing to the east, and it would be dangerous to keep the men out on the ice much longer. Teulon's battalions were also in position, making the final preparations to move on the armory trenches. He would need to travel to the northern territories to ready the attack forces. The Kangal's general had not accepted the failure of his scouts and was sending more ships every day to patrol the surface. Teulon could not afford to be distracted by a League spy, no matter whom he resembled.

"I am no more a spy than you are Iisleg," the Terran said in flawless Jorenian. "I would know your House, warrior."

"You already do, Linguist." Teulon removed his face shield. "Now you will explain to me how you still breathe when I watched you die two years ago."

"I could ask you the same thing." Reever switched from speaking Jorenian to Iisleg. "I was saved during the battle. We never learned how, but the child who was with me that day may have been responsible."

Teulon recalled the tiny, golden-haired Terran daughter of Cherijo Torin and Duncan Reever. Xonea Torin, an old friend and captain of the *Sunlace,* had told him that in order to protect the child, all records as to her existence had been destroyed. Those who knew of her were either HouseClan Torin or their closest allies.

Still, he had to be sure. "What was the name of this child?"

"Marel."

"Give him back his weapons and release him." He ignored his hunters' astonished stares, gestured to the open ice, and walked with Reever past them.

"How did you come to be here?" the Terran asked when they were out of hearing range.

"The League had reasons to keep me alive." He watched Reever replace a blade in a shoulder sheath fitted as an assassin would wear it. "Do my people believe that I embraced the stars with my kin?"

"The League stated that you ran into an open air lock after your ship was destroyed, and that your remains were lost among the battlefield debris." The Terran halted and checked the power cells on a pistol before glancing at him. "They also claimed that you started the incident by ordering your ship to fire on the League."

"I gave the order to protect my ship from a drone launch programmed to destroy it." Teulon studied the tracks leading away from the crash scene. "Why are you here, Linguist?"

"My wife was captured during the battle and disappeared. She was brought here, as I imagine you were, to be sold into slavery. Her transport crashed on the surface." Reever halted and faced him. "Why are you leading this rebellion, ClanLeader?"

The word made Teulon's head pound. "I have no House, Linguist. Here I do the last of the work left to me, and then my path ends."

The Terran began to say something, and then paused. At last he said, "But you are leading these surface natives into war with the Toskald."

"I am." He saw the skela had been brought into the wreck site. "Your pardon, Linguist. I must attend to this."

Teulon went to the body, where the skela had gathered. "Have the launch shrouded," he told Hasal. "Erase all signs that there was a crash here." To the dead handlers, one of whom had already produced a skinning blade, he said, "Do not take his face."

"Raktar, worgald is always taken," Hasal said.

"The time for tithes is over. The Kangal will not sell any more faces of the dead to grieving kin," Teulon said. "Neither shall we." He looked at the cringing skela, and for once understood why the Iisleg held them in such contempt. "Give him to the cats."

The skela quickly and efficiently stripped the body before they dragged it over to the waiting jlorra.

Hasal snapped out orders, and the scouting party that had accompanied them to the crash site reassembled and mounted their skimmers.

Reever came to stand with Teulon. "Am I your prisoner, or am I free to continue with my search?"

"There is a storm coming. You will have to take shelter soon." He nodded toward the trail across the ice. "You were following someone."

"Two females. The hunters who came to salvage the crash called them vral," Reever said. "I think they may know something about Cherijo."

Teulon gestured for Hasal, who hurried over to them. "What is the closest iiskar to this place?"

His second gave Reever a suspicious look before answering, "There are two. Kuorj, one hour to the east, and Pasala, one hour to the west."

"Which would welcome the Raktar's personal emissary?" Teulon asked.

"Kuorj. Their rasakt has pledged all of his men to the cause. Pasala is smaller, less affluent, perhaps not as loyal to the cause. We have not met with them. The Kuorj would wait to find out the ensleg was your emissary. The Pasala would be too busy feeding him to their pack animals."

Teulon turned to Reever. "Go east. Tell the Kuorj leader that I sent you to find these females, and you may shelter with them until the weather passes." He handed him a transmitter beacon. "This will signal my camp. If you are in need of aid, relay the coordinates of your position. Help will be sent to you." He met Reever's gaze. "I have never seen your wife on Akkabarr, Linguist. Should that change, I will signal you."

Reever nodded and departed, heading east over the ice.

The methane-powered skimmers made the hour-long trip to Pasala iiskar in only a few minutes. Teulon's scouts went ahead to alert the rasakt of the iiskar, who stood waiting with his three highest-ranked men as the Raktar's party arrived. There were several greeting rituals performed, including the declaration of the rasakt as loyal to the Raktar and the rebel cause, as Pasala and Teulon had never met before now.

Teulon thought Pasala might be in earnest with his vow. His men were thin and wore their weapons battle-ready. The women and children were kept completely out of sight. The camp had been erected near natural thermal vents, the heat from which disguised the camp's thermal signature and rendered it invisible to any orbital scan. The entire camp was free of clutter, and the Pasala appeared quite ready to pack up and leave within a few minutes' notice.

"I would speak to your hunters," Teulon told the headman once the formalities had been observed and the last of the greetings exchanged.

The rasakt displayed the command he held over his people by uttering a few words, which had his hunters assembled beside him thirty seconds later.

"Have you been out on the ice today?" Teulon asked the oldest of the men.

"No, Raktar," the hunter answered. "We remained here to help with the repair of some shelters, as a storm approaches."

One of the younger men among the lesser-ranked, the beast master, made a coughing sound, and the rasakt turned and gestured for him to come forward. "What have you to tell, Jaf?"

"I was out on the ice today with the jlorra, at midday," the beast master said.

"You saw the ensleg launch crash?" Teulon asked him.

The younger man nodded. "Kuorj flew in from the east. I saw them land to lay claim to it."

"Did you see anything else?"

Jaf glanced at his footgear. "I may have seen something. Something that was not there."

Teulon tensed.

"You cannot see something unless it is," Hasal said sharply. "Tell us."

The beast master shifted his weight from foot to foot. "Two came on foot, from the south, just as the Kuorj had crossed the ice. They were there and they were not. I thought my eyes snow-dazzled."

"Vral," one of the other hunters muttered.

Hasal made a sound of contempt. "Vral, is it? Next you will tell me you saw winged jlorra and gold-beaked rothawks."

"Hold." The rasakt lifted a hand. "We have heard much talk of the vral. It is said they walk the ice here now, and keep the skela idle."

"Have you seen them with your own eyes?" Hasal asked. The rasakt shook his head. Teulon's second turned to the assembled hunters. "Any of you? Say now."

None of the men spoke.

"It was a trick of the light," Hasal assured them, his voice gentling. "Out on the ice, a man sees things now and then that are not there."

The storm was moving in fast now, so Teulon thanked Pasala and his men and returned by skimmer to the central encampment. There he took reports from his battalion commanders and briefed them on the two females for whom Reever searched, and issued orders that the women be captured alive and brought directly to him.

That night, when Teulon had finished planning the next day's maneuvers with Hasal, he said, "Both the Terran and the Pasala spoke of vral. Who are they?"

"They are nothing." Hasal stowed away the topographic maps they had been using and went to adjust the heatarc's flue. "Vral are not real. They exist only in the old stories."

"What are these stories told about them?"

Hasal looked up. "You wish me to repeat tales told to children who fear the absence of their father?"

Teulon inclined his head.

"As you say." Hasal crouched to prepare their food and drink. "When a man is harmed, it is said that his blood opens the eyes of the gods. If he cries out like a coward in pain, they look away, and he dies. If he is silent and endures, however, the gods open their ears. Only then can they hear the cries of the man's women and children. This makes them take pity on those who will suffer the man's death, and they send the vral to find him. The vral look into the wounded one's heart. If they find him worthy, they restore him to his iiskar. That is all."

"What are the vral?" Teulon saw Hasal about to retort, and added, "What are they said to be in these stories?"

"They are spirit made flesh." Hasal made an uncertain gesture. "They walk as we do, in body form, but they have no faces."

Teulon thought of the skela, prepared to remove the

face of the dead Toskald. "What happened to the vral's faces?"

"No one knows." Hasal looked uncomfortable. "Some say they are the souls of those who died during the journey from the old world to this one."

Or perhaps, Teulon thought, they were the corpses stripped of worgald, brought back by Iisleg subconscious guilt to haunt them. Part of him could accept that. There was not a conscious moment when he was not haunted by his beloved dead. "Why are they so feared?"

"If the vral find you unworthy, they feed your soul to their jlorra," Hasal said. "To look upon them is to see true death, Raktar. Vral may be sent by the gods, and grant a second life to those deserving of such miracles, but no one *wants* to see them."

Teulon considered this. Given the legend, vral might go anywhere on the surface and never be challenged. "How do we find these vral?"

"We could walk the ice until we become as snowblind as that hunter likely was," Hasal suggested as he brought over a plate heaped with boiled grain and vegetables for Teulon, and a thick section of boiled meat for himself.

"That may be so." Teulon accepted the plate. "How do we find two Toskald spies who have disguised themselves as vral?"

Hasal smiled for the first time that day. "Vral are spirit made flesh, but they are not alive. If the legends are true, they would generate no body heat." He took out his thermal scanner and showed it to Teulon. "Spies, on the other hand, would."

When Hasal had gone for the night, Teulon dressed

and slipped out of the camp. Bsak accompanied him to the place they had found during one of their treks, a tiny ice cave hardly large enough to serve as anything but temporary shelter from the cold.

Bsak spied something moving on the ice, and looked up. Teulon made the gesture of release, and the big cat stalked off. He never brought the cat inside the cave; something about the interior seemed to make Bsak uneasy.

He went in and ignited the tiny heatarc that had been left abandoned in the center of the floor. There were no other signs of occupation, except for a depression in one wall where someone had chopped a hole to look out.

Why does she come here?

Time and an ancient vent shaft had carved the small cave from very old, dense blue ice. It absorbed the light from the heatarc more than it reflected it, but kept the cold out. The interior grew warm in a very short time.

Teulon leaned back against one wall and watched the light flicker. The cave was also one of the quietest places he had ever found on the planet, and soon all he could hear was the sound of his lungs filling and emptying, and the meaningless beat of his heart. He closed his eyes and listened for the whisper of her steps in the snow.

Raktar.

The ghost drifted into the cave, formless, nearly transparent, so insubstantial that her passage barely disturbed the light and the air.

"Spirit," Teulon greeted her, as he always did. He wasn't sure how he knew she was female, only that she was. Nor did he reach out to touch her, as he had done the first time she had appeared. He knew she would vanish if he tried to do so. Instead, he watched her go through her ritual of walking the length of the cave three times, going to the depression in the ice once each time before coming to him.

You should not be here alone.

"I am not." Teulon liked the sound of her voice, and the fact that she spoke perfect Jorenian. "You are here."

I am not here.

"I know." He waited a moment. "Are you vral?"

Are you?

She drifted around the cave for a time, gliding more than walking, without purpose. Teulon watched her without speaking, for too many words would also send her back to the otherworld where she dwelled.

You are thinking of her.

"I can do little more," he said.

I am lost to my beloved, and my beloved to me. The ghost moved in closer. *What will we do, Raktar?*

"You will haunt this cave." Teulon studied his hands. He had his father's large, capable hands. "I will make more ghosts."

For the first time since she had come to him in this place, she made physical contact. The mist of her came between his hands and rested lightly against his chest. *It will not bring them back.*

"I know this." He held her briefly, a slim column of something slightly more than air. He didn't understand his deep emotion for this creature, whatever she was. He simply knew she was the only thing on this world sadder than himself. "I would bring you back, if I could."

She moved away from him. *There is still time, Teulon. Time for you to use your hands to build instead of destroy.*

"Wait." Teulon opened his eyes as he reached for her.

Like everything that mattered, she was gone.

Nine

Hurgot heard the shuffling sound of a woman seeking permission to enter his shelter, and finished bandaging the gash on his patient's forearm.

"Next time, keep your braces on," he told the young hunter before pulling his sleeve into place. "Ptar claws can cut through bone." He turned his head toward the flap. "Come in."

One of the younger women who wore the robe covering of a salvage sorter stepped through the flap and to one side before she dropped into a respectful crouch. "I am Ygrelda, Kheder."

Hurgot waited until the young hunter left before he told her to rise to her feet. "What is it?" he asked, feeling impatient. No more men were waiting to be treated, but a woman who came with empty hands boded nothing good.

"I come to ask after Resa, the ensleg female." Ygrelda's voice was soft, hesitant.

"She is not here."

The woman's head bobbed in agreement. "She was taken from the gjenvin master three suns ago."

Like everyone in the iiskar, Hurgot had been aware of Resa's presence, but only in the vaguest sense, through casual comments made by the other men.

Most of what was said came from ribald curiosity, as few of the men had ever tried an ensleg woman. The rasakt had not made her available for general use, and she had not shown herself around the camp to tempt anyone.

That Resa had been removed from the sheds seemed odd to Hurgot, but he had vowed to keep his own distance, so as not to attract any further trouble. "What of it?"

"Resa did well among us, Kheder." The woman stared at his feet. "She was modest, worked hard, and never asked for more than was offered her. She would do the same again if returned to the salvage sheds. Her presence is missed."

So it was the usual female nonsense. This one had befriended the ensleg and now wished a boon to bring her friend back to her side. "I have no say over such things," he told the woman. "Go back to work."

"May I know of how Resa does?" Ygrelda asked, cringing a little. "There has been no word of her."

Hurgot frowned. The women in the camp usually knew everything about everyone; they had nothing better to do than to gossip. If the women didn't know what had happened to her . . . "Where was she taken?"

"To the jlorra caves, Kheder. She was taken by the beast master." Ygrelda gulped. "She has not returned to the iiskar since."

Hurgot bit back a violent curse. "Who gave word to send her there?"

"It is said the order came from the shelter of the rasakt," Ygrelda said.

Sogayi. Had it been Navn to give the order, everyone would know. The headman's wife had dared much this time. "Has the beast master returned to camp since Resa was taken?"

Ygrelda nodded. "Three times."

So Resa had been left with the jlorra, who were known to attack sleeping people when hungry enough. Hurgot went and pulled her to her feet. "Listen to me carefully. You will return to the sheds, and say nothing of this to anyone. I will go out to the jlorra caves to see that she is well, and bring you word. If she is—whatever has happened to her, you will accept it, and you will not speak of this again."

Ygrelda looked into his eyes. "She is good, Kheder. She does not deserve to be harmed. She did nothing wrong."

"She was born ensleg, and she did not die on the ice. That is reason enough for some." Unable to stand the weight of her eyes, Hurgot tugged her head wrap over her face. "Go now. I will send for you when I return."

It had been too cold to leave the shelters after sunset, but it was only midday, so when Ygrelda left, Hurgot put on his heaviest outfurs and prepared to go. After some thought, he put some food and tea in his medical pack.

Leaving the camp without being noticed was not difficult, for few paid attention to Hurgot anymore. He took care to leave casually rather than with a show of stealth, so as not to make his trek too obvious. To any eyes that spotted him, it would appear as if he were going to gather, as he often did, the medicinal molds and ice plants that grew around vent shafts.

There were no naturally occurring ice caves in the immediate vicinity of the camp, so Iiskar Navn's beast master had constructed artificial caves for his jlorra, stacking hewed blocks of ice to form three elongated domes. Several consecutive snowfalls had filled in the cracks between the blocks, and wind had scoured and rounded the surface until the caves looked almost identical to those formed in nature.

Hurgot knew Egil, the beast master. He was the son of a low-ranked hunter and one of the camp's ahayag. Handling pack animals was often a duty given to the youngest men until they gained more experience in hunting. Only when Egil had made a significant contribution to the camp's stores would he be raised to the status of hunter, and another with a less-certain hand on the bow would take his place. As Egil was also one of the lazier men in camp, he had held the position for far longer than usual.

There were no jlorra in the temporary holding pen, also built of ice blocks, on the side of the caves, so Hurgot stepped into the low, wide entrance.

"Egil?" he called out. "Are you here? It is Hurgot."

No voice answered, but the sound of many claws scraping the ice came to Hurgot's ears.

She is dead. Sogayi had him kill her and feed her to the beasts. Hurgot felt angry and resigned, for he had half expected as much as soon as Ygrelda had told him of Resa's removal from the sheds.

He had turned to go back out when Resa appeared, surrounded on all sides by the beasts. She looked directly at him and smiled before remembering to drop into the customary crouch and wait to be addressed. One of the jlorra nuzzled the side of her face as she did so.

"Stand, Resa." When she had, Hurgot inspected her.

She wore ancient outfurs, and her face was smudged with soot marks, but otherwise she looked intact. "You are well?"

"Yes, Kheder." She gestured toward the back of the cave. "Come, I make tea for you?"

More curious now than thirsty, Hurgot followed her to the back of the center cave. The jlorra followed the ensleg silently, not even glancing once at Hurgot.

The center cave had been built around the opening of a vent shaft, which provided some warmth for the beasts and their handler. Someone had fashioned a crude heatarc over the opening, and on it sat a salvaged pot and several other odd items, including some chunks of stone.

Resa first picked up a scrap of cloth and removed one of the stones, wrapping the cloth around it before offering it to Hurgot.

"Hold," she said when he frowned at the bundle. "Make hands warm."

Hurgot felt foolish—men did not feel the cold as women did—but he could indulge her this much. As soon as he clasped the cloth-wrapped stone between his mitts, the heat radiated into his palms and fingers. The mild ache he usually felt when on the ice vanished.

Resa was busy with filling the makeshift cook pot with meltwater and adding clumps of damp tea plant. "Make hot tea," she said, glancing over at him. "Soup, yes?"

Hurgot frowned. "Someone brought you food?" He would have expected Sogayi to give orders to starve the girl. Surely Egil could not have brought down any game, and if he had, it would have been taken to the skela and made fit for the camp's use.

"Cats bring." Resa reached over to run her fingertips around the ears of one jlorra's massive head. "I cook. You sit here, please?" She indicated a pile of furs to one side of the heatarc.

Hurgot sat. The furs were warm from being in close proximity to the shaft opening, and although they were a little stiff, they were surprisingly comfortable. He saw another large bundle of furs to one side that appeared as if Resa had been sleeping in them. Some were ragged, and their irregular shape puzzled him, until he saw the narrow lacings of guts holding them together. Resa had taken the fur scraps from the jlorra's kills, washed them, and stitched them together. He had never seen the like.

"Make fur," Resa said, following his gaze. "Keep me warm in night."

"You are learning to speak Iisleg," he said, just now realizing how well she was able to communicate.

"I speak some, not good," Resa told him as she brought over a cup of tea and presented it. "We talk, yes?"

"Yes." Hurgot sampled the tea, which was weaker than he liked, and had obviously been brewed several times before. "Resa, who brought these things here for you?"

She looked around. "Fur here. Cats bring food. I find things."

He did not want to think about the food aspect, so he asked, "Where do you find things?"

"Pile things." She gestured toward the south side of camp, where, Hurgot recalled, the gjenvin dumped whatever material could not be salvaged. She went back to the heatarc and poured some of the contents of another, odd-looking vessel into a smaller, bent piece of alloy with a shallow indentation like a bowl. She then brought the bowl to him. "Meat only," she said, rather apologetically. "Not know good plants here."

The bowl held a strong-flavored broth with small chunks of meat in it. Because it had no vegetables or spices it was bland by Iisleg standards, but otherwise hot and filling.

To give himself time to think rather than dwell on the origins of what was in the bowl, Hurgot ate slowly. Resa went back to her place by the heatarc and crouched there, warming her hands and sometimes petting one of the cats, who had piled all around her like sleepy, contented children.

"I brought you something," he said finally, when she took the empty bowl and cup from him. "Here." Feeling embarrassed, he took the food and tea from his pack.

"I thank you," Resa said, clearly delighted. She went to the bundle of patchwork furs, pulled one side up, and hid the food beneath it. When she saw Hurgot's expression, she made a face. "I put here or Egil eat all."

Refusing to give food to a man was a serious offense, one for which she could be beaten severely. Yet Hurgot found himself only admiring her ingenuity. Also, like every other man, Egil was well fed every night in camp. It appeared that Resa had been left to fend for herself.

He had to be sure, however. No need to jump to conclusions when someone else might be supplying

Resa's needs. "Did anyone bring you food and furs from the camp?"

She shook her head. "Cats, I find, I make. That all." She looked directly into his eyes. "I not die, Hurgot."

Was she reassuring him, or was she telling him that Sogayi's plan had failed? *She could not know.* "I will see to it that food is brought to you. It will not be much, but you will not starve." He was beginning to wonder if anything could kill her.

"That kind." Resa refilled his cup. "I thank you."

"Aren't you afraid of the jlorra?" Hurgot asked her as he watched her sit down and idly stroke the blue-white fur of the largest male's ridged back.

"Cats? No hurt me." Resa surveyed the animals around her as if they were nothing more than small children. "Cats like me." She began to say something else, and then frowned.

"What is it?"

"Egil beat them." Her dark brows drew together in the center. "I no like that."

"Egil beats the jlorra?" A wave of nausea swept over Hurgot at the thought of the beast master being so foolhardy.

"Sometime," Resa said. "Cats no like. I try, tell Egil no? Hit me." She rubbed the side of her head, ruffling her short, sheared hair. "Cats no like when Egil hit me."

"Hurgot?" A young man in heavy, unkempt furs entered the cave. "I thought I heard your voice, old man. What are you doing here?"

The change in Resa was instantaneous. She immediately put aside the implement in her hand and bent over until her nose touched the shabby boots on her feet, and stayed in that position, unmoving.

"Egil."

"You should have told me you were going to visit; I'd have brought something out with me." Egil's eyes darted from Hurgot to the empty dish and cup Resa had given him. "She didn't make you eat this swill she cooks, did she?"

"It was acceptable."

Egil went around the heatarc, kicking Resa out of his way with no more thought than if she were a bundle of furs. "I can hardly stomach the stuff." Giving lie to his statement, he hunched down and helped himself to the contents of the cook pot. Resa remained curled up to one side, in the position she had landed, still unmoving. The cats, however, shifted their positions, silently moving until they formed a living wall on three sides of her. They also watched Egil with menacing intensity.

"Why come all the way out here, old man?" Egil asked between mouthfuls.

Many of the young men of the camp referred to Hurgot as an "old man," but rarely to his face. "I came to gather some ice plants," he lied. "I stopped in here to warm myself at the vent shaft."

"Ah." Egil nodded, drank the last of the broth from the pot, and produced a loud belch.

Hurgot nodded toward Resa. "What is the ensleg doing here?"

"Nothing of use to me," Egil said. He used the rest of Resa's meltwater to wash his face and hands. "I keep the caves clean, and the beasts hunt for themselves. She does nothing but eat and sleep."

Resa lifted her head and glared at the back of Egil's before noticing Hurgot watching her. She returned to her curled-up position, but her expression was one of anger.

Hurgot had been to the jlorra caves before this day. In the recent past, he had noticed considerable piles of gnawed bones and other remnants of the beasts' kills. They were gone now, and he felt certain that Resa had been the one to clear them out when she had gathered the fur scraps to make her bed.

"Shall I take her back to camp, then?" he asked Egil. "She made herself useful sorting in the sheds; she can work there."

"The rasakt's—the rasakt does not want her polluting the other women with her ensleg ways," Egil said. "I was told that she is to remain here."

By Sogayi, no doubt. The rest of this conversation could not take place in front of a woman. "Walk outside with me," he said to Egil. "We must talk."

Egil went with him reluctantly. "I do not know why you bother with her. She is useless."

"Navn does not know about this, does he?" Hurgot gestured toward the cave. "About her being brought here."

The younger man gave him a stricken look. "Yes. Yes, he does."

"Then I will speak to Navn when I return to camp," Hurgot decided, "and ask him to bring her back to work in the sheds."

Egil pasted a false jovial smile on his face. "Healer, is that entirely wise? With the burdens the rasakt bears for us, he may have forgotten this trivial matter. It is best not to remind him and irritate him."

"He does not know she is here at all, does he?" Hurgot watched the young man's mouth open and close a few times. "A man who takes orders from a woman may as well be a woman himself," he suggested. "If this is made known, you will never hold a bow again."

Egil flushed. "You don't know what it is like. What can be done to one who goes against what is asked of him. Being beast master is not the worst work a man can do."

Hurgot thought for a moment. He had no great affection for Egil, but the younger man was simply trying to preserve his hide. "Navn must be informed of this. I think he has plans for this ensleg."

"I will not tell him," Egil said adamantly. "Unless you wish to spend the rest of the few years left to you curing hides or digging out privy holes, you should not, either."

The image of Ygrelda's pleading face came into Hurgot's mind. "Perhaps we will not have to." He glanced over Egil's shoulder, and saw Resa standing at the entrance to the cave. She had been listening to them talk for some time, he suspected, and if the younger man turned around, he would grab the ensleg and beat her within an inch of her life.

Resa knew this. Hurgot could see it in her eyes. Yet she stood, and she listened to them. She possessed the kind of courage that neither he nor Egil had, and it shamed him so much that he almost went around Egil to beat her himself.

"What are you going to do?" Egil demanded.

"Something," the shame made Hurgot say. "Soon."

Resa turned and walked back into the cave.

* * *

"What do you mean, Stuart's launch *crashed?*" Orjakis rose abruptly, spilling warm, perfumed water over the sides of the carved crystal tub. He thrust the attending drone aside and strode naked across the inlaid tile floor until he stood before his cowering notch.

"I see Janzil Ches—"

"Do not see us," Orjakis bellowed. "Tell us."

"Defense reported that the launch lost control in midflight." The notch fixed his desperate eyes on Orjakis's chin. "It apparently experienced engine failure. A partial distress signal was transmitted by Trader Aledver before the ship crashed. The transmission is unintelligible."

Aledver, one of his most trusted internals. Orjakis felt his rage sink deeper. "Where is it now?"

The notch had to consult his pad. "In the disputed area, Kangal. Defense has sent patrols to search for it, but there has been no success as of yet."

"It has been days since Stuart left Skjonn," Orjakis said through clenched teeth. "And they cannot locate it?" He didn't wait for an answer, but brushed the notch aside and strode into his dressing room. More attendants rushed at him, eager to array him in sky white silken trousers and a matching tunic heavily encrusted with tiny emitters. The emitters, programmed to flash sequenced patterns, were already activated and projecting images of wings, jewels, and other finery.

He ripped the tunic from the attendant's hands and tore it in half. The drone turned and went back to the garment room to select another ensemble.

Orjakis went to stand before the large window overlooking the city. Beneath him, several citizens walking outside the palace stopped at the sight of him. Two women and a man crumpled to the ground, overcome.

I should send for them, he thought. *Make them my ministers. They would kill themselves to please me.*

"We will see Defense in our receiving room," Orjakis told the notch, who had crept in after him. "In two minutes. With answers."

It took longer than two minutes for Orjakis to calm himself, and to select his colors and scents for the day. On his way from the chamber, he said to the Provisions drone, "Have a surface woman here awaiting our pleasure when we return."

Gohliya was waiting on his knees in the receiving room. Orjakis noted the old man's fixed stare and wondered if the notch was becoming more efficient than was entirely necessary. A general warned of the Kangal's ire was a general prepared to make excuses.

"The launch," Orjakis said, too agitated to take his customary seat. "Where is it?"

"I see Janzil Ches Orjakis, Kangal of Skjonn," Gohliya said. "The launch has crashed on the surface, somewhere within rebel-controlled territory."

The Kangal strode up to the general and grabbed him by the front of the tunic. "That is not the answer we wish, Defense. Where are they?"

"They are dead, Kangal."

Orjakis struck the older man in the face and turned his back on him. Denying Gohliya the sight of his beauty was only a minor punishment, and not a very satisfying one. He would have the decrepit fool strung up in the courtyard and whipped. He would have him made into a bath slave. A toilet slave. A bed warmer for the garrison—*wouldn't the soldiers love that?* The possibilities were endless. He summoned a drone to clean off the hand that had struck Gohliya.

"Before the Kangal has me tortured in some creative manner," Gohliya said softly, "I would speak one last time."

"We should have cut out your tongue when our father died." Orjakis walked to the throne and sat down. He made a regal gesture. "Speak, then."

"The League will not hear the news of Colonel Stuart's loss with happiness," Gohliya said. "If such tidings are delivered correctly, they will come here. They will look for him. They will see the rebels and how they have made the innocent below suffer. They will act as our allies."

"If Stuart was League, which we find very hard to believe, we do not need his superiors to control our planet," Orjakis reminded the general. "That is your job, and you have failed miserably at it."

"I was not permitted to send an escort with Stuart," Gohliya said. "By your orders, he and Aledver went alone."

"Aledver was going to ferret out his true reason for coming to Akkabarr, and then slit his throat and leave him as a feast for the carrion eaters." Orjakis had never bedded Aledver, either. He had died, ignorant of the ultimate of all pleasures.

The ache in Orjakis's head made him gesture blindly for an attendant, who approached the throne and knelt before him. He pointed to his temples, and the female went around the throne to stand behind it and begin a gentle massage of his scalp and neck.

"The Kangal has long desired to strengthen ties

with the League," Gohliya said, his tone more considerate now. "This provides the opportunity for the Kangal to do so, if the Kangal is willing to invite League troops to Akkabarr."

"The League does not serve us," Orjakis snapped. "They are mongrels and mercenaries, unfit to look upon us." But they were also the most powerful alliance in the galaxy, and possibly ruthless enough to exterminate the Hsktskt. If they did win this war of theirs, it would be within their power to outlaw slavery. "Why are we tormented like this? Is it not enough that we must serve the people every moment of every day, devoting every second of life to maintaining our perfection exclusively for their benefit?"

Gohliya did the unthinkable. He did not answer.

"We are aware of your feelings for us, General," Orjakis said, extinguishing the tiny flicker of pity he had once felt for Gohliya. "Someday we will grant your wish and separate that hideous head from your shoulders. But until that time, you are sworn to serve us. Sworn by the same oath that your father and his father took."

The general inclined his head, almost breaking eye contact. "What does the Kangal order me to do? Shall I pursue finding the crash with our own resources, or shall I contact the League and enlist their aid?"

Orjakis gave him his instructions, and then left the receiving room and walked back to his chambers. His mind kept returning to the image of the devoted Aledver accepting his mission to interrogate and kill the League colonel.

I will find out what he conceals from the Kangal. Aledver's eyes had been a rare color, almost as unusual as the colonel's eyes. The devotion in them had been absolute. *He will tell me everything the Kangal wishes to know.*

Now poor Aledver was dead, and his body being torn apart—oh, gods, and eaten—by the animals below. The obscenity of those thoughts staggered Orjakis. Aledver had been one of his best internals, as well as one of the most beautiful men in Skjonn.

Aledver, forgive us. You above all did not deserve this fate.

Tears were winding down his cheeks as he closeted himself in his bedchamber. One of the female animals that had been sent to him as tithe tribute knelt in a trembling, submissive pose at the base of his bed. She was so ignorant of how to behave that she kept her gaze fixed on the floor.

"Look at us," Orjakis heard himself tell her as he drew one of the small ceremonial daggers he wore at his waist.

The woman lifted her eyelids. She must have been the most comely of the tribute women, but the ravages of cold and work had burnished any hope of beauty from her face. She looked upon him with hope, and fear, and, yes, longing. He was the most beautiful thing she had ever seen.

He thought of Aledver, who would never see him again, and looked into those dark eyes.

Orjakis walked naked into the bathing chamber thirty minutes later, his face and hands soaked with blood. Small bits of flesh and bone fell to the floor as he handed his ruined dagger to the nearest drone. "It is contaminated. Destroy it." To his notch, he said, "Have our chamber cleaned at once."

Orjakis could not enjoy the same treatment. He would have to wait for the drone to remove the remnants of the woman from his body before he could sink into his tub.

He looked down at himself, vaguely surprised by the amount of gore. He had never taken one of the little animals before, but it had been a pleasant surprise. He had not gagged her, and yet through all that he had done to her, she had not made a sound to distract him. Perhaps he need not sell all the women they sent him from the surface. The exercise might prove beneficial.

He had been wrong about her potential, as well. Her dark, slick blood provided a unique foil for his smooth, firm skin. *On me, she looks quite beautiful.*

TEN

After Hurgot's visit, Resa guessed that someone would be sent to the caves to take her back to the camp. From listening to him talk to Egil, she knew he was going to tell the leader of the people that she was alive.

She knew she was supposed to be dead.

Egil had told her himself that as soon as he left her, that first night, the cats would devour her. He had suggested she make cuts in her arms so that they would not play with her. It had not happened, even though these cats were not the same as those Resa had stayed with before she had found the camp. These strange cats had accepted her just as the others had, treating her as if she were one of their own kind.

Another way I am not like the people.

She sat by the heatarc she had constructed, and wished she had enough of their words to find out why the woman wanted her dead. She knew she was different, not like the people in many ways. She knew some, like Ygrelda, could accept this. But the one who wanted her dead the most—the one whose name everyone whispered—would find another way.

I did nothing to her, and she wishes me dead. Try as she might, Resa could make no sense of it.

She did not wish to die. Not alone on the ice, and not at the hands of the people. If she was to die, she would choose the moment. Perhaps she would walk out onto the ice in the night, and let the one of the things that prowled the darkness take her. She knew places where they gathered. The jlorra would not kill her unless they were starved, she thought—the others had dragged her to their cave when they had found her wandering in the snow—but surely she could sneak out just after they fell asleep.

There was no way to avoid death unless she stayed here, with the cats, but the people would not permit it. She also suspected she might die of loneliness, or fear from the dreams she had been having.

The dreams began the same way, each night: She was bleeding on the ice, reaching out to someone standing over her. A woman with long dark hair.

Dahktar, she told the woman. *I am a dahktar.*

As the woman bent over her, Resa lifted a weapon and shot her in the head. But it was her own head that exploded with pain, her own face that turned wet with blood. Then light surrounded her, and wrapped her in chains. A jlorra licked the blood from her face, and the woman was there, holding her hand, watching her.

Resa looked at her and saw her own face on the woman's. Heard her voice coming from the woman's mouth.

Dahktar. I am a Dahktar. A Dahktar. The woman produced a chain and bound their wrists together. *So are you.* She lifted a dagger over Resa's chest. *For that, you must die.*

Resa would wake up, covered with sweat and shaking, white-hot pain in her wrist.

Egil did not come the next day, but a storm did, and Resa was glad of the food Hurgot had brought her. She tried to share some with the cats, but they preferred their food bloody-dead, and refused it. As soon as the skies cleared, the entire pack left the caves to hunt, and Resa was once more alone.

I could go and look for other people, Resa thought as she busied herself stitching together some fur pieces. *Ygrelda said there are many iiskars spread out over the ice. Perhaps another camp would not have a woman who hates me for no reason.*

She used a sliver of bone to pierce the edges of the fur scraps and form small holes, through which she passed lengths of sinew she had softened in warmed water. When the sinew dried, it tightened a little, sealing the seam. Today she was fashioning an undergarment to wear, for the old outfurs she had been given were worn in many places and would not keep out all of the cold.

Resa held up the garment against her body to assure she had made it large enough. She used a long, narrow wedge-shaped piece of metal that she had found in the discarded salvage heap and sharpened to trim some uneven tufts. It would not win admiring looks from anyone, but it would do. She started to finish the last seams, and felt a little disappointed that the strange pleasure in putting together the thing would soon be over.

What was the word Ygrelda called it? Sewing. Resa liked sewing. Her hands seemed to crave it.

The day drew on, silent and empty. Resa tidied the caves, sorted through her stores, and prepared a stew for her evening meal, but after that, there was nothing else to do. She dressed to go out and look at the colors of the sky, and watch the sun start to drop. The shift in light made the shadows on the ice move and change shape, and for a time she tried to see things in them. But soon that, too, grew tedious.

If the cats did not return by sunset, Resa knew that they would take shelter somewhere else and wait for the sun. Without the warmth of their bodies around her, she would have to sleep closer to the heatarc.

Resa walked around the caves, warming her limbs with the exercise. She tried to make the sweet strings of sounds that some of the women in camp did, what Ygrelda called singing, but discovered the sounds that came from her throat were flat and rather unpleasant by comparison. She could not sing, so she practiced her words out loud, repeating all she had heard, and trying to make sense of the order and meaning.

"How does she live?" she muttered under her breath. "She carries no furs, no food, no weapons. The demons protect her. No. Who are you?"

She understood most of that now. Except for *the demons,* which she thought might be another word for the jlorra. She did not know the answer to the last words—*Who are you?*—but she did not think she would ever know.

Resa took out the piece of metal she had used to cut things. One side of it was shiny and showed a slightly distorted image of her face. She remembered the first time she had looked into it, when she had not known her own face. Even now it looked strange to her.

If she had been important, special, beloved, someone would have looked for her. She did not know exactly how long she had been in this place, but she had not just come here. She had the distinct feeling that she had been here for some time before her earliest memory of the cats.

Is there no one who knows who I was?

She did not think of her past as belonging to her anymore. Who she had been was lost to the darkness and the pain. In fact, Resa was almost afraid to remember it, because knowing would mean missing everything she had loved in her former life. Whether or not she had been loved, she had felt love for others, she felt sure of it. She had begun to love Ygrelda, and it had not seemed like a completely new feeling. Nor had the odd affection she felt for Hurgot, although that puzzled her even more. She did not feel desire for him, and knew he did not like her.

Why did she still feel this kinship with the camp's healer? He was old, and a man, and of a different kind. She felt certain that he didn't even *like* her.

A soft growl made her look over her shoulder. The cats had returned, their claws and muzzles stained with bits and patches of red ice. Despite their gory appearance, she was happy to see them and went to greet them with affectionate hands.

"You do well?" She looked at the pack and saw the remains of a carcass they had dragged through the snow. Since the jlorra devoured their kills as soon as they caught them, she knew the meat was meant for her.

They feed me like a cub too young to make her own kills. "I thank you," she told the big male, and started to walk back to the caves with them.

"Egil!"

The cry made Resa stop and look in the direction

from which it had come. There was a skimmer down on the ice, perhaps three hundred yards from the caves, and a hunter half on, half off it. Something was atop him, something twice his size.

Beside her, the largest male in the pack sniffed the air, catching the scent of fresh blood. He was well fed, however, so his interest was only casual.

"Egil, help me!"

Resa understood that the hunter had mistaken her for the beast master, but that was not the problem. She had been given no serrats on her boots, possibly to keep her from attempting to go back to the camp. The worn soles of her boots made it impossible for her to run to him. They were also too far from the camp for the hunter's cries to be heard. She was as useless as a child, or a cub—

The cats think of me as a cub.

"You carry me?" she asked the male, stroking him with reassuring hands as she went around to his side. She had never tried to ride one of the cats, but she had seen both male and female carrying their cubs on their backs when the young grew tired—and when they were going on a hunt. If the male objected, she would get off immediately.

As soon as she was seated, the big cat started toward the skimmer. Her weight on his back made no difference in his stride, and he displayed no displeasure when she grabbed on to the thick fur clump between his shoulders to keep from sliding off.

Resa looked ahead. The hunter was now huddled over, his arms over his head, crying out each time the avian's sharp beak struck him from behind.

The jlorra stopped a safe distance from the skimmer

and moved his shoulders, as if to tell Resa to climb down. His narrowed eyes, she saw, were focused on the huge avian ripping and tearing at the hunter's outfurs, trying to get at the flesh beneath. The creature had wings twice the length of the skimmer, and claws that were as curved and sharp as its beak. A length of thin, sheared rope hung from its neck.

Snare cord, Resa thought. She had seen some of the netlike traps that the hunters used. *Why didn't he kill it before he put it on the skimmer? Stupid man.*

As soon as Resa was on her feet, the jlorra snarled and bounded forward, jumping from the ice to knock the avian from the hunter's back. The two tumbled over and over until the avian landed on the ice and the jlorra lunged, mouth open, teeth bared to sink into the avian's thick, corded neck.

The avian struck the big cat directly in the face, nearly taking out one eye. The big cat instinctively rolled off, head down, and the avian used the opportunity to launch itself from the ice into the air.

Resa saw it fly up and then make an abrupt turn, diving back toward the ice. It was not coming for the jlorra; it must have realized that it was no match for the big cat's bulk and power. Instead, it hurtled down directly at the skimmer.

The hunter, who had risen from his huddled position, did not see the avian until he pulled the hood back from his face.

"Down!" Resa shouted, but the hunter now saw death coming for him and became like a pillar of ice, unable to move.

Resa was not aware of running toward the hunter, but somehow she reached him before the avian did.

Her position put her directly beneath the attacking creature, and she shoved her arm up, driving the blade in her hand into the center of its neck. Her knuckles slammed into its leathery hide, and she jerked the blade to the side, severing two neck tendons and the gullet.

The avian screamed through its own blood. Its wings swept forward, closing around the hunter and Resa as it scrambled to thrust away from them with frantic clawing, and then its body went stiff. It fell back and onto the ice, where the waiting jlorra pounced on top of it.

Resa watched as the big cat crushed the avian's gaping throat between its massive jaws, and shook it fiercely, making the bones snap and crunch. The wings dangled, the killing shake rendering them limp and motionless. She looked down at her hand, which was still clutching the wedge of metal.

No. She remembered how she had thought of it as she had used it on the avian. *Blade. I used it as a blade.* Resa's stomach clenched as she saw her face reflected through the blood on the blade's shiny side. She had never used a blade like this. *How could I know how to do this?*

"You." The hunter stared at Resa with almost as much horror as he had the avian. "You are not Egil."

Resa knew him. He was the son of Navn, the rasakt. Ygrelda had pointed him out one day. He was also waiting for her to say something, judging by his expression. What would be the safest response? "Egil not here."

The hunter moved away from her and wandered in a circle for a time, muttering and shaking his head. He would stop, stare at the dead avian, then at her, and take up walking nowhere again.

The jlorra, which was not interested in the avian's carcass, came over to her and nudged her hand. Resa stroked him, not sure what to do about Navn's son. She did not wish to stay near him, as he was acting as if he was angry with her. Yet she could not go back to the caves until he told her to go. Ygrelda said that was one of the most important of the people's rules: to wait for the men to say what to do.

"Why did you do it?"

She looked up into the hunter's face. "Do?"

He jerked his head toward the avian. "Kill the ptar."

"Help man." That was what the people's women were supposed to do, always. "Woman kill creature . . . bad luck?"

The hunter's eyes seemed to bulge out of his head, and then he began to make the *huh-huh-huh* sound that the women made when they were happy or amused. The sharp sound he made wasn't like theirs.

"You killed it," he told her when he was finished making the sharp sound. "You saved me. I am Aktwar, the son of Rasakt Navn. Do you know what that means?"

"No." She hoped it did not mean he would kick her and hit her, as Egil had done.

Aktwar put his hands on her wrists, but he did not hurt her this time. "It means that I owe you my life. Come." Still holding one of her wrists, he led her to the skimmer. Resa looked back at the jlorra, who gave them a long look before seizing the ptar's carcass and dragging it off to the caves.

As Resa climbed onto the back of the skimmer,

where Aktwar fastened her to the strange chair part of it, she wondered if this would be the last time she saw the big cats. Then the skimmer was rising, not far from the ground, but enough to make her clutch at Aktwar's back.

Flying through the air felt exhilarating and frightening at the same time. Resa tried not to cling to the young hunter, but by the time they landed outside the iiskar she had her fists curled tightly in the shreds of Aktwar's outfurs. He helped her down, his hands still not harsh or hurtful, and gestured for her to follow him into camp.

Resa followed as slowly as she dared. If owing her his life made Aktwar angry, he could do whatever he wished to her. She sensed from Ygrelda's words that he was important, perhaps almost as important as the rasakt. Perhaps that she had saved him from the ptar would make Navn feel more kindly to her. He might let her live out in the caves, with the cats, and, after a time, perhaps return to the camp to be with the people.

That possibility quickened her step a little.

Aktwar led her to the rasakt's shelter, where he pointed to a spot outside the flap. "Stay here. I must tell him first." He stepped through the flap.

Resa stayed there for a long time. She ducked her head each time a man passed her, but she could feel the weight of his eyes. For the first time she realized how much she smelled—she had not been able to bathe properly while out in the caves—and now there was ptar blood all over her outfurs.

When the young boys of the camp started loitering near the rasakt's shelter to stare at her, she pulled her hood forward, trying to hide her face. She did not have the bit of cloth she had been using as a face wrap with her.

At last Aktwar came out. He did not look particularly happy. "My father is not here," he told her. "He will not return until nightfall."

Resa brightened. "I go back caves?"

"No. You will stay here, with my mother, until my father returns. Come." He went back through the flap, and feeling helpless, Resa followed.

The interior of the shelter was very warm, and the scent of food tickled Resa's nose. If she were back at the cave, she would be eating the stew she had made before Aktwar and the ptar: her only meal of the day. There had been no time, however, and now her stomach felt hollow and was making growling sounds.

There were two other men inside. Both were older men, hunters whom Resa had glimpsed in the past. Neither seemed particularly happy to see her. A woman came out of the back room of the shelter carrying a tray with bandages and a bowl containing a pungent mixture.

"That isn't necessary. I'm only bruised. I want you to know . . ." Aktwar turned to Resa and frowned. "What is your name, woman?"

"Resa." She watched as the other woman set down the tray and walked toward them, her movements slow and deliberate. Resa thought of the white snakes she had seen slithering out of vent shafts.

"Mother," Aktwar said, "this is Resa."

"I know." Sogayi smiled. "Come, sit. Tell me how you saved the life of my son."

* * *

Navn considered staying the night at Iiskar Sverrul. The rasakt, Knab Sverrul, was an old friend, and with the rebellion upon them it might be months, even years, before they saw each other again, if at all.

Knab, who had already sent his men to serve the Raktar, had been philosophical about his decision to back the rebellion. "I do not wish it, but I have little choice. It is not as if we have never fought before. Our fathers' tribes went to war, as did their fathers, and their fathers. Men fight." He shrugged. "It is the way of men."

"The tribes before us fought each other over hunting territory. The windlords are our masters. We displease them, and they withhold our food, and we starve." Navn shook his head. "The rebels are fools."

His old friend's gaze turned shrewd. "How much meat is on your table of late, Deves? How long has it been since your women baked bread? Do you think the vral will come to find your iiskar worthy?"

"I do not believe in vral."

"Neither do I, but the hunters begin to." Knab rolled his eyes. "I think the rebellion preys on more than our stores."

Since the windlords had stopped sending the foods that could not be had on the planet, all the iiskars that had not allied with the rebellion had been gradually using up their stores. Some said the Iisleg might adapt to eating nothing but meat—the beasts thrived on it—and their hunters could provide meat for a hungry tribe, but only for as long as the game held out. Navn knew as well as Sverrul that there were now too many tribes competing for the same food. In time, that would dwindle, as well, and the Iisleg would turn on each other or sicken and die. They needed the synthetics and foods the rebels were growing in the abandoned trenches to survive. Word had been sent that the only tribes permitted to share in the bounty were those who joined the rebellion.

The Raktar was no better than the windlords.

"Even if your tribe does not join the rebels," Knab told him, "the windlords will not reward you for it. I have friends in the west, and they have attested to the fact that the few loyal tribes have received nothing from above. The rebels will not share their food with those against the rebellion. There is no alternative." He gave Navn a pained smile. "You must send your men to fight."

"We trade one cruel master for another," Navn said bitterly.

His old friend gave him a pitying look. "That is also the way of men."

Before he left the iiskar, Navn embraced Sverrul, and once more refused the gifts his friend wished to make him. "Your hunters serve the Raktar now," he told Knab. "Save your stores, for you will need them if the rebels are defeated. I will look after my own."

"Send word if you decide to move on," Sverrul asked as he embraced him. "If we survive this, I want to know where I can find you."

Navn thought about his friend's request as he mounted his skimmer and took to the air. Part of him valued Sverrul's counsel, and part wondered if his friend had promised more than men to the rebellion. *Does he wish to know where my iiskar goes for his sake, or so that he may report our movements?* Another reason to despise this Raktar—he made Navn question the word of a worthy ally, as well as a friend he had known and trusted since his boyhood.

Navn had gone to Sverrul alone, so he was by himself when he arrived back at camp. Most of the men were out hunting, while the rest were at work repairing storm damage to the shelters. He nodded to the respectful greetings he was given, as always, but noticed the close looks his men gave him when they thought he could not see. Also remarkable was the absence of all the women.

His men might have any reason behind their furtive glances, but there was only one thing that kept all the women inside: One of them had done something to earn a severe punishment. Women always scattered and hid like terrified children when that happened.

Navn felt the tightness of anger in his head and chest as he entered his shelter. Sogayi would tell him what it was, as she always did, while she massaged the tiredness from his head and neck. These days, she was his heart's only shelter. *Why cannot the other women be like mine?* No wonder so many men envied him his wife.

Navn came to a stop just inside the flap. In the center of the shelter, a half-naked, limp body hung from a discipline pole, baring a back covered with lash marks and trickling blood. Two of his strongest hunters were plying their whips with rhythmic ferocity, adding more ghastly stripes.

"Hold." He strode forward, intent on seeing the woman's face, his rage swelling like a poisoned wound. Only when he saw that the prisoner was the ensleg, not Sogayi, did he find his voice again. "What is this?"

"Punishment, Rasakt," the oldest hunter said, lowering his gaze and his whip. "This female fashioned a weapon, and used it."

Sogayi's serene, beautiful face swam before his eyes. "Whom did she kill?"

The two hunters exchanged glances, but before the oldest could speak, Navn's wife rushed to crouch before him. He was so relieved that he lifted her in his arms and embraced her tightly. Over her head, he said, "Get out."

The two hunters bowed and left the shelter. For a long time all Navn could do was hold his woman, and stroke her hair, and savor the sound of each breath she took. Only when the ensleg stirred did he set Sogayi at arm's length.

"Tell me what has happened here."

Sogayi's cheeks gleamed with tear streams. "I was so afraid, my husband. I prayed you would come, and you are here. Surely I am the woman most blessed by the gods." Overcome, she covered her face with her hands and sobbed.

Such a gentle creature, to be subjected to such ugliness. Navn almost drew his blade to slash the ensleg's throat. But the alien female only moaned a little before her head fell forward again.

It took Navn some time to calm his wife, and what she told him when she could speak made his heart grow cold. The ensleg female had come to the shelter, her garments covered in blood. His own son, Aktwar, had brought her, claiming she had saved him during an attack by a wounded creature.

"I invited her to sit with me, and talk with me," Sogayi said, sniffing back new tears. "She told me that she threw herself at our son when he was fighting the beast. She said she had used . . . that she had made for herself . . ." Unable to speak, Sogayi lifted a hand and pointed to an object lying at the ensleg's feet.

Navn went to pick up the object, which was a very sharp wedge of metal coated in dried blood. "This?" He held it up. "She made this? Used this?"

Sogayi nodded.

Navn studied the metal. It was no more than a sharpened scrap piece, too small to use as anything but a cutting tool. "What happened then?"

His wife clasped her hands together. "Two of my husband's men were present when the ensleg spoke to me. I—I summoned them to be here, because I was afraid. She was covered in blood. They saw her display the weapon and invoked punishment. I did not know what to do but to hide."

Of course, she could not do otherwise. Sogayi was a proper female and knew better than to challenge a man's decision. "What was the punishment?"

"It is what is always done, for her to be beaten until dead." She gave him a brief, wretched look. "I would have begged them wait for you, but all Iisleg, even women, know the law."

A woman was forbidden from fashioning, touching, or using weapons. It was one of their more common laws, but Navn was not sure that the ensleg had been made aware of it. She had been here only a short time; she did not yet speak their language. *This is why you should have had her killed, the first day she came to camp.*

His wife glanced at the ensleg and shuddered. "I am glad you are here now, so that you may dispatch her."

"Father?"

Sogayi's mouth opened and closed as Aktwar entered the shelter.

Navn's son looked pleased to see his father until he caught sight of the ensleg. "Why is this woman being beaten? She saved my life."

"With this?" Navn showed him the makeshift dagger.

"Yes. She cut the throat of a wounded ptar that was trying to eat its way through my back. Who ordered her to be beaten?" Aktwar went to the discipline post and untied the ensleg, lifting her sagging body into his arms. "I am taking her to Hurgot."

"No." Navn closed his fist over the metal piece. "You will not."

Aktwar stared at him. "Father, if not for her I would be dead, my body torn, my eyes pecked out of my head."

"She used this to kill the ptar?" Navn showed him the dagger, and when Aktwar nodded, he sighed. "She has violated the law. Yes"—he lifted his hand when his son began to protest—"I understand that it was to save you, and for that I will always be grateful to her. But the law is the law for a reason."

"This is nonsense. I owe my life to this woman, Father." Aktwar gently lowered the ensleg's body to the furs covering the floor. "She had no reason to help me. She is ensleg. It would not have surprised me if she had stood and watched that ptar kill me."

"My son, she may have meant to hurt you, and killed the ptar through clumsiness," Sogayi said in a low, hesitant voice. "Or perhaps she did this thing to gain your trust, knowing you would bring her back among the tribe, where she might use her weapon again, but this time on the living."

"That is enough." Hearing such scheming words coming from his beloved's mouth made Navn feel sick. To his son, he said, "If she saved you by any other means, Aktwar, I could reward her."

His son's brow furrowed. "The only other way she might have saved me was to give herself up to the ptar so it would take her instead of me."

Sogayi nodded sadly. "That would have been the proper thing for her to do. There is nothing more glorious than for a woman to give her life so that a man may live."

"If this thing is to be done," Aktwar said, his voice harsher than Navn had ever heard it, "then it will be merciful, and by my hand." He drew his blade and crouched by the ensleg, lifting her chin.

"No." Navn thought of Sverrul's tales of the vral, and concealed his terror at the prospect of watching his son slash the ensleg's throat. *If he does so and she will not die . . .* "There is the other punishment."

Aktwar frowned. "What other?"

"Sogayi, leave us." Navn waited until his wife was gone before he told his son, "She will be taken out of the camp."

"It is not more merciful to allow her to slowly freeze to death," Aktwar snapped.

"She will be cast out." Navn turned away so he no longer had to look upon the ensleg. "She will be made skela."

ELEVEN

Skjæra did not need to sleep as the other skela did, and so she was the first to hear the skimmers as they landed. She recognized the sound of the propulsion devices that made them fly, and heard the heavy footsteps of the hunters. She did not rouse the headwoman. Hunters who brought the skela's portion of the meat came only to drop it outside, so the sound was ordinary to her ears. Only when a shout rang out did it startle her and wake Daneeb.

"What is it?" Daneeb came out of the crawl, already wearing her day garments.

Skjæra thought for a moment, trying to recapture the memory of the sound. Recently she had begun remembering things, but only when it served her own purpose. Rarely did anything interest her enough to trouble herself. Even speaking still seemed unnecessary most of the time.

The headwoman went to the view hole. "Skimmers," Daneeb said. "Too many. Stay here." She jerked on her outfurs and hurried out into the bitter cold.

Skjæra paid no further attention to the matter, and went back to contemplating the amber red light of the heatarc. The beautiful colors changed constantly, blending and reblending into new shades. She could see a tiny universe of heat and light in the heatarc, and it was seductive. She could not bring herself to go too near it, not since the explosion, but she could sit and watch it for days. She would have done so, many times, if the sisters had left her alone.

On the ice I was born, and on the ice I will die, but this entire world will never be as lovely as this small heart of the stars.

Solitude and silence were not to be hers now, it seemed, for Daneeb returned and shouted for all the sisters to rouse themselves.

Skjæra rose to retrieve her outfurs.

"No," Daneeb said, and pointed to Skjæra's crawl. "You have not slept."

She did not respond, but simply looked at the headwoman and waited for the rest of it.

"I know what you are thinking, and I tell you again: no." Daneeb's face darkened as some of the sisters stopped dressing to watch them. "You will obey me here, Skjæra. You will go into your crawl, stay there, and sleep. Go now."

Skjæra thought of walking past Daneeb and outside to see what the hunters wanted. She thought of climbing into her crawl. Decisions, too, were not an easy matter for her.

Daneeb gave her a different look, the one that begged without words.

Skjæra went to her crawl, climbed in, and waited in the dark narrow space until she heard Daneeb and the other sisters leave. When they had gone, she climbed back out and dressed.

Outside it was still dark, and the cold had sharp teeth. Skjæra pulled up her hood to conceal her face and scanned the front of the skela's caves. A group of men stood before the sisters. A small bundle of cloth lay in the snow between them.

"If she fails," the lead hunter was telling Daneeb, "you may do as you wish with her."

Skjæra liked hunters. They did not taunt and curse the skela as the gjenvin often did, perhaps because they understood that the skela, too, served a purpose on this world. Mostly the hunters brought them a portion of the meat the skela butchered for them and otherwise left them alone.

People who left her alone were always in favor with Skjæra. She often regretted not living among the hunters.

"As you say, Kheder." Daneeb bowed her head.

The men moved away, mounted their skimmers, and flew up into the sky. Daneeb snapped out orders for two of the sisters to help her lift and carry the bundle inside.

Skjæra smelled blood, saw dark stain lines on the cloth, and followed.

The skela did not carry the bundle to the lidded square pit in the ice where they kept their meat, but instead carried it into a portion of the cave they rarely used for anything but storage of extra furs.

The sisters placed the bundle gently on the floor of the cave, and furs were brought even as Daneeb unwrapped the cloth. Skjæra frowned as a woman's face appeared uncovered. She knew that face. She knew . . . but she did not know. She could not be sure.

It did not seem worth the time or pain to try to remember.

For a long time no one said anything. The sisters

stared at the woman, and the woman stared back at them. The woman was pale and her expression was one of wariness and concealed fear. The sisters simply seemed shocked.

"It cannot be her," Malmi whispered, her voice sounding like a string pulled too tightly. "It cannot be, Skrie. She was—"

"Close your mouth," Daneeb snapped. She turned back to address the strange woman, who was looking at everyone with visible bewilderment. "Do you know where you are?"

"No."

"What is your name?"

"Resa."

Daneeb said nothing, and Skjæra thought she might be shocked now, too. The tension of her body, the way her gaze would not settle, the manner in which she bit the inside of her lip—all signs that the headwoman felt disturbed, possibly even threatened.

The silence did give Skjæra time to turn the name over and over in her mind, which sometimes brought the memories back to her without much pain. *Resa. Resa. Resa.* She knew no one called that name.

"What this place?" the woman asked. She spoke as if unsure of the words.

She does not speak our language. Skjæra remembered the fair-haired ensleg man whose face she had repaired. *Like him.*

"This is the dwelling place of the skela who serve Iiskar Navn. You have been cast out. Your once-life there is over." Daneeb bent to wrap furs around the woman's shivering form, and then stepped back. "You must show that you are worthy to join us."

Malmi surged forward. "No, Skrie, please, do not make her—"

Daneeb slapped the skela's face with her bare hand before she addressed the strange woman again. "Are you prepared to show your worth?"

Resa struggled to stand, and pulled the furs around her tightly. "Yes."

"Callai, Fren, Opalas," Daneeb called out. "Bring the choices."

The three skela left the area. The remaining women drew back, taking places against the wall and leaving their headwoman and Resa standing facing each other in the center of the floor. Skjæra took the opportunity to slip back to the cave to retrieve her pack of medical supplies. As soon as Daneeb finished tormenting the woman, she would need her wounds attended to. On her way back, Skjæra saw Callai and Fren dragging a fresh carcass in from the butchering room, while Opalas carried a box from the salvage pile.

"Put them before her," Daneeb said when the three skela returned, and the box and the carcass were set on the floor before Resa.

Skjæra checked her pack to see if she had the proper antiseptic and ointments. From the way the woman was holding herself, she had back injuries. The bleeding through the cloth did not appear to be significant, but she would have to examine the wounds. Skjæra felt a strong surge of impatience with whatever game Daneeb was playing with the stranger. She knew the skela had their ways of deciding things, but the headwoman had better hurry up with it. Resa was in pain.

"Before you are two choices," Daneeb told Resa, and pointed to the box. "In that are rations from an ensleg vessel. They are sealed in things that keep them fresh. You may eat what you like from them." She pointed to the carcass, which was far less attractive in appearance. "This is a beast given to us as a portion for our work. It must be made fit eating." She threw a dagger into the carcass. "You may have all the meat if you butcher it by yourself. Choose one or the other."

Resa eyed the box, and then the carcass. She swallowed a few times before she crouched down and took the blade from the dead animal. She stared at it, and held it out like an offering. "Hunters beat me for touching, using blade." She produced a strange smile. "I use blade to save hunter life."

Malmi turned away and made a strangled sound. Daneeb said nothing.

Resa studied the faces around her for a long time before she crouched and began cutting open the belly of the carcass. Her hands moved easily and with considerable skill.

Skjæra pushed some of the other skela out of her way to go to Resa. She pulled the woman's hands away from the carcass and looked up at Daneeb. Skjæra took the knife from Resa and put it aside, and then tugged down the furs covering her back.

"Are you healer?" Resa asked her.

Skjæra's native language was not Iisleg, so it had taken her some time to learn it after she had come to join the skela. She sometimes practiced it when she was alone or with the jlorra, mimicking the intonations of the other women until she could speak as fluently as any of them. She didn't know why, but it seemed important, as if part of her knew she would have to speak to them someday.

Perhaps Resa's arrival meant the time for silence had come to an end.

"I am." Skjæra turned Resa gently so that her back faced her. "Were you whipped?"

Daneeb gaped at her. "What did you say?"

"I was." Resa, too, stared at her. "How did you know?"

Skjæra wasn't sure, exactly. The blood on the cloth could have come from any part of her body. "I guessed." She glanced up at the headwoman. "I am a healer."

"So you are." Daneeb gestured to the other skela with a hand that shook. "Take away the choices. The rest of you, go back to the crawls." When everyone had cleared out except the headwoman, Resa, and Skjæra, Daneeb came to crouch beside them. "Tell us what happened to you."

"I use blade, kill ptar, save hunter. They beat me, cast me out." Resa shrugged out of the furs and unwound the ragged cloth around her body until her back was exposed. "Not beat me much. Cold make feel better."

"Daneeb, fetch some warm, clean water," Skjæra told the headwoman as she gently peeled back the cloth clinging to the fresh lash marks. "I will try not to hurt you, but these must be cleaned and sealed, or they will fester."

Resa nodded.

Daneeb was staring at Skjæra with wide eyes. "You are speaking as if—"

"My tongue has always functioned. I cannot say the same for your ears." She noted the depth of the weals and which would have to be sutured. "Daneeb, I still need that water."

The headwoman rose and went out.

"I smell. No clean myself long time." Resa turned around and touched the edge of Skjæra's face wrap. "Why wear? No men here see you."

Skjæra did not show her face before strangers, and she had hidden it for so long that she never felt at ease with it exposed. Keeping it covered made the sisters feel more at ease, too, and she had to wear the mask when she did the work.

But Resa had pleased Daneeb with her choice, and would be one of the skela now.

Skjæra pulled back the wrap and exposed her face. At first Resa's eyes widened, and then she touched Skjæra's cheek. "You look like me."

Something happened in that moment. Skjæra was not sure precisely what, but feeling Resa's hand on her cheek made her head swim. She looked into the other woman's eyes and saw the same confusion.

"Who are you?" Resa asked softly.

There was an answer to that, but Skjæra did not want to go into the place in her head where it was waiting. That place was filled with pain, and not just her own. Pain that no one should see, no one should feel.

Skjæra placed her hand over Resa's and pressed it to her face.

The crash. The cold. The child. The weapon. The light. The pain.

The vagueness that had embraced her for so long abruptly dissolved, and Skjæra saw Resa clearly. The eyes, the nose, the mouth—they were all the same. She remembered exactly who Resa was now.

No wonder Daneeb had acted so strangely. She had known this woman for two years. They all had. Resa's was the first life Skjæra had saved since becoming skela. She had operated on her, repairing the damage from the terrible head wound she had suffered. Resa's body had slowly recovered, but her mind had not. The wound had induced madness to a degree that Resa had to be restrained. Skjæra had kept Daneeb from killing Resa, and instead had nursed her for months, trying to bring her back to sanity. Then, one day, Resa had somehow freed herself from her chains and walked out onto the ice.

Since losing Resa, Skjæra had cared little for anything but the work of saving others. Now she had returned, and what did that mean? *What do I say to you? Why have you come back to me? Why don't you recognize any of us? Why did you run away? Why are you still alive?*

"Who are you?" Resa repeated, more insistently now.

"Jarn," Daneeb said as she rejoined them. She set down a basin of meltwater. "Her name is Jarn."

Skjæra glanced at the headwoman. "I am called Skjæra."

"You are *Jarn,* and you will *answer* to your *name,*" Daneeb said, her tone ominous. "Now that you have found your tongue, it is time you stopped living as if you occupy another world and the one where the rest of us dwell does not exist."

"Jarn is pretty name," Resa said politely. Her gaze moved from Daneeb to Skjæra, unsure.

Skjæra meant "Death Bringer," and she certainly

was not that. Now that she remembered everything, even those things that made her want to scream until her throat swelled shut, she could not return to the vagueness that had protected her. She understood why Daneeb was so insistent, as well. If Resa was to stay with them, and be skela, Skjæra would have to abandon everything that had kept her insulated and safe.

It would keep Resa safe, too.

"Turn around," Jarn told Resa. She held out a cloth to Daneeb. "Soak this in the water."

A vibration shimmered across the ice floor of the cave, and the three women went still. It continued only for a few minutes before it died away, and the ice was still again.

"Tremors," Daneeb said. "Deep below."

"Yes." Jarn looked at the ground beneath their feet. "But what is making them?"

The Toskald defense forces expected the rebels to attack during the hours of darkness. They still patrolled the skies during the daylight hours—their leaders were taking no chances—but the bulk of the patrol ships came down from the skim cities as soon as the sun set over any territory.

Teulon had expected this, and compensated by moving the last of his troops into position only during the brief periods of time when the patrols were in mid-change, or had already flown over the battalion's present position. Otherwise, the rebels stayed under cover and remained where they had been ordered to camp.

At times it seemed maddening, even to Teulon, but they had to wait. For the attack on the armory trenches, they were waiting specifically on the perfect conditions under which they could carry out a successful campaign, and take all the trenches on the same day.

"They will not detect us if we move at night or day," Hasal often argued. "Why do you not give the order?"

Teulon refused to move one unit. "We wait until the planet is ready to help us."

Akkabarr finally obliged him with the storm he had wanted. It rolled in from the east, a fierce squall that pulled more winds and ice into itself until it swelled into one of the rare storms that covered most of the inhabited surface. The storm was immeasurable, an enormous blanket that settled over the planet and expended its violent energy on anything that dared move out of shelter. No ship could fly in such weather, and the Toskald retreated to their cities, confident that the rebels would do the same.

That was the moment Teulon gave the order.

The battalions, which he had stationed in key positions, received the order and sent their troops down into the tunnels they had been burning out by redirecting vent shafts under the ice for the last year. Like the armory trenches, the secret, complex maze, now reinforced to provide safe passage for those who used it, was carefully mapped and well-known by the rebels who had built it. The storm kept the Toskald's subsurface monitors from transmitting any images of activity below, so no one in the skim cities would know what they were doing or could respond to it. The rebels were free to move through the tunnels to the walls of the armory trenches. There the demolition squads began cutting through the plasteel with harmonic cutters salvaged by the Iisleg and repaired by their Raktar.

One hour after the order went out the first squad signaled that they had cut through.

"Trench F417 has been breached," Hasal said, breathless from running through the tunnel the troops had burned out from the communications shelter to the Raktar's HQ. He handed Teulon the datapad, on which was listed the complete inventory of the trench. "No casualties."

Teulon skimmed the list. "Drones?"

"Disabled." Hasal grinned. "The surge torches you designed worked exactly as you said they would."

Teulon had known that the automated security systems were impervious to cold, pulse weapon fire, or any sort of mass reprogramming. He could not use standard demolition ordnance or flamethrowers, either, for that would set off the contents of the trenches.

The drone designers, however, had been too confident of the primitive surface conditions. They had never considered that the Iisleg might take advantage of the natural bioelectric power present in their environment. The surface dwellers were never permitted anything but the most basic technology, and that was never improved. The designers even considered the ice that encased the trenches impregnable.

In his former life, Teulon had been an engineer and a shipbuilder. As experienced salvagers, the Iisleg had been hoarding components and alloys for years, learning slowly through trial and error how to use the simplest of them. They did not know how to reactivate the malfunctioning drones that the Toskald had replaced and discarded over the years, but they collected and stored them, all the same.

Teulon showed them how to deprogram the drone before reactivating it, which was when they discovered the drones' one vulnerability. He then designed the weapon to exploit it: the surge torch. With his knowledge, and the Iisleg's hoarded tech, they built their own armory.

The weapon gathered bioelectricity from both body friction and the surrounding atmosphere, concentrated it, and emitted it in a focused stream. The stream was not particularly powerful—it could inflict only an unpleasant jolt to any living being—but it did not have to be lethal to living flesh. The drones guarding the armory trenches had been designed to withstand only conventional weaponry. By experimenting on the reprogrammed, reactivated units, Teulon discovered that they were utterly helpless against surge torches' streams.

The inventory list from Trench F417 listed some interesting items, Teulon noted. He indicated on the pad which ones the rebels were to take for themselves, which they were to leave behind, and how he wanted the trench mined and resealed. What he was interested in was what the squad leader had reported as "clear rocks with strange markings."

Crystals.

"These clear rocks are etched crystals. I want them wrapped, packed, and delivered to the battalion commanders before the storm breaks," Teulon told Hasal, showing him the item on the inventory list. "Send a signal to all trench search teams and give them a description of the crystals. They are to retrieve any they find within the trenches and also have them delivered to their commanders."

Hasal frowned. "Why must we retrieve rocks? Even if they are decorated, we have no use for such baubles."

Teulon handed him the datapad. "You have your orders."

"As you say, Raktar." His second pocketed the device. "There is an emissary who arrived from the east just before the storm descended. He says he flew around it, but it is unlikely that is true."

Teulon had been expecting another assassination attempt, but not so soon. "What iiskar does he claim?"

"Navn. He says he is the rasakt's only son. There is something else." Hasal shifted his weight from one foot to the other. "Iiskar Navn is located in the center of the territory beyond the Kuorj and the Pasala. They, too, were within distance of the ensleg launch crash site."

"Close enough for these vral the Terran saw to have come from their camp?" Hasal nodded. "Why did you not say before, when we were out there?"

His second flushed miserably. "Truth be told, Raktar, I forgot."

Teulon considered this. He counted on Hasal's excellent command of intelligence, and had never known him to fail to present the right facts. His second never complained of exhaustion, but the strain was evident on his face.

I demand too much of him. "Tell me of Navn."

Hasal's expression lightened, and he almost stumbled over his words as he related what he knew about the rasakt. "Navn is a traditionalist. An isolationist, as well. He trades outright only with Sverrul. Since he became headman after his father's death in battle, he has been consistent, if somewhat unimaginative, with his tribute to Skjonn. His people are excellent hunters and metalworkers." Hasal thought for a moment. "Navn's father was a fierce warrior, and a vengeful one. He slew many during the tribal wars, and became a legend among the eastern tribes. Even if Navn the Younger is not the man his father was, he was likely brought up to follow the oldest ways."

The Iisleg who followed the oldest ways were some of the finest warriors Teulon had ever seen. Unfortunately, they also remained loyal to the Kangal long after other tribes had turned to the rebellion. Such traditionalists believed that the best ensleg was a dead one stripped of its worgald. Teulon had been hard-pressed to bring them over to the rebellion. "Is Navn a declared loyalist?"

"I cannot say. With Navn's son here to petition to join the rebellion, likely not." A peak formed in Hasal's lip. "Doubtless Navn's people grow hungry. They were some of the first to be cut off by Skjonn."

Orjakis. Yes, this made more sense now. "I will see him shortly. Leave me."

Teulon sat in darkness for a time, clearing his thoughts and preparing for the meeting with Navn's son. If the emissary did not try to kill him, Teulon might actually learn something that could aid Reever in finding his wife, and confirm one of his own suspicions—that the Toskald had sent spies down to infiltrate the rebellion. The fact that Navn was a traditionalist would help—the tribes that followed the old ways were also among the most superstitious—

and Navn's son might become worthy of his grandfather's blood.

One raid on an unguarded storage depot had yielded some interesting garments, which the battalion commander had forwarded to Teulon's headquarters. The Raktar reserved several for his personal use, and now went and changed his robe for one of them. After he had armed himself, he signaled for Navn's emissary to be sent alone into his planning room.

The man turned out to be a boy, barely large enough to fill out his hunter's outfurs. "Raktar, I bring greetings from my father, Deves Navn, rasakt of Iiskar Navn. I am Aktwar Navn, his son." Aktwar bowed, although it was obvious that he could not see Teulon.

Teulon stayed in the shadows. "Why do you come here, son of Navn?"

"My father petitions the Raktar and bids him allow the men of Navn to join in defending Akkabarr from the depravities of the windlords and their ensleg allies." The boy presented a scroll with a slight flourish.

"We do not defend Akkabarr," Teulon informed him. "We will attack the windlords first and take their cities."

"I spoke in ignorance, Raktar." The boy went down on his knees and bowed his head. "My father wishes to support the rebellion in any manner the Raktar sees fit. Forgive my clumsy tongue for implying otherwise."

Teulon rose from his chair and walked into the light. "Look at me."

The boy slowly lifted his head. His eyes seemed to bulge out of their sockets for a moment. "You are not

Iisleg. You are ensleg." He eyed the Toskald uniform Teulon wore. "You are a windlord?"

"I was their slave. As you are now." Teulon crouched down to put himself on eye level with the boy. "Will you and your tribe still fight for me?"

"I—my father—"

"Go back to your iiskar, boy." Teulon rose and stood over him, leaving himself open, waiting for him to strike. "I have no use for your kind."

"You ensleg are everywhere." Aktwar rose and began to move toward the shelter flap.

Teulon seized his shoulder and spun him around. "What did you say?"

"Nothing." Aktwar cowered.

"What other ensleg have you seen?"

"It was no one. Only a woman. My father cast her out." The boy grimaced. "He should have let me kill her. It would have been better for her to die."

Teulon grabbed the front of his furs and dragged him up onto his toes. "Describe this woman to me."

"She is not like you." Aktwar swallowed hard. "She is human, like us. Only she is not like us. She is not like any woman I know. She killed a ptar with a piece of metal and one strike."

Teulon released the boy and turned away. "Your father, he killed her?"

"No. She is skela now." Aktwar's gaze shifted, and his voice lowered. "Some of the hunters say she cannot die."

He looked back at the young hunter. "What?"

"Nothing kills her. Not being alone on the ice, not being given to the jlorra, not the ptar, not beatings, nothing." Aktwar's shoulders moved. "Had she no face, she might be vral, spirit made flesh. They say they have come to walk the ice daily now."

"She might also be a drone, modified to look and act and smell and bleed like a living woman," Teulon told him.

The younger man gaped. "There are such things?"

"In the skim cities, there are all manner of drones." He checked the hour. The largest storms never lasted longer than a day and a night, Hasal had told him, and it would take until dawn for the battalions to breach the remaining trenches. By the time the Toskald realized that every weapon on the planet was now in rebel hands, it would be too late. In a week the rebels would be in position to launch their first assault on the skim cities.

Teulon could lead the attack on Skjonn from Iiskar Navn as well as anywhere. "As soon as the sky clears, you will take me and my men to see this ensleg woman who will not die."

Twelve

Rasakt Kuorj would not lend Reever a skimmer, something for which he apologized.

"My men need them here, to be ready for the time when the summons arrives," Kuorj explained as they walked through the small encampment. "Once the armies are ready to make their attack on the windlords, an alert will be sent, and all of my men must take up arms, go, and join them."

"All of your men?" Reever had counted twenty, if that.

"Only I am permitted to remain behind, with the women and the children," the headman said. He nodded to one of the hunters passing by. "It is the same with every iiskar. I would say this general of ours wants no challenge to his leadership."

"If the fighting draws close, you may have to relocate the camp," Reever said.

"We have made ready to move at any time." Kuorj made a casual gesture toward the shelters. "The women can do it by themselves."

Iisleg women, Reever was learning, could do a great deal without help from their men. Yet they were utterly subservient. He looked out at the large patch of darkened ice just beyond the camp, where the hunters' game was butchered. While telling Reever about Iisleg customs, Kuorj had given him scant information about the outcast women.

Reever had the distinct impression that there was more to the skela than he was being told. "When you relocate, what happens to the skela? Do they accompany you?"

"No." A flicker of distaste crossed Kuorj's face. "They are Navn's concern, not mine. He has the largest iiskar in this territory." He followed Reever's gaze. "You show peculiar curiosity about them, and you should not. We have no contact with the unclean, ensleg. They are as the dead are to us."

They were also the only Iisleg permitted to remove bodies from crash sites in this territory. One of them had to have seen Cherijo. "If this is true, why do you allow them to make your game fit for your consumption?"

"They handle the dead. I do not know how it is for ensleg, but we cannot." Kuorj glanced at his wristcom. "You have eight hours before the light is gone. It will take you three to trek to your destination, four or five if you tire easily."

"I have not said where I intend to go."

Kuorj glanced at the stained ice. "From this place, there are few destinations." He called to one of the hunters, and asked for his bow, which he handed, along with an elongated pouch of bolts, to Reever. "Ensleg weapons do not always work out on the ice," he told him. "Best to carry this, in the event that yours fail you."

Reever slung the pouch and bow across his back, hunter fashion. "I thank you."

"There will be other hunters out on the ice today," the headman said. "They will not cross your path if you keep yourself out of theirs." He sighed. "I begin to sound like my father in his final years. Next you will hear me call for more furs and a larger heatarc."

"I appreciate your concern." And Reever did. The old rasakt had taught him a great deal about the Iisleg, and had the sort of wisdom that came only after many years of leading other men.

Kuorj clasped the top of Reever's forearm with his hand. "May the vral's work not be made wasted today."

"Farewell." Reever inclined his head and started out on the ice.

The sky was a hard, glassy dome of white that settled without seams over the polished bone plate of the world. Had there not been patches of the dense blue ice showing through the surface snow, Reever might not have been able to tell up from down. Even Kevarzangia Two, with its emerald skies echoing the lush verdancy of its surface, had not been so monochromatic.

The magnetic fields on the planet rendered directional-guidance equipment useless, and the ice fields offered little in the way of landmarks. Reever reserved his thermal scanner and used the Iisleg's method of navigating, shadow shifting, which he had learned during his last visit to Akkabarr.

Reever had not taken twenty paces on the ice before the imperative began burrowing in his mind again. *Go. Find her. Hurry.*

He cleared his thoughts and concentrated on the ice. It wasn't enough to watch his footing and keep a steady pace; he also had to look for the discolorations and cracks that heralded crevasses and hidden vent shafts. He regularly came to narrow chasms in the ice that were barely two or three meters wide but appeared to be bottomless and hundreds of meters in length. Probably created by earth tremors and submantle magma shifts, the gaps sometimes sported snow bridges and inner walls lined with innumerable icicles waiting to tear into any flesh falling into or past them. So far none of the gaps had proved to be too wide to jump across, but Reever tested the other side of each gap before he leaped, to assure it would hold. He had ice stakes and safety lines in his survival gear for the chasms he could not go around or cross.

Did she walk this way? Reever scanned the vista from right to left, trying to imagine his wife following the same path, and her reaction to such a place. It wouldn't have been a happy response; Cherijo didn't like extremes in temperatures. She had been kept in near-total isolation by her creator for most of her life, but as far as he knew, never in such a frigid climate. After living happily on Kevarzangia Two, the garden of border territory planets, and being exposed to the outrageous alien beauty of Joren, the home of her adopted people, Cherijo would hate this place. *There is no color, no life here except where it can cluster and hide from the wind.*

How long has she been here? Reever wasn't sure. The reports were vague; she might have been trapped on Akkabarr anywhere from six months to two years. *How long was it before they found her?*

Reever knew Cherijo had survived. Because his wife had been bioengineered to be virtually indestructible, it would take much more than a crashed ship to kill her. He saw her clawing her way out of a wreck, and walking across the ice alone. No protective clothing, no survival gear. No knowledge of where she was. No hope of escape. No means with which to contact him.

She doesn't even know Marel and I are still alive. The rage, always there, burned deeper, until the imperative swept over it, as it did everything.

Go. Find her. Hurry.

Reever stopped at Akkabarran noon, as the sun overhead erased the shadows and created visual whiteout, making it impossible to continue on without becoming disoriented. He ate some of the preserved food Kuorj had given him, and walked in a circle to keep warm until the shadows shifted into view once more.

Kuorj had told him that the skela who served his iiskar lived in shelters built of ice blocks that adjoined the natural caves inhabited by their pack beasts, and after two and a half hours, Reever saw color interrupt the line of the horizon. As he drew closer, he identified the color as a wide patch of stained ice—black instead of dark red and brown, as it had been outside the camp—and several collected salvage heaps and a single pile of bones. Behind the debris stood two large ice caves and the skela's built-on shelters.

Reever waited and watched the open entrance to the caves as well as the narrow space between the ice blocks that made up the shelters. There was no movement, light, or sound, and no sign of heat being used within. He breathed in and smelled cooked food, damp animal fur, and cured hide. People occupied the place.

Snow crunched behind him, but he turned a moment too late. The tip of a blade pierced his clothing and stopped short of inserting itself between the second and third ribs on his right side.

A woman dressed like a hunter but wearing a modified face wrap stared up at him. "Drop the bow." Reever allowed the weapon to slide from his shoulder. The woman kicked it out of the way but kept her knife in place. "To the crawl. Slowly."

Reever could have disabled her with one sweep of his arm, but decided to humor her and began walking toward the crawl. "I thought you respected men on this world."

The knife jabbed him, drawing blood. "You are not a man. You are stupid. Men never travel alone."

The narrow opening in the ice blocks was actually a hatch that had been recovered from a troop freighter. It slid inside, and a familiar form appeared.

"Malmi, what—" Daneeb peered at Reever and took a step back when she recognized him. "You."

"Me." He glanced down. "Would you ask this woman to remove her knife from my abdomen?"

"Malmi, leave him." Daneeb pulled the hood of her parka over her head before stepping outside. "Go inside and wait."

Malmi removed her face shield, revealing her features. Her skin had the bloom of a young woman, but milky cataracts covered one of her eyes. She turned her head slightly, looking at Daneeb out of the clear cornea. "Skrie, he is *ensleg*."

"Go." Daneeb waited until the door to the crawls

closed again before she spoke to Reever. "We meet again. Why is that?"

Because you lied to me. "I need your help."

"Again?" Daneeb glanced at him. "We tended your wounds and kept the hunters from killing you. Is that not enough?"

"I will explain, but I am not as accustomed as you to this climate," Reever said, and gestured toward the salvage piles. "Will you walk with me while we talk, so that I may keep from freezing?"

"Skela do not have conversations with ensleg," she pointed out.

Reever saw her mitt slip into a side seam of her parka. "No, I believe you only remove the faces from their dead bodies. I am still alive, fortunately."

She gave him a disgruntled look. "Fortunate for whom?"

Daneeb did walk with him out to the salvage piles, which were an interesting jumble of useless components, scorched scraps of alloy, and melted lumps of plas. Reever stopped to pluck a length of frozen wire protruding from one-third of a stripped communications panel.

"How is your friend?" He inspected the pile of bones, but they all appeared to be from small to large animals, not humans. "The other woman who poses as vral?"

Daneeb shrugged. "She is as she always has been."

"She cannot speak, can she?" Reever waited for an answer, and when he didn't get one, he added, "I got the sense that something is wrong with her mind."

"She can speak. She is quiet, that is all." Her tone changed. "What of it?"

Now, why would she lie about the other woman's disability? Was it some sort of taboo? Or— "There is something wrong with many of you, isn't there?"

Daneeb took in a sharp, quick breath. "Wrong, you say. Is it wrong to be born blind in one eye, as Malmi was? Or to lose a hand to flesh rot, as old Ganna did? Not pretty, perhaps, not womanly, but wrong?"

Reever could feel the tension vibrating from her, and quickly wrapped one end of the component wire around his left hand. "I had not realized."

"You are ensleg. Why would you?" She stared out at the ice. "You had better leave now. It will take you the rest of the light to make it to a camp."

"I have one more question for you," he said. "When you came to help me, the last time we met, why did you not tell me that you and Jarn are skela?"

Daneeb snorted. "Why would I? You are ensleg. You know nothing about us."

"Kuorj told me about you and the skela. How you are the only people on this world permitted to handle the dead. How you are sent to search every crash site for the dead." Reever saw the tiny flinch she gave. "If anyone had found the woman for whom I am searching, it would have been one of you." He waited a beat. "Was it you, Daneeb? Did you find her in the wreckage, still alive?"

"I do not know of what you speak, ensleg. I am going back; I have work to do." Daneeb started back for the shelter.

He caught up to her. "You did, didn't you? You found her, and she was still alive."

"No." Daneeb turned away and dipped one shoulder.

Reever caught her by the throat and wrist, using the loop of component wire to hold the dagger in her fist away from his face. "Where is she?"

"She is dead." Daneeb made a strangled sound as his hand tightened. "Dead."

Rage became a silent roar in his head as Reever wrenched the knife from her, threw it away, and dragged her close. "You will tell me." If he had to beat it out of her.

Daneeb's gaze shifted, and Reever heard a whistling sound just before something collided with the side of his head.

The white of the world turned black.

"General Gohliya," one of the subordinate officers said from the strategy chamber's entryway. "The Kangal signals."

It was the Kangal's seventeenth signal of the morning. His last sixteen had come in at ten- and fifteen-minute intervals, with unceasing demands for reports on why the surface defense grid was still off-line from the storm.

Gohliya looked up from the latest recon scans. "I am not here."

The young officer paled. "God be, General, I am not able to lie to the Kangal."

Gohliya turned to one of his senior staff, a lieutenant who was not a native of Skjonn. "Are you able to lie to the Kangal?" The man nodded once. "Go and tell him I am not here."

The lieutenant saluted and left, the anxious younger officer following and protesting in his wake. Once the door panel closed, another staffer secured it.

"Orjakis is going to be trouble," Lopaul, a senior commander and Gohliya's second, said. "Even if we do get the drone communication grid back online today."

Gohliya grunted and changed the surveillance scans to view the next in the series. "He cannot be anything else."

Gohliya had considered killing the Kangal, and had goaded him to the point of committing suicide himself, for over a year. Frustration had run high among the Defense troops, and Gohliya knew precisely who was responsible for it—the Kangal, who knew as much about running a defense force as he did manual labor. He would have assassinated their fool ruler a long time ago, using the men loyal to him to stage a coup and take over the skim city. It had been his father's deathbed request, in fact, that Gohliya do exactly that.

"You can defend the city against the others," General Qohudit had told his son, several times. "They have become weak and self-indulgent above all else. You could take over the world."

The problem was the means with which to do it. The Kangal had severely restricted access to the skim-city armories, cleverly using drone guards as he did with the armory trenches on the surface. Patrol ships were allocated only enough fuel to perform their scheduled flights; weaponry was kept under strict count, and no more than two units could be armed simultaneously.

Then there were the command override crystals, which the Kangal kept to himself. He had one for every Toskald ship, and could use them to take control of those ships anytime he wished.

Just as he could use the crystals kept on the planet to summon an army to defend his throne.

The Kangal were more than rulers. They were in complete control of Akkabarr, and all its treasures. Only Orjakis knew how to disarm the drones guarding both the skim city and the surface armory trenches that belonged to Skjonn. Even if Gohliya could take over the city, access to the offworlders' crystals, kept below on the surface, would be lost to him the moment he cut the Kangal's perfumed throat. As insurance, it was enough to stay Gohliya's blade and keep the general on his knees in front of a man whom he'd considered a waste of breathable atmosphere all his adult life.

Gohliya focused on the scans. "There has been no movement for forty-nine hours. You are quite sure about this."

"All of our orbital scanners are functional, General. We have run diagnostics to be certain of it." Lopaul brought up a comparison screen and looped it to show progressive scans. "None of the scanners detected any new heat signatures or topographical changes. It is as if they have disappeared off the face of the planet."

There was something very wrong with that, particularly when it coincided with the first massive failure of the surface defense grid.

They are animals. They have no technology, and none of the equipment they would need to dig down to the trenches. And how would they disable the drones before they sent out an alert?

Gohliya felt better for thinking it through. "What about the camps?" His patrol ships had been menacing the surface for weeks now. The rebels had likely run back to their iiskars to hide behind their cringing women.

"None have relocated," his second said, displaying several scans of the iiskars. "We have seen no increase in thermal activity."

"No." Gohliya struck the screen with his fist, splintering the plas. "Fifty thousand rebels do not disappear into the wind."

"Commander?" One of the junior staffers came forward.

"Leave us," Lopaul said. When the rest of the men had left the room, he brought out the first aid pack. "They may have tried to move during the storm." Carefully he removed the shards of plas embedded in the side of the general's hand. "It was one of the largest and worst of the year. If the Raktar was so foolish as to send his men out into it—"

"He would not do that." Gohliya felt ridiculous for having lost his temper. "Whatever this Raktar is, he is not a fool."

"Neither is the Kangal."

Gohliya understood the bitterness in Lopaul's tone. Like the general, his second's father had been one of Orjakis's advisers. He had been killed down on the surface after being sent there to monitor the tribal wars. A short time later, Lopaul's devastated, lovely young mother was summoned to the Kangal so that he could comfort her. She never left the palace again, and Lopaul was sent to the youth academy.

A signal chimed on Gohliya's private console, and after a nod from the general, Lopaul went to answer it. The encoded message was brief and to the point.

Lopaul acknowledged it before destroying the relay and his own reply.

"Our League contact reports that the body of Colonel Stuart was found three days ago, hidden in a cargo hold of a troop freighter," Lopaul said. "DNA was verified. He was not missed because he was on official leave just before his body was discovered."

"Was he murdered?"

"No, he died of disease six weeks ago," Lopaul told him. "The leave Stuart took was medical, and he died while undergoing treatment. His body was taken from the facility by a male Terran claiming to be a family member. The death record was deleted from the hospital's database before its routine upload."

"So the Terran is not Stuart, but stole his body, erased his death record, and took his place. I knew something was wrong with his story. Get me a drink, 'Paul." Gohliya sat down and stared at the scans of the Iisleg camps. "League, then?"

"Our contact would have indicated that, if it was so," his second said as he made the drink at the prep unit. "His loyalties are to those who pay him, and we pay him very well."

"This Terran comes here looking for a woman," Gohliya said, thinking out loud. "He petitions the Kangal—knowing that is risky, but willing to gamble—and is granted permission for a search. He agrees to permit Orjakis's man to pilot him to the surface. He hijacks the launch, crashes it deliberately, kills Aledver, and disappears. The only DNA from the recovered remains belonged to Aledver—is that still so?"

"Yes, General. We also have received a report from the surface that the Raktar is now searching for a pair of females who may be working as spies against him." Lopaul brought him a glass of firewine. "That story was not planted, and as we do not use women . . ." He lifted his shoulder.

"A third party has become involved. Yes, that is rather obvious at this point." Gohliya swallowed some of the wine and savored the way it burned down his throat. "Now our task is to identify this third party."

"It would not be the League. They are entering into negotiations with the Kangal, and they would not risk those," Lopaul said.

"Yes, they do adhere to their tiresome diplomacy with fanatical devotion of late." Gohliya considered other powers within the region. "It would not be the Faction; they won't use warm bloods. That, and it is more their style to conquer the planet than spy on it."

"Mercenaries," Lopaul suggested. "Working for non-League, non-Faction worlds. There is a growing coalition of them, some say."

The general shook his head. "Mercenaries are limited in what they can do. If they could get to Akkabarr, they would not spy while they were here. No matter who paid them to come, they'd be at the slave pits or attempt to abduct the Kangal."

"I can't think of anyone else."

Gohliya considered the small amount of wine left in his server. "Let us imagine that the Terran is an independent. He came here for the woman for personal reasons."

"He is insane, then," his second said.

"I have an easier time believing that than him coming to spy. There was something about him that made me very uneasy. Do you recall? The way he moved, the set of his face. Those strange eyes of his, as well. He looked out of them as if he were more drone than man." Gohliya knocked back the rest of the wine, rose, and went to another scanner table with an intact view screen. "Show me the site where the Terran's ship crashed."

Lopaul brought up the image. "We believe it was here." He pointed to a small discoloration in the largely white image.

"Zoom out and show me the surrounding camps and any history of rebel movement." Gohliya watched as his second adjusted the display. "Six camps. Navn the largest settlement. Navn." Although he had little use for the surface natives, he recognized that name.

"I show no tracked rebel activity for this area, General," Lopaul said.

"None?" Gohliya knew the rebels changed locations constantly, and guessed that they had been doing so for much longer than anyone had suspected. Since creating his useless army, the Raktar had kept it on the move. It was one of the reasons the Toskald had been unable to capture him; any intelligence on his whereabouts was good only for a matter of hours.

"The area lies within the eastern part of the inhabited territories." His second adjusted the display to show all known Iisleg settlements and average climatic conditions. "It is colder, and the indigenous food supply smaller, so the population of the eastern tribes has not shown significant growth since settlement of the surface was initiated."

Since the Toskald had abandoned their former slaves, was what Lopaul meant. Gohliya had no love for the conquered or captured, but like many of his generation, he saw the loss of revenue as tragic. The slaves had been well in hand when they had finished digging out the ice for the armory trenches. Whoever had ruled at the time should have rounded them up, taken them off the planet, and sold the lot of them.

So much nonsense might have been avoided, had the Iisleg's ancestors been removed from Akkabarr. The Kangal might never have developed their hysterical vanity, a practice originally begun to instill awe in Iisleg tithe slaves, to keep them docile and cooperative. No, selling off those abducted Terrans certainly would have saved Gohliya a considerable amount of grief now.

"Let us say that the Terran is a field agent for our unknown third-party interest," Gohliya said. "He crashes his vessel in an area where there is no rebel activity. Deliberately?"

Lopaul raised his eyebrows. "Perhaps. But if he is to spy on the rebels, why? Would it not make more sense to join the rebellion, infiltrate it?"

"We cannot know the thoughts within such an alien mind." Gohliya froze. "That is it." He uttered a sharp laugh. "All this time before me, 'Paul, and I did not see it."

His lieutenant gave him a blank look. "I don't follow, General."

"The Terran." Gohliya tapped his chin with his finger. "I have long suspected something very odd about our rebel general below. He does not seek security, only concealment. Only predators do that. He does not attack directly, but he persuades these squabbling tribesmen to stop sending tithe to the Kangal. Thus he strikes a blow directly at the vain heart of the Toskald.

The Iisleg know the result of this will be starvation, and yet they obey. Do you know what it takes to inspire that sort of allegiance? To make men risk dying a slow and debilitating death for you?"

"They think they will win," Lopaul said, still puzzled. "He has convinced them to believe so. Some leaders possess that kind of power."

"My father was one. I would have died for that man, gladly." The general examined the scan again. "He was not like other men. He left our world and traveled to others. He learned many things from other generals and other militaries. He returned a changed man. Had he not become ill, I believe he would have taken over this planet."

"I don't understand, General."

"I could never predict what my father would do, because his education was largely conducted offworld," Gohliya said. "It is the same with this Terran. We can't explain his behavior, see a pattern in it, or even fathom why he is here. And it is the same with the rebel general."

"You think the Raktar is an alien? But—"

"Think, Commander. We would know if he was Iisleg. Their ways are familiar to us. We have observed their tribal squabbles for decades. The only thing the Raktar does like an Iisleg is to live on the surface." Gohliya met his second's astonished gaze. "No, this Terran shows us why the rebel general is not Iisleg."

"If this is so, how did he reach the surface?" Lopaul asked.

"He was brought here as a slave, I imagine." Gohliya thought for a moment. "Somehow he escaped the skim city and made his way down to the planet."

"That is not possible," his second protested. "We have never had an ensleg slave escape the cities."

"Not alive." Gohliya remembered marching a prisoner to the edge of an abandoned dock. He had wanted to execute the man cleanly, but the slave had insulted the Kangal, who had insisted he be thrown off the platform to be torn apart by the kvinka. "I will need the records on all slaves brought to Skjonn and put into the service of the Kangal two years ago."

Lopaul frowned. "That could be as many as three thousand records."

Gohliya had forgotten the slave's name and number, but he remembered that face. "I want only to see the records for humanoid males with blue skins and white eyes."

"I will retrieve them from the database. What of this Terran?"

"He would not have had time to leave the eastern territory before the storm hit." Gohliya would have preferred to capture the man, but he had other priorities. "Send down an attack unit and kill anything that moves."

"Yes, General." Lopaul glanced at the door. "And the Kangal?"

"Say that I have gone to personally inspect the city security hub in order to get him the answers he requires." Gohliya refilled his server with firewine. "Then disable his relay."

"He will take your head for that," Lopaul warned.

Gohliya looked through the view panel down at the blue-white blur of the surface. "Not if I bring him the Raktar's first."

THIRTEEN

Resa dropped the femur she had taken from the bone pile to use as a makeshift club, stepped over the unconscious man, and helped Daneeb up from the ice. "You hurt?"

"No." Daneeb rubbed the front of her neck. "Bruised. For a moment there I thought he would snap my neck." She looked into Resa's eyes. "You could be killed for what you just did, if another man had seen it."

"No man here but him." Resa regarded the body. The ensleg male was dressed oddly, and his face appeared very pale. She bent to check his pulse, which was still strong. "What do with him?"

Daneeb retrieved a knife from the snow and stood over the unconscious male. "Go back to the crawls, Resa. Keep Jarn inside."

"Too late for that."

Resa looked over at the healer, who was standing a short distance away. "Man hurt Daneeb neck," she told her, hoping it would not result in another beating. "I hit man in head."

"Yes, I saw." Jarn did not look at her; she was busy staring at the man. "Put away your blade, Daneeb. You are not skinning him."

"You don't know who he is, Jarn—"

"He was at the crash site. I remember." Jarn opened her pack. "You are not ruining a face I fixed."

Resa watched the exchange with intense curiosity. She regretted having to hit the man, but he was bigger than she and looked much stronger, and she couldn't think of another way to get him off Daneeb.

She understood why Daneeb wanted to kill the man. He had been trying to strangle her, and would probably try again as soon as he woke up. She understood why Jarn wished to prevent his death, too. It was Jarn's work to heal the wounded and keep people from dying.

Healers make a vow not to harm people. Resa's vision wavered, and pain began pounding above her ears. *I know this. I know.*

"I will need help to carry him inside," Jarn was saying.

"Let him freeze. The jlorra will enjoy the meat more." Daneeb sheathed the knife, stood, and strode off.

Jarn looked at Resa. "Are you well enough to help me?"

Resa moved her shoulders. Whatever Jarn had done to her back last night had taken away all the soreness and ache. "Yes. I help carry?"

"Take his feet." Jarn went to slide her hands under the man's shoulders, and when Resa had a grip on both of his ankles, she lifted him. "He is heavier than he looks," she muttered.

Resa helped Jarn carry the unconscious man inside. "You know this man?"

From the way she was holding her head, Jarn was

staring at his face. "Daneeb and I found him when his ship crashed here. He is an ensleg."

"Like me."

Jarn's head lifted. After a moment, she said, "We are all the same under our skins."

Someone opened the door to the crawls, but Jarn told Resa to carry the man into the jlorra caves. There she discovered that Jarn had set up a place with things that she had once sorted in the salvage sheds.

"It will be better to keep him here, with the cats to guard him," Jarn said.

After they had put the man on the board Jarn had wedged between two square blocks of shiny metal, Resa stepped back.

"I get your pack from crawls?" she asked Jarn.

"I keep another one here." The healer went to a natural shelf in the ice and took down a fur pack. "Can you take off his jacket?"

Resa examined the strange garment with some doubt. It was made, not of fur, but of a glossy material that was dark blue in color. "Cut off?"

"No, there are fasteners down the front." Jarn pointed to it. "Lift the flap of cloth there."

As soon as she studied the fasteners, Resa could see how to release them. While she dealt with the jacket, Jarn brought a humming device over to the man, and passed it over him before looking at it.

Resa put the jacket aside and came to look at it, too. The square in the device had tiny marks on it, and seemed very familiar. "What is that?"

"This tells me if he is bleeding inside his head, which he is not." Jarn made the marks go away and put the device aside and turned the man's face to study the bloody place on the side of his head. "You struck in the ideal spot, Resa. If you had hit him that hard at the back of the skull, he would be dead now."

"He want to kill Daneeb." Resa studied his face. It was obvious that he wasn't Iisleg—his skin and hair were the wrong color—but he looked almost familiar. "Kill woman he look for?"

"Perhaps." Jarn, too, studied his features. "He may be one of the slavers from the windlord city."

"But you help him."

"For now." Jarn bent close and held the scanner over the wound.

Resa looked around the room, went over to a box, and selected a container, which she brought to Jarn. "Use this man's head?"

Jarn checked the markings on the bottle. "This is antiseptic." Resa nodded. "Can you read this label?" She showed her the markings on the bottle.

Resa peered at them, but they were not like the few of the markings the people made that she had learned. "No read."

"Yet you knew what it was." Jarn studied her face. "You've had some sort of training as a healer."

Resa frowned. "I not remember."

Two male jlorra came into Jarn's room and sniffed at the ensleg's feet. The larger male yawned, flashing his lethal teeth before he nudged Jarn's hand.

"No," the healer said absently as she used the antiseptic to clean the man's head wound. "You can't have him."

Resa smiled at the cats and went down on her haunches. Both cats ambled over and sniffed her thoroughly before rubbing their heads against her knees and arms. She gave both a good scratching around the ears and muzzle, smiling as they closed their eyes in silent enjoyment.

"You have an affinity with the cats," Jarn said.

Resa stood. "Sisters say cats like you. Why people fear cats?"

"The jlorra are not particularly fond of people. They treat most of them like walking food." Jarn lifted the man's head to wrap a bandage around the back of it. "I don't know why the cats like me. I have done nothing to deserve their affection."

"Cats judge smell," Resa said. "We not Iisleg. Maybe we not smell like food. We maybe smell like little cats."

Jarn secured the bandage. "That is an interesting theory. They do treat me like a cub." She glanced up. "How did you know I am not Iisleg?"

Resa pointed to her face. "You look more like me, not them. Cats bring you food?" When Jarn nodded, Resa chuckled. "Me, too."

Resa noticed the larger cat sniffing the man's leg and inspected the area. There was a hole in the material covering his flesh and flecks of blood. "Man hurt here, Jarn."

"Jarn!" Daneeb's shout echoed in the cave.

"I must settle this with her," the healer said. "See if you can remove his pants so we can tend to his leg. I'll be back in a few minutes."

Resa found the fastener for the man's pants at his waist and had no trouble with it. The ensleg's clothing was bizarre; ties were so much easier than the complicated things holding his together. Yet it seemed familiar, too, as if once she had worn such garments.

I am ensleg. Of course I did.

She worked the trousers down to his knees, exposing a wound on the side of his left thigh, from which a piece of blackened metal protruded. After a glance at the empty cave entrance, she pulled his trousers off and put them with his jacket.

The metal would have to come out; it was lodged deep in his flesh and would poison it if left there. She went to Jarn's pack and found a probe, a pair of hand coverings, clear wash solution, and a suture laser. She also took a square transparent container and placed it between his legs, and folded a length of bandaging.

She probed the wound and felt around it with her fingers. The shrapnel was relatively small, but it had gone deep into his leg. If she removed it, there was a risk of more bleeding, but the edges of the wound were already an angry red. Carefully she tested the metal, wiggling it and tugging on it gently before stopping to observe. The flow of blood was minimal; it did not feel as if the shrapnel had twisted itself into his flesh. With the bandage ready in one hand, she quickly jerked out the metal and pressed the bandage down hard over the wound.

The wound bled freely, but not dangerously, and a quick wash showed minimal tissue damage. She used the suture laser to cauterize two bleeders, and examined the depth of the wound. He was very lucky; another two centimeters and the metal would have cut into the man's femoral artery.

The rest took a few minutes. She was careful to repair the tear in the thigh muscle before closing the edges of the wound. He would need medicine to prevent infection and keep any fever from escalating.

Resa cleaned the leg and used another bandage to dress the wound, and then dumped the bloodied instruments and bandage into the container, which she set aside. Covering his legs with his jacket to keep them warm, she looked around the room for some water to use to clean her hands.

Jarn stood at the entry, watching her.

Resa suddenly felt uneasy and not a little confused. "I fix leg."

"Yes, I saw you operate on him."

"You angry?" Resa couldn't see her face, and Jarn's voice gave nothing away. She felt stupid for doing something like this without permission, but it had seemed so necessary when she saw the wound.

"No." Jarn came over and checked the man's leg. "Very good work. How long have you been a healer?"

Resa frowned. "I am a healer?" Jarn nodded. "I not remember."

"Yet you remembered how to perform minor surgery on this man," Jarn said, in a language that was not Iisleg.

Yet Resa understood her perfectly. It was the same language she herself had been thinking in while working to repair the man's leg.

Terran.

Confusion became a whirlwind spinning through Resa's head. Surely she could not be a healer. But she had known what to do; she had felt utterly confident while doing it. She could not tell Jarn what she had done; she didn't have enough words, but even if she had, it would be difficult. There were no Iisleg words for some of the things she did.

And she had done it all while thinking in Terran.

Resa looked down at her hands. Her right wrist throbbed now, as hard and as painfully as her head. "You be healer, Jarn," she said, groping for the words. "Not me. I . . . should not."

"No, Resa." Jarn came to her and placed her hands over Resa's. "You don't have to be afraid. You are among friends here."

"Friends." The word felt uncomfortable on her tongue, as if she was not accustomed to using it. "You and I?"

"We speak the same language." Jarn smiled a little. "The language of this world, and that of the homeworld. It is all right for the two of us to speak Terran when we are alone. No one has to know."

"Terran. Terra." The words felt strange on her tongue. "Our homeworld."

"Yes, for what it's worth. Daneeb will be grateful," the healer told her, speaking in Terran again. "She has never liked the work. She does not know how to do anything but kill them, and she refuses to learn."

The work? Them? What was she talking about?

"War is coming." Jarn's voice went low. "There will be many like him, many who wish to kill each other. Many will perish, but there will be some who may be saved. Saving people is more important than killing them; do you agree?"

The throbbing eased a little. "Yes."

Jarn went to the pack and took out a stiff circle of material. After a few moments, it seemed to melt into her hands. "Daneeb was the one who actually found this. It was in the wreck of a . . . a ship. It is alive. I think it knows what we think, because it makes itself into what I wish."

It was a blob, and yet she spoke of it as if it were some magical thing. Resa's stomach clenched as she regarded it. It was flowing over Jarn's hands now, as if made of some thick water that would not drip. It changed shape as muscles did when they moved, only more so. "What is it?"

"I don't know." Jarn placed the thing in one hand, and removed her head wrap with the other. Then she placed the thing on her face.

"Jarn," Resa shrieked as the thing stretched out and completely covered Jarn's face from scalp to neck. She ran to pry it away, to keep the healer from smothering.

Jarn lifted one hand. "No, don't be alarmed," she said in a perfectly audible voice. "I can still breathe, and see, and speak. It does no harm." The thing on her face did not move. "When we go outside into the cold, it does grow stiff, but I can do the same out there."

Although she knew it was a mask, Resa felt her stomach churn. "Why put on face?"

"It makes the Iisleg believe I am an instrument of the gods." Jarn held her hand in front of her face, and the blob came off onto it. "To help them, we must first terrify them." She looked at Resa. "Could you do that, to save a life?"

Before Resa could answer, a huge, explosive sound shook the caves, causing a shower of ice crystals from the upper roof to pelt the two women and the unconscious man.

Jarn and Resa both went to the ensleg and shielded him with their own bodies as a second, more powerful burst rumbled through the ice beneath their feet.

* * *

"Personally gone to inspect the hub?" Orjakis opened his eyes, disturbing the eyelash treatment the face drone was applying. He swatted the hover unit away and removed the delicately petaled mash from his brow, cheeks, and nose. He left the depilatory treatment on his chin and jaws, for the solution might create a rash if it had to be applied a second time in one day. "This takes precedence over answering our signal?"

"I see Janzil Ches Orjakis, Kangal of Skjonn." The notch, who had lately taken to standing near or behind solid objects, looked around the treatment room's doorframe. "The general's second said he had gone to inspect the hub. It could never, not even in the imagination, take precedence over the Kangal's signal."

"You offend our nostrils and our ears, notch." Orjakis waved a hand. "Go away."

"I see and obey Janzil Ches Orjakis, Kangal of Skjonn," the notch said, "and before I am delighted to follow the Kangal's orders, I must inform the Kangal that the League liaison has arrived and is awaiting the Kangal's pleasure in the Kangal's receiving room." The notch waited for the final dismissive hand gesture, which Orjakis gave him, and then scurried away.

Orjakis would have stayed in his dressing room and contemplated the magnificence of his visage while deciding how to disassemble Gohliya with a blunt blade, but the League liaison had traveled several dozen light-years to attend him. He would have to be allowed a glimpse and a moment of Orjakis's attention. After the depilatory was finished removing the stubble from the three disgusting hairs that had resisted stim treatment and kept growing back on his face, naturally.

Orjakis chose glorious gold and severe black as his color theme and, once properly adorned, permitted a half-ceremonial presentation. Full would have been more appropriate, of course, but he wanted time to deal with Gohliya, and so enjoyed only the partial deference due him as he was escorted by his attendants into the receiving room.

The humanoid male waiting for him did not look anything like Colonel Andrew Robert Stuart, that lying, murderous walking refuse heap of a being. No, this male was much worse; unsightly with age and overweight, he wore the same drab brown uniform, but the fit was ill to the extreme. He also reeked of misplaced authority; he was not even making a motion to go to his knees.

Orjakis nearly withdrew to change his garments to a thunderous crimson purple of offended sensibilities, but his ears were already being assaulted by the League male's voice.

"I have been waiting here for three hours," the officer said, without the slightest note of respect in his tone. "I'm Captain Hark Deyin. Who are you?"

Orjakis had never actually fainted, so he had no basis of comparison, but felt what he suspected might be very close to it. "Clear the room," he said in a trembling voice.

The drones and his attendants disappeared. It was left to Orjakis to seal the doors himself. He did so to give himself the chance to compose his outraged senses. There was no question that Captain Deyin would die before the sun moved another inch through the heavens. But how he would die—now, that required careful consideration, even more so than the matter of Gohliya. Orjakis thought he might have to spend several days thinking it over.

Deyin would simply have to wait in the death pit until he had settled on something.

"Is this thing not working?" Captain Deyin muttered, checking the translation device on his wrist. "Who are you?"

"We are Janzil Ches Orjakis, Kangal of Skjonn." Orjakis realized he had never had to tell anyone his name. Not once since the day of his birth. Deyin's tongue would be the first thing he would pry out of his head. "We are ruler here."

"You signaled League Headquarters to inform us that a"—Deyin looked away from him to study a datapad—"Colonel Stuart, Andrew R., was killed on this world by rebels." He finally made eye contact. "Is this correct?"

"You know nothing about Toskald protocol." Orjakis circled around him, oddly fascinated by the man's fearlessness. "Not how to behave, or speak, or look upon us? Do you?"

"I am not a diplomatic liaison." The League officer actually waved a hand in front of his bulbous nose to disperse Orjakis's mood scent. "We assumed this was a civilized, progressive world. If you want some sort of honorific, I'll need to talk with your chief protocol officer, but I'd rather hear more about what happened to Stuart."

Orjakis considered the fact that this ugly, ignorant, abusive, offensive, fecal-brained ensleg had no idea whatsoever that he was a dead man for his words alone. He represented the League, however, and Orjakis wanted them to avenge Aledver more than he wanted the man's death.

Just a beating, perhaps. Something to cripple and disfigure him for life.

"Such protocol is hardly necessary, under the circumstances," Orjakis lied. "This Colonel Stuart came asking permission to search for a woman whose ship crashed on the surface two years ago. We granted it, but sent one of our men with him. He killed—"

"Hold on." Deyin was not looking at him again; he was fiddling with his pad. Suddenly he looked up. "Andrew Robert Stuart died weeks ago, two systems away from here. His body was stolen from a morgue and his death records erased. He's never been to this planet."

"That is how the man identified himself to us."

"Do you have vids of the man?" Deyin squinted at him. "Your kind *do* know *what* vids are, I hope?"

Deyin would lose his eyes, long before he died, for that remark. "Yes, but then we Toskald are a slightly progressive, civilized people. Over here."

Captain Deyin followed him to the room console that Orjakis had never actually touched. Pulling up the security stills taken of Stuart during his visit to Skjonn did not present a problem, however, as Orjakis frequently used the console in his privacy chamber to access the security system.

A pity Gohliya does not realize that. "The man," Orjakis said, indicating each scan, "his vessel, and the identification he presented to us."

"Brilliant forgeries. He must have paid heavy creds for these." The captain peered at the screen. "You said he was here looking for a woman?" He jerked back from the console and stared at Orjakis. "Was it a Terran woman?" he asked, his voice shaking with some sort of strong emotion. "A Terran woman physician?"

Orjakis was fascinated by the complete change in the man's behavior. Excited and fearful, over a slave. This obscene lack of respect had gone so far beyond any realm of Orjakis's imagination that he was mesmerized.

"Yes, we believe that was how he referred to her. You may listen for yourself." He replayed the audio recording of the reception.

Stuart's voice came out of the panel. *This slave female has knowledge of certain events which, if manipulated by our enemies, could prove damaging to League treaties. . . . I have been ordered to find her and bring her to Intelligence Headquarters for interrogation and detainment. . . .*

Orjakis cut off the audio. "He spoke of the Jado Massacre."

"There was no massacre." Deyin scowled for a moment before he recovered his exhilaration. "I need to send a priority message over this panel. Did he find her, do you know?"

"We don't know." Orjakis came to stand behind him and watched as he typed furiously on the keys. Deyin might be the ugliest male that had ever offended the Kangal's eyes, but his hands were attractive in their competence. *I will have them cured and made into ring holders.* "Shall we summon one of our drones to assist you in encrypting this message?"

"No, it's already coded." He finished the transmission and enabled the transponder. "They find her down there, they'll give me a medal or something, you know that?"

"We knew how vital and sensitive the matter with the woman was," Orjakis said, memorizing the code and the relay frequency and channel Deyin used. "Under the circumstances, we felt we had to contact the League."

"Everything they say about her. I always wondered if it was true." Deyin shook his head. "I've seen some of the records—QI keeps the good ones classified, of course—but they distributed the general-info file to every security detachment in the League."

"Do you have that file on record in your database?" Orjakis asked.

"On my ship, yeah, but it's League business." The captain looked up from the console briefly. "Sorry, I can't give you access."

No offering of crystal. That made things simple. "Never worry, Captain." Orjakis used one of the floor taps to signal his personal drone guards. "You may yet change your mind."

Deyin, who wasn't listening to him, stood up and turned around. "I'll need to set up a security command post somewhere in this place." He looked around as if seeing the room for the first time. "If you have some men you can spare to help me, I'll need them, too, and some dignitary accommodations for when the old men arrive."

"The old men?"

"The big brass, our quadrant commanders. I wouldn't be surprised if QI sends every ship they've got in the quadrant here within the next seventy-two hours." Deyin gestured toward the view panel. "You'd better have your people prepared to receive them."

Orjakis released the door panel to admit his guards. "Escort Captain Deyin to the Preparation chamber."

Deyin stopped on his way out and seized Orjakis's hand. "How do I thank you? What you've done is going to change everything for me."

"No need." Orjakis smiled. "There are more changes to come for you."

FOURTEEN

Hasal had recommended killing Aktwar Navn, but Teulon was satisfied with having the boy kept at the front of the detachment escorting them to Iiskar Navn.

"You could be walking into a trap," his second protested when Teulon ordered preparations be made for the journey. "Navn has waited a very long time to declare his loyalty to the rebellion."

"Navn's people are starving," Teulon said. "I trust their hunger, not their declarations."

Hasal stayed behind at the main encampment to finish coordinating the second phase of the attack, but vowed to fly out to join the Raktar as soon as all of the battalion commanders had their troops in place. He handpicked the men to accompany Teulon and had them arm themselves to the teeth.

Teulon preferred to travel light, and knew most tech weaponry was useless on the ice, so he brought only his sword and his blades. The skimmers the detachment used were modified with scan scramblers to prevent patrols from tracking their movements, and had been outfitted with white shielding as aerial camouflage. The Raktar's own skimmer was modified to accommodate Bsak's bulk.

The fact that a jlorra would voluntarily fly on a

skimmer always impressed the men, but Aktwar Navn was terrorized by the sight of the big cat climbing on behind Teulon. Only when Bsak settled into a crouch behind the Raktar did the boy shut his mouth and climb onto the back of one of the escort skimmers.

The big cat rested his chin on Teulon's shoulder so it could watch the way ahead of them. Behind them, five guards brought up the rear.

Teulon rarely indulged in any flying himself, so the long, chilly trip to the eastern territory was something of a novelty. It also gave him the chance to oversee the different territories from which they would launch their attack against the Toskald cities.

His gaze shifted. Skjonn hovered above them, a dark smear on the pristine white of the sky. It had been two years since the Toskald had taken him from the death pits and marched him to an abandoned transport dock. The general of Defense himself had been sent to perform the execution, probably as a punishment.

On that day, Gohliya had sent the guards away. *You tried to kill him.*

Teulon had. *I failed.*

I will not, Jorenian. He had drawn a pulse weapon. *This is no death for a warrior. I will make it swift.*

That is not necessary, General. Teulon had stepped to the edge of the platform hatch, and glanced down. The kvinka was a river of air, furious and unforgiving. *I am already dead.*

"Raktar," one of his men transmitted. "There is something ahead."

Teulon and all the pilots wore short-range headgear, salvaged from a Hsktskt wreck, which allowed them to communicate effectively during skimmer flights. Because the tech was designed not to be detected by League monitoring devices, they could use it without risking alerting the Toskald patrols.

Bsak lifted his head.

"I see it," Teulon said.

On the horizon the air was changing color; bursts of yellow brightened, then faded.

Patrol ships, firing on the surface.

Teulon's troops had already raided the trenches in this region and left, but that made no difference. The Toskald had found something to attack. "Assume strike formation. Edin, take Navn's son to the iiskar, and have his men come in over the ice."

The patrol, a well-organized unit of some thirty ships, was flying attack patterns above a large hunting party pinned down on the ice. The flat plain had forced the Iisleg to use their skimmers as cover and there was no sign that they were returning fire.

Bodies of men and game lay in pools of frozen red slush.

Teulon waited to see the skimmer carrying Navn's son break off before he moved up to take point. The patrol ships had not yet detected their approach. "Seek out the navigational cluster before you attempt anything else. Don't ram the engine cowlings; they've been reinforced. Bring them down intact if you can."

Bsak crouched low in the skimmer, muscles coiling against Teulon's back.

The skimmers spread out, each acquiring a ship and breaking out of formation to move in. Teulon flew under three skimmers to emerge just beneath the lead vessel. All Toskald patrol ships possessed standard hulls insulated against temperature and atmospheric debris. Yet because the ships were used exclusively on the planet, and the Iisleg were not permitted any weaponry, the builders had not bothered with protecting certain vulnerable points.

Teulon moved into position and extended modified docking clamps to fix his skimmer to the hull. Once he had a stable platform, he shut down the skimmer's engine and drew his sword. The central processing unit for the patrol ship's navigational system lay behind an access panel, which he pried open with his claws. A single thrust of his sword into the aperture destroyed the ship's primary and secondary guidance and maneuvering systems. He dropped down onto the skimmer and immediately disengaged the clamps; the patrol ship's pilot had already lost his helm controls.

Teulon flew straight down, crouching low to avoid the jetting debris as the ship he had sabotaged collided with another and exploded in midair. He circled up and went to the next ship.

The Toskald, now only too aware that they were under attack, redirected their weapons and opened fire on Teulon and the rebels. Their tracking systems could not lock on to the skimmers, however, as the camouflage shielding also absorbed the reflective scans, and the barrage was almost completely ineffective. Three patrol ships crashed on the surface, while five more made fairly successful emergency landings. Ten were destroyed in flight, as were four skimmers.

The remaining patrol ships suddenly retreated, flying up into the higher atmosphere where the skimmers could not follow. After firing a few more useless volleys, they flew off on course for Skjonn.

Teulon scanned the ice below. More skimmers were coming from the south, along with men on foot. Toskald infantry poured out of the ships that had landed safely, and began firing pulse weapons at the skimmers as well as the Iisleg still trapped on the ice.

"Land beside the patrol ships," Teulon told his men. "Engage the infantry."

For two years Teulon had awaited this moment. He had counted the hours and, at times, in the darkness, the minutes. He had remembered every face, every decision, every moment, that had brought him to this place.

The first had been Teulon's own decision. He had decided to travel to the Liacos Quadrant with his HouseClan, and stop a war that was devouring systems and destroying millions of lives. As a show of trust, he had also agreed to jaunt over to the League flagship by himself to meet with their commander and arrange the time, place, and goals of the initial talks.

Those were the last free choices Teulon would make for some time.

"I know you came here to negotiate peace between the League and the Faction," the League general said after his guards seized Teulon. "But that is not why we brought you here. There will be never be peace, and it is time that your people learned that."

"Think carefully, Shropana," Teulon warned. "You know Jorenian law. If you kill me, my HouseClan will not rest until you are dead."

"That is easily remedied."

Now, at long last, he had the army, and the crystals, and the means to avenge himself. The time to fulfill his promise to his dead kin had arrived.

He landed by the nearest vessel and jumped from his skimmer. Bsak, at his side, hissed. Three soldiers rushed at them from opposite directions, firing their weapons.

The seven-bladed sword blazed through the air as Teulon decapitated the soldier in front of him, and turned to skewer the one behind him. Bsak permitted the third a short scream before biting his skull in two. Teulon shook the blood from his blades and strode out onto the ice.

Shropana, standing at the console, had issued the order personally. "Signal the CloudWalk. *Tell them that we are sending some Jorenian passengers over to dock with them. Then launch the drone ship." He turned to smile at Teulon. "Something the Bartermen bought for us from the Hsktskt. It will make it appear as if the stardrive malfunctioned." He nodded to the guards. "Take him to interrogation."*

In the corridor, being dragged by the guards. Killing them. Finding a com panel. Sending the final signal to his brother on the CloudWalk. *"Fire on all League vessels within the vicinity of the ship and destroy them—"*

At last. Releasing the beast inside him to run with Bsak was almost painful; it had been tethered for so long. As a soldier charged at him, Teulon snapped his forearm dagger into his left hand, pivoted, and slit the Toskald's throat. Hot blood spattered his chest and face. *At last.*

The guards who had recaptured Teulon shot him in the chest, arms, and legs. He had been barely conscious when they dragged him to the view panel, where Shropana's voice, an oiled snake, sank its fangs into him.

"Congratulations, ClanLeader. You'll be happy to know that your signal—which I recorded—did get through to the

CloudWalk. *Your people successfully destroyed the drone launch before it docked with your ship. Unfortunately, they also fired on three scout ships of ours that were sent to investigate. I have so notified command, and I have been given the order to defend the fleet and return fire."*

The pain of his body had been nothing then. The House was greater than any one of its Clan, and for his House, Teulon would beg. "There are women and children on board the ship. My bondmate, our ClanSon. He has only three years." He fell to his knees. "Be merciful. Spare them."

"Spare women and children who would pursue me to the ends of the universe for killing you? Permit a three-year-old to live who will grow up wanting nothing more than to dig out my guts with his claws? I think not."

"I will shield you and you can kill me without fear." Teulon bowed his head. "Spare them, I beg you, and I will do anything you wish."

"Yes, I'm sure you would." Shropana gestured to the guards. "Hold him up."

Pulse fire became sporadic as the patrol's weapons reacted to the temperature. Men cursed and flung pistols and rifles into the snow as they ran for cover. The Iisleg hunters who had been trapped there now stood and fired their crossbows. The hail of bolts was like a scythe. Men stopped and fell into the snow, cut down as precisely as yborra grass beneath a honed blade. Bsak became a darting streak of wet crimson fur and flashing teeth.

The guards had difficulty holding Teulon, flesh and garments slick with his own blood.

"Hold on to him. No, keep him right where he is," Shropana told his guards. "I want him to watch. I want him

to remember what happens to those who threaten the League."

Teulon felt the life pulsing out of him from his wounds. He could not take his eyes from the sight of the CloudWalk, *surrounded and outnumbered. The Jado's ship was badly damaged, yet still returning fire.*

Shropana sighed. "Valiant to the end."

Teulon felt the madness roaring inside him as he cut his way through the Toskald troops to join the hunters, now fanning out onto the ice. He kept in front of them, leading them against the frantic patrol troops, severing heads and hands and limbs. Bolts whistled through the air past him, reaching some of the Toskald before his blades did. Mouths sagged. Bodies jerked, spun, tumbled.

The CloudWalk, *and every member of HouseClan Jado save one on it, swallowed by brilliant white light as the ship exploded.*

Teulon killed every Toskald in his path.

Fewer screams punctured the air now. The sun poured merciless light over the battlefield, illuminating the faces of the living and dying. The snow turned pink and then red before it froze into a gory slush. Bsak walked from body to body, inspecting, nudging, gnawing.

That final conversation, before he was taken away.

"You cannot declare me ClanKill, Teulon Jado." Shropana appeared serene, even complacent. "You need kin present to do so, and I have just obliterated all of yours."

Teulon was the ClanSon of a shipbuilder. As a student, he had studied and followed the path of Tarek Varena. He had trained as a warrior, as did every Jorenian, but had vowed never to use a weapon against another living being unless to defend his kin. He had told his HouseClan that there were better paths to be found. He had dedicated his life to making a path of peace.

That path, that life, had ended. He met Shropana's amused gaze, and uttered the three words. Words that meant he would not rest until each and every member of his HouseClan was avenged. Words that made a monster out of an honorable warrior. No Jorenian since Tarek Varena, who had witnessed the slaughter of most of his kin, had spoken these words. No Jorenian had ever lost all of his family, as Teulon had. "I Choose Death."

"You no longer have the privilege of choice, slave."

Some of the Toskald survivors tried to retreat back to their ships, but Teulon saw that Navn's men had arrived and taken up positions there, waiting for them. Crossbows twanged, and the sound of bolts hitting flesh peppered the air, while ghosts whispered behind Teulon's eyes.

"Jorenian male, sold to Trader Ivicis for one thousand credits."

When the last death cry faded, more than two hundred Toskald lay dead in the snow.

"Gift to the Kangal of Skjonn, Jorenian slave, male, from Trader Ivicis."

Teulon came back to himself slowly. He found he was standing over the headless body of a Toskald officer, sprawled on the ship ramp up which he had tried to run before meeting the Raktar's sword. In his hand was a timed explosive device that had been activated.

"Presentation of prospect nine-two-one."

The Toskald knew what the Iisleg would do to their ships, and preferred to destroy them before they could.

"Do not clean him. We like how the blood and the sweat make his skin gleam."

Teulon knelt to disarm the handheld bomb, and set it aside. He sensed the hunters drawing close, gathering around him. Many were hurt, bleeding, exhausted. All were silent as they watched him stand and face them.

Bsak padded over to sit at Teulon's side.

"He tried to kill us. Look, we are bleeding! Give him to the kvinka."

A few moments before Teulon had boarded the launch to fly to Shropana's ship and begin the peace negotiations, Teulon's bondmate, Akara, had suddenly flung herself at him and embraced him. It was not unusual for bondmates to show strong emotion at being separated even for short periods of time, but this was different. Akara was sensitive to many things, and for some unknown reason, she had been frightened.

She had, in fact, been terrified.

Standing in the light now, blood dripping from his sword, Teulon again heard the last words Akara would ever say to him. She had whispered them against his skin. She had burned them forever into his soul.

Do not go, my heart. I fear for you.

She had been right to fear.

"It begins now," Teulon told them. "What is done here can never be undone. There is no apology that can be made. No tithe will pay for this. No Toskald will ever forgive us this. They will know we are no longer their slaves."

Teulon knelt beside the body, and used his claws to tear open the man's uniform. With a second swipe of his hand, he did the same to his belly. He buried his hand inside, digging deep, and wrenched out a steaming mound. He lifted the man's intestines up over his head, displaying them for his men, and for the dead who were all around him now.

"Now." He looked at the pale, bloodied faces, saw the reflection of his trophy in their eyes. "We fight, or we die."

Resa reached up to touch the smooth mask the blob had formed over her face. Just as Jarn had said, she could see, breathe, and speak through it.

"It will not hurt you," Jarn promised as she tested the depth of the snow with her walking staff.

"It grows hard." It had a smell to it, as well, sharp like cold air was to breathe, but Resa was growing used to it. Still, she would rather have covered her face with a wrap. "Must wear?"

"Yes. Cloth falls away when you are bending over someone." Her tone changed. "There will be many, from the sound of it."

The terrible noises, Jarn had told her, were from ships firing at the surface. The healer had little more to say than that as she prepared her medical packs.

Daneeb had arrived after the worst of the noise died away, and had immediately raised strong objections to Jarn's taking Resa with her to see to the wounded.

"At least I know how to put on the charade," the headwoman had argued. "She can barely speak coherently, and you only began talking again last night."

"We both speak fluent Terran, so we can communicate easily," Jarn had said, "and we do not have to talk to the wounded. Stop your worrying, Daneeb. I will not let anything stray from us again."

Resa had not been with the skela long enough to judge, but she wondered at times if the healer deliberately meant to provoke the headwoman. Their conversations were never very quiet, at least, not on Daneeb's side. Jarn always seemed a little odd whenever she spoke about Resa. As if she was angry with Daneeb over her.

Before they had left, the worst argument of all happened.

"What about him?" Daneeb jerked her chin toward the unconscious ensleg.

"The cats will guard him." Jarn helped Resa into the strange clothing that she said she had to wear to go with her.

Daneeb seized Jarn by the arm and turned her around. "He tried to kill me. I have the right."

A blink of the lashes and Jarn had Daneeb pinned against the ice wall, a blade poised at her throat.

"Not one hair on his head will be out of place when I return," the healer said. "Not one drop of his blood will stain your hands. I will have your word on this."

Daneeb eyed the blade. "You cannot kill me, Jarn."

"I don't have to kill you, Skrie. I only have to hobble you." She moved the blade down, down, leaning sideways until she slipped it behind Daneeb's knee. "Your word."

The headwoman considered this, and nodded slowly.

Jarn called out a strange word and two cats appeared. "We will be gone for a long time. If we are caught in the dark, we will find shelter."

"No one will take you in," Daneeb said, wiping a drop of blood from the tiny cut Jarn's blade had made in her flesh. "One day you will walk out there and not return. You know this as well as I." She regarded Resa. "Have you nothing to say? Do you wish to follow her into death?"

"I help," Resa said softly. "Jarn need help. So do men."

"So do we all." With a disgusted sound, Daneeb left.

The trek to the place where the ships had fired on the surface took less time than Resa had thought. Jarn hitched three of the jlorra to a pack sled, and had Resa ride on the back of it with her.

"We must be able to transport the wounded," Jarn said, "and leave quickly. The rebels will return for the ships."

At first it confused Resa, to see the dark, looming silhouettes of the ships on the ice, instead of properly in the air, where they belonged. Then she saw what the ships had been firing on, what they had left on the snow.

More men than Resa could recall ever seeing alive lay dead all around them. Hunters, men in bleached furs, and other men in strange garments.

"So it has begun," Jarn said, her voice very low. "Again."

Resa stared at the dead. "So many."

"Yes. Don't release the cats." Jarn tethered the sled to a stake and looked out carefully over the ice field. No one had been left standing, but there were sounds. Groans. Snow shifting. Muttering. "The ones in the white outfurs are rebels. The others are soldiers of windlords." She paused. "The soldiers will likely all be dead."

So many bodies, and only she and Jarn to tend to them? "How do we do this work?"

"Standard triage," Jarn told her before they went to the first Iisleg hunter lying on the ice. "Check for a pulse first. Clear airways; slow bleeding; dress burns. Pack open wounds and exposed bone. Say nothing unless you must."

The hunter, a young man with a ghastly head wound, was already dead. So, too, was the headless body closest to him. Jarn stepped over him to see the third.

This hunter was older, and not as grievously wounded. His outfurs were scorched in several places, and he had a terrible energy burn to the side of his head and neck. But he opened his frost-crusted eyes the moment Jarn touched him.

"Vral," he whispered. "Find me worthy."

Jarn took a syrinpress in a warming sleeve from her pack and infused the man's neck, rendering him unconscious within seconds. "Scan for internal injuries before you dress his burns," she said to Resa in Terran. "Use the sled to carry him over to one of the ships, and put him inside where he can be made warm." She moved on to the next casualty.

Resa hesitated before reaching into her own pack. She couldn't remember being a healer, and for a moment she resented the way Jarn had ordered her to act as one. What if she made a mistake? She would not know if she did; only Jarn would—and Jarn was ten yards away, her hands busy probing the chest of a fallen rebel.

Fear faded and was replaced by another, more powerful emotion. *I am a healer. Like Jarn. This is my work.*

Resa took the burn medicines and bandages from her pack and went to work on the hunter.

The sun moved over the two healers, shifting the shadows around them. Resa soon discovered that the majority of the men left abandoned on the ice were already dead. The few who had survived were in shock, most suffering from injuries that could not be healed. More than one died as she worked on him.

With so many dead around them, Resa expected the jlorra to be restless, but they merely stood and watched until they were needed to haul men over to the ship Jarn wanted to use as shelter. One man who had been brought to consciousness and needed only a broken arm bound began helping them load the others onto the sled.

"I will take them," the rebel said, and drove the sled for Jarn and Resa on the second trip from the ice to the ship.

Daylight was an hour from fading when they had finished the work. The survivors, sheltered now in the ship, were as comfortable as they could be made. The dead were left where they lay. The hunter who could walk recovered an abandoned skimmer and told Jarn he would go to Iiskar Navn to summon help to transport the men from the ship to the camp.

He hesitated before climbing onto the skimmer, and looked back at Jarn and Resa. "I thank you for finding me worthy, vral."

Poor Hurgot, Resa thought as she watched the hunter fly away. *You will be busy tonight.* She noticed that Jarn was staring at one of the other nearby ships. "What is wrong?"

Jarn seized her arm. "Run to the sled. Quickly."

"But we cannot leave—" Resa stopped as she saw rebels in bleached outfurs running from the other ship toward them.

"Now, run." Jarn dragged her down the ramp.

They didn't make it to the sled. Rebels surrounded them on all sides and trained their crossbows on them. They moved only to make way for a very tall male accompanied by a scar-faced jlorra covered in blood. This man's face was shielded, but he was far too large to be Iisleg.

"Vral?" the man said to one of the rebels, who nodded. "Take them to the ship."

FIFTEEN

Teulon listened to Navn's tale of the ensleg Resa. He refused food and drink offered by the headman's ked-era, Sogayi, who said nothing but managed to project silent displeasure at his refusal, just the same.

"Why did you not kill her when she violated your law?" Teulon asked when the rasakt had finished the convoluted story.

"I had . . . thought to be merciful," Navn said, almost stammering. "She did save the life of Aktwar, my son. It seemed appropriate to allow her life."

"As it seemed appropriate to allow her into the camp."

"Yes."

"To work among your own women."

"To earn her place here, yes."

"That is not the truth." Teulon rose. "You follow the oldest ways, Navn. Your own son told me how you despise the freedoms given to women in the western tribes. Yet you allow an alien woman into your iiskar? You permit her to contaminate your women with her off-world ways? And when she makes and uses a weapon, an offense for which you would kill any Iisleg female, you spare her?"

"I was confused." Navn's expression turned resentful. "I have never had to deal with ensleg."

"You lie again. You did all of these things because you feared her." Teulon loomed over him. "Was it because you feared that she could not die?"

"No." Navn looked sick as he turned to his wife. "Go, fetch fresh water for the basins." When Sogayi had left the shelter, the headman slumped back in his chair. "You are right. I was afraid of her. Of what she is. She is very like . . . but it can't be the same woman. The one who was brought here was too badly wounded. It was too long ago."

Teulon paced the wide interior. "How long?"

"Eight seasons. Perhaps nine." The headman covered his eyes with one shaking hand. "I have not slept well since the day they brought her back to show me. That one, not even the skela could kill."

The ensleg that would not die had arrived on Akkabarr at the same time Teulon had. "Tell me about her."

Navn composed himself, and tucked his hands in the ends of his sleeves. "We saw the ship go down. The gjenvin went to work the wreck, as always. A League transport vessel, it was. A small one. There were two on board. The male was dead when the skela recovered his body. The female had survived. Some of the skela committed a sacrilege and were put to the ice for it. The gjenvin master told me the Skjæra shot her with a pulse weapon, but that did not kill her."

"What is the Skjæra?"

"A skela who puts the dying out of their misery." Navn's voice grew rich with disgust. "Iisleg warriors do not slay the helpless."

"Go on."

The headman made an empty gesture. "That is all. The gjenvin brought the ensleg female here, to show me. The woman barely breathed, but they were afraid. So was I. I was about to take her head when the jlorra broke from their harnesses and took her. They dragged her out of the camp. It is their way to attack the wounded and devour them. I swear to you, that is what happened."

This Resa was not Cherijo Torin, Teulon decided. No living being, no matter how enhanced her physiology was, could survive under such conditions.

"If that female who would not die was a drone, no beast on this planet could have eaten her." Teulon pulled on his outfurs. "Your healer is attending the wounded that were brought here?"

"Yes, but there are so many, and he is old and only one man." A crafty look came into the headman's eyes. "These vral, if you permit them to live, they may prove of more use to us. They saved many of your men, did they not?"

They had, and that was the only reason Teulon had allowed them to live. If they were drones, perhaps he would even reprogram them. "Prepare your men to leave camp."

Navn was taken aback by this order. "You are taking my men?"

"You pledged them to me when you joined the rebellion." Teulon put on his face shield and left the rasakt's shelter.

The guards waiting for him outside escorted him from the camp to the temporary command post they had constructed just outside the battlefield, where the dead were being dragged by sled to be thrown into a nearby crevasse. Teulon had given orders that the skela not be summoned and worgald not be taken from any of the bodies.

"Neither of the females will speak, Raktar," Edin, who had been posted outside the makeshift detainment unit, said. "The packs they carried have ensleg medicines and such in them. No weapons except for this, which the smaller one carried." He showed it to the Raktar.

Teulon examined the weapon. It was a slim, narrow stiletto a fingertip in width and two hand spans in length. "Is this the sort of blade used by the Death Bringer?"

Edin looked uncomfortable. "I believe so, Raktar."

Teulon nodded and slid the blade into his sleeve. "I will question them."

Inside the temporary shelter, both women were sitting together in a corner, their backs to the walls. Both were conscious and showed no signs of abuse. Teulon knew the only reason for this was that most of his men remained convinced that they were vral and would not go near them.

He performed a thermal and bio scan of both females. They were not camouflaged drones, and they carried no subdermal devices or implants. Both were approximately the same age.

"I am the Raktar of the rebel forces," Teulon said, setting aside the device. "Who sent you here?"

Neither woman responded.

"I know you are not vral, or spirits, or sent by the Iisleg God." Teulon saw no reaction, but they were both still veiled. "Show me your faces."

When the women did not remove their head wraps, he strode over and tore them off, one in each hand. The masks beneath startled him, but only for a moment.

"I can remove those, as well," he advised them, showing his claws.

One of them reached up and held her hand in front of her face. The mask oozed from her head into her hand, where it became a slowly undulating blob. It had concealed a small, narrow human face with high cheekbones, a prominent nose, and tilted dark eyes. Her sheared hair was dark with a prominent streak of white.

The other woman removed her mask in the same fashion, but kept her face averted. Her long dark hair helped by acting as a shroud.

"Show me your face," Teulon said to the second female.

"Show yours," the first one said.

Perhaps frightening them would provoke more of a response. Teulon reached up and removed his face shield.

The first female frowned, but the second glanced and then stared through the curtain of her hair. He crouched in front of her, reaching to move the hair from her face.

The long-haired woman bolted, running for the entry. Teulon caught her by the back of her robe and dragged her around. Her face was exposed now, the bright emitter overhead showing every detail of her features.

She looked enough like the other woman to be a sibling.

"No," she said, twisting to try to free herself with

hysterical fervor. She snatched the blade from his forearm sheath and held it between them. "Let go. *Let go.*"

Teulon seized the knife and flung her away from him. She landed in a heap and did not move again. As he turned to drag her to her feet, the other woman barreled into him, knocking him off-balance and falling with him to the floor. She pounced on top of him and pressed something sharp against the side of his throat.

"I use blade, kill ptar," she warned him. "I do same thing to you."

"Is that why you were sent? To assassinate me?"

"We came, help hurt men." She looked disgusted. "Would like kill you for hurting Jarn."

Teulon rolled, dislodging the wedge of metal she had at his throat, and pinned her beneath him. "Never make threats you cannot carry out. Drop it."

She struggled for a moment, and then released the makeshift blade.

He looked over at the long-haired woman. "Her name is Jarn?"

"Don't hurt her," she spit in his face, speaking now not in Iisleg, but in Terran. "Slit my throat if you wish, but she's done nothing." She glanced over at the dark-haired woman, who was unconscious. "She came here to help your men."

Teulon rested the blade against her throat. "Why are you here? Who sent you?"

"We came on our own." She lifted her chin. "Go on. It's all you know how to do, isn't it? Kill me."

The shift of her face made something glimmer, and Teulon used the blade to ferret it out. It was a vocollar, a linguistic translation device made and used by Jorenians. He had not seen one since the slavers ripped his from his neck. "Where did you get this?"

She covered it with her hand. "It is mine."

Teulon lowered his blade. Two years ago. A Jorenian vocollar. An ensleg female who would not die. He reached farther back, recalling the image of a Terran female physician on his display. The relay had been distorted slightly by the dissimilarities in their com equipment, but she, too, had had dark hair with a single white streak. At the time, he had known of her—everyone had—but that had been his only contact with her. He could even remember some of that one, brief conversation they had shared.

Your kin have arrived, and we will keep them safe.

May the Mother watch over you all.

"What is your name?" he asked the woman under him.

"Resa."

Resa, the newly arrived ensleg who Navn claims does not remember who she is. The one he fears came here two years ago. Teulon stood, and held out his hand. "Come. Stand. I will not hurt you."

She let him help her up, and yet watched him with wary eyes. "Why not?"

He considered telling her exactly that. "You say you are here to help us. You have saved many lives. You did not try to kill me when you held the blade at my throat." He gestured to Jarn. "I believe you are what you say you are."

"No, we are not," Resa admitted. "But it is the only way we can help the wounded." She frowned. "You speak Terran, like we do, but you are not Terran."

"I had dealings with Terrans once." Teulon saw

Jarn's head lift and her hand sweep the long dark hair from her face. "Is she Terran, like you?"

Resa nodded. "How did you come here? As a slave?"

"I was sold in Skjonn." He went over and helped Jarn to her feet. "I escaped two years ago."

There was no change in Resa's expression. "From the skim city? How?"

"I was sentenced to death and walked off the edge of an open platform. Only I caught an edge as I went over, climbed under it, and hid. Later, I stowed away on a supply ship. It brought me here." He felt Jarn trembling, and to her said, "I will not hurt you."

"You say one thing and do another," Jarn said. "I do not trust you."

She was unsteady on her feet, so Teulon held on to her. There was something very strange about the Iisleg woman. She seemed not of this world. She reminded him of other, equally insubstantial things—things that soothed him with sorrow, and burned him with shame —

Like the spirit of the cave. Teulon closed his eyes. Holding Jarn in her vral garments was as if he were back in the small cave, trying to embrace a column of air. He looked down at her. "Do you know me?"

"No." She backed away from him. "Perhaps I will after you wash off the blood from your last victim."

Teulon studied his hands as she did, and saw the dark red stains. "I fought men who would have killed me had I not. They were opponents, combatants, not victims."

"They lost, did they not? These men who follow

you into battle"—Jarn gestured toward the entry—"do they know you are ensleg?"

"The ones I trust do. Healer, being that you and your friend are Terran, I do not think you are in a position to criticize me for my lack of veracity." There was something that bothered him about Jarn, as well, but Teulon couldn't place it. "Do you intend to keep searching for wounded and treating those you find?"

"It is our work," Jarn said. "We are healers."

"You will be dead healers if you continue to wander the ice without protection." Teulon couldn't let them go, especially not Resa, not now that he knew who she was. She might prove to be more valuable than the crystal. And in some strange fashion, Jarn shared a connection to the otherworldly creature from the small cave.

Was it her? He had always thought the ghost he had encountered there a true spirit. *Spirit made flesh.*

The long-haired healer gave him a level look. "What do you want, Raktar?"

He had already planned to keep Duncan Reever on the planet. No one on Joren could know that Teulon was alive. One of these women was Reever's wife. The solution was a simple one. "You may join us and fight for the rebellion."

"Oh, yes, that is what I wish. Arm me. Let me shoot the men I have healed." Jarn made a disgusted sound and turned her back on him.

"We cannot fight," Resa reminded him softly. "We are healers."

"You came closer to killing me today than any assassin the Toskald have sent after me for the last year," Teulon told her. "I would not ask you to fight. You can follow the army and treat the wounded." While he kept Reever busy elsewhere, away from Resa and Jarn.

It was a cruelty, perhaps, but not a permanent one. Teulon could also safeguard both women until it was safe to permit Reever to leave Akkabarr.

"Just like that?" Jarn asked. "While you keep us well supplied with patients? Permit me to express my lack of gratitude now."

"War is upon us, Healer. Men will die whether you wish it or not." He saw something dark move in her eyes. "You will go on healing whether you are with the army or not. With us, you will be protected."

"While we watch you butcher them. I thank you, no." Jarn covered her face. "Are we permitted to go now?" She walked to the entry and waited there.

"Before the patrol came here, they fired on an iiskar to the north. Sverrul, it was." Teulon saw her back tense. "Do you know the camp?"

"I know the Sverrul, yes." Jarn turned around. "What happened?"

"What usually happens when a fully armed Toskald patrol decides to punish the Iisleg. The rasakt and every woman and child in the camp were incinerated." Teulon glanced at Resa. "They were not armed. Their men had left to join the rebellion. I doubt the women even came out of their shelters when they heard the ships."

Jarn was shaking her head slowly.

"If we went with you, your men will not permit us to treat them." Resa picked up the blob that had rendered her faceless. "That is why we use these. So that they will think we are vral."

Something else that Teulon now found very convenient. "You will have to maintain the vral illusion except when you are alone or with me. Would it be so difficult?"

Resa turned to Jarn. "He is right."

"He is a killer." Jarn went to Teulon. "What do you want from us?" she demanded. "You are a man. You would not be this generous without a reason."

"A general who commands two vral will encounter very little resistance from the loyalist tribes," Teulon said. "You will give me the final sanction I need: the sanction of the Iisleg God."

The two women looked at each other.

"I cannot decide this," Resa told Jarn. "This is your work. I follow you."

"They will discover what we are—*who* we are," Jarn protested.

Resa thought for a moment. "Not if we are careful. We must have our own shelter. We cannot share it with anyone else."

"You will have it," Teulon said.

"I don't have enough medical supplies." Jarn rubbed her eyes. "I have used here today most of what I have been able to salvage."

Teulon nodded. "I will obtain that which you need."

"We will also need shelters that we can set up near the battlefields, so that the men can be treated under cover," Resa suggested. "Someone to help us with moving and treating the wounded."

"The skela," Teulon said. "No one would question their presence, as they are death handlers. The skela already know what you are."

"The ensleg," Resa said suddenly. "We cannot leave

him." To Teulon, she said, "An ensleg came to the crawls looking for us. He believes we know where his woman is. She was lost here, on Akkabarr. He is Terran, and wounded."

Teulon wondered how Reever could have found both women and not realized one of them was Cherijo. He would have to lie now, something that disgusted him, but could not be helped. "Terra is part of the League. The Toskald are forging an alliance with the League. Whatever reason he has come here, it is not to look for a woman. That is only an excuse."

The two women fell silent. Jarn's expression was not visible, but Resa's was troubled.

"There may be more that we require," Jarn said to Teulon at last. "It will not be a simple thing to conceal us."

"No path worth traveling is simple." Or entirely revealed to the traveler, but Teulon kept that portion of the Jorenian adage to himself. "We seem to follow the same direction."

"No, we do not." Jarn pulled the wrap from her face and looked into Teulon's eyes. "I will not kill, ensleg. Not for you. Not for anyone."

She seemed to believe the words she spoke, and yet she carried the blade of a Death Bringer. "Agreed."

Jarn closed her eyes. "We will join your rebellion."

War

SIXTEEN

"You fight well, for an ensleg," the rebel in the abandoned trench said to Reever as he offered him some of the dried meat from his pack.

The skirmish Reever and the rebel had survived had been intense and bloody. There were still men straggling in from the ice, wet and exhausted.

"No, I thank you." Reever took some emergency rations he had salvaged from a patrol ship the week before and put a liquid pack to thaw by the heatarc. "How long have you fought for the rebels?"

"Two seasons, since the beginning of the war." The rebel was an older man with the dark skin and callused hands of a builder. "You?"

"The same." Reever had woken up in Iiskar Kuorj to find he had been knocked out and operated on by one of the skela. Kuorj knew nothing of how he had been brought to the camp, only that he had been found by one of the renser women going to gather clean snow for meltwater. Reever had gone back to the crawls as soon as he was well enough to travel, but found them abandoned. Stories of the vral on the battlefields had already begun to circulate by then, and when Kuorj's men had been summoned to fight, he had gone with them. "Have you seen the vral? Have you seen a Terran woman with them?" he asked the rebel, as he asked every Iisleg he met.

"Once, yes." The hunter shuddered. "I fought beside them. They make a man feel like a woman. What is a Terran?"

Reever leaned back, resting his head against the trench wall. "An ensleg, I meant. It doesn't matter."

"There are more vral than rebels on the ice now," another man listening to the conversation put in. "They appear on every battlefield to kill our enemies before they heal those Iisleg found worthy."

"Not every battlefield." Reever had yet to encounter the faceless healers, of which there were stories that numbered them in the hundreds.

"They only fight with the Raktar's army," the hunter beside him said. "Mind your pack before it melts, ensleg."

Reever plucked the liquid pack from the trench floor and held it between his fur mitts. It had grown too hot to open, so he waited for it to cool and studied the faces around him. They were thin, dirty, and tired, but so was every face on Akkabarr.

Victory was near, but whose it would be was still undecided.

The Toskald began attacking as soon as they had learned that the Raktar had emptied their armory trenches, evidently overnight, during the worst of the seasonal storms. How the rebel general had accessed the heavily guarded bunkers, let alone moved the massive amounts of ordnance out of them, remained a mystery. Reever had seen some of the tunnels the rebels had burned through the ice by redirecting vent shafts. The process of tunneling had not been easy, for the water from the melted ice had to be relocated. Reever estimated it had taken the Raktar's forces close to a year to tunnel their way to the trenches.

No one knew where the weapons had gone, and those who did would not speak of it. It was, as every rebel said, the Raktar's will.

Reever was far more interested in the vral. Since the beginning of the war, they had been sighted regularly, and then constantly, wherever the fighting was worst. They came to heal at first, and then they were seen fighting alongside the rebels. They were always accompanied by special detachments of heavily armed rebels who flanked them on either side. Reever had never heard of a vral who had fallen in combat.

Somehow the two vral had multiplied. Reever had verified from other rebels who had survived large-scale engagements all over the inhabited territories that the vral now numbered in the hundreds.

"They kill the windlords, and save us," one rebel who had survived an enormous skirmish in the west told Reever. "That is how I know our cause is just. If it were not, they would kill everyone."

"Hundreds of them," one wide-eyed rebel whispered to Reever in the dark of an ice cave they had shared as temporary shelter. "They drift over the red snow, but it never touches them. They kill faster than anything I have ever seen. Then they lower their cradles for our worthy, and carry them away." He swallowed. "Some of our men are seen again. Some are not."

Reever understood that the rebel general was using the vral both as his field medics and an attack force; that much was obvious. But how he had managed to turn two into hundreds, and make them kill as well as heal, remained a mystery.

A trio of pilots climbed out of the tunnel into the trench. "We need men to defend Iiskar Bjola," one called out. "All who are able, come with us."

Reever was conscious and not wounded, which counted as able, so he rose with the others and went out onto the ice. The transport waiting for them was a refitted Toskald scout ship, captured and reconfigured as a mini-troop-carrier and skimmer launch platform.

"Patrols attacking from the north, forty ships," the pilot shouted over the sound of the engines. "Ground forces have surrounded the camp and are returning fire, but they are outnumbered. Your skimmers carry two plate charges. Land when you have planted them and support the ground defense."

Reever had never attached the explosive devices on the Toskald ship, so he mounted behind a rebel who had, to provide cover. The crossbows the rebels used were useless in the air, but he could man the pilot controls while the rebel planted the charges.

The sun was just beginning to rise, showing a fiery horizon line where the Toskald patrol was firing on the encampment.

"Stay low," was the carrier pilot's final instructions. "They have improved their targeting devices. The ice and God protect you."

The mission was a simple one. Reever and the other rebels would fly in under the patrol ships, mine them, and land to join the infantry. The Toskald still had difficulty tracking the skimmers in the air, but equipment modifications allowed them to lock on for short periods of time. The skimmer pilots, who were accustomed to flying in linear formation, had to compensate by resorting to degrouping and flying in erratic, zigzag solo patterns.

Reever looked down to see the rebel forces encircling the defenseless iiskar. Bjola had been evacuated some weeks ago, as had many other large camps. The women and children were now kept safely hidden in empty trenches far outside the battle zones. The rebels still used the shelters left behind, however, and if there were enough warm bodies, their thermal signatures would attract a Toskald patrol.

"Ready?" Reever's pilot shouted.

Reever slapped his right shoulder, and the pilot engaged the engine. The skimmer launched from the open side of the carrier into the icy air, and dropped immediately and changed course to prevent attracting attention to the larger ship.

The Toskald's forty-ship patrol was now only some thirty in number, with a dozen ships grounded or smashed into debris. On the ice below, four clusters of rebels with antiaircraft cannon were firing up at the patrol. In the air, skimmers darted around the attack vessels, weaving between pulse blasts until they could maneuver beneath a ship. The reinforced lower hulls had defeated the rebels' attempts at sabotage for a time, until commanders began issuing explosive charges that would blast through the alloy.

Reever's pilot found a hole in the cross fire and shot through it, coming up beneath a ship already partially crippled by ground fire. "Take over," he called to Reever as he engaged the stabilizer clamps and throttled back on the engine before standing up.

Reever slid forward, taking hold of the controls and

watching for spot gunners. The Toskald had mounted pulse turrets on the back of every patrol ship, with gunners whose sole duty was to spot, target, and destroy rebel skimmers and their pilots.

The plate charge clanked as it adhered to the hull of the patrol ship, and the pilot grinned down at Reever. "Disengage the—" The rest of what he said was lost as a drone arm seized him and dragged him off the skimmer.

Reever snatched at the pilot's leg, but the hull drone, a spiderish, former maintenance device that crawled along the outside of the ship, dragged the pilot out of reach. Reever drew his pistol and aimed for the drone's drive center, but a bright bolt of cannon fire struck it, blasting it and the pilot's body to pieces.

Half-blinded and deafened by the blast, Reever disengaged from the patrol vessel and dropped down. He wasn't injured, but he couldn't see well enough to fly to the next target. He rolled the skimmer out from under the ship and made for the surface.

The landing was rough, but the skimmer stayed intact. A man rushed up to help him off, while another checked the skimmer. "How many?"

"One," Reever told him. The ice all around him was dark with scorch marks, debris dust, and old blood.

"We have the other." The two men mounted the skimmer and took off, leaving him where he stood.

The patrol was still hammering the surface with a barrage of pulse, deton, and incendiary blasts. A huge blast went off near Reever, deafening him and throwing him to the ground. He tried to wipe the blood and sweat from his eyes as he crawled for cover. Most of the iiskar's shelters had been razed, but the debris heaps still afforded a small amount of protection. He discovered a gash on his forehead was responsible for the blood that kept running into his eyes, and pressed his palm against it hard, hoping to stanch the flow.

His vision blurred, sharpened, and then blacked out.

The stench of blood, carbon, and cooked flesh pressed in around him. Somewhere a latrine pit had been uncovered or overflowed, and was burning. The wind cut through his threadbare furs, but it blew much of the odor away from his face. The noise was not so bad, either, but Reever could not hear anything clearly.

He was blind, and almost deaf.

"Wounded?" someone asked him, voice muffled as if by a heavy cloth.

Reever shook his head. He didn't have to see to know that there would be far worse casualties than he here.

A hand touched his shoulder, squeezed it. A heavier fur dropped on top of him, covering his torso and the upper part of his legs. "Stay here and rest, brother."

Brother. That was how all the rebels referred to each other. As if the war had made them all one large, affectionate family. In a way, Reever supposed it had. There were no ranks in the trenches, or out on the ice. The battle cry of the rebels was one of union, too. A union upon death.

We fight, or we die.

Time passed. The blood coagulated on Reever's scalp and stopped seeping into his eyes. He dozed, but he couldn't sleep, not with the noise, which was growing louder by the moment. The patrol was throwing everything it had at the cannon, but they were firing off twice as many blasts. The ice shook and trembled beneath Reever as ships crashed. There were shouts from the rebels, and screams from the Toskald. Both sounded desperate and furious. Together they cleared the last of the ringing from his ears.

"They're coming from the north fields."

"Over there—release the cats."

"Target acquired. Fire!"

More shouts. Growls. Voices in anger, cries of pain. The business of killing was not a quiet one. The arena had been silent only when the last slave fell.

Reever had never fallen. He would have crawled through hell for his wife, but this hell would not end. He had told her he would wait, and he had. Almost three years now. He had promised her.

It had been the last thing he had said to her. *I'll be waiting for you,* Waenara.

And she had made her promise as well. *Not for long,* Osepeke.

Cherijo wouldn't have lied to him. She loved him. She had given him a child. She had saved him. She would never have made him wait like this. She would have run naked into hell after him.

Go. Find her. Hurry.

Silence settled all around him, as deep and still as the thought crystallizing in his mind. What if he never found her? He hadn't found her. Had he failed? Was this the moment he had dreaded since the *CloudWalk?*

"Open your eyes, ensleg."

Reever obeyed the low, feminine voice speaking Iisleg. A shape hovered in front of him, a shape without a constant form, a thing of light. He wanted to tell it to go away, that it had no business here. It would end up smeared on the ice, like everything else that lived and spoke and cared.

"Head injury. Reacts to sound." The weight of the extra fur went away, and small hands searched him. "Malnourished. Lacerations. This one can go to the unit. Where is the next?"

Reever knew that voice. Knew it as he knew his own. *"Waenara?"*

"I need transport over here," his wife said.

No, it could not be her. He was hallucinating. He seized one of the hands and dragged it to his face. On the fingers was her scent. "Cherijo."

"Delirious." The hand tugged gently, trying to free itself. "You will be well, soldier."

"Cherijo." Reever clamped his hand around her wrist. "I can't see you. *Cherijo.*"

"You can't see anything. You're battle-blind." The hand twisted, a little more insistent now. "Infuser."

Someone else was there with her. Reever squinted, trying to make out her face. But there was no face. There was nothing but a smooth patch of ivory. Then he felt the instrument at his throat, and fell back against the rubble. "Cherijo?"

"Rest now." The fur covered him. "All will be well."

Of course it will, Reever thought as the drugs dragged him down into the dark. The imperative driving him mad was now silenced forever.

Reever had found her.

Orjakis paced the length of his balcony, not bothering with privacy screens. These days few people had time to walk the streets of Skjonn, and those who hurried along below did not spare the time to look up anymore. The Kangal stunned himself by how little he cared about the lack of homage. How could a ruler pay attention to the proper priorities when half of his army was dead and the other half was losing a war they should have won the second day it was declared?

Losing to slaves. To slave animals, left to breed unchecked. How was this possible?

All the mirrors in the palace had been smashed by Orjakis and the pieces removed, and the Kangal had not bothered with a full-body treatment in weeks. He did not dare look upon his image now. The strain alone had been enough, he was convinced, to have turned him into Gohliya's twin.

"I see Janzil Ches Orjakis, Kangal of Skjonn," a protocol drone said from the arch leading into Orjakis's bedchamber. "Representatives from the Allied League of Worlds have arrived to offer crystal and assistance to the great Kangal and his cherished kindred."

"They were supposed to come here last season," Orjakis snapped at the drone.

"The Hsktskt blockade prevented that—"

"They are too late." The Kangal gave a delicate sniff. "We do not have time for them now." He flicked his hand. "Send them away."

"General Gohliya suggests—"

The Kangal wrenched a slat from the delicately carved mock palisade. "We ordered you never to utter his name in our presence." He struck the drone with all his might, knocking its cranial case from its chassis.

"I see Janzil Ches Orjakis, and so can the citizens of Skjonn," Gohliya said, stepping out onto the balcony.

He caught the slat before the Kangal could club him over the head with it, and tossed it over the side. "You will have to improve your timing, Kangal, or you will never kill me."

"Kill you?" Orjakis was so angry he could only whisper the words. "No, our dear inept fool. You are to be kept alive for years. Decades. We are planning every moment of them."

"We will all die very quickly if you do not convince the League to help us win this war," the general said. "They have finally broken through the Hsktskt blockade and have their ships in orbit. They have brought the crystal you demanded in payment. Where is that liaison officer they sent here, just before the war started? Deyin, wasn't that his name?"

"Yes, Deyin." Orjakis took a moment to savor the memory of what he had done to the League captain. It had been one of the last pleasures he had enjoyed. "Which portion of him do you want? You should be very specific; there are many."

Gohliya shook his head. "I will have to do something about this."

"Do you threaten us?" Orjakis had tolerated an exorbitant amount of disrespect from the general since the trenches had been taken, but Gohliya had never crossed this line. *It is the final one. I don't care how important he is to the army, or who will run it in his stead. He dies today.*

"I mean Deyin," the general said. He glared at Orjakis. "They are expecting him to debrief them on the situation."

Orjakis waved a hand. "We will say that the animals killed him."

"That is another thing, Kangal. You must stop calling them animals." Gohliya turned his back on Orjakis and walked into the chamber. "They are rebels. That is how the League refers to them. They will not know who you are speaking of if you do not call them that."

Orjakis considered wrenching off another slat, but his hands hurt and his head pounded. He pressed his hand over his heart—he was too young for it to fail, surely—and took several deep breaths, calming himself before he walked into his chamber. He did not summon the detainment drones. It was a bitter thing, but he needed Gohliya alive until the end of this war.

"We cannot see them until we have had a treatment." Orjakis felt a little better, hearing the calmness of his own voice. He did have a very melodic voice, much better than Stagon's had been. "Tell them to come back in a week."

"In a week there will be nothing for them to return to. I had thought we made progress at Bjola, but—"

"You lost fifty ships at Bjola, and a thousand men." Orjakis waved away the dressage drones and selected his own garments. "Fifty crystals. How is this progress?"

Gohliya gave him a narrow look. "I did not know you were aware of the losses."

Orjakis went to view himself, cursing under his breath when he remembered how he had taken apart a drone with his bare hands and smashed all the mirrors.

"Kangal, who reported the casualties at Bjola to you?" The general sounded different now.

"What you mean is, how did we discover your latest ineptitude?" Orjakis sprayed himself with scent.

"We are aware of everything that has happened in this war, General. Never forget that."

"The point is, the rebels were not prepared for the secondary attack. They have no intelligence on our movements, and their ability to communicate between battalions is severely limited. Five hundred Iisleg died at Bjola. The Raktar's resources grow thin. We have eradicated most of his underground hydroponics labs, so they are entirely dependent on synthetics for food. He cannot synthesize new troops. We have the League, ready to help us."

"Only because they believe the trenches are still intact." The Kangal made a bitter sound. "When they discover that we no longer hold the fate of ten thousand armies in our hands, do you think they will be quite as accommodating?"

"That is why you must handle these men," Gohliya said, his voice oddly urgent. "Not in the usual manner, but as commander of the Toskald armies. You have proven yourself a worthy leader, Janzil. The other Kangal would never have given control of their troops to you, had you not. Forget your vanity for once and be the ruler we need now."

"We need a manicure," Orjakis murmured, studying his hands. "Perhaps the treatment unit can be persuaded not to tint our nails so pink this time. Do you have a spare pistol we may take with us?"

Gohliya sighed and rubbed his eyes. "You destroyed the last of the functioning treatment units three weeks ago."

"Oh." He frowned, not remembering the particular incident. "Was that before or after I ordered all the animal—*rebel*—slaves executed?"

"After. You wanted to watch."

"Come here and help us with this," Orjakis said, taking down his heaviest ceremonial cloak. "What do we wish to obtain from the League?"

Gohliya helped to drape the weighted, padded shoulders of the cloak over the Kangal's. "Crystal, of course," he said. "The loan of five hundred scout/strike vessels and one hundred troop carriers. We will also need infantry."

"Allowing League troops on Akkabarr is dangerous."

"We will not permit any of their troops to leave it. Lift your chin." When Orjakis did, Gohliya fastened the jewel-encrusted collar. "There is something else. As they came through the blockade, the first signal the League sent us was to inquire about a Terran clone. The same one the man posing as Stuart mentioned to you."

"Deyin was very excited about her. We found nothing of importance in his database, however." Orjakis applied a thin layer of sparkling tint to his lips. "She was cooked up in a lab by some insane Terran genius, now dead. We cannot understand why anyone would want that female. She is only a surgeon, and not even an interesting one."

"Deyin would not have had the interesting files on his database," Gohliya said as he took the headdress that matched the cloak from its storage case and set it carefully on the Kangal's head.

"True." Orjakis pursed his lips as soon as the tint had set. "So they came for her, as well."

He had meant to interrogate Deyin about the female, but once he had entered the Preparation chamber, where his guards had chained the League officer next to the open display case with all of Orjakis's favorite implements, such thoughts had rather slipped his mind.

"We will need to accommodate the ships and troops they give us at once," Orjakis told Gohliya. "Make ready for them. We want the city prepared for the attack."

"What attack?"

Poor Gohliya. His spies were so much less efficient than Orjakis's. "Even as we speak, the rebels are preparing to launch their final attack. They are coming for the cities now, General. You had better make your men ready to defend us."

Gohliya came around to face him. "From where are you getting your information? How? This is not the first time you've anticipated something the rebels intended to do."

"Why would we give you one of the two things that keep you from assassinating us, General?" Orjakis swept out of the room.

The League contingent was a small army of officers, diplomats, and representatives from a dozen League worlds. Orjakis had to instruct the drones to herd them all into his ballroom; they wouldn't fit into the receiving chamber.

Orjakis insisted on full protocol presentation, which took another hour. The League were marvelously courteous and carried out their part in the ceremonial introductions with few errors.

"I see Janzil Ches Orjakis, Kangal of Skjonn," the senior ranking officer said once he had offered crystal and had been invited to speak. "I am Allied League of

Worlds General Patril Shropana, Kangal. I sent Captain Deyin to respond to your request for assistance. Could he be brought to debrief us on the present situation?"

"We would be happy to summon him, General. Unfortunately, Captain Deyin was killed by rebels just as war broke out." Orjakis produced a sad sound. "He died saving our life, as it happens. He was given an appropriate memorial service, one fit for who he was."

"I see." Shropana's expression tightened. "We must then petition the Kangal for permission to search the surface of the planet for our missing property."

"The Terran clone physician for whom you have half the galaxy searching, we presume?" Shropana nodded once. *And you hate her,* Orjakis thought, seeing it in the other man's eyes. *More than you love your life.* "The rebels have her now. Many of our brave men have died trying to retrieve her."

"So have mine." Shropana broke eye contact to murmur to one of his aides. "Perhaps the League can be of assistance to the Toskald people in this conflict."

Orjakis smiled. "Perhaps you can."

Seventeen

"How is that chest wound that came in?" Jarn asked Resa as she washed the blood of a dying rebel from her hands in the basin.

"Holding steady. I've put Malmi to watch him. She will come if there is any change." Resa pulled the disposable surgical shroud away from her robe. The shrouds had come from a supply ship that had run afoul of the surface blockade and crashed mostly intact, which had also provided their field hospital with badly needed medicines. "These are convenient, but I wish there was some way we could recycle them." She dropped the stained overgarment in the refuse bag. "Your patient?"

"I was wrong; the liver was destroyed. He won't live past dawn. I gave him the last of the valumine to keep him asleep." Jarn pressed her hands to the dull ache throbbing at the small of her back. "We should do rounds before the senior caregivers come on for the night. The three we had brought over from Bjola are here."

Resa nodded and pulled on fresh gloves. "Any change?"

"The snowbite will have to have that foot amputated. I'll talk to him now. The others from Bjola are still sedated but stable." Jarn picked up the datapads they had converted for use as patient charts and led the way from surgery into the ward.

The field hospital was arranged as a treatment center, not a true hospital. They moved too often to keep any sort of a permanent ward. Yet while they were at a battle site, Jarn and Resa insisted on providing as many beds as they could for the surgical patients who had a good chance of survival, as well as those who could not tend to themselves alone.

Malmi, who was with the patient Resa had operated on, stood as soon as she saw the two women enter the ward area. She had been the skela who had taken to nursing with the most ease, and was now their caregiver supervisor in the unit.

When they were on the ice, she was one of their deadliest killers.

"The drainage continues, Healer," Malmi told Resa. "It is streaked with blood, but not a great amount."

"Good." Resa went over to check the patient's vitals and inspect the surgical site. "Send someone for me if there is any change."

Jarn went to the young rebel with the gangrenous foot. He had been caught in a shelter collapse and lain there three days before someone found him, and only then by seeing a twitch in the blackened foot sticking out of the rubble. He was awake and lucid now. "Are you in any pain?"

"No." He looked around him with large eyes and shivered with awe and fear. "Am I with God? Did the vral bring me to the otherworld?"

"You are in a hospital," Jarn told him, tucking the furs up around him. "We are healers."

He frowned at her. "Healers are men."

"Men are soldiers. For now, women are healers." She didn't think he would give her trouble, as some of the older men did. Much had changed between the men and women of Akkabarr since the beginning of the war. "Do you remember about your foot?"

"It is black." He stared at it. "That means I will lose it and be a cripple. I should keep it so I may walk when I give myself to the ice."

"You were found worthy by the vral, were you not?" Jarn watched the doubt fill his eyes. "We need men to protect the women and the children in the trenches. These men need not walk, only monitor the defense systems and activate them if there is a threat. Could you do that for your Raktar?"

The young man nodded eagerly.

"Good. Then rest, so you will be ready for the morning." She moved on to the next bed.

When Jarn and Resa had finished rounds, they stepped into a curtained corner where they donned their vral masks and robes. They wore the disguises whenever they went beyond the walls of the field hospital's shelter. The few times that there were enough shelters for them to sleep outside the unit, they left the masks off there, but otherwise never revealed their identities to the men.

Resa felt it was becoming unnecessary. The faceless vral fought alongside the rebels now, and they were respected as soldiers. Most of the men had their suspicions, although they never voiced them. Jarn was the one who had insisted on maintaining the illusion. When they were vral, they were untouchable.

Without their masks, they were women. Worse, they were skela. The men would not fight with them if their suspicions became known facts.

The rebel encampment was small and well concealed beneath an enormous portable canopy of reflective material that mimicked the surface crust in appearance and when scanned by the Toskald patrols. Sometimes the canopy was taken down to be carried to their next location; sometimes the camp moved only with the canopy, propped on pack sleds, still shrouding them.

"Vral." The word chased the wind whenever Resa and Jarn walked under the sky. Rebels who carried the blood of the dozen men they had slain that day would draw back in fear. Other, more knowledgeable souls would bow. Everyone knew they belonged to the Raktar now, and saved the men who fought for him because he was worthy. The Raktar had become more than a leader; he was a god among men, for he commanded the vral.

"Hold." Hasal came out of a shelter flap and intercepted the two women. He treated them with a combination of suspicion and mild contempt, but the general's second seemed to regard everyone save Teulon as a potential threat. "Is the work finished for the day?"

Jarn inclined her head.

"The Raktar would see you in the training shelter." Hasal walked ahead of them, glaring at anyone who stepped into his path.

"I didn't know he had returned," Resa murmured. "Usually he comes to the unit first."

The Battle of Bjola had been a difficult campaign for the rebels. They had deliberately repopulated the iiskar, hoping to lure patrol ships within range of their cannon, at first concealed by flimsy tents that only imitated Iisleg structures. The initial phase had been successful, and they had brought down ten ships. It had been while they were salvaging the crash sites at dawn that the second wave of forty ships had converged on the rebels. Half of the men were killed before they could cross the ice and take cover. Those who stayed inside the wrecks were not spared, either; the Toskald now destroyed all of their grounded ships.

As soon as word filtered back to the general's encampment, Teulon had sent up his reserves, but it had not been soon enough, and three companies of rebels were lost.

Hasal stopped outside the training shelter and waited for the two women to go inside. He permitted Resa to pass, but held Jarn back with one raised hand.

"What is wrong?" she asked him.

"This." Hasal handed her one of the mouth straps the rebels all carried. This one was bitten through and stained green. "It is the tenth he has discarded this moon."

Jarn hated the silencer; the men used it when they were wounded to keep from screaming. She also knew Teulon was not wounded, at least, not where anyone could see, or anywhere she or Resa could fix. "This would be the Raktar's private concern, not mine."

"The men are concerned. They have heard him now, several times." Hasal looked around before adding, "He needs rest, but he hardly sleeps now. Battle does not tire him. Neither does walking the ice, or visiting that empty cave he favors."

Jarn knew what the Raktar's second was asking. "We are not here to play ahayag."

"You sleep with the wounded." Hasal gestured abruptly toward the unit. "Would you deny him the comfort you give to the infantry, or the pilots, or the other women?"

"I would deny him nothing." Jarn meant that, too. She had not trusted the Raktar when she and Resa had joined the rebel army, but as the war raged she had grown to know him. He led countless charges into battle. He fought through until the last of the enemy fell. He never asked any of the troops to do that which he would not do himself. "But he has never asked—"

"He cannot. He believes his heart is dead." Hasal placed the strap in her hand and closed her fingers over it. "It lives at night, Jarn. It screams in the night."

She tucked the strap into her robe and went into the shelter.

"Follow my movements," the Raktar was saying out loud. "Up, then down. Side to side. Slowly, now."

Resa and the general were standing beside each other. Both were armed with Toskald ceremonial swords, which they were moving in tandem. Behind them, forty newly arrived skela were following their movements.

The integration of the skela into the army had been inevitable, had anyone truly thought about it. At first

Jarn and Resa had used their skela sisters only to transport the wounded and, once they had discovered that the blobs they used for their vral masks were replicating themselves, made them into a small army of vral. Everyone on the battlefield was at risk, however, and the skela turned vral had been repeatedly forced to defend themselves. That was when Teulon saw, as every man did, that the dead handlers were faster and more experienced with hand blades than most men.

Teulon ordered the vral armed. Jarn and Resa had argued against it, of course.

"They were not brought here to engage in combat," Resa had told him when he proposed enabling the skela to fight as well as carry out the wounded. "They came to help us, not to kill for you."

"Only the Death Bringers can do that," Jarn added, "and only when commanded to do so."

"Skela know how to kill game that are brought to them still alive." Teulon looked at both of them. "You command the vral."

"No." Jarn had walked out, and after a moment, Resa had followed her.

It had been Daneeb who had settled the matter. She had engaged the first Toskald in battle when an infantryman ran at one of the wounded she had been carrying off the ice. She had killed him with her first blow. That night she had come to the Raktar and asked that the skela be issued long blades. When Jarn and Resa had opposed it, she had turned on them.

"They attack us as if we were rebels," the headwoman told Resa. "We must defend the injured."

"You are talking about killing, not saving."

"This is our world, too. We wish to fight for it." Daneeb turned to Teulon. "We can be held in reserve. We can continue to mask ourselves as vral. Only arm us."

Now Jarn waited, not understanding why she had been summoned to the training session, but sensing it would be several minutes before it was complete and the Raktar dismissed the skela. She found a curious joy in observing, as well. Watching Resa and Teulon practice together was like seeing jlorra move.

"Halt and lower blades. Jarn." Teulon gestured for her to come forward, and took another sword from the pile that had been cleaned and repaired by one of the armorers. "Take it."

Jarn folded her arms. On this subject she had been adamant. "I will not use weapons."

"I have need of the men who have been guarding you on the battlefields." He extended the sword to her. "Take it."

"Am I to understand," she said, making no move to touch the weapon, "that you have acquired a case of amnesia? Perhaps that is why you forget what I told you when I joined this rebellion."

"I do not expect you to kill for me. I expect you to live." He did not lower the sword. "The Toskald are learning to leave their energy weapons on their ships. At Bjola they carried nothing but swords. You can no longer go onto the ice unarmed, Jarn."

He was right. He was right and she hated him for it. Jarn heaved out some air and took the weapon. "I will likely stab myself with this thing rather than defend myself."

Teulon gave her a shrewd look. "You have better defenses than half my battalions."

He was obviously in the grip of some bizarre whim, so Jarn indulged it and practiced the sword movements with him and Resa and the other skela. The weapon was heavier than it looked, and reproducing the simple strokes he showed them more difficult than she imagined.

"You should spar with Resa," Teulon said after dismissing the other women. "She is your match with a blade."

Jarn was sweating and her arm felt as if it were made of stone. "It is one thing to wave a blade in the air," she said, feeling guilty for enjoying it as she had. "Another to skewer someone's body with it."

"When someone tries to skewer you," the Raktar said mildly, "I hope you will not wave yours in the air." He shrugged into his outfurs. "We are prepared to move into the third phase. It is only a matter of days now. I thought you should both know, since we will be leaving you here."

"The rumors are true, then," Jarn said. "You have found a way to reach the skim cities."

He did not respond, but covered his face and left the shelter.

At first everyone thought the Raktar meant to deplete the Toskald troops by battling them on the surface. But two battalions of rebels had been sent to places unknown to the rest of the army, and it was presumed the weaponry liberated from the armory trenches had gone with them.

Jarn did not see how they could fly to the skim cities. The few operational ships and pilots capable of traversing the kvinka could still not carry enough troops to take over one of the flying cities. Skimmers could, but they were too flimsy and their engines stalled if they flew too high. They could never cross the zone of violent wind keeping the surface dwellers from their former masters.

"I need to bathe, and sleep," Resa complained. "So do you. Let us worry about ourselves tonight."

"We cannot." Jarn took out the silencer strap, holding it tightly in her hand for a moment before offering it to Resa. "We must decide what to do about this."

"You have not eaten this day," Hasal said as Teulon stripped out of his sparring garments.

"I had a session with the vral," Teulon said.

"That should not have taken long." His second brought him a bowl of stew and a server of water. Teulon had issued the last of the tea to be distributed among the men. "They saved the men at Bjola, it is said."

"Jarn took up the blade tonight." Teulon drank some of the watery stew. "I gave her no choice, I suppose."

"That one will not suffer," Hasal told him. "Her tongue alone could slice through a hull. She should spar with her twin. There is no one faster with a blade."

Hasal always referred to Jarn and Resa as twins. There was something faintly eerie about how alike they were, too. They moved like mirrors of each other, or parts of the same person. They finished each other's sentences. They were rarely seen apart.

Teulon saw their differences more clearly. Resa gave him companionship, loyalty, and understanding, and she did so without reserve. Jarn did the same, but there was a wall between her and the rest of the world, and she would not permit him to see over it. Sometimes she would not allow him within sight of it.

Jarn, he suspected, knew who Resa was. Just as he did.

"Do you have any final orders for me?" Hasal asked after Teulon had finished his meal.

"See the stores master and have enough synthetics set aside for seventy thousand women and children," Teulon said. "If we fail to take the cities, it will be up to you and the reserve troops to keep them alive until the planet recovers."

The war had destroyed much of Akkabarr's already limited resources; the holdout tribes had also decimated what game had escaped it. Teulon had no doubt he would be victorious, but he would not leave the helpless behind to starve on the barren ice if he had miscalculated.

He noticed his second was scowling. "What is it?"

"You have told me nothing of this attack, so I do not know of what you speak." Hasal removed the dishes and dumped them into a washbasin. "I am useless with women and children. Let Edin see to the people, and take me with you."

"You are the one I trust to see the Iisleg through this if we fail." Teulon looked up as someone stepped through the flap. He did not put his knife away when he saw it was one of his guards. The men knew better than to intrude without invitation. "What is it?"

"An urgent matter, Raktar. Aktwar Navn has returned from Bjola," the guard retorted. "He has brought a windlord prisoner and wishes to relay vital information."

Navn's son, Teulon recalled, had been assigned to ordnance and recovery after proving himself a coward by running from battle. "Send him."

Navn's son entered a few moments later. "Raktar." He gave the diagonal salute of Iisleg respect and pulled back his shoulders. "I have news of the windlords that you must hear. It may well turn the tide of the war."

Teulon waited for Hasal to make one of his usual caustic comments, but his second had vanished. "Speak, son of Navn."

Aktwar took out what appeared to be the collar from a Toskald uniform. "I found one of the enemy cowering inside a privy hole," he said, showing Teulon the insignia on the collar. "A Tos' commander who begged for his life. He offered information if I would spare it."

"What did he say?"

"The commander told me that there are five hundred League ships orbiting the planet, and that Orjakis is preparing to make pact with them." Aktwar gestured toward the roof of the shelter. "They will resupply the windlords with ships and fresh troops if the windlords give them the ensleg female. From how he described her, it is the woman Resa who saved my life."

Teulon had been counting on the Hsktskt blockade to hold a little longer. "When will the League troops arrive?"

"The commander does not know." Aktwar made a casual gesture. "If he had, he would have told me."

Teulon had blades in both hands now. "I gave orders that no prisoner was to be tortured."

Navn's son didn't have the sense to cringe. "It was necessary, Raktar. The man commanded the patrol. He had much knowledge to impart to me, once I began cracking his bones."

He would have to summon Jarn and Resa from their beds. "Take him to the healers' shelter."

"I cannot," Aktwar admitted. "He escaped."

Or was permitted to. Teulon tightened his grip on his blades. "Can you do nothing right?"

A woman rushed into the shelter and threw herself at Aktwar's feet. "Forgive my son, I beg you, Raktar." She tore her face wrap away, displaying a pretty, plump face painted with Iisleg cosmetics. She looked beyond his shoulder. "He only wished to contribute something of importance to the Raktar's glorious coming victory."

Teulon vaguely recalled the woman as Navn's kedera. Whoever she was, she had no business being in the camp. "Why are you not in the trenches with the other women and children?"

"My son permits me to travel with him, so that I may care for his needs, Raktar." Tears spilled down her face. "His father was killed during the avalanche at Elsil. I have no one else. If he dies, so do I."

Teulon saw the only solution. "Navn, take your mother to Mnomo trench. Stay there with her and help guard the others."

Aktwar's jaw sagged. "But, Raktar, the information I brought you—surely this proves I am worthy of joining your personal staff—"

Greed and ambition. That was all the boy had in him. Today five hundred men had died on the ice, and Aktwar Navn had tortured an enemy for information, let him escape, and was now worried only about securing his promotion to the inner circle.

Navn had even brought his mother to take the blame for his mistakes.

He is too stupid to be a spy. "Get out." When neither the boy nor the woman moved, Teulon shouted it. *"Get out."*

Bsak, who was recovering from a bolt wound he had received during the last battle, rose and padded forward into the light. The sight of him released Navn and his mother from their shock, and they stumbled over each other running from the shelter.

The League's arrival was a disaster. Teulon had to take the Toskald cities before the League sent reinforcements to the Kangal. Which meant launching the final phase before schedule.

The next day could well decide the war.

Teulon pulled on his outfurs and armed himself. He could not spend another minute sitting in this shelter. Bsak came to stand before him. The cat gave him a strange look, as if he intended to stop Teulon from leaving.

"I need air." When the cat didn't move, he crouched down to put them on eye level. "You cannot come with me. Sleep. I will need you when we go to Skjonn."

Bsak nuzzled his face once before slowly walking back to the pile of furs where he slept.

Outside, the night air rushed into Teulon's lungs and tried to freeze them. The men had gathered around an open-air heatarc propped over a vent shaft, and were quietly talking while sharing some rations. They all fell silent when they caught sight of the Raktar, standing outside his shelter. A moment later they had their weapons slung as if ready to escort him.

"No. I go alone." Teulon walked off.

He was too far from the small cave now to trek to it, so he made a circuit of the camp. Most of his exhausted troops were asleep. The only light came from the healers' shelter. He was tempted to go and seek out Jarn and Resa, but they would know he was troubled. They always did.

He would go back. He would sleep tonight, so he would not be weary when the dawn came. It might well be his last.

When he returned to the shelter and secured it for the night, Teulon stretched out on the mound of furs opposite Bsak. He did not think he would sleep, but he still tied the silencer over his mouth and closed his eyes. He hated the dreams, but he hoped this night they would come for him. It might well be the last time he shared with Akara, their son, and the House-Clan that had been their lives.

Jado, come to me, he thought, opening his heart to the darkness. *Stay with me, this last walk on the path.*

Slowly he drifted into the twilight world, but no dreams came. Perversely, they were going to leave him in the dark, and that, more than anything, convinced Teulon that the rebellion would fail. Hope was truly done when not even the ghosts of the past would come to haunt his soul.

Or it has come to the moment when I no longer have a soul.

Weight settled near him. Bsak often climbed onto the furs beside him to keep him warm. Teulon reached out from his sleep and stroked silky hair. Akara had possessed the most beautiful hair. Black as the night, falling like dark silk to her hips, and as soft as their infant son's shorter, unruly locks. Teulon had spent hours brushing and braiding his wife's hair.

How I honored you, my heart. How I failed you.

Akara came to him. She did not look frightened this time, as she always had. She seemed only sad. *I am where I am to be, and you have your path. Follow it.*

He reached out to her, and she came into his arms.

Only know the price, she whispered.

There she began to burn, silent, looking up at him through the flames, her cerulean skin darkening to black, peeling away, her bones charring. In her arms, their son huddled as he, too, burned to ash.

This is how I honored them.

His muffled scream jerked him out of the dark, and he sat up, the sweat pouring down his body, his frame shaking. Something was making a soft sound. There were hands stroking him, arms embracing him.

He lifted his hand to untie the strap, but smaller fingers were already at the knot. Another hand brushed the hair back from his eyes. A third hand rubbed a soothing circle over his chest.

"You were dreaming," Resa whispered in the dark to his right, where she lay against him. She turned only for a moment, to throw away the shredded strap.

Teulon felt long hair stream across his chest as Jarn, on his left, wiped the blood from his mouth with her hand.

Eighteen

"Will I be blind?" Reever asked the woman tending to him.

"No." Hands adjusted the furs keeping him warm. "The blindness is only temporary, from the flash of the blast. The healer has checked the insides of your eyes and they are still functioning. She says it will take a few days before you may see again."

He had woken up in some sort of primitive hospital, alive, but with most of his head swathed in bandages. There were seven other men around him, survivors of Bjola, he presumed, and two women moving around the ward who were tending to them.

All were Iisleg.

"Are you thirsty?" the woman was asking him. "The healer said you may have water, or some soup."

The healer.

"There was a healer who found me, at Bjola," he said, choosing his words so as not to alarm the nurse. "If she is here, I must speak to her immediately."

"I do not know who found you, but Jarn and Resa led the vral to rescue the wounded. It was likely one of them, but I will ask. No." Her hand kept him from sitting up. "Stay as you are. You are still weak from the bleeding, and you cannot see to move around, remember?"

Reever took the time the nurse was gone to check the rest of his body. He was battered and bruised all over, and he had a ferocious headache, but he was able to move without impairment. He considered tearing off the bandage, but he didn't need his eyes to recognize his wife.

It was enough to know that he had found her.

An hour passed before she came. "You asked for me?"

"Yes." He turned his face toward the sound of his wife's voice. She said nothing more, and he remembered the bandages. "Do you know who I am?"

"I know you are an ensleg, and you do not have enough sense to take adequate cover during a patrol barrage." Cherijo's cool hands touched the exposed part of his face. "Your fever is gone. I'm very pleased with you. Once your eyes heal, you may rejoin your unit."

She didn't know him. Reever was stunned into silence. *She didn't know him.*

There were a thousand possible reasons as to why, but that didn't matter. All Reever had to do was link with her, and show her the memories of their life together. That would erase whatever had been done to her mind.

"Give me your hand," he said, reaching out.

"Here." She placed her hand in his. "Don't be afraid. Your vision will return, I promise you."

As Reever held his wife's hand, he hesitated. He was not a physician, but he knew that amnesia was not always attributed to physical injury. Sometimes the victim forgot the past to protect the mind. Then there was Cherijo's unique physiology, which was far different from a normal Terran's.

What did this to her? Why doesn't she know me?

He couldn't risk a link until he knew what had happened to her. For that, he needed to see her. He lifted his hands to the bandages.

"No." She drew his hands back. "I know your eyes are itching; it is from the medicine that I put into them. You must not rub or scratch at them."

"I have to see you."

"I am flattered, ensleg, but you can see me tomorrow. Leave the bandage alone until then, and try to sleep while you can." She moved away to check the patient in the berth beside him.

Reever tracked her movements through the ward, and listened to her voice. She spoke flawless Iisleg, and used their idioms, yet also used League medical terms. She would not have been able to recall them had she not remembered something of her past.

Squilyp will know what to do. The Omorr Senior Healer on board the Torin's ship knew a great deal about Cherijo's condition. In the past he had operated on her hands and treated her for a mental aberration that had almost got her killed. He was a skilled surgeon and doctor; he would have an answer to this.

For now, Reever had to get her out of this war and off the world.

As soon as Reever was sure there was no one in close proximity to him, he checked his wrist. Because he was an ensleg, they had left his wristcom in place and activated to translate his voice. Carefully he deactivated it, removed it, and inverted it, and then concealed it in the furs by his head.

The message was prerecorded, so he did not have to speak into the unit before transmitting. There had been only one message that he had ever intended sending. All he had to do was press a switch, and the tiny, powerful transponder inside his wristcom was activated.

It sent a coded signal on a secured channel with an encryption that no one but Xonea Torin could read, so it would make no sense to anyone else who picked it up on relay. The message was very brief.

I have found her.

Reever pressed a second switch. It removed the message and cycled the signal tone only, making it into a beacon. The repeated tone was also something Xonea would understand. It meant that Reever needed assistance getting off Akkabarr.

Now, Xonea, Reever thought as he began working the bandages loose, *show me how much you honor my wife.*

As soon as Resa and Teulon were asleep, Jarn slipped out of the shelter and walked through the bitter cold to the field hospital. The ward nurses were busy inventorying supplies and indicated there were no problems with the patients, who were all asleep.

All but the Terran, Jarn discovered as she went out onto the ward. He was trying to work the bandage from his eyes.

"You must not remove this," she told him as she sat down beside him and removed his hands from his face. "I will put you into restraints if I must."

"I would not recommend you do." He turned his head toward her. "You sound tired."

"I could not sleep." Jarn tucked in a loose fold of linen. "My thoughts are the wind tonight."

"So are mine." His mouth curled on one side. "Tell me about yourself, Healer. How did you come to join the rebellion?"

She could blame Teulon for persuading her, but in truth what she had done was her own fault. "It seemed an intelligent thing to do at the time. Now I have my doubts. What is a Terran doing fighting on Akkabarr?"

"I came to find my wife."

She remembered how he had spoken of her, the first time they had met at the site of the wreck, when she had repaired his facial wound. "Fighting a war is not finding a woman."

"I found her." He took her hand in his. "On a battlefield."

Jarn frowned. "You left her there?"

"In a manner of speaking. She did not recognize me." His fingers felt very warm on hers. "I think she is safer not knowing yet. You are involved with the Raktar."

Jarn thought of Resa and Teulon, sleeping peacefully in each other's arms. Seeing how they looked together had made her feel like an intruder. "In a manner of speaking."

"Do you and the other healer love him?"

What an odd question. "Resa and I are loyal to him. He is a great leader." She inspected his features. "War is not a time for lovers, ensleg."

"When the war is over?"

Jarn sighed. "I cannot say. Now, will you sleep, or

must I club you over the head? I cannot spare the sedatives."

The Terran sat up and brought her hand to his face. "Take off the bandage and check my eyes."

"Or you will rip it off yourself during the night, I suppose?" He nodded. She began unwinding the bandage. "Your eyes have not had time to heal. You will not be able to see anything. Keep them closed until I switch off these lights."

Once the bandage was off, she darkened the emitters near him and returned to his side. "Now, look at me."

The Terran opened his eyes, which were still milky with the medication drops she had put in them to treat the damage. "I can see a little now."

"Good. You heal quickly, Terran." She bent over to replace the dressing. "If you do not acquire an infection from fiddling with your bandages, your full vision should return in another two or three days."

He caught her wrists with his hands. "You are certain of this?"

"It could take a little less time, or a little more."

Jarn wondered if she should use the scarce sedatives on him anyway. "All will be well again, ensleg."

"Yes." He released her. "It will be, soon."

Resa met Jarn outside surgery the next morning, and took the bin with the blackened, amputated foot from her. "How is he?"

"Stable. I was hesitant to use a local, but he was calm enough once we put a curtain in place." After they returned to the hospital, Jarn stripped off her gloves and plunged her hands into the heated water in the washbasin to warm them. The heatarcs were needed for the comfort of the patients, so surgery was always chilly. "How was the Raktar when he woke?"

"Rested." Resa smiled a little. "Grateful."

"When the war is over, he will need someone at his side." Jarn gave her a level look. "It will not be me, Resa. It will be you."

"Who can say what will be?" Resa shrugged. "Teulon left to go to the northern territories. He said it was time to lead the reserves against Skjonn and the other skim cities."

Jarn shook the water from her hands. "It is too soon for that. The third phase was not to be initiated for several days."

"I heard him and Hasal speaking of it earlier," Resa said. "The Kangal is forming an alliance with the League. That will supply the Kangal with all the ships and soldiers he needs, and the war will be over. Teulon must take the cities today."

Men shouting from outside the shelter made Jarn tense. Both women listened as furious protests clashed with one adamant voice.

"That is Hasal." Jarn pulled on her robe and threw one to Resa before running out.

Resa looked down and saw the vral masks sitting where she and Jarn had left them. "Jarn, no." She grabbed them and ran out after her friend.

The Raktar's second was standing in the center of the men, arguing with half a dozen of them.

"No, I have my orders. The Raktar always anticipated this." To another man, Hasal said, "It has been a danger since he came to us. We must continue as he has bidden."

Jarn shoved the men out of her way. "Hasal. What has happened?"

The sight of her made Hasal close his eyes for a moment. "The Raktar's company was on their way to meet with the reserves. They were ambushed." Hasal spit on the ice. "The survivors we found say the only man they took onto the ship was the Raktar. They took him to Skjonn."

"Someone has betrayed us," Resa said as she joined Jarn and Hasal. She looked around the circle. "Who?"

Hasal pulled his knife. "Navn's son. He came last night with tales of League alliances. He told the Raktar that Orjakis was going to get ships and troops from them. He set the plan into motion too soon. He must have done so in order to ambush the general." To one of the rebels, he said, "Fetch him."

Jarn frowned. "Resa, did the Raktar tell Hasal about Aktwar this morning?" She noticed the men staring at her, and reached up to touch her exposed face.

"I tried to stop you." Resa handed her one of the vral masks. "Too late for these, I think."

"You are women," one of the men murmured, his gaze moving from the blob masks to their faces. "Only women."

"It was not me!" Aktwar Navn, struggling between two hunters, was dragged into the circle. "It was them!" He twisted loose and rushed at Jarn, who pulled her blade. He came to a comical halt and spit at the feet of the two women. "Filth, to accuse me of betrayal."

"Actually," Hasal said from behind Aktwar, "it was I who accused you. I heard what you said to the Raktar last night. You lied to send him out into a trap."

"Jarn," Resa murmured, drawing her back. "Teulon's decision to go was based on what this boy told him."

Hasal gave them a quick, hard look, but Navn's son was too busy shouting at the other men to hear what Resa had said. "You see? This ensleg was cast out of my father's iiskar to become skela, like this one. They are filth, and filth always betrays the worthy."

Resa walked up to him. "I saved your life, boy, when you were too afraid to defend it."

He lunged at her and wrapped his hands around her throat. "You will die a proper death this time, ensleg." He stiffened a moment later and collapsed against her.

Behind him, Hasal lowered his crossbow.

Resa lowered the boy to the ground and checked him, but the bolt had penetrated the back of his neck. "He is dead."

"Aktwar!" A woman dressed in a fine robe fought her way to the dead boy's body, and threw herself on top of it. "My son, my son." She sobbed uncontrollably.

One of the hunters said, "You are women. Skela women."

Resa stood and looked at the faces around them. "Yes, we are women. We were skela before we joined the rebellion. So were all the other vral."

"There is not a man here who can say that the vral have not fought as long or as hard or as fiercely as you," Jarn told them. She pulled her hood back so that her long dark hair was exposed, as well.

"No," Hasal said, his voice oddly gentle. "No one can say that."

"It is forbidden . . . ," one of the older men began to say, but glares from the others silenced him.

Resa touched her face. "You could fight with us when you could not see this. I am asking only that you fight with us again, and save our general."

"No," Hasal said. "The Raktar left orders. If the assault on the skim city failed, the remaining troops were to remain on-planet."

Resa felt like wrenching the bolt out of Aktwar and driving it through Hasal's heart. "The assault hasn't failed yet. Edin." The Raktar's commander stepped forward. "Your crossbow." She held out her hand. He placed it in her hands, and she checked it to make sure a bolt was loaded before she leveled it at the woman crouched over Aktwar's body. "Get up, Sogayi."

The Raktar's second stiffened. "What are you doing?"

Sogayi lifted her tearstained face. "You kill my son, and now you would kill me?"

"I will if I am right. How long have you been feeding information to the Tos', Sogayi?" Resa demanded. "Since Navn joined the rebellion? Before?"

Jarn put a hand on Resa's forearm. "Resa, wait."

"No." Resa sighted the bolt. "How did you get word to the Toskald?"

"There have been enough killings this day," Hasal said, his voice harsh. He turned to the men. "Remove the boy's body. I will alert the troops."

Jarn shot a bolt into the ice in front of Hasal's boots, preventing him from taking another step. The circle around them widened. "No, you will not."

"Stop interfering, you idiot female," Hasal shouted.

"While you play with that weapon, our general is dying."

"Dying?" Sogayi gave Resa a look of loathing. "No. He is already dead."

She leaped to her feet and tried to run, but Jarn and Resa had her on the ground before she went a hundred yards. Ice chips flew as the three tumbled over and over.

Resa landed on top and put her blade to Sogayi's throat. "How could you do this? You are Iisleg. These are your people."

"My people." Sogayi spit in her face. "My people made me a whore."

Resa jerked the woman to her feet and turned her to face Aktwar's body. "You killed your own son, Sogayi. For the Tos'."

"My son." Sogayi wrenched free and staggered forward, reaching for the body. "I was sent as tithe to Skjonn. It was better than being camp filth forever, wasn't it? The old rasakt told me that the windlords would be kind. That they would pamper me like a pet."

"Is there anyone else here from Iiskar Navn?" Resa asked.

A hunter stepped forward. "I was born to Navn."

"Does she speak the truth?"

The man nodded. "She was one of the camp whores. She was sent to Skjonn as tithe. The Kangal sent her back as unacceptable."

"How long was she in the skim city?" Hasal asked the hunter.

"A year."

Silence settled over the circle.

"This is the day when all the pretense ends." Sogayi looked past them at the ice. "I was sent by my mother to old Navn, who made me a whore. It was he who sent me to the Kangal. My mother persuaded him to do it. She said it would be better than being made skela for what I had done."

"What was your crime?" Resa asked.

"I fought back when a man beat me for not pleasing him." Sogayi's smile turned ironic. "I did not like it as much as my mother."

"And for this, you betrayed us?" Jarn demanded.

"I didn't," Sogayi said. "I only betrayed Navn. I helped kill the old one. And the young one. And now our son."

Resa's eyes narrowed. "That is the same thing—"

"They have my first child, my daughter. Her name is Poma." Sogayi looked up at the dark blur of Skjonn floating high overhead. "The Kangal told me I would do this or he would kill her. So I said I would. I let him put me in one of his machines. It put things in my flesh. Things that told him everything my ears heard, and told my ears what he wanted. I asked Navn about the general. I gave Aktwar the story. I did everything he asked."

Jarn ran a scanner over the woman. "Transponder implants."

Resa wanted nothing more than to kill Sogayi, but that would not save Teulon. "What will happen now?"

"The Kangal will do something terrible to him. He is very creative. It will take a long time. Perhaps he will do it in front of his new League allies." Sogayi gave Resa a strange look. "He wants you, too. I was to have you captured the next time you went on the ice."

Resa frowned. "Why me?"

"The League has come for you. You belong to them. That is all I know." The Iisleg woman's voice grew dull. "I don't care what you do to me. You have killed my son, but I have saved the life of my daughter. At least one will live."

"No." Jarn grabbed Sogayi by the front of the robe. "There is another life you will save."

The *Sunlace* was on full battle alert as it transitioned into normal space, and turned on a direct heading for planet Akkabarr. On board the Jorenian vessel, every member of HouseClan Torin was preparing for a large-scale assault on the ice world.

"Captain Torin."

Xonea Torin stopped in the corridor and turned to see his Senior Healer hopping out of the medical bay. "Healer Squilyp, there is—"

"—no time left to debate the matter, I know." The Omorr caught up with him. "Our sojourn teams are ready to report to the launch bay on your orders. Medical has prepared to receive mass casualties, as have the Senior Healers on the other ships in the fleet. We have replenished all depleted supplies and tripled our replacement organ stocks."

Xonea relaxed a degree. "I am grateful for your attention to detail."

"It is nothing." Squilyp nodded toward the corridor ahead of them. "May I walk with you to Command?"

The Jorenian captain and the Omorr healer had never considered each other friends, but since Squilyp had taken over as Senior Healer they had come to rely on each other's opinion. Xonea found the Omorr's mind meticulous and efficient, while Squilyp appreciated the Jorenian's uncompromising integrity. They also respected each other's responsibilities, diverse as they were.

"Reever has found her, but he cannot leave the planet," Squilyp said. "The League has most of the Seventh Fleet surrounding Akkabarr. They will not let us take them without a fight."

Xonea stopped to approve a requisition from one of the engineers. When the man strode off, he said, "I know it will not be an easy retrieval."

"Not when the Faction is probably at this moment sending every raider they have within range to attack this world," Squilyp said.

"We will reach Akkabarr before the beasts do." Xonea stopped and faced the Omorr. "I know what you mean to say, Senior Healer. But Cherijo is more than this House. She is a member of the Ruling Council of Joren."

"Captain, if she verifies that the League were at fault for the Jado Massacre—"

"The child is too young." Xonea's expression turned to stone. "Thus we will avenge the Jado as the council has ruled."

No HouseClan on Joren had ever been exterminated before the Jado. The unprecedented slaughter had provoked the Ruling Council to make a horrific decision. If it was ever determined that the Jado had been deliberately butchered, Joren would defend its dead by hunting down every League officer present at the time of the massacre: some forty thousand souls from hundreds of different worlds.

The League had been notified of the council's decision, and returned one of their own. If Joren ever sought such retribution, the League would consider it as an act of war.

"Other worlds will join Joren." Squilyp's voice went lifeless. "Whole systems will be destroyed. Billions will die. Captain, this is not about honor anymore."

"No, not when saving a single life may cost so many." Xonea shook his head. "Sometimes when I cannot sleep, I wonder how many millions of future lives ceased to exist when the Jado were exterminated. We will never know."

"Teulon Jado wanted peace. He died for it." Squilyp rubbed a hand over his face. "Can the child shield the League?"

Xonea's voice grew tight. "Children cannot defend, so they cannot shield. It must be a member of HouseClan Jado, of majority age. They all died on the *CloudWalk*."

"You are sure."

"Think you I have not checked a thousand times?" Xonea shouted. Immediately he made a gesture of regret. "Your pardon, Senior Healer. I am warrior-trained, and yet I never thought to face something like this. It makes me feel a coward. It makes me feel trapped."

"What I ask you now is not a declaration of a threat or an intention, only a hypothetical inquiry," Squilyp said. "If someone killed Cherijo Torin before she verified what happened to the Jado, what would be the result?"

Xonea cursed. "You cannot ask me—"

"Captain," Squilyp said very gently. "Please answer my inquiry."

"That person would be declared ClanKill." Xonea displayed his claws. "I would hunt that person down, and eviscerate that person before the entire House-Clan."

"That would put an end of it. There would be no war between Joren and the League."

"Yes." The words came reluctantly, but Xonea was clear. "That would put an end to it. I do not wish to divert your path, Senior Healer."

"Thank you, Captain. I will not give you any reason to do so." The Omorr turned and hopped away.

NINETEEN

"Raktar of the rebel army," General Gohliya said as he walked in front of the man chained to the wall of the interrogation room. "I had not thought I would meet you alive. Especially not when I discovered who you were before you disrupted our lives, aroused the Iisleg, and tried to take over our world."

Teulon watched him through the damp, knotted curtain of hair veiling his eyes and said nothing.

The old man cocked his head. "It was two years ago, but I am certain that I threw you off that platform myself." He waited for a response before he continued. "Well, slave, you have certainly taken your revenge on your masters. Half my troops are dead; my fleet is virtually crippled. I will yet have my measure, I think. Certainly the Iisleg will be left to starve in the snow."

A younger man entered the room and spoke in hushed tones to Gohliya, who nodded and sent him back out.

"A pity you did not achieve a complete victory," the general said. "It would have made you a hero to the League, who despise us for being slavers like their other enemies, the lizards. Still, only one can win in any conflict, and this time, it was not you."

Teulon knew of two ways he could kill himself

while hanging in the chains, but was not sure how quickly the general might try to prevent it. He would attempt it only if they resorted to drugs.

The general sat at the interrogator's console and toyed with the ornate cuff of his sleeve. At his hand were controls that could inflict ten thousand varieties of pain. "I would give you a soldier's death if I could, but our ruler has decided differently. You will be displayed during his banquet tonight, while he and his new League friends celebrate the Toskald victory. Then you will spend a very uncomfortable month learning just how our beloved ruler obtains his real pleasures." Gohliya looked up. "Unless you would like to tell me what your men did with the contents of the armory trenches?"

Teulon thought of the five reserve battalion commanders, each of whom had specific orders. If the Raktar was captured or killed, each would take command of the third phase. Only one of the five had to be successful. The Toskald did not know that the rebel Raktar had stopped being necessary from the moment the trenches were breached.

"Your men will only waste the weapons," Gohliya said, sitting back in the chair. "Most of them have no idea what a disrupter rifle is, much less how to use one."

The general lapsed into a longer silence, staring at Teulon, waiting for some sign. As the empty room became a vacuum, Teulon turned his thoughts inward. The Kangal's promised execution would call on the last of his reserves, but he would embrace the stars with the dignity and silence that his ClanFather had.

"Very well." Gohliya stood. "We are going down to

take over the surface. It will only be a matter of time." He walked to the door panel.

"I jumped," Teulon said.

Gohliya glanced back. "What did you say?"

"At the platform, two years ago. You did not throw me off. I jumped."

The general smiled a little. "Yes. I believe you did. A pity you landed where you did." He inclined his head and left the room.

"You did not look to see where I landed," Teulon murmured. "That is the pity."

Resa did not want to take Sogayi with them to Skjonn, but there was no one else who knew the Toskald city as well as she. She also claimed to know a place to dock and a way into the palace.

"Transport won't let you dock without authorization," Hasal had warned them after agreeing to use Sogayi's knowledge to retrieve the Raktar from Skjonn. "Even if you destroy the ship's transponder, they'll scan it for ID. They'll know it was lost on the planet, and they'll open fire."

"I know where to put the ship," Sogayi insisted. "There is a place the Kangal uses. It is not known to the army."

"If she's lying," Resa murmured later, as she and Jarn walked up the ramp into the cabin of the patrol ship, "we're all going to die with the Raktar."

"I don't trust her any more than you do," Jarn said as she selected seats close to the helm and sat down. She gathered her dark hair in her hands and began swiftly braiding it. "But if she does not keep her bargain, we have our secondary plan." She glanced at the pilot, then at Resa. "I checked him twice. He can see well enough."

"How is it you always know what I think?" Resa asked, turning the palm blade over in her hand.

"We're both Terran. Too suspicious for our own good." Jarn secured her braid, covering her head with the soft, shimmering hood of her cloak before shrugging into her harness. "Also, your thoughts show on your face."

"Yours do not." Resa clipped her harness into place as the patrol ship's engines engaged. "It is as if you always wear two masks, Jarn."

"She will need both today." Daneeb came out of the lower cargo hold and sat down on the other side of Resa. "I hope this will be brief. The beasts are not happy, especially that silent one." She looked toward the helm. "No one has yet explained to me why we permit this ensleg to pilot the ship."

Resa gazed over at Reever again. She could not club him in the head if he did not behave himself this time. "He is the only pilot at camp who has flown the kvinka before now."

"He is partially battle-blind now, and he crashed the last ship he piloted when he could see perfectly well," Daneeb pointed out. "Could we have not sent to another camp for someone *else?*"

Jarn leaned her head back and closed her eyes as if exhausted. "Daneeb."

"Yes?"

"Shut up," she said in Terran.

Resa smiled at the headwoman's puzzled look. "She says to fasten your harness."

When the ship was off the ground, Daneeb left them

to sit with the other vral. Jarn remained where she was, as still as a pillar of ice.

"I think I will go and sit in the copilot's seat," Resa said, and released her harness. "I may be of assistance to him."

Jarn nodded without opening her eyes.

Resa was not certain why Jarn had permitted the ensleg to accompany them on the rescue mission. He had come from the hospital as they were deciding which patrol ship to take to Skjonn. Jarn had tried to order him back to his berth, but he had drawn her to the side. No one knew what he said to her, but it was enough to change her mind.

It was not as if he were in the best physical shape, Resa thought, studying his thin, bruised face. He didn't act as if he was quite right in the head, either. He caught her watching him, and she smiled. "Are you sure you feel well enough to pilot?"

"Yes."

He was not particularly verbal, either—at least, not with her. He seemed to have a lot to say to Jarn, and Resa wasn't sure how she felt about that. *Well, I did bash him in the skull, the last time we met.*

Resa turned and watched as Jarn, Daneeb, and Hasal went through the final preparations with the other vral for the attack.

"No, you must wear it so." Sogayi bent over to adjust a fold. She looked at another vral. "Too much red, not enough blue. Your brows should be thinner, more arched."

"Have you ever been to one of the skim cities?" Reever asked Resa, distracting her.

The words were innocent enough, but they made

Resa feel suddenly on guard. "No. Well, perhaps. I cannot remember, to be truthful. I suffered a head injury that stole most of my life from me."

"Do you wish to remember?"

Resa considered that. "Sometimes, yes. It is maddening not to know who I was. But I am not from this world, so there are no answers for me here, and since the war started, it seems more important to live in the day."

"What if you must choose between who you are, and who you were?" Reever asked.

"I hope I . . . choose wisely," was all she could think to say.

The flight to Skjonn took only a few minutes, but Reever stayed well beneath the kvinka layer until the vral had finished their preparations. Then he ordered the cargo secured and the rescue team to strap in.

Resa noticed the Terran had become very pale. "What should I do if you cannot make it through the layer?"

"Say good-bye to the others," Reever told her. "Quickly."

The patrol ship jolted as Reever jumped from the temperate zone into the kvinka. The roar of the wind outside filled the ship with an eerie echo, as if it were trying to pry the hull panels apart and get in at them. The view panel was filled with such turbulence that Resa found herself automatically closing her eyes, as if expecting to be struck in the face.

Deeper groans and shudders shook the vessel as Reever maneuvered through the deadly streams of air. Resa saw how he was jumping from place to place, seeking the relatively calm areas and using the more violent currents as conduits to get to them. Behind her, someone was suddenly, abruptly sick.

A final, terrifying jolt made them all jerk in their harnesses, and then the patrol ship was in placid, calm air.

"Skjonn," Reever said, nodding at the viewer panel.

Once the Kangal had retired to have himself prepared for the victory banquet, and the League's ambassador retreated to his quarters to rest, General Gohliya invited his counterpart, General Patril Shropana, to his offices in the palace. They dismissed their aides by mutual unspoken agreement and went there together, discussing on the way a few trivial points of interest within the quadrant, and how the military life often made off-duty time a precious commodity.

Inside his private sanctum, Gohliya had his serving drone bring out one of his best bottles of firewine and two servers before he sent it out and secured the door panel.

"Your ambassador is quite impressive," Gohliya said as he offered Shropana a brimming server of the black red liquid. "Do you have to program him, or does he think up all those polite phrases on his own?"

Shropana was startled into a laugh. "He has had much practice in the art of honorifics and other accoutrements of homage. Fortunate, in this instance. I would have run out of pretty compliments for your Kangal after three minutes."

"That is why I have Lopaul," Gohliya admitted. "He thinks up my lip service for me in advance."

The two men regarded each other for a moment, pleased and guarded.

"How many worlds have had their fate decided in rooms such as these," Gohliya wondered out loud, "by men such as us?"

Shropana sampled the wine. "Not enough."

Someone had to make the first foray into the territory of truth, so Gohliya played polite host. "Things have been much better since we captured the rebel leader."

"I would like a word with this man," General Shropana said, trying to sound casual. "That is, if he is still alive."

Gohliya looked over the rim of his server. "Oh, yes, he is. The Kangal reserves the right to inflict the full punishment of the law whenever he desires. He desires this man. No one else is permitted near him, I fear, so I must refuse your request."

"Indeed. I have the sense our Captain Deyin did not run afoul of your rebels, but of your Kangal." Shropana shook his head. "You need not comment. We should not have sent him here alone. No, I have the greatest sympathy for you, General. I have gathered the impression that you contend with much here."

"Motivation, General, is a marvelous thing." Gohliya set aside his wine and silently produced a scrambling emitter that would prevent their conversation from being overheard by any of the listening devices Orjakis had planted in his offices. He set it out in front of Shropana and activated it. "We will talk about the Terran woman now."

"She is not a negotiable point." Anger made

Shropana's eyes small and hot. "Your Kangal promised her to me."

"Everything is negotiable. He will make promises, our Kangal." Gohliya smiled. "I believe he made several to Captain Deyin. I would verify this with the recipient, but my guess is that he occupies any number of places in the disposal pits."

Shropana made a disgusted sound and subsided. "I thought as much. Do you intend to take over as soon as the rebels surrender?"

Gohliya chuckled. "I have already taken over. The Kangal simply doesn't acknowledge it."

"A little neuroparalyzer at the banquet tonight, and you can have him in a position to acknowledge anything you wish."

"The monarchy of the skim cities is hereditary, General," Gohliya told him. "I am a soldier's son, as common as an engineer or a sanitation worker. Our people have certain standards in rulers. In truth, I could not take over Skjonn if I had ten armies at my command."

"Which you could, if I am persuaded to lend them to you," Shropana said smoothly.

"I do not wish to be the Kangal." Gohliya removed a transparent crystal from his inner jacket and set it on the console between them. It sparkled like a phantom jewel. "I only wish to control his power base. The most valuable ice on Akkabarr, General."

Shropana took it into his hands. "Permanently etched?"

Gohliya nodded. "Stored here for centuries. The first exchange of space for crystal began with one world. They gave us the command override codes to control their fleet, etched on indestructible crystal, which we verified. They also agreed to defend Akkabarr should we ever call upon them. In exchange we provided them with safe storage for their ordnance. Once we had proved trustworthy and did not use the crystals to take over their fleet, or sell their weapons, they recommended our services to their allies. Thus, word of our services spread. Our entire civilization was built on our reputation for safe, secure storage. There is no armory safer than Akkabarr."

"Or was, until your rebellion," Shropana reminded him.

"Akkabarr is not a vault so easily defeated. The rebels have no ships, and no experience traversing the kvinka if they did, so they cannot leave the planet." Gohliya moved his shoulders. "They have done what I could not, however. They took the keys to Akkabarr out of the Kangal's control."

"Rebel ice." Shropana smiled at his own joke. "When you have all of the crystals, will you use them?"

"We already do, to provide the security we crave, by not using them," Gohliya said. "The rebels don't know what they are, and even if they have some idea, they can't use them. I propose to put them back precisely where they were, only with my guard drones in place instead of the Kangal's. That is where you would come in."

"You want help getting them back."

"I don't know where they are. I will need your men down on the surface with mine to search these rebel encampments." Gohliya poured more firewine into his server and offered the same to Shropana, who shook his shaggy head. "We have only a short time to find and relocate them. We can supress news of the crystals being taken from the trenches, but not forever. Many of our clients have already made some anxious inquiries."

"That can be done." Shropana drained his glass. "In return, of course, you guarantee me the Terran woman."

"I would like to know more about this woman everyone regards as so valuable." Gohliya pulled up a data file on his console. "The files Deyin carried were unclassified; they only list the decision to classify her as a nonsentient, and the criminal charges against her. Collaborating with the Hsktskt is the most serious, I presume?"

"She sold me and my fleet to the lizards," Shropana snapped. "Hundreds of my people were butchered. Some were eaten."

"Regrettable. I have heard rumors of a bioengineered clone that escaped a Terran laboratory. This clone was female, and allegedly the first true immortal bioconstruct." Gohliya switched off the viddisplay. "Is this the same female?"

"We don't know. She is very hard to kill, that much I can attest to." The League general rose. "Whatever she is, she is my price for providing assistance to you."

Gohliya weighed the demand. He needed the crystals to gain irrevocable control over the Kangal. On the other hand, what man would not be tempted by the prospect of immortality?

"Her value would surpass that of your crystals," Shropana said, his voice rough, "except that she also carries a Hsktskt blood price on her head."

That decided it. Gohliya would not antagonize his

suppliers in the Faction for what was only a slim chance at immortal life. If this Terran woman was being hunted by the Hsktskt, she would need ten armies to protect her.

"If she lives, she will be yours." He checked the time and stood. "The banquet will be starting shortly. Let me show you to your quarters so you can freshen up for the festivities."

Janzil Ches Orjakis had watched Gohliya's attempt to interrogate his former slave. The general had not employed the console, but Orjakis was sure it was not out of respect for the Kangal's demand that the rebel leader remain untouched. Gohliya, he suspected, had ordered three of his men to methodically beat the Raktar while he was being transported from the planet to Skjonn. Now the magnificent creature was covered with wounds, and not one of them inflicted by hands that would adore doing so.

It was not the only thing the general had done to cheat Orjakis. *He always has to spoil things.*

What had to be dealt with, and soon, could not ruin the Kangal's mood entirely. There were too many pleasant things happening for Orjakis now. The League ambassador, a charming male with the most elegant turn of phrase, had made many significant promises. *The Toskald need not continue being made to serve slavers;* now, that had been particularly inspired. The League was willing to forget all the unpleasantness of the past and become friends to the Toskald.

All he had to do was make the right impression at the banquet, and slit his Defense general's throat before Gohliya did the same to him.

Orjakis suddenly realized he had nothing to wear to the banquet, and summoned ten dressage drones. "We require new garments brought for our inspection, Senior Dressage. A selection of one hundred to begin."

The drone he had addressed scooted forward. "I see Janzil Ches Orjakis, Kangal of Skjonn. We would happily supply the Kangal with all the Kangal requests, but Acquisitions has no more garments worthy of our Kangal."

"We are not asking for weapons, ships, or men, only that which may enhance our physical perfection." Orjakis frowned. "Why are there no more garments worthy of us?"

"Garments for the Kangal have always been created from materials provided through tithe tribute," the drone stated. "No such materials have been delivered for eight months, nineteen suns, and—"

"Enough." Orjakis waved the drone away and gnawed at his lip. How would he look beautiful for his new League friends if there was nothing for him to wear? "Shall we go naked to our own banquet?"

None of the drones responded, as they had not been addressed directly.

"This is infuriating. *We* are the *Kangal* of *Skjonn*." Orjakis paced around the chamber before he stopped. This repulsive situation might actually solve his other problem, namely finding out what Gohliya had planned for him. All he had to do was have one of the slaves take his place at the banquet for a short time while he searched the general's offices and planted another recording drone. For that, he would need his own disguise. "Senior Dressage, summon Defense's lackey—what is his name?"

"Defense's senior staff consists of Commander Lopaul, Lieutenant Commander Fhren, Lieutenant Commander Appulus—"

"Lopaul. That one is his favorite, and precisely the right size." Orjakis rubbed his arms. "Summon Lopaul to our presence."

Twenty

Reever maneuvered the patrol ship into the abandoned docks using only lift thrusters. It took longer to move the ship into position, but there was less chance that their minimal energy signature would attract attention from the city's defenses.

"The dock is clear," he told the women after scanning the area.

Resa, Jarn, and the other vral were already waiting to exit the ship, and followed Hasal and Sogayi out as soon as the docking ramp had been extended. Reever secured the helm and locked down the ship's controls. Daneeb stayed behind to open the lower cargo hold doors.

Once the other women were off the ship, Reever closed the outer door panels and waited for her. Daneeb slowed her step as she emerged back into the cabin and saw him, but went to her pack and begun to dress.

"I am astonished, ensleg," she said to Reever as she donned her robes. "You did not crash us after all."

"You are welcome." He checked his blades. "Daneeb, there is something I must know before we go into the palace. Why did you never tell Resa what happened, that day on the ice?"

She went still. "I spend every day on the ice. Of which do you speak?"

"You know the day." The images he had taken from the mind of the nurse still haunted him. "The day the child was sacrificed to protect the skela. Why, after that, did you conceal the truth of how that was done from her?"

"I do not know what you mean." Daneeb quickly covered her face. "I have nothing to say to you, anyway. You tried to break my neck. I should skewer you before I begin on the Tos'."

"The sequence of events is not important." Reever came to stand before her. "The two years you have kept your silence are. Did you lie to protect her, or both of them? I must know."

She recovered from her shock quickly. "You speak nonsense. I have a general to find, and windlords to kill." When she tried to push past him, he caught her by the arms. "You are crazy. I have lied to no one."

Reever caught the fist she drove at his face. "You will tell them what happened that day on the ice."

"You know nothing."

"I know everything. Malmi was there, and for a one-eyed woman, she saw a great deal." He met her furious gaze. "This will be your last chance to tell the truth. She leaves with me today."

Daneeb smirked. "You think she will go with you, just so easily? You dream out loud, ensleg. You are nothing in her heart. She doesn't know you. She has forgotten everything about you."

"She will remember." Reever released her. "Tell them everything, Daneeb, or I will."

He opened the hull doors and walked down the

ramp. Hasal was organizing the women into smaller groups and going over with Sogayi how to gain access to the palace through the least-guarded entrance.

"They keep the drone guards at the busiest entries, so they may scan all the people coming in and out." Hasal was walking around, checking the women's robes and faces. "Say nothing. I am your escort; Sogayi is the only one who speaks." He checked the Toskald uniform he wore before glancing at Reever. "You cannot come with us. They will have scans posted of you."

"I will not be caught," he assured Hasal as he pulled on the robe of a slave trader.

"Be it on your head." Hasal turned to Jarn. "Sogayi's daughter is kept with the other children of the palace, in the sublevel beneath the courtyard. When you begin, that is where I will go. I will bring Poma back here to the ship and wait."

Reever scanned the faces of the vral. They did not appear frightened, or even apprehensive, at the prospect of entering the most heavily guarded structure in the city. They knew what would happen to them if their ruse was discovered. It did not matter. Only their Raktar did. He was the center of their small, war-torn universe.

You are nothing in her heart. She doesn't know you. She has forgotten everything about you.

Daneeb's words didn't frighten him. Whether she remembered or not, whether she was willing or not, Reever was leaving Akkabarr today with his wife.

Teulon had heard the general issue the orders that he not be beaten again. They were ignored, for the most part, as two guards dragged him from the interrogation chamber and into a preparation room. One well-aimed baton sent him back into the darkness.

He woke again when an icy splash of water struck him in the face.

"No more, Kallis, he is bleeding from the nose and mouth." A rough cloth scoured Teulon's face. "The general will have our hides for this."

"My brother died at Bjola," the guard named Kallis said. "I want due for my family."

"So do we all, but the Kangal will take it for us. Now prop him up." Cold alloy bands cinched tightly around Teulon's neck, chest, waist, knees, and ankles. "Watch the neck. He can't breathe." The constricting band loosened. "Better. Are we supposed to do something with his face?"

"Why? Let them see the animal for what he is." Another kick landed in Teulon's ribs.

"Enough, Kallis. He has to live through the banquet, at least." Footgear shuffled, and a winch was engaged.

Teulon remained limp, keeping his muscles and chest distended as much as possible. Through the slits of his eyelids he saw they had bound him to a Hsktskt discipline post attached to a glidecart base.

"All right." Hands checked the alloy bonds. "He's secure. Let's move him out."

The pole jerked, and Teulon was hauled out of the room and into a long, wide corridor empty of people. The guards were behind him, steering the cart, so he kept his head hung low while he inspected his surroundings. The corridor opened out into a seven-sided courtyard under a transparent dome. Large tables, lavishly decorated, were set and ready to hold food and drink. Slaves dressed in celebratory livery were setting out the large round floor cushions upon which the guests would recline. A group of drones occupied one discreet corner, where they were making fine adjustments on Toskald musical instruments.

"The old man said to put him in the center of the yard," Kallis said. "Raise him higher. Yes, like that. He thinks himself above all; let him hang there."

The sun was in Teulon's eyes, and he closed them. He understood the necessity to display and humble an enemy before kin, but his people took the matter far more seriously than the Toskald. They did not treat enemies as if they were no more threatening than a place setting or a floral centerpiece.

I should have tried to break my neck with the chains before they took me down.

He had exacting control over his body, control he had learned from his months on the slaver ship. If the Kangal decided to begin his torture here, at this feast, it would not be in earnest. Orjakis would wait until he was away from the eyes that by law had to be on him before he shed his armor of vanity and truly enjoyed himself.

Teulon had seen Orjakis do that. He preferred to die here, now.

Because he had kept his lungs filled and his muscles distended, the bands supporting his body were not as secure as they should have been. The guards had removed his tunic and his footgear, leaving him only his trousers. His body was still damp from the water they had used to revive him. The guards had raised him up almost a meter from the ground. Once he freed himself from all but the band encircling his neck, there would be no support for his body weight. If his neck did not snap and end his life, the loss of blood to his brain would do so.

The sun slowly moved over the curve of the clear dome overhead. Once the tables were prepared, the well-dressed slaves disappeared into the palace. Teulon was left alone with the drone musicians, who practiced short measures and then fell idle, as they were not programmed to play to an empty room.

Men facing death often took notice of things they had never regarded much in the past, and Teulon was no exception. The Toskald's ridiculous table decor was made of real flowers, and it had been years since he had smelled the scent of fresh blooms. None were like the flowers of Joren, but they reminded him of home. The color of the material used as draping and table coverings was almost the same shade as the sea had been when he and Akara had walked together on the dark sands that first week he had spent at her family's HouseClan. The brilliant blue of the manganese tiles on the courtyard floor reminded him of his son Xan's skin.

The shapeless, formless ghost from the little blue cave materialized in front of his face. Or perhaps the pain was making him hallucinate. He would never know, and it mattered not anymore.

"Spirit," he greeted her, and then saw the shapeless light take form.

Bondmate, Akara said, floating in front of him.

Teulon wondered if he had been drugged. *It was you, in the cave, all this time?*

She answered him as if she could read his thoughts. *Two that are made one can never be parted, my heart, but I think this will be the last time I come to you. For there is another now.*

No. He tugged at his bonds, trying to free a hand. *There will never be anyone but you.* He looked into the ghost light of her eyes. "Take me with you."

Akara shook her head slowly. *I will wait, my heart. There is another who will honor you in my place. This is my gift to you, Teulon. I release you from our Choice.*

The spirit of his dead bondmate drifted over him, only the barest movement of the air, and wrapped herself around him. Teulon's head fell back as the scent of her filled his head. Something touched his face. Gradually the embrace faded.

When he opened his eyes, the vision of Akara was gone.

Teulon thought of nothing as he began to work the edge of one claw against the strap at his waist. He did not sever it completely, but made it so that it would snap with one jerk of his body. By the time he had rendered it so, his claw had worn through and snapped off. He waited to assure he was not bleeding again before inching his hand up to the band across his chest.

By the time the slaves began ushering in well-dressed men and women and seating them at the tables, Teulon had all of the straps around his body prepared, and had worked the strap at his ankles loose enough to slip his feet out of it. He went motionless and hung with his head down, pretending to be unconscious when some of the braver attendees came over to inspect him.

One couple discussed the prospect of purchasing him. "My, he is a large, strong specimen. Think of the work that we could get out of this one." The male, a slim and handsome Toskald official, tried to reach up and test the muscles of Teulon's leg with his hand.

The woman with him, a breathtakingly lovely female who looked no older than an adolescent girl, eyed the snarl of hair covering Teulon's face. "Not Iisleg, obviously. Lovely skin. What species is he, darling?"

"Jorenian, I think." The man stepped back to have another look. "I'd have to see the eyes to be sure."

"I may be able to persuade the Kangal to sell him to me," the woman said. "I did give Orjakis that pretty little feral woman he took a fancy to at our last party."

"If he's a Jorenian, dear, that would be a very bad bargain." Her male companion slipped his arm around her and guided her away from Teulon. "You know they never last long in captivity."

Guests soon lined every table, but the balcony directly across from Teulon, where the Kangal would come out to greet his guests, remained empty. Slaves carried out platters of food and took their positions, waiting for the prince of the city to appear so they could begin to serve. The Kangal's highest officials, the last to arrive, were finally in place, and Orjakis still did not make an appearance. The guests began whispering, then murmuring.

General Gohliya rose from his table and walked over to stand beneath the balcony. He held up his hands for silence. "Colleagues, allies, and friends of the Toskald, I welcome you to the Kangal's celebration of victory over the Iisleg rebels."

Teulon closed his eyes.

"Our beloved prince has been unavoidably detained, no doubt in preparations to please us, as he always does. As I am but a soldier in the service of our great city of Skjonn, I cannot hope to greet you with the eloquence he would offer. The Kangal sent a message to beg us all to enjoy ourselves until he can join us. So." There was a clapping of hands. "Let the banquet begin."

Sogayi led Hasal and the vral to the office of the palace steward. The man was so nervous about the banquet arrangements that he raised no alarm over their arrival.

"Procurement said nothing to me about entertainment with whores and animals," he said to Hasal.

"It is a surprise for the Kangal. Here is the order for it." He took out a stunner and shot the steward. To Jarn, he said, "I will go and get the girl now. Wait as Sogayi says, until the music begins."

Jarn had ordered that Sogayi not carry any weapons, but the Iisleg woman had managed to conceal a blade. As the vral entered the corridor outside the courtyard, she fell back and then ran silently after Hasal, keeping to the shadows so that he would not see her. She waited outside the level where the Kangal's children were kept, and met him when he came out, alone and silent.

"Poma?" she asked, looking around him for her daughter.

He looked at her. "She is not here."

"But she cares for his children."

"There are no children here. Only a drone and a disposal pit. I accessed the drone's memory core." Hasal caught her by the arm as she tried to go around him. "She is dead. They are all dead."

Sogayi didn't believe him. She had to go inside and find her daughter. So Hasal took her into the execution chamber, and showed her the remains of the infants and young children that had been dumped there.

"We will return to the courtyard," he said, looking down into the pit of bones. "The vral need—" He crumpled to the floor.

Sogayi pulled her blade out of his back and wiped the blood on her robe. "I need," she said as she stripped him out of his uniform. "I need."

Once she had put on the uniform and tucked her hair back in Toskald fashion, she left the chamber and headed for the level where the Kangal's private chambers were located. It was there that she saw him walk out. He was dressed in a Defense staff uniform, and his face was clean of his usual cosmetics, but it was him. He headed in the direction of the courtyard.

The vral did need help, and Sogayi was sorry she had killed Hasal. Here was something she could do. She caught up with him. "Commander."

He looked back at her, annoyed. "We are—I am in a hurry. What is it?"

To do what was necessary, she needed to get him away from the palace. She had only a blade, and there were too many drones here programmed to respond to his voiceprint.

You will spy for us, or we will throw your daughter to the kvinka.

"Defense sent me. The rebel leader escaped," she lied. "He is pinned down at the abandoned docks."

Outrage made his mouth spring open. "What?"

"The men are afraid to kill him until the Kangal arrives to pass judgment," Sogayi assured him. "Yet the Kangal cannot be found. No one knows what to do."

"We will see to it." He turned and strode off.

Sogayi followed him to the docks, where he turned and looked for the rebels and his guards. He saw her. "Where is he, you idiot?"

"I see Janzil Ches Orjakis, Kangal of Skjonn," Sogayi said as she removed the headgear and shook out her hair. "Do you remember my face?"

Orjakis scowled. "God, not you. You were supposed to stay with the rebels until this is over. Go away." He looked down at the blade in her hand, and a smile crept over his face. "You would threaten me? Have you forgotten about that brat of yours?"

"Of ours, Kangal. You sired her on me. Why did you have her killed as soon as I left to join the rebellion? I did everything you asked of me."

"I do as I please. You can't do anything to me." The Kangal laughed. "You're only a woman."

"Yes."

Orjakis saw her eyes and took an involuntary step back. "There was a mistake. I am in the mood to be merciful, given your service to me. You can have a place in the palace."

"No. There is only one place for me now, Kangal." Sogayi threw her blade into his right arm. "At your side."

She ran toward him as fast as she could. She didn't stop when he took out a pistol with his only good hand and fired at her. She didn't stop when the pulses struck her body, or when he ran down the dock. She didn't stop when he ordered her to, and then begged her to. With the last of the life in her body, Sogayi slammed into Janzil Ches Orjakis and jumped with him into the swirling vortex beneath the docks.

The kvinka swallowed them.

Teulon heard the sounds of pleasure and greed as the slaves brought forward the platters of sumptuous food. He could not remember his last meal, but it had been the same thin soup of native meat and synthetic compounds that he and the rest of the Iisleg had subsisted on for many months now.

The drone musicians began to play low, elegant Toskald music. Utensils clinked; wine gurgled into fluted servers. A single, staccato laugh rang out and just as quickly broke off. Feminine voices passed around him and drifted out of the courtyard. The scent of wine became heavy.

"Now that the ladies have gone for their cake," Gohliya's voice, somewhat blurry now, said, "let us have our small entertainment."

The man chuckled and laughed, until a jlorra snarled.

Teulon opened his eyes.

Twenty robed women came into the courtyard. Rather than drift in on hover cushions, as the court prostitutes always did, each rode on the back of a snow tiger. The jlorra had been tethered and muzzled.

The sight of so many helpless women astride the deadliest creatures on Akkabarr made the Toskald men go still with shock. The offworlders, oblivious to the danger, applauded. Someone made a spluttering sound as he choked on his wine.

When the women and the beasts filled the center of the courtyard, a drunken Toskald voice called out,

"You see, ensleg? Skjonn has entertainments like no other city."

That seemed to be a signal to the other Toskald men, who produced somewhat convincing laughter. Teulon saw Gohliya nodding to the musicians, who began to play the music to which the prostitutes would dance.

The women dismounted and shed their outer robes. Beneath them were scanty, stylized fur bands that barely covered their breasts and loins. Their faces, painted with delicate cosmetics, were more lovely than those of the Toskald women who had left the banquet.

"General!" a laughing voice called out. "Alert the city guard, the rebels have at last invaded Skjonn!"

More, genuine laughter filled the courtyard.

Teulon watched the women as they stroked the jlorra with their hands, making a small dance of the petting, caressing each beast as if it were a man. The guests were too busy joking and drinking and ogling the prostitutes to notice that as they danced, the women were unfastening the tethers and muzzle straps on the cats.

Just as the women fanned out around the cats, there was movement above them on the Kangal's balcony.

"Janzil Ches Orjakis, the Kangal of Skjonn," a drone announced.

Teulon saw the men look up to watch the entrance of the ruler. The women dancing turned in unison to face the balcony, as well, but did not stop their dance. They moved out, leaving their beasts sitting in the center of the courtyard, and wove their way around the banquet tables. They teased the courtiers, trying to draw their eyes away from Orjakis, but the courtiers were too well trained, and the dancers had to be content to stand behind the men and rub their hands over their bodies. Once they had teased the guests, the women moved on to undulate in front of the guards.

Orjakis, cloaked from head to toe in a hooded scarlet robe, moved into view on the balcony in slow, princely fashion.

Teulon saw one of the women pull the rifle from a guard's shoulder. She turned slightly, and her face and hair began to melt from her head, turning into the same blob that had made the vral faceless. The same thing was happening to the other dancers, who were also playfully disarming the guards.

The guards who could not look away from the Kangal.

"Now," one of the women shouted.

The prostitutes, armed with the pulse rifles they had taken from the guards, stepped back and trained the rifles on the Toskald.

"Over there. In the center," one of the dancers ordered. When one of the guards lunged at her, she shot him in the leg.

The jlorra rose on all sixes and shook off their tethers and muzzles.

The band around Teulon's neck disappeared. "When I release these, can you jump down?" Resa's voice asked from behind him.

"Yes."

"Be ready." She cut through all the bands. "Now."

Teulon jumped and landed on the polished tile. Two guards rushed at him, but Bsak was there and knocked them both to the ground in one leap. The other jlorra had worked their way through the assembly and were menacing the guests.

Resa handed Teulon a rifle. "I am happy to see you still alive, Raktar."

He pulled her into the circle of one arm and held her at his side as he assessed the situation. The cats would keep the guards at bay, but not for long. "We will leave."

Several Toskald men shrieked in horror, and Teulon looked up in time to see one of the presentation drones push the Kangal over the balcony. He fell screaming to land with a liquid thud on the courtyard floor.

General Gohliya fought his way over to the body of the Kangal and pulled him over onto his back. It was not Orjakis in the Kangal's robes, but a slave who bore only a superficial resemblance. He looked up, meeting Teulon's gaze. "They are only slave women," he shouted to the guards. "Use your swords!"

The first soldier who charged a dancer, his sword ready, fell back and collapsed, the front of his uniform burned. A jlorra pounced on top of him and gnawed with enthusiasm at his head.

No one moved after that.

"Go." Resa slipped out of Teulon's hold as she gestured to the entrance from which she and the women had entered. "Jarn is waiting outside for you."

"You will follow me."

She smiled up at him. "Very soon."

Teulon strode to the entrance. Outside the courtyard, Jarn stood armed and waiting. She wore, not the disguise of a prostitute, but that of a female merchant.

"Raktar." She handed him the cloak and his seven-bladed sword. "Have you had your fill of court?"

"Yes." He covered himself and his blade. "Do you have a ship ready?"

"At the abandoned docks. We must—" Jarn pivoted away from him and threw the blade in her hand. Something fell to the ground behind Teulon, and he turned to see General Gohliya, a disrupter pistol sagging in his limp hand. The hilt of Jarn's dagger protruded from his right eye socket. The healer went over, bent down, and checked the general's neck with her fingers before wrapping her hand around her blade and tugging it out of his head. She looked up at Teulon.

"I was wrong." She touched the blood on the blade, coating her fingers with it. "We are the same." Hand trembling, she smeared the blood over her face.

"Jarn." Teulon barely caught her before she hit the ground. Her head lolled on his arms.

Then Resa was there, staring in horror at the limp body of her friend. The other vral gathered around them. "Teulon, is she dead?"

"No." Teulon lifted Jarn and held her cradled in his arms. "She killed for me."

Reever stepped out of the shadows. "They are here, although I do not know from where they came."

The light dimmed all around them. Teulon looked up into the darkened sky above the city dome, where innumerable ships hovered. Ships of every design from League to Toskald to Hsktskt.

Ships that bore the scars of crash landings, and rebuilding. Ships that bore the symbols of every iiskar on Akkabarr.

Daneeb frowned. "How?"

"I am the ClanSon of a shipbuilder. I was also a

pilot," Teulon said, staring up at them. "The Iisleg have been collecting derelicts for centuries. All they needed was time, someone to show them how to build the parts back into ships, and someone to teach them to fly."

Reever looked up at the rebel fleet. "That is why they made you Raktar."

"Yes." Teulon looked down at Jarn's face. "I gave them ships, and taught them to fly them. So they could have their war."

Twenty-one

The day after the rebel fleet conquered the skim cities of Akkabarr, Hsktskt raiders formed a new and much larger blockade. The League, unable to leave orbit without risking an engagement they could not win, and finding no sanctuary in the rebel-held skim cities, appealed to Captain Xonea Torin of the *Sunlace* to intervene as a neutral third party.

"Your people are experienced negotiators," League General Shropana said over his emergency relay to Xonea. "We have every confidence in you."

Xonea watched the sweat bead on the man's upper lip for a few moments. "The Hsktskt are not a threat any longer, General. The rebels have the skim cities and the crystals from the Toskald vaults on the planet. They are the ones with whom you must negotiate."

"Their leader is said to be one of your kind," Shropana said. "He will listen to you."

"Will he?"

"You may use my command ship for your talks if you like."

Xonea sat back. "I will not be drawn into another League deception, and I have no desire to speak for your actions here at Akkabarr. No, General, if you wish to negotiate, you will come here, to my ship, and speak to the rebel leader personally."

Shropana did not think it over for long. "When?"

Xonea told him before terminating the relay. He looked across the console at Duncan Reever. "That much is done. Were you successful with the Hsktskt?"

"I contacted them and asked for a representative to be sent for the negotiations," Reever told him. "They are sending TssVar."

Xonea rubbed his face. "Has there been any signal from Skjonn?"

"No. He will come at the time he said. He has no reason to avoid it." Reever looked through the viewport at the white sphere that was Akkabarr. "You are not to interfere. No one is. Make that known."

"Duncan—"

Reever rose and left the room.

Xonea signaled the Senior Healer. "I want a full medical evac team in the launch bay in one hour."

Shropana was the first to arrive. He and his contingent of diplomats observed every known Jorenian courtesy in greeting Xonea Torin and his flight crew.

"We will hold this meeting in launch bay," Xonea told the League general as he escorted them there. "It is the only place on my ship large enough to accommodate all three parties."

"So you were able to convince the lizards to send someone? That is no small feat." Shropana had to trot to keep up with the Jorenian's long strides. "I suppose if anyone wishes to leave, launches will be provided?"

Xonea's expression remained blank. "I doubt anyone will wish to leave."

OverLord TssVar arrived with a detachment of heavily armed Hsktskt centurons. The eight-feet-tall, six-limbed reptilian commander said nothing to the Jorenians, and remained silent as he was escorted to the launch bay, where he and his men took up positions opposite the League contingent. His saucer-sized yellow eyes watched everyone and everything.

Reever escorted Raktar Teulon and his three vral guards to the launch bay. The rebel leader had kept his furs and borrowed only a black cloak, which he wore with the hood drawn over his face.

Outside the launch bay, Reever paused and looked up at Teulon. "This would be the last opportunity you have to change your mind, Raktar."

"I will not." He gestured at the door panel, which Reever silently opened.

Jarn and Resa stayed on either side of Teulon, while Daneeb followed behind them. The women wore their vral masks, and the sight of their faceless heads seemed to startle the League men. TssVar and the Hsktskt merely watched in silence as Teulon walked up to exchange greetings with Captain Torin.

"Linguist Reever has not been very forthcoming about you," Xonea said after they had exchanged greetings. "All I know is that you are Jorenian. Of what House, Raktar?"

Shropana strode forward to interrupt. "You Jorenians can conduct your family reunion another time. There are four thousand ships out there, poised to fire on each other. I want safe passage out of this system for my fleet. What will it cost me?"

"Far more than you think, General." Teulon pulled back his hood.

Shropana's eyes widened, and he became a statue. "You're dead. They told me you threw yourself to the wind."

"The wind threw me back." Teulon looked at the Hsktskt OverLord. "I am Teulon Jado, ClanLeader of HouseClan Jado, taken prisoner by the League during the Jado Massacre, sold as a slave to the Toskald, and left to rot on this world."

"You have an interesting manner in which you rot, General," TssVar said.

No one moved as Teulon removed his cloak and handed it to one of the vral.

"This man is a slave and a liar," Shropana said. "If he intends to blame us—"

Teulon did not draw his seven-bladed sword. He removed a handful of transparent crystals, the surfaces of which were etched. "The treasure of Akkabarr." He handed them to Xonea. "There are forty thousand more down on the planet." To the Hsktskt, he said, "These are crystals permanently etched with the command codes needed to issue orders to the fleets, armies, and military forces of ten thousand systems within this galaxy. These command codes use corresponding crystals in the command database on each vessel to override any other commands issued by anyone or anything. The matching crystals are set in a matrix, invented by the Toskald, that cannot be removed from the databases or destroyed unless the ship is. I possess all of the override codes to these crystals."

"You cannot use them," Shropana said. "You do not have the means—"

"The command transponders in each of the skim cities are now manned by my men and women," Teulon said. "I have but to issue the order, and the crystals will be activated." He watched Shropana draw a small weapon from his tunic. "Killing me will make no difference. The order will be issued if I do not return to Skjonn in one hour."

"What is the order, Raktar?" TssVar walked forward. "Do you intend to use these forces to attack the League, or the Hsktskt? We are not responsible for the Jado Massacre."

"The League will fight," Shropana said, but his face had gone ashen, and there was no strength left in his voice.

"ClanLeader Jado." Xonea Torin handed the crystals back to him. "You have the right to declare ClanKill on those responsible for the death of your House. Do not make that into a war."

Teulon's face became an impassive mask. "General Shropana issued the order, but my kin embraced the stars because we were asked to negotiate peace between the League and the Faction. Both sides are responsible."

"Even with your crystals, you cannot destroy all of us, Raktar," TssVar said softly. "You will have to choose to take your revenge of the League, or the Hsktskt."

"I was told, long ago, that I no longer had the privilege of Choice." Teulon drew his sword and pointed it at Shropana. "You informed me of that, General, before you handed me over to the slavers bound for Akkabarr."

Xonea grabbed the general and dragged him in

front of Teulon. He forced Shropana onto his knees. "Take him if you must, Jado, but let this one life suffice."

Teulon looked down at the League general. Instead of cowering, Shropana straightened his shoulders and kept his gaze steady. "You said so many things on the day you slaughtered my kin," Teulon said. "Have you nothing to tell me now, General?"

"I am a soldier," Shropana said. "I followed my orders."

Teulon's claws shot out.

One of the vral came forward. She made no move to protect the general, but stared at him. "When the battle is over, everything terrible and strong falls. It becomes sad and helpless, like him."

No one moved as the vral removed her mask, revealing Jarn's face.

"We vral have carried the wounded and the dead from your battlefields," she said, turning so that she addressed every warrior present. "Some of us have fought on them." She gazed at Shropana. "I have killed for you, Teulon Jado. You will listen to me now."

The Raktar nodded.

"The battle is over here. Teulon, you can ignore those who have fallen. You can give them a merciful death. Or you can save them. It is in your hands now." She looked at the mask in her hands, and let it fall to the floor.

"What would you have me do, Jarn?" Teulon asked.

She inclined her head. "No one can take that choice from you, Raktar. No one can make it for you."

It seemed an eternity before Teulon moved. He

lifted his sword above Shropana's head, and then slowly replaced it in his shoulder sheath.

"I shield General Patril Shropana," he said, his voice clear and strong. "As I shield all those who were responsible for the Jado Massacre. The sacrifice of my HouseClan was for peace. I will honor this by completing the mission I began two years ago. I will negotiate peace between the League and the Hsktskt."

The war was over.

The Hsktskt and the League agreed to a temporary cease-fire to allow each other's forces to withdraw from the region. Before they left the *Sunlace*, Shropana and TssVar agreed to relay Teulon's offer to reestablish peace negotiations to their superiors.

"I think there is hope for this peace," Xonea said after the two commanders had gone. "Considering you possess the means to destroy either side at your whim."

"For a time." Teulon pulled on his cloak. "If they wish to continue the war, all they need do is contact the worlds of ten thousand systems and inform them that the Toskald no longer possess the crystals, but that I do. A way will eventually be found to remove the databases, which will render the crystals useless."

"Which systems use the crystals?" Xonea asked.

Teulon glanced out at the stars. "That is why it will take them time. They don't know which systems to contact. You must have the crystals to know."

"I hope you have them where they cannot be found," Xonea said. "There is something else I must tell you, Teulon."

Now that the dignitaries had departed, other members of HouseClan Torin entered the launch bay. One small, blond girl ran across the deck to Duncan Reever, who picked her up in his arms.

"She is a beautiful child." Teulon frowned as he saw a taller, sturdy boy of the same age walk over to greet Reever. His skin was a beautiful blue, the same as Akara's had been. The same as— "Who is that boy?"

"Do you not recognize your own ClanSon?" Xonea asked.

Xan Jado looked over and smiled Akara's smile. He asked Reever something and, when Reever nodded, hurried over to Teulon and Xonea.

"Your pardon, Captain, but I would like to meet my ClanFather," Xan said. To Teulon, he said, "I regret I did not know you. I was only a baby when we were parted."

Teulon crouched down before his child. He seemed almost afraid to touch him, and then he held out his arms and took the boy in a close embrace. Over Xan's head, he asked Xonea, "How is this possible?" He set Xan at arm's length. "I saw the ship explode. You were on it."

Xan's expression turned sad. "Captain Torin has told me of how our HouseClan was lost. I was saved by Linguist Reever's daughter, Marel. She brought me and her ClanFather to the *Sunlace*."

"How?"

"We are not sure," Xonea admitted. "Just before the *CloudWalk* exploded, Marel, Xan, and Reever materialized on the helm of the *Sunlace*. I witnessed it myself. Marel told us that she brought Xan and Reever with her, and then fell unconscious. She had no memory of it, or how she had done it, when she woke. Reever believes she has the ability to teleport from place to place. It would explain how she was able to move all over the ship when she was younger without any of us seeing her."

As Teulon reacquainted himself with his son, Marel interrogated her father.

"Daddy." She squeezed his neck tightly. "Is she here?" He nodded and Marel looked around until she spotted Cherijo. She frowned. "Why doesn't she come to see me?"

"She does not remember you, Marel." Reever set the child down on her feet. "Why don't you go and say hello to her?"

Teulon watched the little Terran child walk toward him. She was small and fair compared to the Jorenian children, but she looked very determined. "Here is a rebel I would not wish to engage in battle," he said to Resa, who was meeting Xan.

Marel wandered past Teulon and Resa and stopped in front of Jarn. She held up her arms, and Jarn automatically picked her up. Then she pressed her hands to Jarn's cheeks. "Mama, what happened to the white in your hair? It's not all dark in Daddy's photoscans."

"I am not your mother, child," Jarn said gently. "Perhaps I look like her a little, for I am Terran, too."

"You *are* my mama," Marel insisted. "I remember you, before you went away. You crashed on that white planet." When Jarn nodded, she sniffed at her neck. "Your hair is different, but you smell the same." She laid her small blond head against Jarn's shoulder.

"Jarn?" Resa looked confused. "What is the child talking about? You did not crash on Akkabarr."

"I did." Jarn stroked the little girl's fine golden hair.

"The skela found me, and cared for me. In time I became their healer." She started to say something else, but glanced at Daneeb's face and fell silent.

"I remember." Resa's gaze became faraway. "When we found you."

"No." Daneeb tore off her vral mask and stepped between the two women. "It is as Jarn says. There is no reason to speak of it. Put the child down now. We must return to Skjonn."

"I remember," Resa repeated. "She was in the launch that crashed, the day I killed Enafa." She blinked. "Daneeb, I am Iisleg. I was skela. I am Jarn." Her face paled. "I killed that child."

"No, you did not. You have things mixed up, that is all," the headwoman said quickly. "There is no need to talk about this. It was a long time ago."

"Tell her, Daneeb," Reever said quietly.

"Tell her what? Tell her that she shot herself in the head instead of this ensleg, as she was supposed to?" The headwoman flung a hand at Jarn. "The ensleg saved your body, but not your mind. You went mad. You said you were the ensleg, and she you. We had to keep you in chains in the end, and still you escaped. You put on her ensleg's clothes, and walked out to give yourself to the ice as payment for Enafa." Daneeb shoved Reever before she turned on Resa. "So know the truth. I killed Enafa. Not you."

Resa's face had drained of all color. "But I held the blade over her heart. I remember."

"Yes. And I broke your wrist when I thrust it into her heart. We were all going to die, and still, you would not do it. And then you . . ." Daneeb shook her head.

"I do not remember that part," Resa said slowly.

"I do," Jarn said. "I watched it happen. I saw how you tried to stop Daneeb. Then you came to me, and shot yourself in the head."

"And I picked up the pistol, and shot you twice," Daneeb told her, her voice thick with unshed tears. "But you did not stop breathing. You would not die."

Daneeb told the rest of the story. How the gjenvin had taken Jarn to Iiskar Navn, and how the jlorra had dragged her back, still alive, to the skela caves. How quickly Jarn had healed, and how she had nursed the real Jarn back to health. "There were stories of vral, spirit made flesh. That was all that made sense to us. I did not know you blamed yourself for Enafa," she told Resa. "Not until that night when you escaped us and gave yourself to the ice."

Jarn looked down at Marel, who had fallen asleep against her breast. "I was this woman, Cherijo? This is her child? The child of my body?"

"She is our daughter, Marel," Reever said. "I am your husband, Duncan. Your name is Cherijo Torin."

Jarn shook her head abruptly. "I am not your wife, Linguist. I was born that day on the ice. Whoever this Cherijo was, she died on Akkabarr." She held Marel close. "I will take good care of her daughter, that much I promise you. It is our way."

"I know you will," Reever said. "We both will."

She gave him an uneasy look. "I am not staying here. The little one will go with me, to Skjonn." When Xonea started to protest, she looked at Teulon. "You said no more children would be taken, and she is all I will ever have." To Reever, she said, "It is the way of my people now. Children are not to be taken from their mothers."

"The Iisleg are not your people, Cherijo," Xonea said. "We are."

"I only look like this child, and him," Jarn said. "You cannot be my people."

"The Jorenians adopted you. You are many things to many people," Reever told her, "but you cannot stay with the Iisleg. You belong here, with us. We will help you remember who you were." He went to her and put his hands on her shoulder. "You belong with me."

"Teulon." When the Raktar came to Jarn's side, she handed him the little girl. "We are taking her with us. The Iisleg are my people; I don't know any of you. I am Jarn, not Cherijo, and you cannot stop me."

Squilyp surged forward, but Xonea caught his shoulder.

"I challenge your right to take her from me," Reever said. "I am her father. We are the only family she knows."

"You have each other. I have nothing." Jarn pulled the blade from her waist. "No, Reever. You will not take her from me."

"Squilyp." When the Omorr joined them, Reever asked, "Is what she says true?"

"I will have to run some tests, but she has suffered at least two point-blank pulse fire shots to the head," Squilyp said slowly. "If there was enough brain damage, the cells would have regenerated, but the memories belonging to Cherijo would not. Cherijo would, in essence, no longer exist."

"We will leave now," Jarn said.

"You would kill anyone who tried to take your

daughter away from you, would you not? Is this the way of the Iisleg women now?" Reever asked her. When Jarn nodded, he said, "So would I. Anyone but you."

"Jarn." Teulon handed Marel to Resa. "He is right. You cannot take the child away from him. You do not know her."

Jarn shook her head. "I will come to know her again. He cannot take her away from me."

"You will have to kill me to take her," Reever said calmly, taking his own blade from a forearm sheath and offering it to her.

"Duncan." Squilyp was horrified.

"You would die for her." Jarn circled around him, both blades ready.

"I would die for both of you," Reever said.

"I know this feeling." Jarn stopped and glanced over at Teulon and Resa. Slowly she replaced her blade, and offered Reever's to him. "Do you have any other wives? Other women?"

"No."

She studied him from head to toe. "Will you take me as your only wife?"

"Yes. There will be no others for me."

Jarn nodded. She walked over to Teulon and Resa, and took Marel from her friend. "I must go with him and the child," she told Resa. "You understand."

Resa nodded, and embraced her. "I will miss you."

"And I you." Jarn ran her hand over Resa's short hair once, and then stepped back. "Teulon, take care of her."

The Raktar nodded.

Jarn carried Marel over to Reever. "Well, ensleg, it

seems that we are yours. We are tired, too. Where on this ship do we sleep?"

Resa found Teulon in the former Kangal's sleeping chamber. He was standing at the wall that looked out over the city.

"It seems so strange, not to have ice beneath my feet," she told him. "Nothing feels right here, especially now that Jarn is gone. I mean, Cherijo."

"We will be leaving soon, too," Teulon reminded her. "The peace talks are to be held on Joren, my homeworld."

"Are you sorry that Jarn chose to go with Reever?"

"No. I think they belong together." He turned to gaze down at her. "What of you? Hasal always said you and Jarn were like twins. And the memories returning . . . it cannot be a happy thing."

Resa could remember most of what had happened to her after finding Jarn in the crashed launch. "No, it was not. Enafa was so young; she did not deserve to die as she did. But I know now that I tried to save her. As you tried to save Akara and your HouseClan."

"When peace has been made between the League and the Hsktskt, I would like to stay on Joren. Edin and the other commanders here have things well in hand. The crystals are where no one will ever find them." His battalion commanders had been dropping them, one by one, into deep crevasses for several months now. "Xan and I are the last of the Jado, and it is left to us to rebuild our HouseClan."

She drew back. "I understand. You want me to stay here, so I will not interfere."

"I want you to come with me." He took her hands

in his. "Be with me, Resa. Not as a kedera or a bond-mate, but as whatever we will be to each other."

Resa thought of Jarn's prediction and smiled. "Yes. I will be with you."

Reever went immediately to his quarters as soon as he was off duty. Xonea had offered to give him several days to spend with Cherijo and Marel, but he had refused.

"She needs time, Xonea," he told the captain. "Time to heal."

"She has become a stranger, Duncan. She refuses to answer to anything but this 'Jarn.' She walks the ship armed with more blades than I own. She asked one of the women where she could kill something and cook it for a meal." The Jorenian sighed. "I fear you have a long road ahead of you."

"We will travel it together. She is with us. That is all that matters."

Reever entered his access code and walked into his quarters. Most of the furnishings were gone, as they made Cherijo uneasy. Pillows and bed coverings littered the floor. The cats had taken refuge with Salo and Darea Torin, for neither of them had recognized Cherijo, and Reever had been worried she might try to kill and eat them while he was on duty.

He looked in their bedroom, but the sleeping platform was empty. An arrow of fear shot through him as he strode across his quarters and opened the door to his daughter's room. Her bed was also empty.

Reever was about to summon security when he heard a soft sigh come from under the bed. He got down on his hands and knees, and saw Cherijo and

Marel nestled together on a blanket under the sleeping platform. In Cherijo's right hand was a wicked-looking blade. Her left arm was curled around their daughter. Both were fast asleep.

Reever stripped out of his tunic and crawled under the bed. He would have to do something about the bed. Perhaps raise it. He stretched out behind Cherijo, and put his arm around her before closing his eyes.

She is with us. That is all that matters now.

Explore the frontiers of speculative fiction from

S.L. VIEHL

STARDOC *0-451*-45773-0

A young female doctor discovers the startling truth of her origins in this unique and gripping science fiction medical thriller.

BEYOND VARALLAN *0-451*-45793-5

Dr. Cherijo is living the perfect life—if you think that finding out you're a clone, then being declared "non-sentient" by your father/creator is your idea of perfect.

ENDURANCE *0-451*-45814-1

The further adventures of Cherijo, a genetically-enhanced human engineered to be the model of perfection—if she can survive.

SHOCKBALL *0-451*-45855-9

Cherijo Grey Veil is searching for a place where she'll be safe from the demented man who created her. But she soon finds that she can't just run from her past-she must destroy it.

ETERNITY ROW *0-451*-458915

Cherijo and her husband have found safety aboard the star vessel Sunlace. But they have promises to keep-—promises that will endanger everything she ever fought for—including her solemn oath to protect life.

penguin.com

S563

Roc Science Fiction & Fantasy
COMING IN FEBRUARY 2006

DREAMS MADE FLESH

by Anne Bishop

0-451-46013-8

Set in the realm of *The Black Jewels* trilogy, this collection features four brand-new revelatory stories of Jaenelle and her kindred.

THE KING'S OWN: A BORDERLANDS NOVEL

by Lorna Freeman

0-451-46071-5

When Rabbit joined the Royal Army of Iversterre, he was just trying to get off the family farm. But with Iversterre sliding towards the abyss, Rabbit needs to master his powers quickly—before someone else does it for him.

MECHWARRIOR: DARK AGE #20: TRIAL BY CHAOS

by J. Steven York

0-451-46072-3

The Raging Bears have begun their occupation of the planet Vega with the hope of restoring order amid relentless violence and civil ruin. But their bold move may prove to be the chance their enemies have waited for.

Available wherever books are sold or at

penguin.com

Finally, someone is doing something about the weather.

The Weather Warden series by

by Rachel Caine

Ill Wind

0-451-45952-0

Joanne Baldwin is a powerful Weather Warden, charged with keeping the world's weather in balance. But she's been framed, charged with corruption—and murder. With a fast, classic car, and a powerful Djinn under her control, she just might escape with her life.

Heat Stroke

0-451-45984-9

Joanne Baldwin has been hunted down and killed by her veangeful colleagues. Reborn as a Djinn, she senses something sinister entering Earth's atmosphere—and her only allies are dropping fast. Who said being all-powerful would be east?

Chill Factor

0-451-46010-3

Restored to her original form, Joanne Baldwin is ready for a rest. But now, a deeply disturbed kid is holed up in a Vegas hotel, bringing on the next ice age—and she's the only one who can stop him from destroying the world.

Available wherever books are sold or at penguin.com